I0572514

MISTRESS OF
ANIMALS

Karen Myers

MISTRESS OF ANIMALS

The Chained Adept: 2

Karen Myers

PERKUNAS PRESS • Tyrone, Pennsylvania

Mistress of Animals

The Chained Adept: 2

Perkunas Press
2635 Baughman Cemetery Road
Tyrone, Pennsylvania 16686
USA

PerkunasPress.com

Author contact: KarenMyers@KarenMyersAuthor.com
KarenMyersAuthor.com

Cover and Illustrations: Jake Bullock, http://ohbullocks.com
The Kigali, Zannib, Rasesni, and Ellech languages:
    Damátir Ando,
    http://damatir-ando.tripod.com/conlangs.html

© 2016 by Karen Myers
ALL RIGHTS RESERVED
Published 2016. First Edition.

Trade Paperback
ISBN-13: 978-1-62962-032-9
ISBN-10: 1-6296203-2-7

Library of Congress Control Number: 2016932083

ALSO BY KAREN MYERS

The Hounds of Annwn

To Carry the Horn
The Ways of Winter
King of the May
Bound into the Blood

Story Collections
Tales of Annwn

Short Stories
The Call
Under the Bough
Night Hunt
Cariad
The Empty Hills

The Chained Adept

The Chained Adept
Mistress of Animals
Broken Devices
On a Crooked Track

Science Fiction Short Stories

Second Sight
Monsters, And More
The Visitor, And More

See KarenMyersAuthor.com for the latest information.

CONTENTS

Chapter 1	1
Chapter 2	6
Chapter 3	10
Chapter 4	14
Chapter 5	21
Chapter 6	26
Chapter 7	31
Chapter 8	35
Chapter 9	40
Chapter 10	45
Chapter 11	49
Chapter 12	53
Chapter 13	57
Chapter 14	63
Chapter 15	68
Chapter 16	73
Chapter 17	81
Chapter 18	85
Chapter 19	91
Chapter 20	97
Chapter 21	101
Chapter 22	105
Chapter 23	110
Chapter 24	114

Chapter 25	119
Chapter 26	124
Chapter 27	130
Chapter 28	135
Chapter 29	142
Chapter 30	146
Chapter 31	153
Chapter 32	157
Chapter 33	162
Chapter 34	167
Chapter 35	173
Chapter 36	177
Chapter 37	184
Chapter 38	189
Chapter 39	196
Chapter 40	202
Chapter 41	207
Chapter 42	213
Chapter 43	218
Chapter 44	223
Chapter 45	228
Chapter 46	232
Chapter 47	237
Chapter 48	242
Chapter 49	247
Chapter 50	253
Chapter 51	258
Chapter 52	262
Chapter 53	265
Chapter 54	270
Chapter 55	277

Chapter 56   281

Chapter 57   286

Chapter 58   290

Chapter 59   294

Chapter 60   301

Guide to Names & Pronunciations   306

If You Like This Book   320

Also by Karen Myers   321

Excerpt from Broken Devices   322

About the Author   330

<h1 style="text-align:center">CHAPTER 1</h1>

"Demon, I swear I'm going to eat your ears for breakfast."

Penrys halted her horse, dismounted, and stomped back past her three pack horses to the beginning of the string of seven donkeys, the first of which had dug in his feet on the trail of the High Pass and was bawling like three demons instead of one.

The other donkeys fidgeted nervously and seemed inclined to join him, so Penrys probed to see if there was anything more than a fit of donkey sulks responsible.

Demon's dominant mode was generally offended pride, but this time his mind showed her something different.

Najud, something's wrong. I think he's afraid of something.

Her companion's mental voice chuckled. *Sure it's not you he's afraid of, Destroyer of Demons?*

After three weeks, the joke had worn thin to her. Perhaps the wizard they had destroyed had deserved the name, and maybe this donkey did, too, but she found the full title, applied to her, both ridiculous and embarrassing.

Guess Najud's not going to bother to dismount and leave his own string to take a look.

She ran her hands over Demon and scratched under his chin in the spot he liked, and gradually he calmed down, placated by the attention. The others took their cue from him and settled.

She looked down their back trail. The view of the southern part of Neshilik, laid out below them, had been lost two days ago. Now only the steep scrambling slopes on either side were visible, along with the winding trail itself.

Footsteps behind her made her turn. Najud had come back to check on the donkeys, after all.

"Is he all right?"

"See for yourself."

Najud had been making progress on his mind-probes of animals. He was cautious about relying on it—as he said, "I can *see* the start of a pack sore before the beast begins to feel it."

"He's calmer now, but you're right, I think. Something alarmed him," he said. "You can see why many clans put donkeys with the sheep herds, to act as guards against wolves."

"Do they fight the wolves, or is it just the braying that makes them run away?"

Najud snorted.

Penrys scanned the area. "There're no other large animals around, except our own."

"The wind has shifted. Maybe he smelled something, and now he doesn't."

Despite the rock walls, the pass was high and fairly exposed, significantly colder and windier than the sheltered, settled land behind them. And it would only get colder, the further south they went, with the autumn solstice two months past. Penrys had never experienced winter in the south of the world and was still adjusting to the concept that "south" implied "cold."

"Let's get going," Najud said. "We'll see the other *lud*, late today, if we don't keep stopping."

"How do you know that? I thought you'd never taken this route before, over the border between Kigali and your *sarq*-Zannib?"

Najud grinned at her. Since the weather was dry, if cold, he still wore his small turban, the blue one today. Penrys was grateful for the wide-brimmed hat pressed upon her by the tailor back at Gonglik—it kept her shoulder-length hair from blowing in her face.

"It's described in one of the travel stories," he said. "Each landmark is a part of the tale."

He waved his hands in the air. "We tell each other these stories so that we can know a place before we see it. The *lud* are some of the characters."

The little gods, the Zannib called them—the special places or objects, a crooked tree, a rock formation.

It sometimes seemed from conversation with Najud that the *lud* were everywhere. She wasn't sure how seriously he thought of them.

"Remember the one we passed two days ago, the last spot for a view?" he said.

There *had* been something unusual about that lone, massive rock that seemed to keep watch over the trail.

2

"She's a character in the story. When you come from the south, she opens the door so the traveler can finally see the green of Neshilik spread out in front of him. Coming this way, she waves farewell. See?

"The travel story of this trail starts in the south, in *sarq*-Zannib, and it helps you find the exact spot where the trail to the High Pass begins. Going the other way is simple—just start at Jaunor, and that's easy enough to find—so that's where the way-back story starts, in the inn-yard."

Jaunor was part of the circuit of market inns that surrounded the southern cove of Neshilik, named "Cold Wall" for the border range at its back and the chilly winds that plagued it when the weather was bad.

"They told us there'd been no travelers through here for a couple of years."

Najud shrugged. "They don't come every year. The Kurighdunaq clan holds their *tarizd* below, the route of the migration, unless something has changed." He hooked his thumb south, at the trail ahead of them. "It's their young men who would get together and make an unplanned visit, during the *taridiqa*, to pick up courting gifts and special supplies for the *zudiqazd*, the winter camp. Not a formal trading caravan."

"Like the kind you're thinking of setting up," Penrys said.

"That's right." He smiled at her. "Besides, it's too late in the year to meet anyone up here. The Kurighdunaq would have started their *kuliqa*, their turn-home, two months ago. We'll have to make very good time to join a *zudiqazd* once we get down, the nearest we can find, and not be too picky about whose clan it belongs to."

"There it is."

At Najud's call, Penrys lifted her head from her horse's footing. His string of four horses some distance in front of her had stopped, but the leader was out of sight around yet another bend in the enclosed trail.

There was still light in the sky, but no shadows were cast in the narrow passage, the sun having been invisible for a while. She hoped for a wide spot for their camp. Bad enough that they had to pack fodder for the animals all the way from Jaunor to make up for the bare, rocky, trail—the limited water they could carry was running low. Najud had told her of an unfailing spring just the other side of this next *lud*, this landmark, and she hoped they could make camp there.

Najud's horses didn't move, so Penrys dismounted to walk up and join him. He hadn't seen the view before, either, and she could share that with him.

After she passed the horses, she found him, bent over a pile of something on the east side of the trail. When she raised her eyes, she saw that the trail curved to the left, and the western rock face fell away from a wide and level extension of the trail, leaving the lowering sun free to illuminate the corner of the eastern wall where the trail passed it, where Najud stood. The texture of the stone changed in that spot, and small embedded crystals sparkled in a patch twice the height of a man.

This must be the lud.

As she reached him, her eyes were carried involuntarily to the promised view. The trail curved down to the left and turned again, out of sight, but nothing blocked her view to the south and west. The sun blanketed a soft and rolling land with broad strokes and long shadows. On either side, low spurs of the range extended.

She couldn't see directly below her, where the pass began, but Najud had told her there was a sheltered cove there, and those spurs must be the arms around it.

"You're right," she said aloud. "It's a wonderful view. Looks like there's even a good spot for a camp."

Najud's silence drew her from the view and she turned back to him. He hadn't moved from his spot and was still staring at the base of the *lud*.

Am I disturbing something… religious for him?

She was reluctant to intrude, but his posture conveyed worry or even alarm to her. She walked over to see what he was looking at.

There were half a dozen packs on the ground, ordinary trail packs, like a man might carry, not the large packs used for animals.

"Are they gifts for the *lud*, those packs?" she asked quietly.

He shook his head. "The *lud* don't need gifts, just respect. Sometimes a flower, or a pebble, maybe a bit of honey—simple recognition."

He straightened and looked down the short fragment of trail that was visible before the next bend.

"This is wrong."

His taut posture declared his uneasiness. "I'm going to look down the trail before we stop for the night. You stay here, with the animals."

Penrys raised her eyebrows but took the order in silence, and Najud walked down and out of sight.

She checked for mind-glows around them, but there was nothing except themselves for a mile or two, other than the small creatures that managed to live in this barren place, and the larger ones that lived on them.

The packs on the ground were not all the same, she realized. One was quite small, the size a child might carry. But Najud said it was just the young men who used this trail, not families.

They looked relatively fresh—she couldn't imagine they had already experienced a winter here. But in Jaunor they said no one had come over the trail for two years. Where did these people go? Didn't they need what was in those packs?

Najud reappeared, ascending the trail. His face was troubled.

It's bad, but whatever happened, it was at least a couple of months ago. Nothing we can do about it tonight.

"Demon had cause, this morning," he said, as he joined her. "Dead horse. The wind must have brought him the scent, before shifting."

CHAPTER 2

Penrys took her own look down the trail before the light faded entirely, after the horses and donkeys had been unloaded and fed.

A dead horse lay in its tack at the side of the trail, mummified in the drying winds and well-nibbled. That was bad enough, but it was the scattering of belongings that raised the hackles on her neck. Why were they abandoned there?

Najud was uncharacteristically quiet as they set up the camp at the wide spot, by its spring, overlooked by the presence of the *lud* on the far side of the trail. Its surface sparkled occasionally, reflecting the flicker of the fire. Their supply of wood was limited, carried all the way up from Jaunor and intended to last for three more days to get them through the pass, so the fire was just large enough to heat water for their meal and to take some of the chill off.

By unspoken consent, they'd set up their small tent, partly to keep the wind off but more, she thought, as a barrier against the sinister debris they'd found.

She wrapped her hands around the warm mug of trail stew and cleared her throat. "So, what are you thinking? Have you ever seen a horse and packs abandoned like this before?"

Najud looked up. "No, nothing like this."

He bestirred himself to give her his full attention. "Of course. I forgot for a moment that you aren't a Zan. You wouldn't know."

He glanced off into space to collect his thoughts. "This trail is used for trade between Neshilik and *sarq*-Zannib. And sometimes for refugees—Rasesni came this way when Kigali cleared out Neshilik, a couple of generations ago. But these are Zannib goods, all over the trail, so it's not refugees from the north.

"No Zan would desecrate a trail. That horse should not be there. It would have been butchered for meat, perhaps, or at the very least stripped of its gear and pulled off of the trail and covered with rocks, as much as possible. And the tack would never have been abandoned. What you saw—there was no respect shown the animal. And men on the trail do not abandon useful things."

"Maybe they had more than they could carry," Penrys suggested.

"That's not like the Zannib, either. We are nomads, we plan everything around what we can carry and what we need."

He searched her face. "You saw the small pack, over there?" He cocked his head in the direction of the *lud*.

She nodded.

"That's a child's pack. From the day we can walk we begin to learn how to carry what is needful. And below, I found these."

He reached into his pocket and pulled out two small objects which he tossed to Penrys.

One was a cloth doll the size of her hand, dressed in a Zannib robe. The face had painted eyes and mouth, and bits of dark wool attached as hair. It was soft, easily stuffed into a pack or a pocket. When she sniffed it, no scent remained except the dust of the trail. The other was a dingy brown horse, the same size as the doll. Bits of leather were sewn on as a saddle, and a mane and tail of dark fleece had been attached.

"Children?"

He nodded. "I had toys like this, most children do. When I was, maybe, four or five years old. You don't understand. It's very rare to take children that young on the *taridiqa*. And no one would take them over the High Pass. So, what were children doing here?"

One obvious possibility suggested itself to her. "Could they have been fleeing something and forced to try the pass?"

"I thought of this, but where are they, then? And why are their goods still here?"

Penrys shifted her position uneasily. "Maybe they weren't alone, Maybe someone found them and took them away."

Again, he nodded.

"And left their goods behind. It's possible. But who made the pile of packs at the foot of the *lud*? Only the Zannib would do that. If they were taken by other Zannib, why would they take people but not gear? And in either case, why involve the *lud*?"

"What does it mean, these packs to the *lud*?," she asked. "You said they weren't offerings."

"They're not. It's hard to explain about the *lud*. They're not gods, the way the Kigaliwen and the Rasesni think of gods—

something that directs the world and may reward or punish them. The creator of our world does not take such an interest in us. He made our world good for us, and it's up to us to keep it so.

"What the *lud* do is show us where the *dunaq wandim*, the world that surrounds, shines through for us to see, piercing the veil of illusion that is our life. Yes, I know that is just a rock formation over there. But it is also a hint of something…"

"Sacred?" Penrys suggested.

"Yes, sacred. A reminder. We owe it respect because of that reminder. We speak of the *lud* sometimes as if they were little gods. This one is the husband of the other one at the north of the pass. They've been married a very long time, hundreds of years, and they don't talk much to each other any more, but they are still *yuj*, a married pair, and not separated very far. It's a silly little story, and they are not little gods, not really, but it makes things more comfortable for people, stupid as we are."

"I understand, I think. But what does it mean, then, those packs?"

Najud shook his head. "A plea for help? A pledge to endure?"

He lowered his voice. "A farewell to life?"

Penrys lay awake after Najud finally subsided into an uneasy sleep. There was no laughter under the robes tonight.

It was strange to her, this withdrawn mood of his. He was cheerful in the face of his own troubles, but the presence of children in this sinister scenario had been a blow to him. That, and the uncertainty over their fate.

All the way down through Neshilik for three weeks he'd been bubbling over with eagerness to get home, free for the first time in his ten years of self-imposed exile, even though the time of year would keep him from reaching his own clan's winter camp before the snows set in. No one had bothered them as they moved south through the chaos in Neshilik—not the Rasesni occupiers, once they'd shown their safe conduct from Menchos, a high-ranking Rasesni officer now based in Gonglik, and certainly not the Kigaliwen who recognized non-Rasesni foreigners and were glad to be rid of them.

The bigger problem had been the occasional encounter with Rasesni priests in the towns they passed through, wherever a temple had been rededicated to Rasesni gods. The news of events at the north end of Neshilik, and the death of the Voice, the wizard-tyrant that had so threatened Rasesdad, had spread from the temple school in Gonglik, and along with it Penrys's role in his defeat, the one that had led to a Kigali tailor referring to her as "Destroyer of Demons," the somewhat comic title she was still living down with Najud.

These priests had wanted to make a fuss once they realized who they were, and more than once Penrys had been grateful to the tailor's wife for the scarves she wore around her neck, obscuring the chain that marked her. She was very tired of explaining to them that, yes, the Voice had also worn a chain like hers but, no, she didn't know who he was.

She hoped to spend a year or so in *sarq*-Zannib, some of it with Najud's family, before deciding what she should do next. If Najud would have her that long…

Would their intimacy survive once they were back with his people and no longer alone on the trail? If she would be moving on in a few months anyway, maybe she should encourage it to attenuate into a professional relationship, one wizard to another.

That would be wiser—he would be settling with his clan, as most Zannib wizards do, now that he was a master wizard and no longer a journeyman, and what could she offer him that would fit his life? The endless circle of the annual migration? Children? Whatever she was, she doubted she could bear him children, and this was a man who wanted them, who had deferred them too long. She didn't want to watch him make his choice of a wife, and she couldn't stay indefinitely—there was no place for her there.

She wasn't ready to give him up, not yet—she'd been alone far too long for that—but she was determined to try.

CHAPTER 3

"We should bring what we can with us," Najud said.

He was reluctant to disturb the packs at the base of the *lud* in the morning, especially since someone had gone to the effort to arrange them there, but there was no point leaving everything to rot, not when they had capacity in their pack train now that some of the fodder and fuel had been consumed.

"We can at least get it off the pass and take it to the clan."

"Do you know which clan it is?" Penrys asked.

"I know the markings."

He showed her the arc of the world-bow, the blessing after rain, cut into the leather of the packs. "That's Kurighdunaq, my cousin Zaybirs's clan. My mother's sister Qizrahi married into it, to everyone's surprise. It's unusual to marry out-tribe like that—made quite a stir when she brought her herds into their bloodlines."

"Is that the clan we were hoping to meet?"

He nodded, unhappily. For all he could tell, his cousin's pack was here somewhere, and he among the missing. He'd never met the man, and now he feared he never would.

"You can see the *zamjilah*, the eye-of-heaven, on our goods, for my clan. That's what we call the spoked ring in the center of a Zannib *kazr*, where the smoke rises up."

He would be glad to shift to a warm, round *kazr* from the flimsy traveling tent they were using, once he could buy or make one. Waiting for one until he reached his family was not appealing, not as the weather got colder.

"I didn't know what that was," Penrys said. "Thought the symbol might be a wheel."

He kept forgetting she was a foreigner to his land. The intimacy of the mind-speech and her fluency with his language made it seem as though they knew each other well and, of course, there was the sharing of their bodies. But she was still a stranger, not some Zan woman, considering a marriage. And he was years past the sudden, impulsive passions that snatched a woman from around the fire and arranged with the *tayujdaj*, the marriage broker, to speak with her family and count her herds.

And then, they were both *bikrajab*, wizards, and she something alien and strong and solitary, with that chain around her neck and her unknown origins.

There were so few woman like him. He could live alone, or try to make a life with a mind-deaf woman, one who would dislike and resent the differences between them, the way the old songs demonstrated. He'd always expected to end up unmarried, settled in his clan with all of its families and children, making a fuss over his nephews and nieces and maybe sharing time with a widow, now and then, to keep away the loneliness.

Penrys thought the donkeys he was bringing home, to breed mules with, were the main purpose of his present little caravan, and that she was just keeping him company to learn more about the Zannib and their practices. He didn't dare tell her the rest of his plan, that he thought of her as a cautious wild creature that he was luring along, crumb by crumb, hoping to make her comfortable in the warmth of his family, since she had none, hoping she might stay and build something with him, anything.

And like any wild animal, he had to be careful not to alarm her. He didn't want her to feel his attention on her, the way the hunted animal can tell it's being watched. When they mind-shared, he sensed her withdrawing a little more each day, as though she were anticipating a parting, and it worried him—he wasn't ready to bring a discussion about the future into the open, and scare her away.

"Come, help me stuff these packs into the donkey loads. We won't look into their contents now—that's the clan's business, not ours. Then you can help me pile some rocks on that horse, once I cut its tack off and free it from constraint."

"How's your hand?"

Najud's question was a welcome distraction from the mindless work of piling a rock cairn over a dead horse. They'd been at it for a couple of hours and were finally nearing the end. The tack Najud had cut off of the body made a forlorn heap near the road, ready to be stuffed into another donkey pack.

"It's fine. The glove keeps it protected," Penrys replied.

Her left hand was healing quickly. Though she was used to the speed with which her body healed, leaving no marks after the worst of wounds, it had been a surprise to her when her left hand began rebuilding the four fingers, lost in her desperate fight with the Voice only a month ago. The first two were already fully grown, and the third nearly so. The fourth was still a stub, since the slice that took them all had been diagonal, and it had the longest way to go.

How old am I? No marks on m'body at all, not wrinkles, not childbirth.

She had no memory older than three years, when she was found in far away northern Ellech, in the snow, naked except for the chain around her neck.

The Voice had also been chained, but she'd learned nothing from him—neither where he came from nor any information about his own past. She'd been brooding about it for weeks now. *Someone must have made us, but why? Can he control us somehow, through the chains? Are there more of us?*

She shook it off and stood up, bending and stretching to relieve her muscles. *No point worrying Najud about it—not his problem. Just another reason to end it before it's worse for both of us.*

She'd been alone for three years, isolated at the Collegium in Tavnastok in Ellech. She could get used to it again. She shivered a little in the chilly air, and headed for her horse to tighten its girth and resume her cloak.

Najud placed his last rock, and then scooped up the stripped tack. The bright colors of the abbreviated Zannib-style saddle were dulled from a couple of months of outdoor exposure, but even so the day seemed a bit less vivid to her, once they were stuffed away into a pack.

Once they'd passed the debris in the general vicinity of the *lud*, there was nothing else to be found. After a couple of miles of trail, Penrys stopped looking for it and relaxed back into the work of the trail, keeping close behind Najud's string and watching after her own.

From five horse-lengths in front of her, she heard Najud's voice raised in a sad, solemn song. He stopped himself, abruptly.

"Join me," he called. "Do the harmonies. The right ones, mind."

Then he started over again.

She tapped him for his expertise in singing, to share the feel of how a song like this should go, how it should sound, and then she raised her own voice in wordless harmony to match his.

As she heard the words she could follow the meaning, but since she didn't know what the words would be in time to sing them, all she could do was provide a counterpoint for his voice. Verse after verse it continued, a commemoration for the fallen.

CHAPTER 4

Two days later, they were still picking their way cautiously downhill, hemmed in by the rock walls of the lower pass. Every now and then Penrys got a bit of a view which helped her judge how much closer they were to the end of this trail. Last night's heavy autumn rain had laid the trail dust, but it had taken the animals a while to shake off the chill and settle into their work this morning.

For a distraction, she picked up one of her incomplete conversations with Najud, fifty yards ahead of her.

You expected to find this particular clan. Do they always take the same route, every year?

The tarizd, the migration route, is like one petal of a many-petaled flower. The base of the petal is the zudiqazd, the winter camp. From there, they travel in a big loop, never exactly the same, but planned to hit the important grazing places. In the center of the flower are the zudiqazd of all the nearby clans in that tribe, and each petal goes in a different direction.

Penrys pictured for herself a round circle of petal-like routes surrounding the winter camps. Local geography probably interfered with the perfection of that image.

Does it ever change?

Sometimes the petals blow back and forth, and the routes shift, sometimes just once, and sometimes for years. Marriages can change routes, if enough new alliances are formed with the same clans. Sometimes groups want to travel adjacent routes.

She could almost hear the shrug in his voice.

Things change. Nothing is constant. That's why children learn the landmarks for the tarizd of every clan in their group. Each year, at the zudiqazd, the next year's tarizd is planned for each clan while all those clans are together, so there will be no misunderstandings.

Penrys wondered how they resolved conflicts about favorite grazing spots. Was there always consensus, or did some tribal leader step in?

Thinking of conflict, she again scanned the surroundings. This time, she found the mind-glows of people, not far away.

Three men coming, and horses. Wiriqiqa-Zannib speakers.

She felt Najud's surprise, and then his swift evaluation. *I see a wide spot ahead. We'll wait for them there. Tie your string to mine, then ride up and join me.*

Najud and Penrys sat their stolen Rasesni mares side-by-side at the upper end of a wide spot in the trail, he on his Zannib saddle, with its minimal structure, and she on the Kigali cattle-herding one, with its heavy leather construction and the prominent horn, the horn that had been so helpful while her hand was useless.

Penrys took her hat off and ran her fingers through her hair before resettling it, and Najud took a moment to make sure his turban was straight and tidy.

The low murmur of voices and the clatter of hooves heralded the appearance of the strangers before they could see them, but then one of Najud's pack animals stamped his foot and the voices stopped. Only one animal continued forward, judging by the sound, and then a rider appeared, in Zannib robes and turban on a horse in light Zannib tack. The young man inspected the two of them waiting and the first horses in Najud's string, and made a brief bow from the saddle.

He called back over his shoulder. "Strangers, traveling."

He pulled forward and off to the side to make room for his companions.

These were the first Zannib Penrys had seen, besides Najud and the illustrations in the books she'd read in the Collegium. She couldn't tell if they shared the same dark curls under their turbans, but their faces all had a broad resemblance to Najud's. It was hard to be sure, but she thought they were all younger.

They were armed, each of them, with a long curved sword slung from their saddles under their left leg.

The second one to arrive rode a few steps forward and bowed his head. "Greetings, *tulqaj*. I am Jirkat, son of Mishajmarzuwi of clan Kurighdunaq, and these are my clan-kin."

Najud returned the bow. "I'm Najud, son of Ilsahr of clan Zamjilah."

Jirkat said, "I've heard of you. Isn't your mother Kazrsulj, the sister of Qizrahi, and you therefore the cousin of some of my clan?"

When Najud nodded, Jirkat continued. "Your stock-lines do well with us. I hope she left your family some few animals to get by on." He grinned briefly at Najud, and now Penrys was sure he was a few years younger.

"You've retaken your name, I see. You are now a *jarghal?*"

"It is so. I've completed my *nayith* and am returning home to Zamjilah. This is my *bikrajti* companion, Penrys, lately of Ellech."

Eyebrows on all three faces raised at the mention of the distant country, and Penrys could feel their eyes noting the foreign look of her.

Najud urged his horse forward a step. "I bring you bad news of clan-kin, from up the trail."

Jirkat said, "That's who we're looking for. Are they on the trail above, or perhaps in Neshilik? Living or dead?"

"We found no one on the trail, living or dead, and they haven't been seen in Jaunor. But we found their belongings, and what we found we've brought with us."

He gestured at the trail behind them, at the string of animals that continued out of their sight.

"What we found disturbed us greatly. We'd like to tell you about it and return what we found to their clan-kin."

Jirkat nodded. "We've made a camp at the foot of the trail, those of us on the search. Come guest with us and tell us your tale."

When the trail finally widened and the grassland sloped down before them, Penrys took several deep breaths as though her lungs had been stifled from the enclosed journey of the last few days.

Her vision was still restricted directly to east and west by the encircling ranges that sheltered this spot, but spread out before her the grass rolled unrestricted to the horizon.

It was different from the valley of the Mother of Rivers. This landscape was drier, providing no promise of an immense river lurking just beyond some fold of land, and the grasses were not the same variety. They waved in dull yellows swaths, reflecting the waning of the year.

Further out in the cove were three of the round tents Najud had described to her, what he called *kazr*. All three were small, more for travel then longer-term dwelling, but they looked cozier than the tent the two of them were using, with their wrappings of felt and their decorated canvas covers, and the gaily painted wooden doors. They were arranged in a small circle, their doorways facing inward.

Beyond them were small herds of all sorts—horses, sheep, cattle, and even a few goats, and the four mounted herdsmen keeping watch over them broke away from their duty to ride into the camp to greet their returning kinsmen and the guests. One older woman opened the wooden-framed door of her *kazr* and stepped out to join them, her black and curly hair pulled into a horsetail by a colorful scarf.

Penrys scanned the area and found no one else. As they got close enough for the others to see their faces, she felt the wave of disappointment wash through the camp.

We're not who they wanted to see.

Najud stopped outside the circle and waited for everyone to arrive, and Penrys attached her string to the end of his and moved her horse up to join him.

She looked them over, and her heart sank.

They're so young, they make me feel elderly.

Except for the woman on foot, Jirkat was the oldest one there, and he was clearly a few years younger than Najud. He and his two companions were the oldest of the men, perhaps twenty years old. The herdsmen were two younger men and a woman three or four years younger, and a girl of maybe ten. Penrys pegged the woman on foot as the mother of the girl.

Jirkat addressed the gathering. "Our people were not on the High Pass trail. These *bikrajab* have just come through there from Jaunor, and they say they have bad news for us. I know of this *bikraj*—he is cousin to our clan, sister-son to Qizrahi, whom you all know."

The woman stepped up and bowed to both of them. She was dressed like the men in breeches. Her low embroidered boots with upturned toes and her boiled wool overrobes blocked the chill air.

"Be welcome to this camp, *bikrajab*, and accept our poor hospitality. We have no *kazr* large enough to guest us all, but please dismount and share our food, while we water your animals. We're desperate to hear of our kin."

Najud bowed low in his saddle to her, and Penrys took her cue from him, dismounting when he did.

The woman waved the girl and young woman to their horses, and they took them in charge, leaning from their mounts to seize the reins, and taking the pack string with them. Penrys watched them lead the animals to the spring on the west edge of the camp. Najud paid no attention—this must be a customary form of hospitality, and he seemed content to let it take its course.

The riders who brought them also dismounted, and handed their reins to the two younger men who took them along after the others to the spring.

The woman ducked back into her *kazr* and carried out an armful of small rugs which she laid on the grass on top of pieces of canvas, and gestured for them to sit. Penrys took the rug next to Najud when he folded his legs with dignity and sat down.

The woman returned with wicker baskets that held cheeses and small, freshly-baked, flatbreads, and her third trip produced an iron kettle and three stoneware cups. The odor of steaming *bunnas* filled the air.

Najud eyed Penrys. *Pretend you like bunnas. This is a matter of hospitality.*

She nodded silently.

The woman called, "Jirkat, if you will bring cups for your companions, there's enough for everyone."

"Thank you, *lijti*." Jirkat hooked a thumb at one of his friends who bent through the doorway of another *kazr* to fetch cups for the three of them.

The woman lowered herself carefully to her chosen rug, and urged the food upon her guests.

Najud tore off a piece of flatbread for both of them and used his belt knife to cut slices off the cheese, then handed Penrys her portion. At the woman's urging, they began to eat, and the woman joined them. Cups having appeared for Jirkat and his friends, soon all four of their hosts were sharing the meal.

Doesn't seem right not to offer some of our own trail food in exchange, but there must be rules about this I'll have to learn.

The cheese was soft and crumbly, with a distinct tang to it, and the flatbread did double duty as a plate.

By this time, the four younger folk had returned. They picked up rugs and made seats in an outer ring around the six older people. One of the boys and the young woman sat together.

Najud emphatically brushed the crumbs from his clothes onto the grass beyond the rug and placed his cup on the ground before him.

Jirkat took this as his cue. "This is Hadishti," he said, nodding at the woman. "She left our *taridiqa* at the summer encampment to take her elder son to begin his work as a *nal-jarghal*, an apprentice, to the *jarghal* Anitqizat, about a hundred miles east of the summer camp. She brought her younger son, Dimghuy, and her daughter Sharma with her, and they stayed for a little while before she returned, hoping to meet the *taridiqa* at the autumn camp. When she crossed the route between the summer and autumn camps, the one that was planned, she found no trace of them and turned back toward the summer encampment to see why they were delayed."

He used a stick to draw a map on the trodden ground, showing where they were, the summer encampment to their south, and the autumn camp south and west of that.

Hadishti and her children, the girl and the younger boy, nodded to attest to the accuracy of this account.

Jirkat pointed to his map and drew a line far to the west from the summer encampment, then he gestured to his companions.

"These two are my brother, Khashghuy, and our friend, Ilzay. We were sent from the summer encampment by Umzakhilin, our *zarawinnaj*, the leader of our *taridiqa*, to bring back a full load of *shaimur*, dried fish, for our winter food, all the way to Shimiz, in the west, five hundred miles and back. Our clan has taken to bypassing the caravans and going directly, but this is the first time we have done so in three years."

Must have been an honor for one so young to be entrusted with this responsibility.

"As the *lijti* did, so we expected to find our people in the autumn camp, and we, too, crossed the route without seeing signs of travel, and turned north in the direction of the summer encampment to find out why."

Jirkat paused to sip his cooling *bunnas*. He nodded at the boy and girl sitting together. "These are Winnajhubr and his sister Yuknaj. They left the summer encampment to visit with our neighbor clan Akshullah, just to the east. When they decided to return, they, too, headed for the route to the autumn camp, on the way to the camp itself. They met Hadishti along the way and joined together, and we found them all moving north along the unused route, headed for the summer camp."

Najud asked, "And did you find the summer encampment, and were they there?"

"No, *bikraj*. The camp was there, every *kazr* in place, but no people. No one had been there for a while. It's hard to say for how long, but some of the *kazrab* had begun to sag. Some of their possessions were intact, but not all. When we searched the *kazrab* that were our family's homes, much was disturbed and most of the food was gone."

Khashghuy broke in. "It was the same in the other *kazrab*, too."

At a glance from his older brother, he looked down, abashed, and Jirkat continued.

"We looked for the herds, of course. We could see where they'd been, but the trail was one or two months old. We found some strays, but not the rest." He gestured around them at the miscellaneous animals.

"I thought to see if they had taken the High Pass for some reason, though no trail led there, since we were close enough that it wouldn't cost us much time to be sure. The others agreed, and I brought us here from the summer camp."

It sounded to Penrys as if he were relieved to have described the problem to someone older who might know what to do.

Najud listened impassively to the account.

"I assume you searched for any trail of horses or people on foot leaving the camp, in any direction." he said.

"Of course, *bikraj*, but much time had passed. The trail of the herds should still be visible, but people—perhaps not."

Najud nodded to himself as if he had expected the answer.

"Thank you for your report, *lij*. It was clear and detailed, despite its alarming nature."

Penrys watched Jirkat sit up straighter in response to the praise from an older man.

Well-handled, Naj-sha.

"I'll tell you our story, and we'll see how it intersects with yours," Najud said.

CHAPTER 5

Najud shifted his position so that all could see his face, and spread his hands.

"I am Najud, son of Ilsahr of clan Zamjilah, of the Shubzah tribe, and my mother Kazrsulj is the daughter of Khashjibrim of the same clan. You know her sister, Qizrahi. I have never met my aunt's new kin, and I greet them now."

He bowed low from his seat.

"My companion is the *jarghalti* Penrys, of Ellech."

He lifted an eyebrow at her, and was gratified when she bowed in turn for the audience, her face expressionless.

"Our story is complicated, but I'll be brief, to bring you your news."

He glanced down to collect his thoughts, very conscious of his position as oldest male in this collection of lost and worried sheep, out-tribe though he may be. They were already looking to him for answers, and he had none for them.

"I was in my tenth year of my *tulqiqa*, my travel time, and I was sent by the Ghuzl mar-Tawirqaj in Ussha to Kigali to join an expedition at the Meeting of Waters. The tale was that the Rasesni had invaded Neshilik, and Kigali wanted to know the truth of it, from the reports of their nearest large cavalry force. There were rumors of *bikrajab*—wizards, as the Kigali say—and so they wanted one to join them."

With amusement, he watched Khashghuy nod eagerly to confirm whatever they had heard about Neshilik themselves, while his older brother frowned at him for his unseemly display.

"Penrys, here, came from further away—that's too long a tale for right now." *Or maybe ever.* He shook himself and continued. "When we reached the Gates, we two were sent with other scouts over the old passes behind the Gates on either side, to see what the truth of the story was. We found many things, most importantly that the Rasesni have had wizards all along—they call them mages—and that some *qahulaj* had arisen and driven many of them to flee into Neshilik seeking survival."

At the word of a wizard performing forbidden magic, even Hadishti's sober face revealed her dismay.

"To shorten this story, Penrys defeated and killed this *qahulaj* a month ago, and I earned my *nayith* and took back my name. When we left them, the two nations were negotiating. Neshilik is at peace, for now."

He slashed his hands horizontally in front of him to shift the topic.

"And so we took the High Pass at Jaunor. It's been too long since I've seen my family, and I wished to visit them and share my news."

He took a deep breath to resettle himself. "When we reached the Grandfather *lud*—you know the one?"

There were a few nods.

"There we found several packs, piled around its base."

It was so quiet, he could hear the grazing horses tearing the grasses.

"Just below that, we found more on the trail—discarded possessions, things dropped by the way, all scattered on and off the trail. And, on the trail itself, a dead horse, still in its tack."

Dimghuy's gasp disturbed the silence.

"We moved the horse and freed it from encumbrance, then piled a cairn over it. And we took everything we found and brought it with us, in our packs. I'd like to return it all to the clan-kin it belongs to."

Hadishti leaned forward. "But no bodies? No sign of a fight?"

"The horse had been there perhaps one month, perhaps two," Najud said. "Any signs would be gone. But, no, we found nothing that attested to a struggle, just the inexplicable debris on the trail and the packs around the base of the *lud*."

He stood up and looked at Penrys. *Let's leave them to talk in private, and bring them what we found.*

She rose and joined him, and they walked over to where their donkeys were staked on a line for grazing, still bearing their packs. Their hosts hadn't been sure that their guests would be staying, so they chose not to delay them by unloading the packs. It's what Najud had expected, but now he didn't know what to do. It was only mid-day, but it was likely they would be spending the night with these strays.

They collected the three donkeys that they had used for the things they'd found on the pass and he make a short pack string of them. He led them as slowly as he could back to the *kazrab* where an intense discussion between Hadishti and Jirkat was taking place.

At Najud and Penrys's approach, everyone quieted. Najud stopped outside the circle of the *kazrab* with the donkeys, and then Sharma, Hadishti's daughter, stepped up shyly to hold the lead rope for him. He smiled down at her in thanks.

All the Kurighdunaq folk gathered in front of them solemnly. Najud put himself in their place and shuddered. They would be looking for evidence of members of their family and friends.

With Penrys's help, he pulled out each pack and laid it gently in a long line on the grass, followed by the loose items. There were more than a dozen packs altogether, and no one rushed to open them. The accumulated marks of the world-bow on the leather surfaces were like blows to the silent audience. Last was the forlorn pile of the horse tack he'd pulled off the beast.

"Would you help us, Sharma, by returning these donkeys to the others?" he asked. He didn't want her there when the packs were opened and their owners identified.

She glanced to her mother for permission, and then obediently led the string off.

After her back was turned, Najud reached into his pocket and removed the two toys he'd found, and laid them gently on top of the one small pack.

A low moan came from the young woman, Yuknaj. "Those are Anasha's!" She bent down over the pack and looked inside, then clutched it to her chest while her brother wrapped an arm around her.

Winnajhubr explained, "Our mother and her father came from the *zudiqazd* to see our father on some matter of importance, and brought our little sister as a special treat to see the *taridiqa* that she would join in a few years. We decided to do our clan-visit with their little traveling *kazr* so that they could take our places in the home *kazr* with our father until we returned."

He waved a shaking hand at the smallest *kazr* of the three.

Najud looked at Penrys. This was not for strangers. *Come, let's go keep Sharma company.*

Najud walked slowly away with Penrys, down to the grazing near the spring where Sharma had finished staking the three donkeys.

The girl looked anxiously toward her elders in the camp.

Penrys bespoke him. *Better let her go to them. They're her relatives, too, and her mother will do whatever she thinks is right.*

Najud nodded, and called to the girl, "We'll look after our beasts now. You go join your family."

She flashed them a nervous smile of gratitude and ran back to her kinsmen.

Penrys found a tussock of grass to her liking and sat down on it crosslegged, out of the way of the grazing animals but still within sight of the camp. Najud chose another nearby and joined her.

"What happens now?" she said.

What indeed? They need help.

"I don't know. This is some sort of disaster," he said. "Must have happened more than two months ago, since that's when they would have moved to the autumn camp. I've never heard of anything like this."

"If we don't know 'how,' then just ignore it for now," Penrys said. "Let's go for 'what.' What are the possibilities? Sketch them out for me."

"At the worst," he said, "they're all dead somewhere, maybe one or two hundred people, and we just haven't stumbled across the bodies."

That made his stomach clench.

Then he looked at Penrys and realized she didn't understand the implications. "If their herds can't be found, then the winter camp, where the non-travelers live—that could starve. The old, the young, the injured, the mothers… maybe another fifty or sixty people. That's the whole clan. They'll have other food—they grow some—and that Jirkat and his friends have brought dried fish, and the other clans in the tribe will help, but that might not be enough. The slaughter of the excess beasts is what feeds the people through the long, cold days, and well into the new year."

He leaned forward to make his point. "All the warriors are with the *taridiqa*, except for a very few left to support the *zudiqazd*, and this Undullah tribe is not overlarge. This clan will vanish, absorbed into the other clans of the tribe."

Cocking his head at the eight people gathered around the packs in mourning, he said, "They're the walking dead. They haven't thought it through yet, except maybe Jirkat, but they probably don't even have enough people to fetch the remaining wealth of the tribe home."

At Penrys's inquisitive look, he said, "The *kazrab* and everything in them. The rugs made by the women, the leather work done by the men. All the work of their hands that is not in the *zudiqazd* is rotting, a gift for thieves and the weather and the little scavengers. The people in the winter camp may not be able to ride out and salvage it, especially without the pack animals. Whatever these people can carry, that's what they will own."

Penrys swallowed. "Well, if that's the worst, then what we need to do is help them find the people and the herds. They have to know, one way or another."

Najud's heart warmed at her response, but he shook his head. "I'm not of their clan or even their tribe."

"I saw how they looked at you," she said. "Besides, you have relatives here…" Her voice trailed off as she realized what that meant.

"Yes, and they're likely to be among the dead," he said, quietly.

"The missing! Not the dead. We don't know that yet."

I wonder how many children my aunt Qizrahi had? When I last learned the family names, it was only the one, Zaybirs, but that was ten years ago. All gone, like the water from that spring, trickling back into the earth?

CHAPTER 6

Hadishti's son, Dimghuy, walked down to Najud and Penrys about an hour later.

They'd spent the time moving the tethers for their animals to give them all fresh grass to graze. Najud was eager to either move on or make plans to camp here, but they would have to invite him to stay, and he couldn't hurry that decision in the shock of what they'd brought from the High Pass.

The time that was passing was mute evidence of how much they needed someone to lead them, to make those decisions unhampered by inexperience.

The young man bowed to both of them. "My mother asks you to make your camp with us this evening, and to join us in our discussions."

Najud glanced up at the circle of *kazrab* where everyone was watching, and then looked over at Penrys, who nodded her agreement.

"We would be honored," he said, and the look of relief on Dimghuy's face was evidence of how formal the request had been.

The young man waved his arm at the camp, and all the men walked down through the long grass to help with the unloading of the animals.

Every time Najud set his hand to a pack, one of them was before him, lifting it down on his behalf. At first it amused him, but a throttled word of exasperation from Penrys, who was getting the same treatment, finally prompted a response.

"I have been traveling on my own for ten years, *barqahab*, and am perfectly capable of unloading a horse, or even a donkey!"

Dimghuy looked shocked. "But you are *bikrajab*. It's not fitting."

Najud snorted. "I am many things, but helpless isn't one of them." He could hear Penrys's suppressed chuckle in the background.

"I'll tell you what I need," he said, "and we'll do this together. Yes?"

The young men nodded, and things went more smoothly after that. They left the horses and donkeys loose in a herd of their own, accustomed as they were to each other, and clustered the packs, frames, and tack on a platform of rocks under their waterproof canvas covers, secure from any sudden rain.

Their helpers wouldn't let them shoulder the *kamah* and the rest of their camp gear, so Najud gave up and followed them to their designated site, some distance behind Hadishti's *kazr*.

At least it's relatively private.

He shook his head at Penrys's remark.

Yes, but they'll be scandalized when they realize there is no barrier between the male and female sides.

I wonder if that's what Hadishti was thinking of when she picked this spot? I owe her my thanks, if so.

Najud smiled privately, and then stepped up to direct the erection of the simple tent. Penrys was going to discover just how little privacy there really was in the *taridiqa*.

Penrys pitched in with the chores around the camp, or at least she tried to. She spoke to Hadishti about sharing supplies, but was turned down, politely but firmly. When she offered to help with preparations or cooking, the woman just shook her head, kindly. "This is no trouble, *bikrajti*, no need for you to concern yourself."

The youngest Zannib had resumed their herd duties, all but Yuknaj who was helping Hadishti with dinner, and they rode the perimeter of the grazing animals, encouraging them to stay settled in the vicinity of the spring. Penrys turned to Najud for some employment, but found him deep in conversation with the other young men. Even from a distance, Penrys recognized the "getting acquainted" tenor of the discussion and thought her presence would disturb it.

Left to her own devices, then, she located the highest rock in the nearby terrain, within sight of the camp, and waited. Some of the packs from the High Pass had been claimed and doubtless each of the *kazrab* had its share. From her vantage point, she saw the remainder resting in a forlorn heap, not far from the central fire where Yuknaj was tending to a stew. The smell of flatbreads baking rose from Hadishti's *kazr*, making Penrys's stomach grumble.

Not easy to fit in here. I'm a foreigner, wearing the wrong clothing, and a wizard. That last designation is the one they seem most comfortable with—at least they know what to do with that. Maybe Najud is right, maybe we need some sort of status in their eyes to be sharing a tent. Their country, their rules.

One thing I can do. That's a lot of animals they're trying to control. Wouldn't hurt to get a good count, even if they already have one.

She settled into a comfortable position and did a detailed scan, segment by segment, around a full circle—five times, once each for the horses, donkeys, cattle, sheep, and goats. It was easier to count the species one by one. Almost forty horses, including their own, their seven donkeys, twenty-two cattle, thirty-five sheep, and seventeen goats.

With three or four herdsmen? How can they possible control that?

Even as she thought it, all three of the outriders trotted in from their posts, stripped the tack from their sturdy mounts, and tethered them near the edge of the camp.

Even so simple a meal as goat stew and fresh flatbread was a welcome change, after more than a week crossing the High Pass eating even simpler fare. The conversation around the fire was subdued and it deliberately avoided the topics on everyone's mind.

Grief warred with hope in most of the minds Penrys touched, the dread engendered by those mute packs versus the uncertainty, the possibility that their friends and family could yet be found alive.

Hadishti kept her eye on everyone, and when she laid her empty bowl down in front of the bit of carpet she used as a seat, all of her campmates did the same, and the conversation stopped.

She spoke to Najud, across the fire. "We of the Kurighdunaq clan thank you, *bikraj*, you and your companion, for the kindness you've done us, bringing us this unhappy news of our kinsmen. You see us here, three families, unable to decide on our next action."

Jirkat nodded from his own spot, in support of her statement.

"We have spoken," she said, "all of us, about what we should do. With one thing we all agree."

Najud listened attentively.

"We want you to advise us," she told him.

Penrys held her face expressionless. Najud was not surprised, she saw—he had expected something like this.

He raised one hand our, palm up, diffidently. "I am just a *tulqaj*, a traveler. Out-clan and out-tribe."

Hadishti nodded, and waited.

Najud spoke confidently. "If it were me, I would return to the summer encampment, which you say is not far. I'd make an appraisal of what's gone, and I'd do a careful search again for your missing kin. The herds especially can't have vanished without a trace. It seems to me that so many, even after two months, would leave a trail we can see."

He raised his finger in the air. "I don't say you have not already done this. But this is what I would do."

Jirkat said, "Yes, we've done this. But we were in a hurry, I confess, expecting at any moment to find our families, and rushing to seek them."

He looked down. "We haven't found them. Now it's time to retrace our steps and start again."

He exchanged an enigmatic look with Hadishti, then he bowed low from his seat to Najud. "*Bikraj*, you are clan-kin through Qizrahi, and no one can deny it. You are well-traveled, you are older than all of us here, except Hadishti, and you and your companion have seen wonders. You have been on the *taridiqa* in your own clan for many years—you are not strange to our ways."

Penrys noted his hesitation. *What are they leading up to?*

"We, all of us, would like you to be *zarawinnaj* for us, to lead us to our *zudiqazd* after we search again, as you advise, and there to guest with us for the winter."

This time Najud was surprised, Penrys saw, however he tried to hide it.

Hadishti added, "We need a man of your experience, *bikraj*, and we need *bikrajab*, too, for if this is not wizard-work, then I don't know what else to call it."

Najud lifted an eyebrow at Penrys, his expression unusually sober.

She shrugged. *We must winter somewhere, you said, and they seem to need us. Besides, you can't leave something this... whatever this is... uninvestigated.*

"I will swear the oaths of a *zarawinnaj*," he said to Jirkat. "We'll see you to your winter camp and do what we can to find your missing along the way."

CHAPTER 7

"Not what you expected, is it?" Penrys said late that night, careful that her voice didn't carry beyond their tent.

Her question met with silence, so she tried again. "Came home to be a master-wizard, and instead… I suppose this is just a different sort of mastership."

She was curled up against his back, and in any case it was too dark to see his face. She left his mind in privacy, all in turmoil as it was, but she wanted to help, if she could.

"The *zarawinnaj* is a position of great responsibility," he said, at last. "It's either the clan leader or someone he appoints, and the man who undertakes it is much older than I am, very experienced, very respected. He holds the safety of the clan in his hands."

He turned over to face her, in the dark.

"I am *not* qualified to do this, Pen-sha. I don't know these people, I don't know their herds. I don't even know the *tarizd*, the route."

"They know that. And they know the route home," she said.

He snorted. "We may not even go back that way. The shortest route, unless there's an obstacle, would be straight back to the *zudiqazd* before the weather turns. We have to get this remnant of the herds back to the winter camp. At least they're in good shape, healthy and fat."

"I can help with that. I did a count this evening and you know I can find them if they stray."

"Good. I'll rely on you for that. We are far too few to make the herding easy."

They lay in silence for a moment.

"Naj-sha," she said, finally, "What do they expect of me, of the… woman of the migration leader?"

"Oh, people come tell her things they don't want to say to the *zarawinnaj* directly. The women and the youngsters, particularly. We won't have that here, I think—too small. And they don't know you. Besides, they'll be shy of a *bikrajti*—it's not likely they've ever seen one before."

"That Hadishti will help," he mused. "Her other son's now a *nal-jarghal* so we can look to her for commonsense about that. But I've never heard of a *bikraj* leading the *taridiqa*—it would never happen."

"It's happened now," she said. "You'll get them home."

"I'll have to," he said, his voice still troubled. "At least it's not very far, just a few days."

"But won't that depend on what we find?"

"That's what I'm worried about," he said.

"And that's why they need you." She tapped his chest with her finger. "Now go to sleep and stop thinking about it. Or else I'll make you."

As she'd hoped, his attention focused on her, and he hitched himself up on his elbow to free up both his hands. "Oh, yes? Show me how you'd do that."

Najud was all business the next morning, up before daylight and packed. He went to each *kazr* and spent time asking about pack animals, food supplies, and special skills.

Penrys made herself useful. She scanned the whereabouts of the herds and came up short for one of the small, shaggy cattle, so she extended her reach and found him. She saddled up her Rasesni mare and went after him.

He was a one-horned stubborn old bull, no longer the herd-leader, and he liked the patch of grass he was in better than the company of the herd which had stopped obeying him. But when Penrys started to crowd him, he grunted in token objection and ambled back to his herd in front of her. Dimghuy was already in place on the herd perimeter and was glad to see them both.

"I couldn't go look for him," he said, "without someone to hold the rest of them."

Penrys smiled at him. "I know. I think this is going to be my job, looking for the strays and bringing them back."

"You, *bikrajti*?"

"It's something I can do to help." She didn't tell him, but she would also be tracking all the people, since there weren't so many.

She could be Najud's eyes and ears on the backtrail. *All strays accounted for.*

Good. Come in to the camp.

Her lips twitched. *He's busy. It's not just the two of us anymore.*

She tethered her mare on the edge of camp, after taking the bit out of her mouth so she could graze more easily.

The tent she'd shared with Najud had been packed, and the last *kazr* was being disassembled before her eyes. Jirkat's group had already uncovered the roof felts and dropped that canvas to the ground, and the rectangular felts themselves were half gone, exposing the thin rafters that ran from the tops of the five-foot circular wall to the roof crown, the *zamjilah*.

Hadishti and Yuknaj stacked the felts into tidy piles and rolled the canvas covers tightly. Yuknaj chased each anchor rope as it fell and coiled it neatly.

The men dropped down to the ground when they were done and stripped first the canvas and then the felts from the outer wall, leaving the light wooden lattice sections standing when they were done. Only two long ropes remained—the one around the top of the lattice, just where the rafters connected, and another halfway down.

Khashghuy ducked through the doorframe into the exposed interior, now stripped of carpets and contents, and steadied the two long poles that propped the multi-spoked *zamjilah* while Jirkat and Ilzay walked around the wall and lifted the crutch of each rafter loose from the top of the lattice wall, and then pulled it out of its slot in the *zamjilah*. Then Ilzay went in to help Khashghuy lower the wheel-like crown. By the time they came back out with it, the ropes were gone from the lattice wall, and Jirkat was untying the bindings lacing the lattice sections to each other.

Penrys watched all this in fascination. The women took each lattice section as it came free and collapsed it into a compact stack of sticks, the leather bindings at the joints holding the lattice-work together. In what seemed like moments, the entire *kazr* lay in its components at their feet—a stack of rectangular felts and rolled canvas sections, coils of rope, five bundled lattices, a pile of rafters, the two roof-crown props, and the door and its disassembled frame. The *zamjilah* itself, brightly painted like the rafters and the props and the door with its frame, leaned jauntily against the tallest pile.

Najud joined her. "Two horse loads, for a *kazr* this size, but that includes all the contents."

He nodded back at the spot where the smallest *kazr* had been, now just a pile of parts. "A very small *kazr*, four lattices like that one, can fit on a single horse, but you need two for a five or six lattice one."

"Can a single person set one up?" she asked.

He waggled a hand. "It's been done, but it's difficult. If you're going to travel alone, you use a *kamah*, like ours. That smallest *kazr*, the one Yuknaj and Winnajhubr borrowed from their mother, held two adults and the little girl. A *kazr* is always more comfortable than a *kamah*, and stronger against bad weather, but not for a solitary traveler."

"How big do they get?"

"In the winter camps, once in a while, you may see a seven or eight section one. Needs long rafters, one like that, and it's not easy to move, so they're uncommon. And even the winter camps shift locations a little bit, every few years. For very big families, it's easier to have two *kazrab*, or even three, sometimes connected, sometimes not."

Penrys surveyed the treeless steppe. "Where do you get the wood?" Their cooking fires had been fueled by dried dung.

Najud surprised her with a broad grin. "You trade for it, from the eastern woodlands. Very precious, it is."

His face sobered suddenly. "More of the wealth of this tribe— their *kazrab*, left behind in the summer encampment."

"Come. We break camp now." He strode away to the ashes of the prior night's fire, where everyone not on herd duty was waiting.

CHAPTER 8

Najud eyed his new clan responsibilities, as they stood and waited for his instructions. Hadishti's children, Sharma and Dimghuy, were already on herd duty, and he would send Yuknaj out to join them as soon as all the pack animals were loaded.

Jirkat's group had a pack string of both trade goods and their travel loads, as Najud and Penrys did, and each of those needed a leader. The small pack strings that the other two groups had been using for their loads also required leaders.

"Today we travel to the summer encampment. Jirkat tells me it's twenty miles. The cattle are the slowest, so we'll go at their pace.

"After we load the pack animals, here's how we'll do it. The outriders will be joined by Penrys. She can find strays and bring them back. It's a... *bikraj* skill."

Penrys nodded to them when they glanced at her.

"I want Jirkat and Hadishti with me as we go. Khashguy will take your string, Jirkat, and we'll add to it Hadishti's four and Yuknaj's three. Winnajhubr will take my string, the horses and donkeys both."

He noted both Winnajhubr's pride at the increased responsibility, and Ilzay's suppressed dismay at receiving no task yet.

"Ilzay, I want you to be scout on our way. Ride out one or two miles and confirm the route. Come back and tell us about hazards. Find us a good spot for the mid-day break. This is not part of your clan's *tarizd*, not until we reach your summer encampment, so stay close."

Najud suppressed a smile as Ilzay almost visibly swelled with satisfaction.

"Penrys will watch our backtrail as well as help the outriders."

He looked at each of them. "Any questions?"

Receiving silence, he waved Yuknaj and Penrys off to the herds and started everyone else on the task of loading all the pack animals for the long day's walk.

Penrys mind-scanned all the way around every half hour or so, first counting the animals that should be in front of her, by species, to make sure none had strayed, and then more widely, looking for others.

Her range had improved from the two or three miles of a couple of months ago, ever since she had pulled in the power of the Rasesni wizards in their fight against the Voice, the wizard she'd killed before she could learn where he had come from, chained like herself. Now she thought she could reach five or six miles. Certainly she had no trouble following Ilzay's meandering path as he scouted forward on the line of march, and back to inform Najud.

She'd been pleased with her one find before the mid-day break, a flock of seven sheep, led by a stubborn old ewe who dodged her for a while before trotting before her into the larger flock moved along by Yuknaj. "These are my mother's sheep," the girl called, and Penrys lifted an arm to her in acknowledgment before fading back to the rear again.

Ever since mid-day, however, she'd been kept busy picking up pockets of strays—horses, mostly, and sheep. The cattle she found were independent minded, reverting to their ancestral behaviors in the absence of people. One bull was belligerent, delaying her until she drove the rest of his little herd forward without him. His nerve broke, then, and he followed them, bellowing defiance at her as he went.

I hope Dimghuy can handle that one.

She kept her mental attention on the boy in case there was a sudden alarm, but it must have worked out all right.

The sun was about two hours from setting when she contacted Najud for more than just a simple update.

How close are we? I've got more animals coming up than I've got daylight to handle.

Half an hour should see us there. We're planning to swing the herds up north of the camp. What more have you found?

Horses, mostly, and more cattle. Sheep, too. Six bunches, maybe more. Haven't felt a wandering goat all day—they must have gone somewhere else.

There was a delay while Najud considered the situation.

We'll be there at least a full day tomorrow. Let's fetch them in then, and you can have Sharma to help.

That'll do.

Penrys rotated her head until her neck cracked. It had been a long day in the saddle, more mileage than just leading a pack string. Lonely, too, without Najud to chat with. She hadn't wanted to interrupt the *zarawinnaj* while he was working.

They'd made their camp in the fading daylight, just on the northern perimeter of the abandoned encampment. Najud had had their *kamah* set up on the edge closest to the looming, unlit structures, marking the margin and serving as a sort of protective barrier, but even so, Penrys noticed the constant sliding of eyes south into the dark, every time a flicker of firelight provided an excuse.

Collecting dried dung for the fire had been no problem, here where the herds had spent some time two months ago. The small group discussed their plans for the next day as they ate a simple communal dinner. Najud had explained to her how unusual that was—normally each *kazr* had its fire and meals separately—but while the weather was clear, he encouraged this gathering for the sake of helping these clan fragments bond together.

Penrys approved. *We'd be cooking outside for ourselves anyway, so I'm just as glad someone else is doing it for the group.*

"Tomorrow," Najud said, "we'll see what we can find in the encampment and around it. Some tasks we know already—Penrys says she's found more of the herd strays in the area, so she'll look for them in the morning with Sharma and bring them into the herds. They'll need an anchor there to receive them, even if we're not going to be moving them—that'll be you, Dimghuy."

"I want to salvage every animal we can." There were nods all around the fire. "Penrys, when you're done, can you get me a count of every horse that shows evidence of having ever carried a pack? Sharma and Dimghuy can show you what to look for."

"All right," Penrys said. It seemed to her that Najud's voice had gotten even deeper with the advent of his new responsibilities.

Heads came up at that. Jirkat said, "What are you planning, *zarawinnaj?*"

"It's only about eighty miles back to the *zudiqazd*, if you take the outward or returning routes from here, yes? And less if we go directly. Is there any reason we couldn't go straight there, anything in the way?"

Najud's gaze was fixed on Jirkat who answered, "No, people do come visit sometimes, like their family." He waved a hand at Yuknaj and Winnajhubr. "We can travel directly."

"Good," Najud said. "That's only six days of easy riding, since we have to take it slow if we want the cattle to keep their weight. We'll spend a day or two here and gather fuel for the journey. Then we'll take everything we can, make packs for every animal that can bear them. I want to salvage it all—all the wealth of the clan, if we can carry it."

Penrys noted Hadishti's clear nod of approval.

"It will mean we make less distance each day," Najud said, "spending all that time loading and unloading the packs, but if the weather holds, what's another couple of days?"

Penrys asked, "Won't we need more people as herdsmen, as we pick up more animals?"

"Not necessarily. The big caravans are mostly long pack trains with a limited herd of spares and food. We'll be the same. Every horse that can carry a load will be part of a string, and so the loose herds shouldn't be unmanageable."

Ilzay said, "But what about our families?"

"We look for them first, in the morning. I want to see the route up from the spring camp, its trace on the ground. Whatever happened, those herds didn't fly out of here, and the numbers Penrys reports don't account for most of them. Anything fresher than the spring trail should be visible. We find the herds, we may find the people."

"Forgive a foreigner for the question," Penrys said, looking around the fire at the others, "but how often do people visit from the winter camp? Is it unusual?"

Hadishti said, "No, each time we stop for the encampment, we tend to get one or two visitors. They know where we'll be, and when, of course."

"That's what I would have thought," Penrys said. "Then where are those visitors? It's been at least two months since this camp should have been moved. If someone came up from the winter camp, wouldn't they have gone back and brought others to search, and to salvage everything, by now? Why is all of this still here?"

The silence was unbroken for several moments, then Najud said, "If we had enough people, we would send a rider to the *zudiqazd* with the news, and they would come meet us part way. Meanwhile, we can't be sure there's been a visitor—perhaps there were none."

He looked around at his little command. "In any case, we can't do everything. Our responsibility is to make one last assessment of what happened, preserve the clan's livelihood, and get to the *zudiqazd* as quickly as we can, in that order. If there's a problem in the winter camp, we can't make it better by not bringing all we can."

CHAPTER 9

When Penrys returned to camp at mid-day, she was eager to get her first daylight look at one of the seasonal camps of which she'd heard so much, even under the macabre circumstances. All the outlying stray animals had been brought in, young Sharma having proved very helpful in rounding them up, once she'd gotten over her awe at how easily Penrys located them.

No goats had turned up, to be added to the current flock, but all the others settled into their new grazing smoothly. It was clear that they recognized their erstwhile herd companions, except for the horses and donkeys that Najud and Penrys had brought. The donkeys were proving to be a problem, not in themselves, but in the shock with which their new equine neighbors viewed them. When Penrys left, Sharma and Dimghuy were busy pushing the donkeys to the outside of the assemblage, to keep them as far from the other horses as possible.

She dropped the bit from her horse's mouth to let her graze on her tether at the edge of the camp, and walked in to take a look.

There were about twenty-five *kazrab* still standing, and fifteen more bare circles in the grass, with the *kazr* components stacked neatly nearby. They'd been arranged in a broad oval with their doorframes facing inward. Jirkat and his brother Khashghuy, teamed with Winnajhubr, were taking another one apart.

Movement caught her eye, and she spotted Hadishti and Yuknaj emerging from another *kazr* bearing bundles and small packs. They added them to a pile of decorated wood which Penrys thought might be furnishings, disassembled, and went back in for more.

She didn't immediately see Najud, so she bespoke him. *I'm back. Where are you?*

Come to the southeast side of the encampment. Bring your horse.

She reclaimed her mare and then trotted down the open oval space between the campsites, lifting a hand to the work teams as she passed. Well outside of the camp she found both Najud and

Ilzay standing on the ground, holding their horses' reins, and arguing about droppings.

"Too recent," Ilzay was insisting, probing the sample in his hand with a knife. "It's dry, of course, but not five months dry."

Penrys hid her smile, and dismounted to join them. Najud turned to explain.

"Turns out that Ilzay is considered the best of the trackers we have, so he and I have been looking for the trail of the main herds. We rode a large circle all around the camp and its closer grazing grounds, and there's no relatively fresh trail. Of course, the herd came in from the spring camp five months ago, and that trail is still there. We're standing on it."

Ilzay nodded his agreement.

"One of two things happened. "Either there is another trail even further out on the grazing range, where we haven't looked yet, or the spring trail was used again two or three months ago, which is what we're debating."

"Or they flew away, as you said," Penrys said, supplying a third joking possibility.

Najud's mouth quirked. "Speaking of flying…"

Penrys gave him a questioning look. *Are you sure you want me to reveal that? Won't it just scare everyone?*

And make me more of a foreigner than I am already.

"I think we have to," Najud said, startling Ilzay who hadn't heard the silent question. "A large circle at the outer edges, and then a long look down the route from the spring camp."

She sighed. "Better warn them, then."

"We'll all come back to camp first, and you can tell us about the herd totals, like a *dirum*, a herd-mistress."

She remounted her horse and followed them. *Some herd-mistress—I can describe what an animal feels like, but not what it looks like. Not too useful for that.*

When they reached the two work teams, they dismounted and called them together.

"Tell us the counts, *dirum*," he said, calling on Penrys.

"We've gathered all the strays I found yesterday evening. There may be more of course, further away."

She had their attention. On these numbers depended their plans for salvaging the encampment and feeding the clan in the winter camp.

"When I first met you, and counting our own stock, there were forty horses. That's now ninety-three."

Najud interrupted her. "How many should there have been, Jirkat?"

"I don't know the real count, from our *dirum*."

"Guess," Najud said.

"Then I would say at least three hundred and eighty. There were about two hundred people, and you see forty *kazrab* here, so the minimum would be two hundred and eighty, just for people and shelter, and more for food and other things, plus the young ones."

Penrys continued. "The cattle have gone from twenty-two to forty-two."

Jirkat looked at his brother uncertainly. "From a hundred and fifty?"

"No change in the goats, seventeen, but the sheep went from thirty-five to eighty-four. And of course, there are the seven donkeys we brought."

Jirkat echoed her. "Maybe three hundred goats, and four hundred sheep, including the young ones."

Hadishti said, "That's about a quarter of the horses and cattle, or so, and less for the sheep and goats."

She looked at Najud. "We found some food—that includes the cheeses that should be here, aging for the winter, and the summer fruits drying, too—but it's not as much as there should be. Still, the fleeces from the spring shearing are here, loaded into their packs, as usual."

When Penrys's grimace caught her attention, Hadishti raised an eyebrow, and Penrys was forced to explain. "It's good news, after a fashion—only the living need food."

Hadishti nodded thoughtfully. "Maybe, but many of the personal packs were left behind. I can't say what every family carried with them, of course, but it seemed to me that for some food and the packs to carry it were what's gone missing. Maybe some clothing, but many things of value were left behind—small, portable things. For others, everything was abandoned."

Khashghuy broke in. "But they left their pack frames and packs, for the horses. Saddles, too. Are they on foot? Why, if the horses are with them? What are they doing for shelter?"

Najud just shook his head and spread his hands.

"I must speak to you now of something else," he said, and motioned for Penrys to step into the center.

"This *bikrajti* is different in some ways from the *bikrajab* you may have heard of. The herdsmen already know how she can reach out and sense your animals from a couple of miles away. We Zannib *bikrajab* can learn this, too—she is teaching me."

Penrys could feel the wariness behind their nods. They knew something else was coming.

"We are lucky," he said, "that she can help us in other ways. By being our eyes in the air."

He cocked an eyebrow at her. She clenched her teeth to keep her face expressionless and invoked her wings. They rose behind her, taller than her head even when held close to her body, the feathers colored like an eagle's in golds and browns. The familiar odd sensation of the clothes on her back sliding unimpeded between what ought to have been solid attachments contradicted the feel of the wings against her shoulder blades and the tail against the base of her spine.

How can they feel real to my body even when you can see daylight where they pass over my clothing?

If they were a specialized magical device, as she believed, it was no technology she had ever encountered.

The startled audience backed up involuntarily, but Hadishti recovered herself and approached to get a better look.

"Is this something our *bikrajab* can learn?" she asked, and Penrys remembered that her older son had just become an apprentice to a master wizard.

"I don't know, *lijti*," she said. "I don't know the principles on which they work but surely it is in areas that the Zannib…"

"…do not usually study, as *nal-jarghal*, like your son," Najud supplied.

She flashed a grateful glance to Najud for his rescue.

"Najud has asked me to check the ground for trails while the daylight lasts, first for the outer range of the grazing. It may be that I can find more strays while I do that."

She nodded to Ilzay. "After that, I'll look down the trail from the spring camp. Sometimes you can see more clearly from the air than from the ground."

Collapsing the wings back to wherever they went when not in use, she remounted her horse. Better to ride back to the nearest of the horse herds and untack her there before leaving, instead of scaring them all by just launching in front of them.

They were too polite to talk about it while she was in earshot, but she could feel the dismay and unease in their minds as she rode away.

CHAPTER 10

Penrys took advantage of the prevailing winds from the west and pulled herself high enough that she could manage most of the work by gliding. Her mind-scan reached no further from the air, but she could cover a much larger stretch of territory when not limited by a horse's long-distance speed.

She worked downwind to a spot about ten miles southeast of the camp, not without marking the camp's landmarks very clearly first, and began a circle to the south. She planned to circle the camp once at that distance. That would be a flight of sixty or seventy miles, two or three hours in the air. If she found many strays, she might have to widen it the next day, but a full circle five miles further out would take much longer, more than she could fly in a single day.

At least, she assumed that was true. She'd never had an opportunity to fly free like this in daylight, for hours, without worrying about witnesses. Did the wings tire, if they were a device? How were they powered? Her back and shoulders felt some of the effort, and her belly, keeping her legs from dragging in the air— what would their limits be? Her only other long flight, in the dark, looking for the Kigali expedition a few weeks ago, had covered about forty miles and hadn't tired her seriously at all.

Assuming this first circuit didn't exhaust her, that left her about two hours of daylight to look down the southeast trail toward the spring camp, maybe thirty miles coming and going. The lowering sun at that time of day should make marks on the ground stand out more clearly.

She would be out of range of mind-speech with Najud the whole time. Unless she found the people they were looking for, she would be all alone, free as a bird.

Najud tried not to worry as the sun set and Penrys had still not returned. It was unnerving, being out of mind-speech range with her. None of the Kurighdunaq clan-kin mentioned it to him, and that worried him in other ways. If it had been a scout that was overdue, all would have spoken of it, with concern. But what he had decided to do at mid-day, showing them her wings, had made her more alien than just a foreign *bikrajti*, and so they held their tongues. Who knew, after all, what a foreign wizard could do?

He hadn't wanted to expose her, fearing this sort of consequence, but it had to be done, for the better survival of the whole group. And now she was out there somewhere in the dark, and he had no idea where.

The work at the encampment had gone well. All the *kazrab* were disassembled and ready to be loaded, and it looked like there would be enough packhorses to carry the camp, barely. He hoped Penrys would turn up more of them, though it might take another day to bring them back to the accumulating herds. Better more horses than trying to improvise packs for the cattle, or even the goats—assuming the Kurighdunaq even trained those animals for packs.

But where was she?

If Ilzay was right, then they needed to take the spring trail southeast out of the camp in hopes of finding the missing people.

He looked up. The moon was half-full, and the sky was clear. She'd flown at night before, he remembered, that night she located the Kigali encampment, and came back to him. That first night he had finally acted on his desire for her, and found her willing. He smiled, lost in his thoughts.

He caught Hadishti's eye on him. She glanced down at his bowl, still untouched.

"She'll be back, *bikraj*. Who could stop her, up in the air? Maybe she was overtaken by darkness and will return in the morning, cold but unharmed."

Could she be simply lost? She has water and the makings of fire, on her belt, and even a bit of food.

He nodded to Hadishti and conscientiously ate his dinner.

The talk around the fire later was quiet, but less haunted than the night before. Packing up the summer encampment had taken some of the curse off of the abandoned *kazrab*.

Najud had tried to stop checking the sky, once he'd noticed that everyone looked up when he did. No one wanted to mention contingencies—what they should do if Penrys were still missing in the morning. Time enough then to discuss it.

Naj-sha, can you hear me?

He jumped to his feet, abandoning all dignity, and faced the south.

Are you all right?

Fine. Sorry to be late. I have news—be there in a few minutes.

Najud tried to convey his relief through the mind-speech. *Come to the fire. We're all here.*

He couldn't keep himself from grinning when he turned to face the others. "She's not far away, and coming in."

He sat down again somewhat abruptly, before his knees weakened altogether.

He rose again a few minutes later when the moon outlined the dark shape of something large gliding in from the south.

Penrys stumbled a bit on landing, and staggered. Najud walked over to take her arm.

"It's nothing," she told him. "I've never flown that long and I'm just tired. The wings can go on forever, seems like, but not the rest of me." She rotated her head until her neck cracked.

All eight of their fellow-travelers had stood up to watch. Hadishti picked up a bowl she had been keeping warm by the fire and a skin of water and held them out. "Come have some dinner and tell us your news," she called.

Penrys smiled at the welcome. She took the skin of water and drained a good bit of it before stoppering it again and laying it on the ground.

She took the bowl and its spoon from Hadishti's hands. "If you don't mind, I'll eat standing. Anything to work the kinks out."

She took her first two bites, and then paused. "I've found strays around the encampment, quite a few of them. And then I took the trail southeast about thirty miles."

Looking over at Ilzay, she said, "I can't vouch for how old it is, but the next thirty miles look the same to me as the part we stood on earlier today. If that was recently traveled, then…"

She took another couple of bites. "Rather than just retrace that path back, the shortest way, I decided to swing west until I was due south of here, figuring that would put me near the direct route to the winter camp. Then I would come back that way. The other two sides of the triangle, you understand. I wanted to see if there was anything along that route we should know about, like more strays. There wasn't quite enough daylight left, but the moonlight would be sufficient."

Privately for Najud, she added, *After all, it's just the mind-glows I needed to see, not the ground.*

"So, there I was, maybe twenty-five or thirty miles south of here, when I found three more strays. Human ones."

She took advantage of the reaction to set the bowl down and pick up the skin of water again. Najud could see her throat working as she swallowed.

After she put the skin down, she patted the air to calm everyone.

"I landed out of sight—didn't want to scare them. My walking in without warning was bad enough. Two boys, they were, and a very injured man. The boys are Zabrash and Birssahr, and the man is your predecessor"—with a nod to Najud—"Umzakhilin, the *zarawinnaj.*"

CHAPTER 11

Penrys answered their questions far into the evening.

"The boys were out herding, three days before the camp was due to move again. They were down in some pocket of land to the southwest, with their sheep, and stayed overnight."

Jirkat commented to Najud, "This is their first migration. We put them together in their first year—makes it easier for them."

"When they came back to camp the next evening," Penrys continued, "they found it like you did. Scared them to death, I imagine, though they didn't say so, of course. There was just one person there—this Umzakhilin."

She swallowed. "The boys think he was trampled. He was sleeping when I saw him and we didn't wake him up. He can't walk—his feet and his legs are broken. The boys say he doesn't talk, either. They can't make him understand where he is, and he doesn't respond to them."

She looked at Jirkat. "I think you should be very proud of these boys. They told me how they sat in the ruins of that encampment"—she hooked her thumb back at it—"and decided what they should do.

"They couldn't abandon the *zarawinnaj*, but he could neither ride nor walk, nor help them in any way. So they built a travois, two long poles with canvas slung between them. They planned to tie it to a horse to drag and take him to the winter camp."

Penrys raised a finger. "Mind you, they only had their own two horses and that one flock of sheep at the time. So before they could go, they needed more horses. They did what we did—they went looking for strays. They didn't go very far, but they added twenty-three horses and more sheep—they've got sixty or so now, I think. They picked up some cattle, too, but couldn't keep them. And they got some of the missing goats, about forty."

Ilzay said, "Just think, nine years old. But they're only, what, twenty-five miles away, after two months? What happened?"

Najud said, "Ambition. Too many animals for two inexperienced herdsmen to control."

Penrys nodded. "That's right. They knew about how far the winter camp was, and in what direction. They knew it was too many animals, but how could they not try to keep them all? Whatever had happened, the clan would need everything they could bring.

"So they ransacked the encampment looking for food. They pilfered two *kamahab*, since there was no way they could raise a *kazr* by themselves, and decided to take it slow. Dragging an injured man on a travois would slow them down anyway, but they hoped they could do at least five miles a day."

Yuknaj asked, "What happened?"

"The herds slowed them down. First one fragment would go off on its own, and then another, and they would have to stop and fetch it back. Winter food for the clan, you understand. It didn't matter how long it took, as long as they got there before the snow with as much food as they could bring.

"So some days they would make two miles, or three. And then they'd have to camp there while they lost all that distance bringing the strays back to the herds. They had to abandon the cattle—too independent."

She rubbed her hand over her face. "I found cattle on that route, when I was returning in the dark. We can probably get them back."

"The horses were a mixed blessing. Some days they traveled well together, but if something happened, one group might split off for ten miles and need to be tracked the next day. The sheep had to be treated as separate flocks—they didn't know how to make the bellwethers cooperate. But the goats, the goats were the worst."

Winnajhubr burst out laughing. "I can well believe it."

"It's a good thing these boys were stubborn," Penrys said, "They sat before me, having guested me hastily with a bit of their dinner, and told me solemnly that if the goats cost them one more week, they were going to slaughter them all and bring back the wind-dried meat instead. You could see that Zabrash, at least, was hoping it would turn out that way."

She half-smiled. "You never saw two more exhausted youngsters, but they're tough. They've kept Umzakhilin alive and set his broken bones. He should be able to walk by now, but they can't get him to try."

Najud asked, "How did you leave it with them?"

"I told them who you all were, and where, and told them a little about myself to explain how I got there, foreign wizard that I am. Then I said I would come again in one or two days and tell them our plans."

Hadishti said to Najud, "Their families, like ours, are missing, too. But they made the same decision you did, *bikraj*, to bring everything back to the rest of the clan at the *zudiqazd*. I don't see any other course than to travel south to meet them, and sweep them up with us."

Najud said, "Ilzay, your trail may be correct, but it's two months cold, and winter is coming. Tomorrow we should round up the strays around the camp that Penrys found, and then, the next morning, set out for the *zudiqazd*. Penrys can return to tell the boys we're on our way when we leave.

He looked around the fire, but no one voiced an objection.

Late that night, alone in their *kamah*, Najud kneaded the soreness from Penrys's back while she melted in satisfaction.

"I don't suppose you'd do this every night?" she murmured.

"Only when you've earned it," he said, and slapped her shoulder lightly to tell her he was done.

"It was exhilarating," she said, her voice muffled from lying on her stomach. "Flying like that, I mean. No one to notice, no one scared of me. Almost hated to come down again."

"They're grateful for your help," Najud told her. "We might have missed those boys, going south, if our routes diverged and we weren't aware of them."

"Yes, but I'll always be some foreign wizard, here. Worse, one with wings. And if they knew about the chain…"

She said it matter-of-factly, but Najud knew it reflected her deep sense of isolation. His stomach clenched, as he recognized that just bringing her to meet his family was not going to be enough to make her want to stay, to give her a home.

Whoever made her had stolen not just her past, but maybe her future, too, unless he could persuade her to make her own future, the way she wanted it.

What they shared was a start, but it wasn't enough, he reflected, even if she purred as he stroked his fingers softly down her bare back.

CHAPTER 12

It took until late afternoon for all the newly-located strays to be brought back. Najud left Sharma, Winnajhubr, and Yuknaj with the herds near the camp, and formed three more pairs for Penrys to lead—Jirkat and his brother Khashghuy, Dimghuy and Ilzay, and Hadishti and himself.

Penrys guided each team from the air until they reached a particular group, then headed back to the camp to take the next pair. By the time the first team had made it back to the main herds with their charges, she was ready for them to go out again.

She landed after Najud and Hadishti had gotten to the last straying flock and walked up to Najud.

"I thought I might go back down to the kids tonight, rather than make them wait another day. What should I tell them?"

He looked up at the clear sky. "Maybe sixty miles altogether, or more, in the dark. You sure you want to do that?"

Penrys shrugged. "There're no clouds to block the moon, and the landmarks are simple. If I do get lost, I'll just wait until daylight again. I'll want to be back to travel with you tomorrow, since there are herd fragments to pick up along the way, and if I quarter your path while you go, I bet I'll find even more. You might not make it in a single day."

Hadishti said, "She's right. The older animals know this is the time of year they come south, toward the winter camp. We might find many of them on the way."

Najud nodded as he considered that. "Be careful," he told her. "Tell them we come tomorrow night, or more likely the next day. Tell them to stay where they are and keep their herds together, until we join them."

"And to hold onto their goats," he added, with a grin.

As Penrys turned to leave, Hadishti called out, "Tell them they'll travel the rest of the way in a good *kazr*—mine. Umzakhilin, too."

Two mornings later, just before mid-day, Penrys rode into the small camp, guiding Najud and their companions.

The boys must have heard the noise of the herds following behind them for some time, because they were ready for them, waiting on their horses.

Jirkat and Hadishti cantered up to greet them, as the eldest presently in the clan. "Well done, sons of the Kurighdunaq!" Jirkat called, and rode up to each in turn, clasping his shoulder with one hand as though they were grown men.

The way the boys' shyness dissolved into pride brought a smile to Penrys's face.

Hadishti waited for Jirkat to finish, then she asked them, "Where's Umzakhilin?"

Zabrash dismounted. "This way, *lijti.*" He led his horse to one of the two *kamahab* and tethered it to the ground outside the flap with hers before leading her inside.

Najud told Birssahr, "We'll stop briefly to eat, and to integrate the herds, but I want to move on another fifteen or twenty miles, if we can, before we camp tonight. We brought food for everyone, and we can sort things out better after we camp."

"Yes, *zarawinnaj,*" the boy said. He rode to the other *kamah* and tethered his horse there, then ducked inside to begin packing.

Zabrash came out of the first *kamah* and saw what his friend was doing, then walked over to help.

With the horses tethered out of the way, and everyone there except the three youngest who were riding the perimeter of the expanded herds, they squatted on the ground for a cold lunch and a quick interrogation.

Najud asked Hadishti, "How is your *zarawinnaj?*"

"I don't know what's wrong with him, *lij.*" She cocked her head at Zabrash. "The boy told me there were hoof marks on the ground, and it does look like he might have been trampled. They did a good job keeping the legs straight, and the feet bound, and it's healed cleanly…"

"But?" Najud prompted.

"But something's wrong. Not the bones—that is, he may have trouble walking again, won't know until he tries—but that's not it."

She cleared her throat. "I know this man well, *lij*, and he no longer knows me."

Her glance included both Najud and Penrys. "I think this is a *bikraj* matter. We have no *bikrajab* in the clan, but we hope my older son will be one for us. When we were young, Umzakhilin thought he might become one himself, but he chose another path. Still, he's the one who recognized my son's potential. He *heard* him."

She tapped her forehead meaningfully.

Penrys looked at Najud uncertainly. "Should we take a look?"

He shook his head. "Tonight, in camp. We have to make as much distance as we can before the snows come."

After meeting the boys, Najud and Jirkat decided that the organization of their march had to change to accommodate the problem of too many animals and not enough herdsmen. By now, they estimated they'd recovered close to half of the herds.

They still fretted about enough food for the winter camp, but Penrys kept her darker thoughts to herself—if their missing people were never found, they had plenty of food for the rest.

The more experienced among them, especially Ilzay, thought they were four days from the winter camp, at the speed of the cattle, perhaps forty-five miles, and no one seemed to think the season's first snow was imminent, so their sense of urgency was somewhat relieved.

The anxiety about their missing clansmen was not diminished, but time had begun to wear their dread to something more like resignation, and they spoke of their kin as lost, as if they would not be found.

Penrys took over the general task of scouting, from the air, keeping them headed steadily south, aimed between two distant hills that, she was told, pointed the way to the winter camp. Periodically, she swung around the perimeter of the herds, looking for breakaways, and listening for more fragments.

Najud and Hadishti rode in the van. Hadishti led a pair of horses, yoked together with a clever arrangement that held them a fixed distance apart. Between them a canvas litter was slung for the injured Umzakhilin. The boys had helped make it, under Najud's direction. Najud led a saddled horse for Penrys, so that she could take a break from the constant flight and still keep up.

Four were now assigned to the lengthening pack trains—Khashghuy and Winnajhubr were joined by Jirkat and Ilzay who took charge of the summer encampment goods. Everyone else, all five of them, rode the back and side edges of the herds, moving them along gently but firmly. Even the goats behaved.

Penrys reveled in the free flying that afternoon, forward for a bit to check the route in front of them, then round the circle of the herd, listening for more strays outside the bounds. She didn't find any more—perhaps they were too far from the summer encampment by now.

The outriders waved to her, when she passed. Maybe they could get used to her, after all.

CHAPTER 13

After dinner, Najud and Penrys joined Hadishti in her *kazr*. They brought lanterns that they hung near the central fire, to shed light on Umzakhilin, lying quietly on his bedroll on the carpets. Dimghuy and the two boys hugged the outer wall to stay out of the way, but Hadishti had sent Sharma to Yuknaj for a little while.

Penrys could see the gleam of Umzakhilin's eyes. He was awake, but when she probed him lightly, he didn't seem aware of his surroundings. At least he didn't seem to be in any pain.

"You or me?" she asked Najud.

"I'll try first," he said. "You watch him."

She held her mind on the injured man while Najud tried to bespeak him. *Umzakhilin, I'm Najud. I'm here to help you. You're safe, you have friends here.*

Penrys could tell that the words were understood but it was as though they didn't matter at all, they just sank away.

"He hears you," she told Najud, while Hadishti sat and watched, worry plain in her demeanor. "But he doesn't care. It's like... well, it reminds me of shock."

Hadishti said, "Two months is a long time for that. But he does follow orders, like a man disturbed that way—he eats and drinks, if we hold it to his mouth, and he gives a sort of warning, to help the boys keep him clean."

"That's not a good sign," Penrys said. "It means he's accommodated himself to his condition and plans to stay that way."

"No! You can't let him," Hadishti protested. She lay a hand on his shoulder. "He's a fine man. Bring him back to us, *bikrajti*."

Appealed to directly that way, Penrys looked at Najud and lifted an eyebrow. He rose to yield his place by the man's side to her, and took her spot.

She thought about it a moment before she began. This man had been the *zarawinnaj* for his clan, a position—as she was beginning to understand from Najud's efforts—of extreme responsibility.

The lives of two hundred people, the future of his clan, were in his hands.

A man who made decisions that might have serious consequences—he should want to come back and help his people. What could make him give up this way?

Umzakhilin, your people need you. They've asked me to show you the way back.

She listened for any sign he understood her, that he cared. When she glanced at Najud, he shrugged, clearly not able to tell.

Umzakhilin, come help your people. Many have survived, and they need you.

He wasn't mind-deaf, Penrys could tell that much. She'd never met a completely untrained wizard before so she had nothing to compare him to. The students who came to the Collegium in Ellech were already far beyond this.

It would help your kinsmen if you could show me what happened in the summer encampment.

That suggestion sparked an immediate reaction—terror—and his face spasmed to match.

"No one can hurt you here," she said aloud, and echoed it in mind-speech. "We are two *bikrajab*, helping your clan. No one here will harm you."

"Hadishti is here," she said. "Her son is now a nal-jarghal, training to bring honor to the clan, all because you recognized him for what he was. She wants to thank you."

That produced an odd sort of resonance, as though it interested him.

"Say something, Hadishti," Penrys murmured. "Reassure him."

"Everything she says is true," Hadishti said, and she leaned down and patted his cheek. "We all want you to come back to us. I look forward to speaking to you again, alone, just the two of us."

Her son Dimghuy looked down, and the two boys stared at him. Penrys suppressed a smile at the little family drama. She'd known from their travel together that Hadishti was a widow, but she had no idea if the injured man had a family, and now was not the time to ask.

"Show me what happened in the summer encampment. It was long ago, months ago." She echoed everything in mind-speech, convinced that using both channels was letting more of it get through.

"Was it daytime or night? Was it raining?"

He didn't reply in mind-speech, but an image began to form that she could see. It was tinged with fear—he was showing her his nightmare, the thing he had retreated so far from that he could no longer speak.

Penrys held her breath as she watched, not wanting to disturb this fragile communication.

Umzakhilin showed her what he saw in flashes, all the unimportant things omitted. First there was a view of the camp, seen from the height of a man standing in the center of the oval of *kazrab*, the ones they had just disassembled.

A young woman screamed, somewhere out of sight and he turned his head. The men and women he could see at the end of the oval froze in place, or fell limply to the ground. A dozen wolves or more ambled into the oval, but they ignored the people they passed. In their midst was a girl, dressed in shaggy skins, wolf skins. She paused and looked at some of the people, as if she were speaking with them, and then she turned and looked directly into his eyes.

You are the leader of this herd, the stallion, the herd-mare. It's mine now.

Penrys could feel his refusal, his horror at what was happening, as if it were fresh again. His last sane thought—that even if he were armed, how could he fight through all those wolves to reach her? He tried to pull his knife, but found he couldn't move.

A stallion neighed and trotted up to her, and the wolves parted for him. He was swollen with male pride, his muscled neck curved, and he pranced away from her when she waved him at Umzakhilin. The blow from the horse's shoulder knocked him to the ground, and he couldn't even scream when his legs were trampled.

The girl called the horse away and then walked over and stood over him, looking down into his face. She released him from his paralysis, but he was too terrified to make a sound. Her face filled his vision, until he shut his eyes to hide from it. Penrys saw it, too, and choked, but restrained her reaction to keep from disturbing him.

The last part of the nightmare was lying on the ground in agony and darkness. All around him he heard movement, but no talking, no resistance. The silence afterward, nothing but the fabric of the canvas covers of the *kazrab* flapping occasionally in the wind, was soothing, and he gave himself up to it.

The man on the bedroll opened his eyes fully, with understanding in them, and the first thing he saw, before she could pull back, was Penrys, leaning over him, the chain on her neck exposed, the same as the chain on the girl who had crippled him and taken his clan.

He roared in terror, that horrifying sound of a man screaming, and Penrys stumbled to her feet and bolted out of the *kazr*.

It was a girl, Naj-sha, with a chain like mine. Make him understand it wasn't me.

Penrys stopped just beyond the entrance and tried to collect herself. The screams continued from inside, and Dimghuy and the two boys fled the *kazr* through the open doorway. They froze when they saw Penrys, and detoured widely around her.

The rest of the camp had gathered outside at the first sounds, and Penrys could feel their suspicion as they watched the boys avoid her.

She was too distressed to try and explain. She turned her back on them all and took refuge in the *kamah* she shared with Najud.

The screaming stopped a few moments later, and she sat on her bedroll, out of everyone's sight, and worked on calming herself. She kept herself from trying to monitor what was going on in Hadishti's *kazr*—Najud didn't need the distraction, and perhaps Umzakhilin would be able to hear her.

The implications of Umzakhilin's nightmare were horrifying enough.

She was still sitting alone, in the chilly dark, when the rustle of canvas as the flap was lifted made her raise her head.

"Thought you might want a light in here," Najud said carefully, and laid a lantern on the floor of the *kamah*.

He picked up a blanket from the foot of his own bedroll, alongside hers, and draped it over her shoulders. Only then did she realize she was shivering, and she pulled it around herself and tucked it in.

He sat himself down crosslegged across from her. "He's awake, now, and talking, some. Hadishti's taking care of him."

Najud cleared his throat. "I heard what you said to him, but I don't know what happened next, just what you told me after he started screaming and you ran out."

"I'll show you," Penrys said, and swallowed.

Directly, mind to mind, she shared with him Umzakhilin's nightmare, and gave him a few moments to digest it.

"If I'd been wearing that scarf from the tailor's wife, 'round my throat…" she muttered. "That's why she gave it to me. For him to wake at last from that vision, to another woman with a chain leaning over him…"

Najud said, "You did the right thing, leaving. Hadishti and I calmed him down. He's confused, but he knows it wasn't you. We're going to let him sleep and try to talk with him tomorrow."

"*Yrmur!*" she spat. "Where are these chained wizards coming from? This one's a child, and no Zan."

"That's not the problem to focus on, Pen-sha. The question is, what is she trying to do?"

"The Voice didn't do anything with animals, that I noticed. He just built a horde and recruited allies." Her voice trailed off for a moment. "Could I control animals the way she's doing? Maybe if that's all I found, all I met? If she remembers nothing, like me?"

She lifted her head and stared through the walls of the *kamah* in the direction of the herds, and the bray of a donkey echoed back from a distance through the stillness of the evening.

She glanced back at Najud. *Well, that surprised him.*

His eyes had widened, but he made a good recovery. "Demon, I hope?"

In spite of herself, she chuckled. "Who else?"

"So, is she making a herd or a horde?" Najud's eye slid sideways to see how she would take that.

She thumped him on his nearest knee, but the bad joke lifted her mood.

"I've got to go after her now," she said, "even if all those people are already dead."

Najud looked at her soberly. "Like the *bikrajab* gather to overcome a *qahulaj*, a wizard-tyrant, because if we don't, who can?"

"Your *qahulajab* are beginning to seem downright ordinary to me—at least they're natural, not man-made. What's making these chained wizards?"

Najud added quietly, "And why a child?"

"In Umzakhilin's nightmare, she looked about thirteen, tall and leggy, but not full-grown—you know how they are."

He nodded, and they sat together in silence for a moment, until Penrys discarded the blanket and made a couple of attempts to stand up, careful of the low headroom.

"Is it safe to go back out?" she asked, sardonically. "They're not all going to pounce on me and hold me for execution come morning?"

"No," he said. "But I think we're going to have to tell them everything."

CHAPTER 14

Najud watched Penrys steel herself as everyone met for the morning meal. No one said anything to her referring to the night before, but he could see how conscious she was of their eyes following her. The two of them sat together to eat their warm porridge, sweetened with honey, having filled their bowls from the common pot.

Only Hadishti and Umzakhilin were missing, and then the door of Hadishti's *kazr* opened, and all heads lifted to watch their old *zarawinnaj* limp unsteadily out, supported strongly by Hadishti. Jirkat rose hastily to assist her, and between them they helped him cover the short distance to the fire and seat himself.

He sat with his legs straight before him, and worked on them, one at a time, kneading the thigh and calf, bending the joints, and trying to rotate and flex his feet. His flesh was wasted and his muscles slack, but he was able to move freely above the waist.

Najud was relieved that the joints still seemed to bend, but he thought the little bones in the feet would probably have healed badly. Still, this man was determined, and muscle could be rebuilt—it was easy to see why he would have been considered strong enough to serve as *zarawinnaj*.

As if conscious of the awkward silence, Umzakhilin lifted his head and looked for the two boys. "Zabrash, Birssahr—come."

They stood up and approached him shyly. He patted the ground next to him, and they knelt, so he wouldn't have to look up at them.

He bowed to them, sitting, as one adult to another, and their eyes widened. "I am in your debt, all honor to you. Hadishti has told me how you not only saved my life and tended to me, all this time, but how you did your best to find what you could and save it for the clan. That I can walk at all is… unexpected, and I am grateful. I'm hopeful that the clan can recover, with the help of everyone here."

Umzakhilin's glance then fell on the rest of the company. "I know you all, and I'm not surprised that you have accomplished so much. Hadishti told me the story. It's wonderful that you've driven so much of the herds with you, and salvaged the remains of the encampment, so few as you are. And I understand that is partly because of these *bikrajab* friends that you encountered on the High Pass."

His gaze turned to Penrys and Najud. Penrys wore her scarf to hide the chain, but his eyes lingered on her throat anyway.

He nodded to her. "*Lijti*, I thank you for pulling me out of the darkness, out of the nightmare. I know full well I might have been trapped in it until I died."

Penrys flushed and dipped her head.

"And you, Najud of the Zamjilah clan. I name you clan-kin in truth, in your own right, not just as nephew to Qizrahi. Our *kazrab* are yours, our food is yours, our horses are yours."

Najud could feel the heat rise in his cheeks. A clan-adoption outside of marriage was uncommon.

"I fear I am an inexperienced *zarawinnaj*," he said, to cover his embarrassment. "I could have done nothing without the help of everyone else."

Umzakhilin smiled. "I see by that you have already learned one of the secrets of the task."

He leaned toward Najud, and said *sotto voce* across the fire, "Don't tell anyone else, or they won't think we have mysterious powers any more."

The laughter around the fire broke the remainder of the tension in the atmosphere and, as easily as that, their old *zarawinnaj* took back the reins of his authority. Najud marveled at how well he did it.

Umzakhilin spoke to them all. "We'll continue on today. The plan you've made is good, and we'll follow it. Time enough once we've reached the rest of the clan at the *taridiqa* to arrange our pursuit of our missing clan-kin. I will ride, myself, with Najud."

He waved off the concern that flashed over Hadishti's face at that announcement. "The sooner I get my strength back, the better."

"But before we go," he said, "I must know more about this *qahulajti* who took our people."

And with that, he pinned Penrys in an unwavering stare.

Najud exchanged a long look with Penrys and then began the story.

"About two and a half months ago, I was still in my *tulqiqa*, the tenth year of my wandering time as a *daril*, a journeyman."

Hadishti paused from her task of fetching Umzakhilin some of the morning's porridge and nodded in understanding. Her older son would be doing this himself someday.

"Word came from the Ghuzl mar-Tawirqaj in Ussha that a *bikraj* was wanted by the Kigali, at the Meeting of Rivers—some problem in Neshilik with Rasesdad." He cocked his head north, back towards the High Pass.

"I crossed at the Low Pass and joined the cavalry expedition that was being sent to deal with it, in advance of the army. While I was there…" His voice trailed off uncertainly.

Penrys took up the thread. "I was in Ellech."

She waited until the murmurs of surprise faded. That was an almost legendary country to them, so far away.

"I was working on a… wizard thing, an experiment, and it went wrong. The Rasesni were working another wizard thing in the cavalry camp, and that… pulled me from my failed working to theirs."

Najud supposed that was as good a way as any to explain it to those who were not *bikrajab*.

"I joined Najud in his work, and we traveled together with the expedition until it reached the Gates."

The head nods reassured Najud that they knew where that was, the northeast corner where the Seguchi River cut its way out of the mountains surrounding Neshilik.

Penrys cleared her throat. "Meanwhile, we… talked. I'm not *from* Ellech. Three years ago, they found me there, naked except for this chain."

She unwrapped the scarf so that they could see it again.

"And I have no memory before that point."

Hadishti suggested, "A blow on the head…"

"No, *lijti*," Penrys said. "It's not hidden from me—I have reason to know. It's not there at all, nothing but an empty void."

Najud contradicted her privately. *Except for what the body knows, its own memories, embedded in the muscles.*

She nodded in silent acknowledgment, and continued. "I am a… strange wizard, from the perspective of the Collegium of

Wizards in Ellech, and so they named me *hakkengenni*, adept, and took me in. The wings… that's part of the strangeness. And the chain that can't be removed—no one had ever heard of that before. I spent three years in their library, looking for more information and I never found it."

She paused a moment, then shrugged. She lifted both her hands and combed her shoulder length hair back from her face, revealing her small, furry, foxlike ears, the same dark brown color as her hair, placed where human ears should be. "And this."

Zabrash started to rise for a closer look, than clearly thought better of it and sat down again.

Najud resumed the story. "Rasesdad had invaded Neshilik. Again. We were sent in to see what we could find out. We heard rumors of something driving the Rasesni out of their lands, someone they called 'the Voice,' and we found him. He was a *bikraj*, with a chain—the same chain Penrys has—and he had become a terrifying *qahulaj*."

He took another mouthful of his cooling porridge as an excuse to compose himself. "This *qahulaj* was a stranger to the Rasesni. He collected a horde of people from the places he passed through, and bought, from plunder, an alliance with some of the hill-tribes to guard him."

"We discovered the Rasesni have *bikrajab* after all—they've hidden them among the priests of their many gods. These mages, as they call them, couldn't stand against the Voice—he killed many of them, and the rest he captured and… used to increase his own strength."

How can I abbreviate this?

"It's an overlong story, but in the end two groups of Rasesni mages and the two of us stood against the Voice. Many died, but Penrys killed him."

Penrys broke in. "I questioned him, but got no answers. When they cut off his head…" She swallowed. "I saw the same ears as mine. Don't know about the wings."

"I do know one thing," she said. "The Rasesni first heard of him roughly three years ago. Oh, and he didn't seem to come from Rasesdad, by his look, nor did we resemble each other."

She glanced at Najud. "This was how Najud earned his *nayith* and became a *jarghal*. He organized the Rasesni wizards to make them stronger and better able to fight."

Umzakhilin waited to see if there was more, and then said, "And this wolf-girl, who has a chain like yours and is no Zan—you think she is another of the same."

Penrys nodded. "I wonder if she's been here three years, too. I wonder if she had no memory, and if animals were all she encountered, when she awoke. Did she ever speak, when you saw her?"

"Only the mind-speech," Umzakhilin said. "She fits your theory, what little we saw of her. Our clan-kin—they are become another 'horde' to accompany her?"

"I don't know," Penrys said. "But she has to be found, and she has to be stopped, and the chain tells me she will be much stronger than your wizards expect, not just a wizard-tyrant to be stopped by half a dozen others."

She surveyed the faces around the morning fire. "You want your people back, of course you do. But how many others will she try to sweep up, in *sarq*-Zannib, if she isn't stopped?"

Jirkat said, "It will be winter soon. No one travels like that in winter in the *khijr*-Zannib, the steppe."

Najud answered for her. "This *qahulajti* won't care. You always lose a few from the herds in wintertime."

No one spoke after that.

CHAPTER 15

Three days later, Penrys watched from the air as the last of the herds crossed through the gap in the two hills that marked their route. Umzakhilin had told her the route from the autumn camp took the same path through the hills, but there was nothing to be found on the trail to their right when they joined it, no sign of usage at all, other than the few spots worn away to rock.

The *zarawinnaj* was riding much better now, sitting his horse with authority. She suspected his legs were still very weak, from their long immobility, but he was starting to regain his strength. She told no tales about the pain it caused him to walk, on his imperfectly healed feet, respecting his determination to overcome any obstacle.

As she circled back to the front to resume her look ahead, she waved at Najud, Umzakhilin, and Hadishti as she passed them overhead, and relayed the news to Najud.

All the herds are through the gap.

Najud looked up at her as she swung by. *We're only a day out, or less. See if you can find the camp.*

She shrugged. *I don't want to scare them—it's broad daylight and what would they make of me?*

She thought about it over the next few miles. *Well, I know the direction. I should be able to pick up a concentration of sixty or seventy people easily enough.*

After about ten miles, she encountered the mind-glows she looked for, another few miles away, but far fewer than she expected. *Must be herdsmen or something—it's not enough for the winter camp itself.*

Still, the direction was right, and now she had something hopeful to tell them all, back on the march. They couldn't push the cattle too hard. Looks like they'd be meeting up with these people tomorrow.

After so many days in the air flying freely, it seemed strange to Penrys to be riding instead, up front with the three… elders. She smiled inwardly at the usage, since Najud was twenty-six, and she doubted Hadishti had left her mid-thirties, nor was Umzakhilin all that much older, but this was certainly a bunch of youngsters otherwise.

She had spread the word that the nearest of the winter camp's outriders was less than a mile away, and she kept her attention on the man, noting the exact moment when he must have heard the noise of the animals behind them.

"He's coming to check out what we are," she told her companions.

Umzakhilin pushed his horse to the fore, as *zarawinnaj*. Penrys could feel him ignoring the ache of his muscles, still unaccustomed to exercise.

When the approaching rider cleared a little ridge in front of them and halted to stare, visible to Penrys only as a turbaned silhouette, Umzakhilin raised an arm in greeting, and the rider kicked up his horse and thundered in, circling around the four of them before pulling back to match Umzakhilin's steady walk. They would talk on the move, rather than stop the herd on this last stretch short of the winter camp.

"Where did you come from? What happened?" The rider openly looked over the two strangers as he spoke.

"It's good to see you, Hubrahi. Have any of the *taridaj* returned to the *zudiqazd* ahead of us?" Umzakhilin's voice was calm.

"You don't know!" Hubrahi's voice rose. "The *zudiqazd* has been attacked."

Penrys could feel the effort it cost Umzakhilin not to slump. "When?" he asked. "Is anyone left?"

Hubrahi's mouth worked for a moment. "Three are dead. The rest are gone." He stared at Umzakhilin. "You're not surprised!"

"Food taken?"

Hubrahi nodded. "Some of it. Not the first cut of hay, though, which is the only cut they made. How did you know?"

"We have a long, sad story to tell," Umzakhilin said. "Who's with you?"

"You remember I spent the year with my sister, meeting her Winnajjinza clan-kin. I invited some of my new friends back to spend the start of the winter with me. We just rode in two days ago."

"How many of you?"

"We are seven, men and women," Hubrahi said.

"The clan calls on you," Umzakhilin said. "We have half the clan herds with us, and only five herdsmen. Ride back to your friends and summon them all. Once we have the herds settled in their winter pastures, and we've told you our tale, I'll need a messenger to each of the other clans, calling the visiting Kurighdunaq home for winter from the other clans, with anyone they can bring."

He leaned forward on his horse and put the full weight of his authority into his voice. "We have much to do and a trail to find, before the snow falls."

Penrys stood in the center of the winter camp with Najud after a tedious day of spreading cut grass out to dry, amazed at how much had been accomplished in just two days.

Coming into the *zudiqazd* had been almost a repeat of their visit to the summer encampment—the same collection of *kazrab* beginning to sag and the same scattered goods—but this time a bier of three cloth-wound bodies was included, courtesy of Hubrahi and his companions who had found them first.

Umzakhilin took the place of the missing clan leader Warzah, and by the time the first riders arrived, an hour ago, from the winter camps of the two clans on either side, the dead had been buried with the proper rites, and the herds settled near their winter pastures, temporarily, held away from the just-cut grasses where everyone who could help was laying out the gatherings to dry, hoping that the good weather would hold long enough to let them bring in this second crop of vital winter hay. It was very late in the year, and some of the nourishment had already retreated into the roots of the grasses, but it was the best they could manage and, with the diminished herds, they hoped it would be enough.

The delayed harvest of the root crops and the other cultivated foods was next in priority but, like the autumn slaughter, it required more people, and Umzakhilin wanted to to start on it tomorrow, with parties from both the other clans to augment their numbers. There were questions about how many animals to slaughter—the end-of-the-year economics were out of balance, measuring available animal fodder versus human needs for meat. The more of their herds they could keep alive, the faster they could rebuild them the following year, and if their missing clan-kin returned, they could always kill some of the secondary animals then. Everything depended on their estimates of what the pastures and hay could support over the winter, and whether or not they needed help from other clans in the tribe, whom they would be expected to feed.

Umzakhilin had prepared for the arrival of an unknown number of visitors. The largest *kazrab* had been set aside for the personal possessions of all the absent clansmen, including everything non-edible rescued from the summer encampment. They would be stored there throughout the winter, waiting for the fate of the missing to be determined. If they were dead, their goods—their *kazrab* and the furnishings, and their herds—would be distributed to the heirs. In the meantime, the camp was a mix of *kazrab* turned into storage, and others, empty except for furniture, available for some number of anticipated guests.

There were fewer *kazrab* than at the summer encampment, reflecting the smaller numbers who lived throughout the year at the *zudiqazd*. Of the eighteen in the camp, the twelve smallest stood ready for occupants, and one large one was reserved for group assemblies. Umzakhilin's companions stayed in their traveling *kazrab*, and Penrys and Najud in their *kamah*, reluctant to disturb the haunted camp, and Hubrahi and his companions did the same while waiting for the others to arrive.

Riders from the Winnajjinza clan came first, late in the afternoon—twelve of them, and Hubrahi took them around the empty camp and explained to them what he'd heard from Umzakhilin and the others. They nodded their heads to Najud as they passed him in camp and stared at Penrys, beside him, stretching to work out the kinks in her back from the hay gathering.

Think they've been hearing stories of flying wizards?

With sufficient herdsmen to hold the animals away from the hay cutting, Penrys was no longer needed to help with the herds. She'd been breaking her back for a couple of days, first with the mowing, and then with the drying of the hay, abusing different muscles than flying, and she was surprised how much she missed her new-found freedom in the air.

Najud muttered, for her ear only. "You didn't really expect that to stay a secret, did you?"

"I could hope," she said, with a sour grimace.

She lifted her head as her mind-scan alerted her to new arrivals. "More riders coming in, from the east this time."

"That would be clan Akshullah," Najud said. "Good. With the *gharqa* here, the tribal leader, decisions will get made."

"That chained wizard's weeks ahead of us. We've got to get going or we'll never catch her."

Najud shook his head at her. "You can't just rush out in the teeth of a Zannib winter like that. She won't be able to travel, and neither will you. It's only a bit more than two weeks to the solstice, the *durmiqa bul*—we're lucky it hasn't snowed yet, nor the ground frozen."

Umzakhilin walked slowly out of Hadishti's *kazr* to welcome the men from clan Akshullah. Penrys and Najud watched the first man lean down and clasp his arm below the elbow.

"And besides," Najud said, "we're going to need help tracking them, and companions on the trail." He cocked his head at the riders.

"We'll settle a lot of this tonight, in the assembly."

CHAPTER 16

After the evening meal, Penrys and Najud entered the one large *kazr* left standing but empty and found a spot near Umzakhilin. Everyone sat on the rugs that covered the ground, several layers deep in spots.

This could go on most of the night. It's a complicated situation.

She thought Najud's warning was well-founded. The people in the *kazr* were settling by clan, the Kurighdunaq's eleven beefed up by another eight called home from the other two clans. That nineteen was about the size of each of the two small detachments sent by the other clans to help.

Hadishti sat next to Penrys, with her children behind her, wide-eyed at the sight of all the new faces and the strange gathering.

She whispered to Penrys, "He went and found his own *kazr*, among the ones we brought back—the one he shared with his sister's family. We'll set it up tomorrow, but meanwhile he rescued a few things."

She cocked her head behind them at the north side of the circle, where a space had been left vacant and a small shrine stood. It reminded Penrys of a larger version of the little leather rolled-up pack that Najud carried in his belongings, the one that unrolled to display his special stones, and the iron thunderbolt he'd found, his personal reminders of something beyond his daily reality. Not gods, exactly, nor charms. Like everything associated with the *lud*, it was ambiguous.

Umzakhilin sat in front of the cluster of Kurighdunaq clansmen, near the center of the *kazr* and its central fire. Several pots of *bunnas* were keeping warm there, and a constant traffic of passed cups from the edges kept the women seated nearest busy pouring.

The leader of clan Winnajjinza sat in the front of his wedge, chatting quietly with his own folk. The third wedge held the tribal leader himself, instead of the clan Akshullah leader, that being the clan he himself belonged to. He took his place in the center, with the rest of his clan.

Umzakhilin stood up stiffly, but without assistance. When he stood, all voices stopped, and only the small crackles of the fire and the chink of *bunnas* cups rose above the quiet rustle of fabric as people adjusted their positions to accommodate the crowd.

He walked into the vacant space before his personal shrine, and picked up a length of antler, padded at the tip with leather. With that he struck a hanging ram's bell three times, and a soft, penetrating note filled the *kazr*. He bowed once to the shrine and said, "May we all find wisdom in our thoughts this night, and make the best choices for the good of the people."

Penrys was startled by the wordless hum that rose from the assembly, in the same note as the bell.

Umzakhilin returned to his spot near the center of the *kazr* but remained standing and spoke to everyone. "Many of you know me. I am Umzakhilin, *zarawinnaj* of the Kurighdunaq for the last eight years. Our *ujarqa*, the clan leader Warzah, is among the missing of our clan, some two hundred people from the *taridiqa*, and another sixty-seven from our *zudiqazd*. Three we know to be dead, and these we have buried. We, here,"—he waved his hand at the people sitting with him—"are what remain."

He paused for breath, and no one spoke.

"I will begin by telling you what happened, and those with me will tell their own tales."

It took more than an hour to tell the full story, beginning with each of the separate travelers—Jirkat's fish caravan, Hadishti and her children, and Winnajhubr and Yuknaj, visiting clan Akshullah and returning.

Najud told his tale again, and Penrys added what she could.

This was followed by Zabrash and Birssahr, abashed before such an audience, but supported by Umzakhilin, who ended with his story of what had happened to him in the summer encampment. When he described the chain around the girl's neck, the girl with the wolves who had made a horse trample him and buried his mind, all eyes turned to Penrys, and she felt her skin creep.

"Tell us, *bikrajti*," Umzakhilin said then, "about these chained wizards, so that all can know."

She wiped her hands on the legs of her breeches, and stood up to do as he bid her.

Silence greeted her story of her own origins, and the chained wizard that overran Rasesdad before she killed him. She sat down again, trying not to feel intimidated. Najud and she were the only wizards in the *kazr*, and there would be little she could do against sixty people if they should decide she was somehow responsible or a similar threat to them now.

"And so, we are here," Umzakhilin said. "I have made Najud clan-kin to the Kurighdunaq, for his services as *zarawinnaj* in gathering the herds and bringing all our goods home. His companion has helped us, too, and brought me out of nightmare. I vouch for them both, friends of the Kurighdunaq.

"Tonight we must decide several things. The easiest, perhaps, is the pursuit of the *qahulaj* who assaulted us in the summer encampment and presumably came here, afterward. Both of these *bikrajab* are eager to pursue her, and there are others who want to join the expedition and rescue family and friends."

He waved his hand at the camp outside the walls. "We must also complete the late harvest as quickly as possible and do as much of the autumn slaughter as we think wise, and then ensure that we have sufficient of both food and people to winter over in the *zudiqazd*.

"And then, we must decide the future, after the winter. If our people are found, and can return, then we will heal. If not..."

Penrys heard the intake of breath throughout the *kazr* at that possibility.

"If not, then we will rebuild our clan, hoping that our cousins within the tribe can help."

With care, Umzakhilin lowered himself down and yielded his place.

Sahrzay stood up then. "We mourn this tragedy with our cousins and bring them help. With me are men and women of Winnajjinza, planning to stay the winter season and to help you prepare. I've also brought Inghiti, a *dirum-malb*, in place of your own *dirum*, to direct the care of your herds."

Penrys wondered how many apprentice herd-mistresses he had that he could spare one.

When he sat down, again, Zamharshat rose up and looked around until all was silent. "I left the *ujarqa* of Akshullah clan behind in the *zudiqazd* to finish supervising winter preparation, because I had an alternative to propose. With me are the men and women you asked for, Umzakhilin."

He paused, and Penrys could feel Najud beside her tense up. *He must suspect what's coming.*

"Would it not be more sensible, *zarawinnaj*, for the remnant of Kurighdunaq to divide and visit its relatives in the other clans for the winter? It would be no burden to the others, few as they are."

When he sat down, Penrys could feel the dismay arising from her travel companions, though they held themselves still.

With great dignity, Umzakhilin stood up again. He nodded his head to both Sahrzay and Zamharshat. "We thank our cousins for their generous assistance—the Kurighdunaq will not forget.

"As to the other suggestion, we remain a clan of significant wealth in herds and goods, thanks to the hard work of our kinsmen and friends. We will find our clan-kin, and we will bring them home."

Najud commented privately. *Those that survive. There were babies here, in the zudiqazd. There will be deaths, in the best possible outcome.*

Penrys nodded silently.

Umzakhilin gestured to Hadishti who rose and joined him. "I will stay, as the anchor for my clan, come what may. My clan-kin will make their own decisions, but Hadishti has agreed to stay with me. We, at least, will be here when the rest of my clan returns, to welcome them home."

Behind him, every member of the Kurighdunaq stood up in support.

Penrys looked at Najud to see if they should join them, and he shook his head slightly. "Not truly clan," he whispered. "This is not for outsiders."

Zamharshat rose to his feet, and nodded. "We will talk again when their fate is known."

He glanced over at Hadishti. "If you wish to invite others, for the winter, it will be allowed."

She must have married out-clan originally. I think widower will marry widow.

Najud's comment made sense to Penrys.

Why only Hadishti? Wouldn't some of the others have, oh, aunts they could invite?

Hadishti will be in a different position. Clan leaders are married, or they aren't clan leaders. Umzakhilin has declared his intentions, subtly, and the wife of a clan leader has her own authority. Zamharshat is also indicating his acceptance of Umzakhilin as clan leader, perhaps permanently, if the old one doesn't return.

Penrys shook her head. *Zannib clan politics. I don't suppose there are any books?*

By her side Najud suppressed a snort of amusement. *I wonder what clan Hadishti comes from, originally?*

Zamharshat, still standing, led his clan members from the *kazr* and Sahrzay followed, once the doorway had been cleared.

The Kurighdunaq who remained gradually began to filter out, tired from their day working in the fields or managing the herds, but Najud put a hand to Penrys's shoulder and held her back until only Umzakhilin was left.

The three of them seemed to rattle in the *kazr* into which sixty people had been recently crammed, but Umzakhilin sat down next to the central fire as though he were in a small, intimate space, to give them a formal audience, and they all gathered closely together.

"You wish to speak of the search for the *qahulaj* and our people?" he asked.

"Yes, and then one other matter," Najud said.

Umzakhilin nodded his approval. "I've spoken with Jirkat, and especially Ilzay who had much to say about the trail."

He leaned forward. "They are on foot. If they were free and alive, they would have returned by now. If they are too far away, they would be wintering already with someone else, and we would have received word. Therefore, I believe they are either alive and with the *qahulajti*, or dead. Certainly many must be dead."

He lowered his head for a moment. "My son Najjilah among them. And his wife, who should have born their first child by now, in the *zudiqazd*. And the rest of my children."

He wiped a hand over his face. "Everyone has a tale like this to tell. I am not unique."

He looked Najud sternly in the face. "This *qahulajti* spoke of the people as if they were a herd, and I can't get that word out of my mind. I fear she won't let them shelter properly for the winter. If any are still alive, they must be freed, as soon as possible, before it is too late and they simply die from neglect."

Najud said, "We could leave tomorrow. We must. You don't need our labor any more."

"I know it must be you that pursue her. Two is not enough. You need trackers, and you may need force to pry our kin away from the *qahulajti*. You realize, from your tale of the packs at the base of the *lud* in High Pass, that she must have reached out and seized them from that far away."

Penrys nodded at that. She hadn't missed that implication.

"So you need companions. Jirkat will go with you, leaving his brother to deal with his family's goods, and Ilzay. Young Winnajhubr, too, if you'll let him. I can't send enough to make a real fighting force—I'm sorry."

"Those would be very useful, *zarawinnaj*," Najud said. "If we find your clan-kin, we can't possibly shelter them all—we'll have to find a clan to settle with for the winter."

"No, you can't pack equipment for so many and expect to make any speed. Jirkat has his *kazr* which will hold three, and I will gift you with my son's *kazr*—you can't do this with your *kamah*, not in winter. If he or his wife is recovered, I will replace it for them with something magnificent in gratitude."

Najud glanced at Penrys. "We'll leave in the morning, *zarawinnaj*."

"Good, then that is settled." He leaned back again. "You said there was another matter?"

Najud rubbed his mouth. "Something for you to think about, for the future. You know how Qawrash im-Dhal in the east sends the Grand Caravan three times each year up toward well-populated Kigali?"

Umzakhilin nodded.

"I've participated in those caravans, several times," Najud said. "I know how the settlement works, where they begin, and how they support the traffic. I know how the caravans themselves function—how they are led, what supplies they need. I understand the business."

Penrys watched, fascinated.

"Now, when we were in Neshilik, I proposed, to both the town council in Gonglik and the Raseni occupiers, that a new caravan route be created, at the High Pass. It would terminate in Gonglik, but might well go on all the way to Dzongphan, in Rasesdad. Three-way trade between the three countries."

Umzakhilin cleared his throat. "Sounds ambitious. And you a *bikraj.*"

"I don't want to just settle as some *bikraj* in a clan, supported by his kin and otherwise left alone or, worse, holed up in some mountain cave." Najud looked over at Penrys. "I've also traveled and seen the caravan trade, and I know I can do this, if the countries will agree. I'll take charge of that part."

"What I want you to think about," he said, "is what role you might want the Kurighdunaq to play, if it happens. The base for such a caravan would be below the High Pass, and no clan claims that currently, is that right?"

"Yes," Umzakhilin replied slowly. "The tribe claims it, but no clan uses it. It's closest to our clan's customary *tarizd.*"

"Then—forgive me—if the Kurighdunaq are truly reduced in numbers, or even if they aren't, you may find yourselves in a position to create such a caravan base. It could be a permanent settlement, a new location for the *zudiqazd,* or even a seasonal settlement, just when the caravans run, like a *zudiqazd* in reverse, empty in the winter. If you have a surplus of goods or herds after your people are found, that would also have a market there."

Penrys smothered a smile. Umzakhilin looked a bit stunned by the proposal, as well he might.

"I know this is a strange idea," Najud said, "but some of the eastern caravan bases originated in this way, before settlement year-round was more common there. Now there are more people in the east that want to trade goods with Kigali than those markets can support. A new market in the west, one that could take advantage of goods from the western fisheries and farms, one that might bring unique goods from western Kigali or even Rasesdad into Zannib, well, that's not a small thing to consider. It would mean new ways for your people, but it would also mean wealth and independence."

Najud smiled, and then stood up. "Thank you for listening. I'll leave these thoughts with you and see you in the morning."

Penrys joined him as he strode out through the doorway with an almost visible bounce to his step. She waited until they were outside and well away to comment. "Pleased with yourself, are you?"

He grinned back at her. "Why not? Doesn't hurt to plant the idea. And it would be a good solution for him if the news is bad, as it probably will be."

"Surely he'd have to contend with his *gharqa*, the leader of the tribe, to do something that radical," Penrys objected.

"That's what being a clan-leader, a *ujarqa*, is all about—finding the best path for a clan, even if the way is strange and new. We'll see what happens."

CHAPTER 17

It was a chilly morning, the overcast skies a reminder of weather to come. Penrys was glad of the thigh-length sheepskin coat Hadishti had found her and her thick gloves. Her warm cloak was rolled and tied behind her saddle, the heavy Kigali stock saddle that was such a contrast to the sparse Zannib saddles with their bright fabric saddle-pads.

All five of them were planning to lead a pack train of the shaggy Zannib horses, five each, and Penrys had hers already in hand, on the south side of the winter camp.

The visitors were awake and beginning the process of transforming the empty *zudiqazd* into a living village again.

Winnajhubr stood by his horse a little ways off and spoke privately with his sister Yuknaj, while Khashghuy on the ground conferred with his mounted brother Jirkat.

Umzakhilin and Hadishti had already bid them good luck and now came over to speak to Penrys and Najud.

"Are you sure you have what you need?" Umzakhilin asked Najud, looking up at him from the ground.

Najud nodded. "The things we left with you, the donkeys and the Rasesni mares, and the goods they were carrying—well, if we send word, someone can take them on to the Zamjilah clan for us, else we'll pick 'em up when we return.

"I've planned the supplies for the best news, that we find a couple of hundred people alive, somewhere, but four or five days away from the nearest *zudiqazd*, and maybe in deep snow and on foot, with only summer clothing."

Umzakhilin nodded soberly.

Najud waved back at the pack trains. "So, we've brought four of the large *kazrab*, stripped of all the furniture—just raw shelter and a place for a fire."

Penrys said, "The rest is our own small shelters and gear, food, grain for the horses. And as many blankets and bandages as we can carry."

A flicker of concern crossed Hadishti's face. "And the pots of salve I gave you, for burns or frostbite?"

"That, too," Penrys confirmed.

Najud said, "We'll find a trail—Ilzay is sure of it, if we can keep the snow off—and we'll only divert to a nearby *zudiqazd* as our supplies need replenishing. If we find anything, we'll send word back."

"News travels slowly in winter," Hadishti said.

"But it does travel." Umzakhilin said. "You said you would find *bikrajab* as you went along."

Najud nodded. "Most of them will come when called to stop a *qahulajti*."

"Even in winter?" Penrys could hear the skepticism in Umzakhilin's voice, but Najud just shrugged.

"We can only try. We'll coordinate all messages either to you, here, or to my family, in the Zamjilah *zudiqazd*. You've got my letter for them, explaining the situation. That's quite a distance, but we don't know yet what direction this *qahulajti* took. If she went west, the word will go to you directly. If east, then perhaps the Zamjilah clan. I think north is unlikely, since she came from there, but south could be a real problem—colder, fewer people, and further away for messages, especially in the winter."

Umzakhilin said, "No use anticipating the problem until you're faced with it."

The noise of a dozen riders entering the camp from various directions drew everyone's attention. They cantered over to the *zarawinnaj* to report. A little while earlier, Ilzay and several of the visitors had ridden from the camp a mile or more to take advantage of the early morning light to see if they could pick up the trails of the stock and people entering the camp, and then leaving again. Each rider had been responsible for a wedge of ground that he examined closely.

"We found it, *zarawinnaj*," Ilzay reported. "The trail in roughly follows the spring route, as we thought it might." This last was directed to Najud, who nodded his understanding.

"There's a similar trail, faint but visible, headed out to the southwest. As long as the snow holds off, we should be able to follow it."

"How old?" Umzakhilin asked.

"Only about a month. They're moving much more slowly than I would expect." Ilzay shrugged. "Hubrahi brought back some droppings to show you."

"Then we'll be leaving, *zarawinnaj*," Najud said. "The season's against us."

Ilzay picked up the lead rope of his pack-string, which had been tethered waiting for him, and Penrys walked hers over a little way to let Jirkat and Winnajhubr hear the news.

As she reached them, she overheard the last of Khashghuy's conversation with his brother.

"Find her for me, *tigha*," he said, and clasped his brother's arm.

Najud, behind her, explained. *They were planning to marry during the magham, the winter festival.*

Penrys grimaced. *None of them will escape sorrow, no matter what we find.*

Half a day out of camp they found their first body on the trail—one of the cattle, a bull by the heaviness of his horns. A broken leg explained its collapse. Little was left besides the bones and hooves, the hide and its hair.

Najud bent over the carcase with Ilzay. "See the tooth marks?" he said.

"Wolves. But look here." Ilzay pointed out some clumsy cuts along the ribs. "Those are knives."

Najud tugged a segment of the crumpled and dried skin loose and looked at the edge where it had been pulled from the exposed side.

"Some of this was cut, not torn."

"So," Ilzay said, "it looks like someone with a knife sawed through the hide enough to peel it back a ways and cut off some meat."

"Probably took more than one man to do it. Why not just grab the belly meat instead?"

"I don't know," Ilzay said. "Maybe the wolves had already gotten it?"

Najud grunted at that. Usually the people killed the animal, and then the wolves got what remained. The organ meats went first, and then the animal was completely butchered until all that was left for the wolves was the scraps. Even the big bones were taken, for the marrow. Horns and hide, anything useful—it would all be salvaged.

This painted a very different picture, of an animal brought down by accident, and maybe killed by wolves, with people coming along afterward, before they were finished.

The image of the wolves with the chained girl that Umzakhilin had described came to his mind. Were the people standing in line with the wolves, hoping for their share of the kill?

"At least some of them still have knives," he commented.

A mind-call from Penrys lifted his head, and he searched the sky to the southwest.

I'm coming in. I found a body.

So did we, a bull carcase.

He felt Penrys's hesitation. *No, a human body. Nothing but bones.*

CHAPTER 18

Najud found it hard to reconcile this version of Penrys with wings, all bundled up in the sheepskin coat from Hadishti, her knit cap and a scarf protecting the exposed part of her face, with the lightly clothed one he'd first seen, a couple of months ago.

The thought of her wings wrapped around him sometimes in the night brought a private smile to his face. *She's like an owl this way, all fluffed up for the winter.*

When she landed, she unwrapped her scarf and gave him a quick, nervous twitch of the mouth. Jirkat and Winnajhubr waved at her from the ground, and she lifted her gloved hand, but even the bull carcase failed to hold her attention.

"A skull," she said to Najud, "Small, it was, and some bones and scraps of clothing. A hundred yards or so left of the trace. I built a pile of rocks on the edge of the trail to mark the spot where you should turn off. Maybe four miles further along?"

She glanced uncertainly at the animal carcase. "Ilzay, I think there were tooth marks on the bones."

"Like these?" Ilzay drew her over to the bull and showed her examples.

She nodded as she looked at them.

"There was much less left, though."

"People are frail," Ilzay said, "not tough, like cattle. Sometimes all you find is a skull—everything else has been carried away."

She swallowed, and Ilzay continued, "By the close of winter, the rodents will gnaw at the hides and bones, and the hair will slip away, or end up in a mouse's nest. If the season is hard enough, nothing of him will remain," he hooked his thumb at the bull, "except the skull and sometimes the horns."

She turned to Najud. "I came back, 'cause... If we're finding bodies on this trail, there must be bodies on the earlier one, too, the one from the summer encampment, though I must have missed the exact route they took when I flew over it."

Najud looked at her in understanding. "You think someone should tell them, back in the *zudiqazd*."

"Don't you? Wouldn't they want to know?"

Jirkat nodded. "Someone should go back to Umzakhilin."

Penrys shook her head. "No, I'll do it. We're not far away yet. You keep going and I'll catch up again. I don't want to lose any more time. Every day we delay…"

Najud agreed with her. "I'll see you when you get back."

She wrapped the scarf around her exposed face and launched again, like an improbably ponderous goose. *I'll get something to eat back there. Don't wait for me. Keep going.*

His three remaining companions looked to Najud for guidance. "This won't be the first person we find," he said. "We'll need to keep the count of the dead as we go."

Ilzay said, quietly, "Let it be me. Jirkat and Winnajhubr have at least one left living in the *zudiqazd*, whatever news we may get on the road ahead. I have none. I'll keep the tally."

He turned to the bull's skull and busied himself with cutting off the horns. Jirkat walked over to lend him a hand so they could get moving again as soon as possible.

Najud left them to it. Umzakhilin had told him, before they left, that the count of people missing from the clan was two hundred and sixty-nine, though there were infants that would have been born in the *zudiqazd* since the *taridiqa* began this year, and some of the aged might have died, so the number couldn't be exact.

He'd seen the sticks used as tally records, the marks a shepherd made to check the headcount of his flocks, tolling them off quickly in couples with the old rhyming words—*ishqa, imgha, nudi, nari*—and so forth, notching the stick for each twelve couple—a *jal*, a flock of twenty-four. The odd one, any half-a-couple extra, was *mawik*.

So, the headcount of the missing was eleven *jal, imgha* and *mawik*. It sent a shiver down his spine to count people as though they were sheep, the way the *qahulajti* had called them a herd.

"The horses have had enough of a rest," Najud called to Ilzay. "We'll mount and eat from the saddle, soon as you're done."

Ilzay raised a hand in acknowledgment, and Winnajhubr reached into one of his saddlebags to grab some food and stuff it in his belt pouch for easier access. Najud decided to do the same.

Four miles to the first mark on the tally stick.

Coming back, two hours later, Penrys spotted her companions from the air where she expected to find them. The horses had been tethered to get what grazing they could but not unloaded, since they would go on from here.

It was awkward to carry things not attached to her body while flying, and the bulky garments which did a barely adequate job of keeping her warm in the cold wind left her few options. After she landed and took a few stumbling steps to absorb her momentum, she hurried to strip off her gloves and unfasten the long, uncomfortable tool, strapped diagonally to her chest.

They all looked up from the rock cairn they were building as the spade Umzakhilin had pressed upon her clanked to the ground, a wooden pole with a cross piece, riveted onto a pointed metal blade.

At Najud's raised eyebrow, she said, "Yes, Umzakhilin said you would be raising cairns, but then Hadishti reminded him that rocks are not always easily found, and so…" She waved her hand at the spade on the ground and shrugged.

"His word was that he would scour the spring route all the way to the summer encampment, weather permitting, and see to the rites. He asked that you save what remembrances you could…"

Ilzay pointed to something on the ground a few yards away, and Penrys walked over to take a look. A thin goat-hide lay there, with a section carved out, and on it was a newly-made leather pouch and, weighted down by a cobble against the wind, a few scraps of cloth and a bone bracelet, child-sized.

"Oh. I see. Do you know…?"

Winnajhubr told her, "That's Khimar, the daughter of Suragh. I know the bracelet—she used to play with my sister Anah-Jilah." His voice choked.

Penrys remembered the child's pack they'd found on the High Pass, in front of the *lud*. Was his little sister's body somewhere on the spring route that Umzakhilin's people would be searching?

They found two more bodies that day and built the cairns for them, and then stopped early to camp by a small stream, depressed and not yet efficiently settled into a smooth routine for the journey.

Despite everything, Penrys was eager to erect the first *kazr* that she would get to use herself. She had helped raise them and take them down several times by now, pitching in on their way to the *zudiqazd*, and then retreating regretfully to the chilly *kamah* she shared with Najud.

They expanded and attached the first lattice sections on either side of the door and its frame, then tied the remaining lattice frames to the first until they met in a circle about five feet high. The two long decorated poles that held the painted *zamjilah*, the spoked roof crown, went up next, and Penrys held the assemblage erect herself, since it was the least skilled job. Najud and Winnajhubr stood outside on opposite sides and inserted the thin, gaily painted roof rafters one by one, first the narrow tongue into the empty sockets along the side of the raised *zamjilah*, and then the hooked ends onto the top of the lattice, where they were lashed into place.

Ilzay and Jirkat coiled the first long rope around the outside of the circular wall, halfway up, to hold the lattice firmly, and tied it off. Then they wrapped a second rope just below the top where the rafters were hooked in, to further support the outward pressure of the roof.

Once all the rafters were in place and the ropes had been adjusted and tightened, the structure held itself erect. Penrys let the taller men lay the felts on the slanted roof and around the walls, and lash the canvas sections over them with ropes tethered to the ground to hold them in place, while she carried in the canvas flats and rolls of small rugs to cover the floor inside.

The interior of a six-section *kazr* like this was about twelve feet across. It felt downright spacious, and far larger than the two of them needed, but there was no declining the gift of Umzakhilin's son's *kazr*. They had left most of the furnishings back in the winter camp to lighten the load, but Najud had insisted on bringing along the two bedframes and the *umaqab*, or rolled pads, that went with them, on rope supports.

"See how the woman's is wider?" he'd told her. "They tell you it's because she may need to take a child into bed with her, but that's not the real reason. You wouldn't need the hangings over it, if it were just for the children."

His wink and leer made his meaning clear, and she hoped for a more private demonstration.

The only other furnishings were a tall table that could be assembled and used standing to prepare food, a low table and two low seats for working, and the simple iron stove that Najud toted in, by far the heaviest item, at twenty-five pounds or so. The metal stovepipe came in three lightweight sections, one bent to connect to the back of the stove, and the end of the top one fit neatly through a metal-protected gap in the *zamjilah*. A screen suspended between the two top pieces kept most of the sparks from reaching the *zamjilah* or the canvas of the roof. Penrys had seen thin metal like that in the Kigali cavalry camp, but couldn't identify it. A flat piece of the same material made a fireproof platform for the stove to sit on.

The narrow box of the stove was less than two feet deep, with a surface that could hold an iron pan and a deeper covered oven for roasting or stewing. A small door below the grate of the main box allowed for draft control, and its legs were long enough that you could cook standing, if bent over.

Along with a spouted pot for hot water, which could sit on the metal floor plate near the stove when the top was occupied, Hadishti had sworn a woman had everything she needed with this arrangement.

Penrys had done little cooking for herself in Ellech, at the Collegium of Wizards, and only camp food on the trail with Najud, but she'd spent a couple of hours getting some basic lessons from Hadishti, and hoped she could cope. She already knew her body remembered kneading bread—maybe it remembered more about cooking than she realized.

Najud helped her position the beds placed along the walls of the *kazr*. "Not together?" she asked.

"It wouldn't be seemly. We have the larger *kazr* and any discussions will be here. It's a… public space, after a fashion. That's why the woman's bed has a hanging for privacy."

She laughed. "Isn't there any way to lock the door?"

He grinned in response. "Oh, we can drop the flap over it. And will. And it'll be respected, barring an emergency."

He looked around the bare space. "It seems empty now, but it'll look more occupied once we bring in our packs. Our homes are portable, but when you move every night, like this, you don't take as much along. They're not as friendly-seeming as the ones that stay put and accumulate…"

"Memories?" she suggested.

"Yes, memories." He beamed at her. "This is ours now, whether or not we find Umzakhilin's son. Do you like the colors? We can make our own memories here, if you wish it."

She heard the coaxing in his voice, but her stomach clenched, still, at the thought of making a life among these strangers. At cheating this man of children—she felt sure that was what would happen. And she would never be able to just accept the mystery of her origin, especially in the face of others who seemed to share that with her. She'd never be content to stay and ignore that.

His face fell, and he started to turn away. She reached out and patted his forearm. "I'm sorry, it's not you."

"I don't have to put a chain around my neck to get you to chase me?" he asked, only half-joking.

"Never say that!" Penrys wrapped her arms around his chest and burrowed in. "It's not that simple."

He enfolded her in his arms and rested his chin on her head. "I know, Pen-sha, I know."

He murmured in her ear. "I'll just have to try and convince you again tonight, after everyone leaves."

She smiled at the sound of his voice rumbling through his chest against her other ear. "I'll take that as a promise," she said.

CHAPTER 19

It was too cold now to stand outside around an open fire, so dinner was made separately in each *kazr*, and they met again in Najud's, afterward.

Penrys was secretly pleased with her own efforts. Trail sausage was tastier fried crispy in a little oil, and the grain cakes with dried berries would serve for breakfast, too, or maybe lunch. She'd even thought to put a handful of the dried beans in to soak overnight for a warm breakfast. Scouring the iron pans clean with a bone scraper and a wisp of grass, she left Najud to prepare the *bunnas* for their guests.

She smiled to herself. *Guests*, indeed. It felt enough like a home already to make that word seem natural. Najud had been right—with all their personal packs stored safely under cover around the walls, there was still enough room for comfort, and the little stove, fueled by dried dung, put out an amazing level of heat in the enclosed, insulated space, unless throttled by an almost-closed firedraft door. The lantern suspended from the *zamjilah* shed a soft light on the colorful wooden surfaces—no plain wood had been left unpainted, not the rafters and *zamjilah*, and not the furniture. Only the tops of the two tables and the seats of the two low chairs were left bare. All the fabrics, from the rugs to the cloths, were a riot of stylized flowers or mythical beasts, sometime both. She wondered if it was to give the eye something to look at in the long, snowy winters.

She glanced around the space. The cloth to surround her bed, suspended by a hook from the top of the lattice wall, was in place, but not spread for use. Hadishti had warned her that every modest woman hung a cloth there for the purpose. Whether it was ever used was another matter, but it was an important symbol. "No one will question what a *bikrajti* does," she'd said, "but you are also a woman traveling with men and living with a man who is not your husband."

When Penrys had opened her mouth to protest, Hadishti raised her hand to stop her. "It's no concern of mine," she'd said. "We are grown women and can choose these things. But it's always best to respect the proper forms." She'd waved her hand at the hanging cloth hooked to the lattice above her own bedframe.

At the sound of a knock on their door, Najud put the steaming pot of *bunnas* on the metal floorplate next to the stove. "Ready?"

At her go-ahead gesture, he walked to the door and opened it. The canvas flap had been rolled up above the door when they set the *kazr* up, but the door had been closed, to keep the warm air in. Now, as Najud beckoned them, the three men stepped in over the threshold of the *kazr*, careful not to step on the threshold itself to break its luck.

Winnajhubr bowed to Najud and nodded to Penrys, behind him. With formal politeness, he said, "What a fine *kazr, bikrajab.*"

Jirkat poked him as he went by and seated himself, casually, nearest the pot of steaming *bunnas*. "And what would you expect the clan's *zarawinnaj* to have given his oldest son, when he married?"

Ilzay's mouth quirked as he joined them, but he nodded to both his hosts before he sat down.

Penrys provided a cloth to use in picking up the pot of *bunnas*, and Najud offered it to Jirkat, who pulled a cup out of the inside of his robe. Everyone except Penrys took a cup, and they sipped it for a moment as the aroma of roasted *bunnas* filled the space. Even Penrys liked the smell, just not the taste.

When no one else looked like they wanted to begin, Ilzay asked, "What does it mean that they still have knives but haven't escaped?"

Najud looked at Penrys. "Tell them about the horde."

Penrys cleared her throat. "That other chained wizard, in Rasesdad, that we told you about…"

She looked at them and they nodded. "He had three groups of people with him. One was voluntary, a bunch of brigands from the mountain tribes. They were a guard, a little army for him. Then there were captive wizards, from Rasesdad—he controlled them directly, stole their power and kept them weak."

"A *bikraj* thing," Winnajhubr suggested.

"That's right. The Kurighdunaq have no wizards to control. And no brigands."

She swallowed. "And the third, well, we called them the horde. They were ordinary folk, and the Voice, he treated them like puppets, like dolls. They did what they were told, they had no choice about it."

Najud said, "He used the power he took from the captive wizards for it." He raised an eyebrow at Penrys, but she shook her head.

"I don't know how he did it," she said. "He kept them fed and watered, but it was no concern of his if they lived or died."

She looked around at their dismayed faces, but it had to be said. "He must have lost a great many of them, before he was stopped."

Penrys missed the little crackle of burning wood that would have filled the ensuing silence if they were outside. *Too bad this fuel makes so little noise.*

Jirkat was the first to speak again. "Did this 'Voice' use animals, too, like the *zarawinnaf*'s story?"

Penrys shook her head. "No, that's something different, something new to me. I can hear animals"—she tapped her forehead—"that's how I was able to find the strays for you, but I've never tried to control them like that."

She glanced at Najud. *But we both know I can probably learn how. Don't want to tell them that, though. But what's she using for power, without wizards?*

Maybe she doesn't need much. Maybe controlling people is a lot like controlling animals.

She winced away from that thought and tried to keep her face expressionless.

Ilzay refilled his cup with *bunnas*. "I have a special pack I have consecrated to carry…"

Najud nodded. "I will prepare your… our three kinsmen tonight and bring them to you in the morning."

"Good. The tally horns will be ready by then."

Penrys had seen them soaking in a pool, downstream of where they drew their water, weighted down by rocks. Najud had explained this would allow what was left of the bony cores to be pulled out so that only clean horn remained.

Najud asked Ilzay, quietly, "Two horns?"

"One for the dead, and one for the living," Ilzay said, fiercely. "We will *not* be too late for our people, not all of them."

Penrys kept Najud company late that evening as he finished the outsides of the pouches of remembrances for the three dead they'd found that day. They shared the low worktable, seated across from each other.

As she'd told him once, her hands seemed to remember leather-working, and she drew the rest of it from his own deep knowledge of it, so he let her finish cutting them from the goat-hides and stitching them together.

"This won't be enough for more than a few," she said, patting the rolled remnant of the hide.

Najud looked up from his light engraving of the surface of one of the pouches. "Umzakhilin gave me lots of these hides, two whole packs full, and many rolls of lacing. We thought of footwear or clothing for survivors, not this…" His gesture took in the sad work in front of them.

He finished the last of the names, cut into the surface of the leather. He rummaged through the small pack on the ground at his side until he found a small stoneware bottle from which he poured a bit of oil into a small, shallow dish.

With a little brush, he carefully stirred in finely powdered charcoal dipped with a bone spoon from a small pouch in front of him. When it was the consistency he wanted, he filled in the engraved hollows, very carefully, with the coloring agent.

"I'll need to paint these twice," he said, "even with the rough surface I've made from the engraving. The first one always soaks into the leather a bit. Once it's had a little time to partially dry, I'll do it again. Then they can dry altogether overnight."

Penrys said, "I'll just watch. Don't think I'm much of a painter." What she meant was that her fingers didn't itch to pick up a brush, watching Najud, the way her hands did, when he held and worked the leather.

With controlled strokes, Najud filled in the engraved name. The intensity of the black faded as some of it was absorbed into the roughened letters, but even so, the letters were neatly formed, somber and plain.

He covered his dish of paint and suspended two of the three empty pouches near the stovepipe for a few minutes to let them partially dry.

"I'm surprised Ilzay didn't want to do this himself," Penrys said.

"They all know how to read and write," Najud said, "but *bikrajab* are considered better at that sort of thing. People often come to the *bikraj* for special work like this, not just the writing, but…"

He waved his hand at the three sad little heaps at the end of the table. Each had bits of fabric, and any jewelry that could be found. In one case, there was a scrap of parchment that said "broken left upper arm." There were two men that Jirkat and Ilzay could think of who had an old injury like that, and they weren't sure which one this was. Maybe the remaining relatives would recognize the fabric. The pouch destined for that one had no name engraved on it, and no paint.

Najud glanced sideways at Penrys. "You know, you'll have to experiment again."

"What, find out if I can control non-wizards directly? Like she seems to be doing?"

"You have to know how the *qahulajti* uses her power, if you want to stop her."

Penrys shook her head. "This isn't the Temple Academy in Gonglik, and these aren't wizards. I can't do this to one of our companions. How would I even explain it to him? He'd hate me, afterward. I have to live with them on this trail for weeks!"

She could feel his sympathy, but it was still impossible. "How about starting with the animals," he suggested. "We don't want mice in our things, do we?"

He waggled his fingers and twitched his eyebrows suggestively.

Despite herself, she chuckled.

"You win. Let's see what I can do with mice."

She let herself feel the tiny mind-glows in their immediate vicinity. To her somewhat appalled amusement, she found them concentrated under and around the two *kazrab*, drawn by the heat, she supposed. Najud, looking on through her perception, let some of his own appreciation show. *Well, who can blame them? They just want to be warm.*

Not in my tent.

She couldn't speak to them, anymore than she could speak to a horse. She tried conveying a sense of menace, and an image of a snake. *This would probably work better if I could send them the smell of a snake instead. How would I do that?*

Still, it had some effect. All of the little mind-glows retreated, especially from her own *kazr*, though less so from the other one which was further away.

"Don't know how long that will work," she said.

"You can check in the morning and see."

"I'm not sure this is what she did. I didn't command them, the way she seems to have done with the wolves and the stallion. I just showed them something that wasn't so to make them do what I wanted."

Najud looked at her patiently. "Maybe that's all she does, too."

"Not with the people, surely. That wouldn't be enough."

He considered. "Maybe that depends on what she shows them."

CHAPTER 20

After a week, the first light snow had blown in, and then mostly blown off again. The crisp, cold temperatures had kept it dry enough that the trail was still plain.

Penrys found it even more visible from the air, while the snow was light and uneven, a faint but wide scar that meandered over the landscape, headed to the south and west. She was on her outward morning flight of twenty miles, looking for the mind-glows of people or larger animals. When she reached her planned distance, she would return, weaving back and forth across the trail to fix the location of anything her companions should be told about.

Ilzay had announced this morning that they were starting to catch up, that the droppings they were finding were now only weeks old, less than a month. Certainly the track they'd been following had wandered over the low grassy hills and ridges, as if it had no destination in mind.

The hope Ilzay's news should have engendered was weighed down by the continuing finds of bodies, some horses or cattle, but most of them the clansmen for whom rescue had come too late. Sometimes nothing remained but a skull, but usually the clothing had helped many of the larger bones stay intact. Building cairns became their chief occupation, and they'd learned to be grimly relieved when several of the dead could be gathered in one place into a single cairn.

From the air Penrys was able to spot many more than would have been visible from the ground, but she knew they must be missing some of them. No one spoke of that. The pack with its Kurighdunaq marking, the rainbow, was almost full. The tally horn that Ilzay carried slung from his neck recorded four *jal*, now, ninety-six, plus another seven couple in the spoken record—*tabith*, in the old counting language Najud used.

The night camps were quiet, and everyone was involved in the making of the little leather pouches. Najud had charred some bits of fallen wood until he had enough to grind more charcoal with the small mortar and pestle he kept with his craft things in the special pack. There was no way to make more of the linseed oil on the trail—when that ran out, he would have to try cooking oil, a poor substitute. Najud proposed to use ink, first, if it came to that.

She was worried about Ilzay's long silences. Najud had told her that Ilzay had ridden west at sunset, alone, last night, and was gone for more than an hour. Jirkat reported that when he returned, he'd said nothing about where he'd gone, or why.

"You can feel him yourself," Najud had told her. "You know how this business buries his spirit. We're going to do something about that tonight."

Penrys curved west as the trail below her did. She'd discovered the most efficient way to handle the cold in the air for these long flights—she tucked her gloved hands under the armpits of her sheepskin coat to make her upper body more compact, and used a loose strap coiled simply around her knees several times to help keep her legs together. She could rig it in the air, and a tug on the end freed them before she needed to land, but it relieved her of some of the effort of holding them together for hours, so that she could take better advantage of the efficiencies of flying. Her human body wasn't designed for it, and her legs were in the way, a drag on her speed.

The gap between the wings and tail and her body had no difficulty adjusting to the increased thickness of her clothing, and she marveled at the complexities of design hinted at by that, more even than the wings themselves. *I wish I had some idea of how a device like this works. None of its principles are clear, not least that the wings behave like flesh, with feeling and even blood. But the chain is a mystery, too, the way it can store power taken from wizards, almost like a living power-stone. Where does this knowledge come from? Where were these devices made?*

She shook her head to free it from her obsessive picking at the old problem. She was almost at the end of her outward flight. Time for one more mind-scan of the landscape.

A man. Someone living. And four horses.

She ignored the trace below her and swung directly toward him. As she got closer, she realized he was another wizard. *Land now, and walk the rest of the way, or drop in on him from the air?*

Before she could decide, a strange mind-voice intruded.

Now that's not something you see every day, bikrajab in the sky.

The humor of it persuaded her, and she swooped in to land a few yards away from him and let her wings vanish.

The man stood not far from the trail, and his tethered riding horse and the three pack horses grazed the winter grasses behind him. A half-built cairn and the rock in his hands told its own tale.

"You have anything to do with this?" he asked, as he dropped the rock into place and dusted off his gloved hands.

She shook her head. "I'm tracking them with the Kurighdunaq—it's their people."

"Since when do they have a flying, foreign *bikrajti* at their disposal?" he said.

"Now that's a long story, it is." She considered him. The gray eyebrows and lined face declared he was in his fifties, but he was hale and confident.

"M'name's Penrys," she said, "I'm traveling with Najud, of the Zamjilah. We were headed home from the High Pass when we came across the Kurighdunaq disaster." Her hand wave included the cairn.

He nodded to her. "I'm Khizuwi of clan Umzabul, of the Maqurrah. We've been hearing stories, and I came out to see. I've been moving up the trail—didn't want to get too far from the *zudiqazd* this late in the year and the track looked too old for me to catch up anyway, going the other way."

She looked down and saw a cloth on the ground, spread with bits of fabric and a buckle. It was all too familiar.

"Find many, did you?" She pointed at the cloth. "Did you do that for all of them?"

"I knew people would be looking and would want to know. I recognized the clan, from the decorations, and figured someone would come, from that direction."

She felt his eyes looking her up and down. "Lose many of them, did they?"

"Almost three hundred missing, just about all of the clan."

At that, he swallowed and pursed his lips.

"Well, you can tell them *tadas* and *mawik* have found their last homes at my hands."

Eleven, she translated—five couple and one.

She sighed, and her shoulder slumped. "Look, we're about twenty miles back on the trail from here. There're five of us, and we build the cairns as we go which slows us down, some, but we'll get here by evening or sooner. Will you wait for us?"

"Assuredly," he said. "This Najud, he is a *bikraj*, yes? Good. There is work for us here."

He waved his hand at her, as if to shoo her away. "Be off with you. I'll be waiting." He cocked his head at the cairn. "Plenty to do."

Once Penrys got within range of Najud, she called to him. *Met a wizard on the trail coming our way. Khizuwi, from clan Umzabul.*

There was a delay and she pictured him telling the others.

Jirkat says he's famous, he is. Maqurrah tribe, west of here. Some relative of Hadishti's—that's her original clan. He's going to wait for us?

Seemed to think that was easiest. And there's a stream nearby, for a camp.

She paused. *He's been piling rocks, he says.*

Oh. How many? She could feel Najud bracing himself for her answer.

Another eleven. And I've spotted several more on the way back.

By then she was in sight of her companions, just starting to remount after building another cairn, a small one.

She dropped down to give them her report in detail.

CHAPTER 21

"Tell me everything!"

After a week isolated together on the trail, Khizuwi was a breath of fresh air for the trackers, and Penrys was amused to see how he charmed them all, even Ilzay.

At Najud's insistence, Khizuwi had cheerfully abandoned his *kamah* to share their living space. Penrys regretted their loss of privacy, but they couldn't leave him to shiver when he could sleep warm in their roomy *kazr*. The nominal bed hanging didn't suit her sense of modesty, but there would be other times.

Now, in the fading afternoon light, he poked busily into everyone's affairs. Once he caught Penrys following him with her eyes, as he moved from Jirkat, cleaning his horse gear, to Winnajhubr, who bowed respectfully, and he winked at her before quizzing the young man about his family.

Only when he came to Ilzay did he change his manner, regarding the tally horn that hung from his neck with a sober demeanor. He laid a hand softly on the pack that held the remembrances of the dead. "We will bless this in the morning, when we add the new ones," he told Ilzay, "and they will all rest the more quietly for it."

He held Najud in conversation for some time as he helped them finish setting up the *kazrab*, teasing all the names of his Zannib teachers out of him, and then asking about his latest expedition in Kigali, his meeting with Penrys, and the chained wizard they'd found there.

When he turned to Penrys at last, he chuckled. "You were right. It *is* a long story."

He drew her by the hand and walked her out of the shadow cast by the *kazr* into what was left of the sunlight. "Let me look at that chain of yours, now."

She stood his inspection, and even showed him the fox-like ears hidden beneath her hair, low on her head in the place of human ears.

"Najud told me about your hand. What was it, six weeks ago? May I see?"

No one had asked Penrys about the thin glove, the whole time she had traveled with them, and she only just realized it now. She stared quizzically at Najud.

*I told them. Seemed the best thing to do."

She shook her head in chagrin at her own obliviousness and sighed. Then she peeled off the glove she refitted each morning. Her left hand hadn't required bandages for weeks now, just a little protection against accidental damage. And curious looks.

"Where was it cut?" he asked.

She drew a diagonal line with her finger across the back of her hand, starting an inch above the wrist and running up below all four knuckles. None of that damage was visible. Only the too-short little finger was left to tell the tale, and soon it would be done re-growing.

Maybe it's time to just leave off the glove. Stupid to just make a habit of it.
She stuffed the glove in one of her pockets.

"And the wings?" He cocked his head and smiled into her face, and she couldn't take offense at it.

She noticed the three young men sidling up for a closer look, too, so she waved them in and let them see. She pointed out the gaps between her body with its clothing and the start of the wings and tail, and explained her conclusions about it being a device, before she stopped dead, having forgotten the attitude toward physical magic cultivated by Zannib wizards.

He glanced at her as she stiffened. "Just because I'm twice your age doesn't make me hidebound yet. Not all of us believe that physical magic makes you a *qahulajti*. We've heard of other practices, some of us."

Najud diverted him. "We think we know one way this chained girl may be controlling the animals. Penrys discovered she could do it, too. With mice."

Khizuwi grinned. "Can you show me?"

A bit diffidently, in front of the interested audience of non-wizards, Najud said, "When we first met, Penrys let me watch, from the inside, when she did things." He tapped his forehead meaningfully.

"May I do so, *bikrajti*, please?"

She answered him silently. *You are welcome to look.*

"Good," he said. "Now, find us a mouse."

"Stand still, everyone," she said. She checked for the tiny mind-glows she usually ignored, and was startled to discover how many mice there were, warmly tucked into burrows under the yellowed grasses.

She concentrated on a single rodent, and a loud squeak ten feet in front of them produced a startled leap from Winnajhubr. She felt that jump from the mouse's perspective—a movement of the air and a thump felt through the ground itself, and the mouse fled.

She shook her head and glared at Winnajhubr, while Jirkat and Ilzay laughed at him. "Quiet down and I'll try that again," she told them.

This time, when she focused in on a new specimen, she tried to project a sense of food, to no effect. She used an illusion of sound instead, the alarm of the other mouse to the footsteps of a man behind it, but subdued, as though it were further away.

The mouse scurried from its hiding place to a new tussock of grass, closer to them and visible, and then froze there in the open, all except for its glittering black eyes.

Seems to be easier to drive it than to entice it.

She felt Khizuwi's agreement. She released the mouse and waved her arm at it, and it fled in terror.

Ilzay whispered, "Is that what the *qahulajti* is doing to our people?"

"I have no idea," Penrys admitted. "I don't know if it would work on a person."

Khizuwi commented sagely to the three young men, "It would be most unpleasant to have a *bikraj* in your mind, eh?"

Winnajhubr stepped forward, looking to redeem himself from the laughter of the others. "I don't care about that. Try me."

Penrys considered the youthful pride of him. "Are you sure?"

He stood up straight. "If you need to find out… Anything that gets us there faster… I'll do it."

That drew looks of respect from both Jirkat and Ilzay, and Najud nodded to him.

Penrys drew a deep breath. "Remember, it won't be real, none of it."

Winnajhubr smiled uncertainly.

Conscious of both Najud and Khizuwi watching through her, she tried to picture a wolf in the high grass, and added a growl for effect.

Winnajhubr started to reach for his knife before he dropped his hand sheepishly and stood still again.

Next she tried to picture a grassfire edging his way. She could manage the crackling sound, but couldn't add the sense of heat or smoke to it.

Even so, Winnajhubr began to edge backward. "I know it's not real," he said, "but I can't help it. It looks as if it might be."

Penrys stopped. "What was it like?"

"Well, the wolf seemed real at first glance, until I realized it wasn't moving. And the fire… no heat. Still, if I didn't expect it…"

"Like the mouse," Jirkat added, and snickered.

Winnajhubr ignored him. "It was real enough, and I think you'd get better at it, with practice."

Khizuwi looked at her speculatively. "I believe she would."

CHAPTER 22

Khizuwi's comment echoed unpleasantly in Najud's mind.

He was waiting after his evening meal for the serving of *bunnas* in his *kazr*, where everyone had gathered to hear the *bikraj*'s story. He wasn't immune to Khizuwi's charm, any more than the rest of them, but he didn't like the way he'd encouraged Penrys to try and do the same things the *qahulajti* had done.

He recognized that some of the churning in his stomach was guilt that he hadn't sufficiently considered how his colleagues might look upon her. He'd gotten so used to both foreign travel and her unique skills that he'd lost his revulsion for devices, for the physical magic that his teachers would consider forbidden. That was the very definition of a *qahulaj*—one who did forbidden things.

He didn't do physical magic himself, but she did, and he'd watched her do it and learned from her. Was she exposed now, were both of them, as targets for other *bikrajab*? He snorted quietly, thinking of the thirty-odd Rasesni mages she'd stripped of power to help fight the Voice.

The Zannib will have a surprise in store for them if they think to overwhelm her with just a few of the righteous. And she's no qahulajti—she restored all the power she borrowed, and the need was great.

But people had died, he remembered. When she poured her own power into the Voice's weakened captive wizards, four were overwhelmed and left dead on the field—he'd seen them fall. He wasn't sure if she knew that, and he didn't plan to tell her.

Casualties of war. Not her fault.

He felt her eyes on him and he looked her way and nodded reassuringly. The *bunnas* was being tended by Ilzay, while she used boiling water from Khizuwi's own pot to steep a special herb he'd brought with him, something he preferred to *bunnas*.

She poured the infusion into two cups, one for herself and one for their guest. When she emptied the pot, she moved it away from the stove and walked over to sit on the rugs next to Najud, and held the thick clay with the tips of her fingers, waiting for it to cool.

He glanced at the low worktable, in the back portion of the *kazr*. The eleven packets of personal scraps shared the surface with today's finds, and he knew it would take hours to engrave and paint the names for all of them, once the ones Khizuwi had brought in had been identified. They'd waited to do that until after their evening council.

Beside him, Penrys cradled the cup in both hands and inhaled deeply. "It reminds me of some of the herbal infusions they use in Ellech."

She took a careful sip, blew on the liquid to cool it, and tried again. "Interesting. Astringent, bracing. Complicated." She smiled broadly. "I can feel the vigor in it, the alertness."

"What did he call it?" Najud asked.

"*Kassa.* Gets it from Shimiz, he said, by ship, from somewhere to the west. He says there are different varieties, like *bunnas.*" She swallowed another mouthful. "Try it."

He took the proffered cup and tasted it for himself. He recognized the alertness she described from *bunnas.*

He knew the name but had never encountered it. They used it in the west, on the shores of Wandat. It was a specialty of the region.

This would make a good trade item, he realized, as he took another sip and returned the cup to Penrys. They already valued *bunnas* in Kigali and Rasesdad, like civilized people anywhere, but he hadn't heard of this herb being used in either country, or even in the rest of *sarq*-Zannib.

Ilzay finished pouring *bunnas* for those who wanted it, and Khizuwi cleared his throat and started to speak.

"My thanks to my hosts," he began, with a cock of the head at Najud's bedframe behind him. "A warm *kazr* and good company are all a man can wish for, when he meets *tulqajab* along the way."

He swallowed a mouthful of his *kassa.*

"I am Khizuwi, son of Urqudham, of the Umzabul, in the Maqurrah tribe, and the Undullah are our respected neighbors."

He nodded to Jirkat, Ilzay, and Winnajhubr, seated together nearest the door, and they returned the gesture.

"I know of the Shubzah tribe, to the east"—this with a nod to Najud—"and I have even heard of Ellech, though, alas, the Collegium of Wizards there is but a legend to us."

He smiled graciously at Penrys. Najud was interested to see that her nod in return was polite but restrained. Perhaps she wasn't entirely under his spell.

"The *zudiqazd* of the Maqurrah clans is northwest of here, and directly west of the *zudiqazd* of the Undullah clans. My clan's route, the *tarizd*, runs northwest from there, up almost to the rough hills we call Wayat mar-Zarqash, the Corner of Zarqash."

Jirkat stirred, and Khizuwi looked at him.

"Yes, you know where that is, don't you? The trail from your summer camp, south of High Pass, to Shimiz runs along the backside of that ridge."

Ilzay nodded.

"There are caves in the Corner, many of them," Khizuwi said. "Our children play in them, during the summer encampment. Sometimes our young men pry colored minerals out of the walls and use them for decoration or grind them for pigments."

He paused. "In the last three years or so, they've acquired an evil reputation."

Najud and Penrys exchanged looks. She had appeared in Ellech about three years ago, and the Voice first became known in Rasesdad at roughly the same time.

Khizuwi watched them, but didn't comment.

"People stopped grazing their herds there, because too many of the animals went missing and couldn't be found. Early this summer, two herdsmen and the young woman that was a friend of one of them—they vanished, too. Wolf tracks were found, but no bodies."

Jirkat asked, "When, exactly?"

"In the second week of *Jibrim*."

Ilzay worked it out. "That's about when we were passing, to the west, on the other side of the ridge. Remember, Jirkat, we stopped and admired that view on our way back, before we swung south of east to intersect the trail to the autumn camp."

Jirkat stared at Khizuwi. "What are you suggesting, *bikraj*?"

Penrys said, "He's suggesting you stirred up a hornet's nest, passing by it unknowing."

She gave Khizuwi a hard look. "Aren't you?"

He replied, mildly. "Perhaps nothing lived in those caves, those caves that were empty before."

Penrys pressed on. "But perhaps this *qahulajti* appeared there, three years ago, and preyed upon your herds, and finally your people, and then when they passed the place"—she waved a hand at the young men—"near enough for her to hear them," she tapped her forehead, "she went and found their backtrail."

The blood drained from Jirkat's face.

"Isn't that what you mean?" Penrys was rigid.

Khizuwi just echoed, "Perhaps."

The grim lines on Ilzay's face aged it by a decade. "The timing works, *bikrajti*. He's right."

Najud told Jirkat, "You didn't cause this. It's not your fault. The lightning struck where it would, and you had nothing to do with it." He glowered at Khizuwi.

The older man shrugged. "Truly, it is not your fault, *barqah*, if it happened that way. But it's best that we understand what she might have done, what might be true, so that we can learn how to stop her, and rescue what's left of your clan."

Penrys thought out loud. "Maybe that *is* how it happened. It might explain a lot. If that's where she appeared…"

She choked, but continued. "Like me… then maybe she never left. Maybe she never found people, only animals. She's young now, and she'd have been younger then. No memory, no language. What would happen?"

"A feral child," Najud said, "Like one that's lost very young and raised by animals."

Khizuwi nodded. "I have heard of this. They never quite become people again, once they're saved."

"And she found your three people," Penrys said. "And she *learned*. But what would she do with what she learned?"

She struck her thigh with her fist. "She became curious. She scanned around her, and discovered…"

She waved her hand with the shortened finger at Jirkat, and he shrank back in dismay, but she didn't notice and went on. "More people. Where did they come from, she'd want to know."

Najud finished for her. "So she went and looked. And found them."

"But why would she kidnap them all?" Penrys asked. "Assuming this is all true."

Najud shook his head, and Khizuwi watched them without comment.

CHAPTER 23

When the camp had been packed up in the morning and the horses loaded, Khizuwi strolled over to the restive horse in Ilzay's string that carried the pack with the rainbow marking and the doleful load of pouches.

Everyone was still dismounted, and they stood in a loose group facing their guest, and watched.

He lay both hands flat on the pack, and the horse calmed. After a few moments, he turned back to his audience.

"These people—your friends, your family, your clan-kin—they've returned to the *dunaq wandim*, the world that surrounds. These little mementos they left behind—those are for you, not for them. They have no part in them any more. You remember them by these tokens, and it's your memories that are light or heavy. It's for you to make them light again, to think of the pleasant times. They don't make this pack heavy or this horse uneasy—you do."

He looked each of them in the eye as he turned his head. "When you make your cairns, you do it for them—for your memory of them and how you think you would wish to be treated. But I tell you, they don't care, and neither will you, when the time comes. Do it instead for yourself, to remember by the labor of lifting heavy rocks that the world is as it is and is only changed, if ever it is, by sweat and toil and the desire of everything living to stay alive, as long as possible, before returning to the peace of the *dunaq wandim*."

Winnajhubr drew a shaky breath. Both his father and his uncle were among those Khizuwi had gathered, and he would see that cairn this morning. The two brothers lay together, what was left of them. Penrys felt the effect of Khizuwi's words on him, overlaying his sharp grief with the beginnings of resignation.

When she monitored Ilzay, it seemed to her that his depression had lightened, that a new element of guardianship had entered his thoughts and squared his shoulders. His hand grasped the tally horn on its thong as if he would protect it, not as if it weighed him down.

When she turned toward Najud and prepared to mount her horse, she murmured to him, "That was… effective."

He nodded soberly. "How long will you ride with us, before you fly?"

"A while. Doesn't take long to do my twenty miles, out and back."

Once she had adjusted her position, she looked over at Najud. "I wish you'd let me go a reasonable distance. We may lose her if enough snow comes."

He shook his head. "Bad enough you have to fly so far beyond the range of your mind-voice. At least this way, if anything happens, we're only a day away at the most."

"It's not the best way to use your long-distance scout," she said. Khizuwi's words might have calmed the rest of them, but she felt a renewed sense of urgency. It was all very well to not over-mourn the dead, but it was the living who needed their help.

Khizuwi walked his own horse up in time to hear the last of this. The cairn he'd been working on when Penrys encountered him the day before was visible to their left. He indicated it with his head, and said to them both, quietly, "They'll call this the 'trail of the dead' from now on, long after they've forgotten who these people were."

She noticed that he kept his voice low enough not to be heard by the clan-kin of these dead.

Then he looked directly at her. "What do you think would happen, *bikrajti*, if you blunder into the attention of this powerful child, dozens of miles from any of us? Who will you help then? Will anyone find *your* bones and raise the rocks over what is left?"

Two days later, Penrys returned from her morning scouting to join Najud for the mid-day rest.

"I've been thinking," she said, "up there in the cold." She ate standing, since she'd be sitting soon enough, swapping to horseback for the remainder of the day.

Najud waited for her to take another bite of her lukewarm beans and sausage bits, unfrozen by the simple expedient of keeping it in a pack nearest to the horse's warm hide, and then pouring boiling water over it. The result was edible, if not exactly hot. He'd tried to convince her to add some of the *wishkaz* spices to it, but she insisted on salt and nothing else.

The food must be terribly bland in Ellech.

She swallowed, and waved her horn spoon in the air to illustrate her point. "I don't think this girl is truly feral, not in the sense of having no language."

She dipped up another spoonful but paused before lifting it to her mouth. "If she was like me, she no longer had her old language, but that doesn't mean she never had one."

Najud took advantage of her temporary muteness as the spoon reached its destination. "So she knew languages, you're saying—she just needed one to use."

"That's right," Penrys said. "And all she found were animals."

Khizuwi was close enough to listen to them, but he was silent, apparently occupied with his food. The other three squatted together, discussing something in low voices that he couldn't make out.

"For three, long years. What did that do to her? Then she found some people, and all of a sudden…" She chewed another mouthful.

"But what's happened to them?" Najud said.

She shrugged. "Maybe they're still with her."

"Not voluntarily," he protested.

"I didn't say that."

She glanced over at Khizuwi.

"What's she using for power, hmm? None of these people were… are wizards."

"What did you use, on Winnajhubr, or the mice?" Najud asked.

"Well, I don't know. It wasn't like fighting against wizards, in the Temple School. It was finicky, and I didn't do it well, but it didn't need much strength. Still, it's a lot of people and animals, and there's some distance involved—think of reaching up into the High Pass, presumably from the summer encampment. That's, what, twenty miles? Thirty?"

She grabbed another bite. "I couldn't do that, and then maintain delicate control with it, too, especially for so many. And this is all guesswork, anyway. I don't understand exactly what she's doing."

"Or why," Najud added.

"And where's she going? I'll say one thing, she's not in any hurry about it. The track meanders all over the place."

Najud lifted his voice and called over to Ilzay. "Didn't you pick up some more droppings today? How old would you say they are?"

He didn't know what to make of the grins that flickered on the faces of the three young men.

Ilzay stood up, and walked over, and the other two strolled along behind. "The horse droppings look only a couple of weeks old now, maybe less. She's taking her time about it, she is."

He reached into one of the pouches slung from his belt. "Maybe you can tell me what you think about this, *bikrajti*—how old?"

He held out two frozen brown lumps, and Najud choked as Penrys furrowed her brow, clearly trying to identify the animal.

Jirkat successfully froze his expression, but Winnajhubr's attempts to stifle his laughter failed altogether. "I told you she wouldn't recognize it," he sputtered to his friends. "Someone that skilled, you know, with her unusual nature... Probably never saw that before. Humans, they're different from birds, you know..."

With that Najud joined the other three in whoops as Penrys's cheeks flamed and she got the joke. Her mouth opened and shut a couple of times as she searched for a retort, but finally she just gave up and lifted her hands in defeat.

"Is it my fault if everyone's too polite to decorate the camp with specimens so I can learn for myself?" she said.

In spite of herself, she grinned broadly, and Najud could feel the warmth of her affection for these friends, comfortable enough with her to make her the butt of a joke.

As the laughter died down, he noticed Khizuwi smiling quietly as he observed the banter but said nothing.

CHAPTER 24

"People coming," Penrys called back to the others. "Two men, about five miles out."

She rode just off the path, as the only one not leading a pack-string, so that everyone else could stay together.

Najud glanced over at her. *How did you miss them in the morning?*

I can only check a trail ten miles wide, with me in the center. If they were coming from east or west and more than five miles away, I wouldn't sense them.

But you can feel them now.

She nodded. "Two *bikrajab*," she said out loud, for Khizuwi's benefit. "And their horses."

Khizuwi asked, "From the east?"

"That's right," she said.

"That'll be Jiqlaraz and maybe his *nal-jarghal*, from clan Rashaban of the Dhajtawhaz tribe. Their trail to the Maqurrah should cross this track somewhere around here."

Penrys glanced around at the low ridges whose base the track had followed for days. The landscape seemed featureless to her, but Khizuwi clearly knew exactly where he was.

They stopped to raise one more rock cairn, for an unrecognized man, and that gave the strangers enough time to come up the track and meet them while they were still dismounted.

Penrys had kept her mind's attention on them the whole way, glad that this meeting would not find her in the air, flaunting her foreigner status. They all straightened up from their labor at the sound of hoofbeats. Khizuwi walked out to greet them, and welcomed the elder one as an old colleague.

The wizard in the lead was in his forties, Penrys judged, with a prominent hooked nose, and he wore the small turban that was so characteristic of the Zannib men. Behind him rode a young turbaned man who looked to be Winnajhubr's age. He led the longer pack-string—four horses, to his master's two.

Jiqlaraz finished speaking with Khizuwi, and he surveyed their group from horseback, until his eyes fell upon Penrys and he glimpsed the chain she wore around her neck.

"Good," he said. "I see you've caught her already and put her to work."

Without hesitation he launched a mind-probe which she effortlessly repelled by raising her shield. She smiled coldly at his surprise.

"You're mistaken, *bikraj*," she said. "There's more than one of us."

Behind him, the eyes of his apprentice widened.

Khizuwi interposed himself between them and began speaking rapidly to his colleague, in tones too low for the rest of them to hear.

A pressure at her back told Penrys that Najud had stepped up behind her, and she realized she was still focused on Jiqlaraz, poised for his next attack. She made herself relax again, though she kept her shield up. As her shoulders dropped, Najud's placed his hand on one of them.

The other three were puzzled, but they moved in closer together and took their cue from Najud.

Khizuwi stopped talking, and Jiqlaraz considered her again. Then he dismounted and Winnajhubr ran up to take his reins and the lead rope for his string. Penrys watched him exchange a nervous grin with the as yet unnamed apprentice as they waited on their elders.

Jiqlaraz approached and nodded to the group now concentrated around Penrys. "I beg forgiveness for my mistake, *jarghalti*, but all the messenger said was female, foreign, and chained around the neck. Perhaps you can understand the error."

"I do understand," she said, warily. "No harm done."

Najud stepped around her and greeted him genially. "We're very glad to have help with us as we pursue this *qahulajti* who has caused so much grief for our friends, the Kurighdunaq. I'm Najud, son of Ilsahr, of the Zamjilah, and this is Penrys."

Penrys held her face expressionless. *I need parents and clan just for these introductions, if nothing else. Sounds too simple this way.*

The strange wizard tapped his chest. "I'm Jiqlaraz, son of Ghayrbarsh, of the Rashaban of the Dhajtawhaz. My *nal-jarghal* here is Munraz, my brother's son."

Penrys thought Najud froze for just a moment at that announcement, but he continued as if nothing were the matter.

Jiqlaraz turned to Khizuwi. "My friend tells me he has been sharing your *kazr*, Najud. No need for that any more. We two have room for another."

Najud said smoothly, "We will be sorry to lose such a pleasant and distinguished guest, of course, but he must do as he thinks best."

Penrys kept her face expressionless. *Something's wrong here. I won't be sorry to get my privacy back, but what's going on?*

Jirkat stepped forward boldly and spoke to Najud directly, ignoring Jiqlaraz. "We should keep going, *zarawinnaj*, we have a lot more ground to cover today."

Ah. That's part of it. These two wizards are much older than Najud. That's why Jirkat gave him the migration leader's title, to reinforce his authority.

"Twelve more miles at least," Najud said cheerfully. "We're catching up—no time to lose."

Khizuwi threw his weight behind him. "I'll fill you in as we go along, Jiqlaraz, and you can tell us all about your journey when we stop tonight."

After building four more cairns, the mood in the camp that night was subdued. They set up the three *kazrab* and dispersed for their separate meals.

Penrys found Najud quiet and inattentive while she was cleaning up the cookware they'd used, until she finally threw a wet dish cloth at him.

"Explain what's going on," she said. "This has you worried and I don't understand all of it."

He picked up the cloth and used it to clean his low worktable for the leather work he would do after the evening meeting. "Sorry. I've been chewing on it all afternoon."

He paused to order his thoughts. "It's several things, all at the same time. First, it's the issue of leadership. For a normal journey— a caravan, the *taridiqa*, even just a few friends visiting someone else—there is always a leader. It doesn't mean much when it's just a few people, but even so, someone bears the title. Someone must be the leader. It's an important day when a young man first takes that responsibility for a group of his friends, like the day when another man first calls him *lij*, like a true adult."

He hung the cloth over a rope near the stovepipe to dry.

"Umzakhilin set me this responsibility for the five of us, and made it easier for them to accept me with the clan adoption. That's why Jirkat called me *zarawinnaj* today."

"I understand that part," Penrys said, as she looked around to check that everything was in order.

"But the thing is, when *bikrajab* band together to restrain a *qahulaj*, that's different. There's usually no one in their group who isn't a *bikraj*, at some level, and it's almost always the eldest who leads. We have stories about what happens when there's a dispute about it. It doesn't end well."

Penrys said, "And until Khizuwi came along, you were also the oldest wizard in this group, more or less." Her own age was unknown, but she looked about the same age as Najud.

"But not any more," she finished. "What's going to happen?"

"That's part of what we must talk about tonight."

He sat down in his customary spot to the right of the stove and patted the rug next to him in invitation.

"It not an easy question. I've never joined others in a hunt like this."

"Nonsense," Penrys said, as she crossed her legs and made herself comfortable. "That's exactly what you did going against the Voice."

"Not in the customary Zannib way, I mean. Khizuwi and Jiqlaraz—they won't understand the experience I have. They'll expect Khizuwi to take charge, and if he won't, that Jiqlaraz looks all to ready to step up instead."

He pursed his lips. "I've heard of Jiqlaraz's family. It's something of a scandal."

At Penrys's raised eyebrow, he added. "That clan only produces *bikrajab* in that one family's line, instead of the talent popping out in various bloodlines unpredictably. They marry the sisters and daughters of other *bikrajab*, when they can't find a *bikrajti*."

"So, when he named himself the uncle of an apprentice *bikraj*..." Penrys suggested.

"His brother and father are *bikrajab*, too—I know the story." Najud said. "It's always awkward to apprentice your own close relative, in any field. It almost never happens for a *bikraj*, but in this family line…"

"Why do they do it? Are they trying to make themselves stronger? Could they make a clan of wizards, all closely related?"

"I've never heard an explanation. Maybe we'll get one tonight."

"This chained wizard… you don't suppose he might think of her as breeding stock, do you?"

Najud blinked. "That's impossible."

"No one tries to redeem a wizard-tyrant, then?" she said. "Who condemns them?"

"There's usually a trail of dead bodies to accuse them," he muttered, "though this one is by far the largest I've ever heard of."

"So, what are you going to do tonight?"

He just shook his head.

CHAPTER 25

After an hour of tooth-clenched politeness, the dispute in Najud's *kazr* broke out in earnest.

Jirkat and Ilzay were resolute in asserting the priority of the rescue of their kinsmen, and Najud agreed with them. Jiqlaraz made the case for the traditional control of the eldest *bikraj* in a hunt like this.

The man's nephew was too young to voice his own opinions, but Najud was rapidly coming to dislike Jiqlaraz with his condescending references to Najud as a newly declared *jarghal.* He wondered why Khizuwi had said so little thus far.

Penrys had refrained from interfering all this time, but he could feel the impatience rising in her, and now it broke out.

She stood up. "If you'll forgive a foreigner's opinion," she said in feigned humility, "this is pointless. I'm sure everyone wants to save as many of the Kurighdunaq as possible, and to do that we have to catch up with her, and then stop her."

She pinned them with an exasperated look. "Until then, we all want exactly the same thing."

Jiqlaraz glanced at her and then looked away. "We will lose too much time on the trail raising these rock cairns. That can wait until we return."

Najud heard the sharp intake of breath from the outraged clansmen, seated together left of the stove. Before one of them could voice his outrage, he tried to inject a tone of reasonability. "We will catch her in another couple of weeks or so. But the snow is overdue, and once it falls we have no hope of marking the dead or confirming their deaths."

"You'll have the survivors, if any," Jiqlaraz said. "That should tell you who you've missed."

Even Khizuwi murmured at this callousness.

Penrys took a deep breath. "Have you heard what Najud's masterwork was? His *nayith?* He discovered a way to organize wizards, to combine their strengths until they could defend themselves against one of these chained wizards, in Neshilik. It had never been done before—the Rasesni lost dozens of their mages before he helped defeat that wizard-tyrant."

"And who saw all that, in a foreign land?" Jiqlaraz asked scornfully. "Who judged it?"

"I did," she said, and glared at him. "And if you think I'm not qualified, you're welcome to test me. Very welcome."

She wasn't tall or imposing, but the menace of her stance was enough to silence everyone. She wasn't often angry, he reflected, but she made up for it in sincerity once something grabbed a hold of her.

When no one took her up on her offer, she backed off slightly. "My point is, Najud is the *zarawinnaj* of this bit of the clan, no one disputes that. He and I have fought against one of these chained wizards before, and we've both organized wizards to work together to stand against them. *You* have no idea what you may be facing."

She waved her hand at Khizuwi and Jiqlaraz. "No idea at all. I maintain that he is well qualified in many ways to lead the attack on this girl himself, despite the experience and worthiness of the two of you. I ask you to set aside that aspect of your tradition to allow us a unified leadership for our team."

She managed a Kigali-style bow and sat down clumsily again.

Before Jiqlaraz could respond, Khizuwi asked, "And what about yourself, *jarghalti*? I suspect you are stronger than any of us, and more familiar with the dangers we will find. Don't you wish to take command, for the same reasons you recommend Najud?"

She shook her head. "It wouldn't be fitting, not while Najud can fill that role. I'm not part of the Kurighdunaq, I'm not even a Zan. And I certainly don't have the experience to be a *zarawinnaj*."

"And if we can't agree to this, what then?" Khizuwi said. "If other *bikrajab* come join us, they'll likely be older than Najud, too—no dishonor to him."

Very bravely, Ilzay stood up and injected himself into this dispute between *bikrajab*. "Please forgive me, *jarghal*," he said, "but without Penrys to scout for us, we will be much slower, and very much blinder. And my clansmen and I are sworn to follow our *zarawinnaj*. It may be that other *bikrajab* will not join us under Najud—I have no say in that. But my *ujarqa* who met this *qahulajti* put his faith in the two of them, and I think you should, too."

"Don't worry about it," Penrys said later, after everyone had left, and Najud had lowered the flap over the *kazr*'s door for the night. Only the light of the banked fire in the stove gleamed in glimpses through the barely open fire draft door.

"What good are these three wizards—or is it two and a half—going to be against a chained one anyway?" she said. "Remember the Voice?"

Najud held her in his arms in her bed, her back curled into him like a spoon, and he could feel the words as well as hear them.

He grunted, still upset by the unresolved leadership issue. The other three *bikrajab* had gone off eventually to discuss it among themselves.

Penrys mused out loud again. "Maybe this one has never met a wizard before. She could've crushed an untrained Umzakhilin with her mind, I suspect, so why did she use a horse instead?"

Najud said, "You see how Umzakhilin has sent messengers out about this *qahulajti*. We're going to have to send word to everyone, eventually—all the *bikrajab*—about these chained wizards. Khizuwi made that clear to me."

There was a moment of silence before Penrys said, in a quiet voice, "And then I will become everyone's dreaded enemy."

"No, Pen-sha, we will explain…"

He could feel the shrug of her shoulders.

"How can you possibly explain, in a message that will be carried by a chain of relays? Can't be done."

Should I tell her it's worse than that? He hesitated, but honesty compelled him.

"The word will filter out to Kigali and Rasesdad, I fear."

She sighed. "Ellech, too, I imagine. D'ye suppose they'll say, at the Collegium, that they always knew I was a monster, it's what they expected?"

There was nothing he could say to this, so he wrapped his arms around her to give her what shelter he could.

She chucked darkly. "I wonder if your team of wizards will wait until we've stopped this girl before they turn on me."

Not for the first time, Najud doubted the wisdom of having all three of the *bikrajab* living together.

In a patent effort to change the topic, Penrys said, "I meant to tell you what I was thinking the other night, when you were talking about *kassa* with Khizuwi."

"Hmm?"

"I was seeing you as a trader, again. It's admirable, the way things keep dovetailing into this western caravan idea of yours—the suggestion for Umzakhilin to found a base, the donkeys for breeding mules, trade goods like the *kassa*. I was impressed."

He snorted.

"No, truly. It's a side of you I haven't seen much of."

"I haven't told you everything," he confided. "If we can get a caravan base started below the High Pass, there's no reason it shouldn't prosper. You could build a library there, too—why not? Start with copies of the books scattered throughout *sarq*-Zannib. Not just the *bikraj* books, but all kinds."

"Another Collegium?" Penrys asked, with a bit of a tease in her voice.

Najud was glad the darkness hid his face. He tightened his hold on her. "Want to come be a librarian again? Show them how it's done?"

"But what about your family?"

What about his family, indeed. "It's not so far, say, three hundred miles—a couple of weeks. Maybe we could go back and forth."

"When you're not leading caravans to Dzongphan," she commented, skeptically. "How can one man do all of that?"

"You start small," he said, "And you just keep going."

He wondered if Umzakhilin had thought more about his proposal. Maybe he had even started to get the word out to other clans.

"That *kassa* would be a good trade item. Lightweight. I wonder why the Rasesni don't use it already? They might like it in Kigali."

"Ellech, too," Penrys said. "They've got other infusions, but nothing this complex, and with the kick of *bunnas*. Think you can deliver it to a harbor for them?"

He smiled in the dark. "Someday… Do you miss things from Ellech?"

"How can I not? It's all I know."

She nestled more comfortably against him. "It's a cold-weather place, too—many similarities. What you call cabbage is lot like something in Ellech, the way it keeps well over the winter. I think of that whenever I smell it."

She rolled over onto her back and lifted a hand to stroke his cheek. "Not your beards, though. None of you in the South can raise a good Ellech beard—not the Zannib or the Kigali, or even those barbarous Rasesni. Some of the Ellech men shave, but the ones that don't… it's like living with a bunch of bears—some tidy, some shaggy, and some downright fashionable."

Najud inhaled the smell of her hair and leaned his head into her hand, glad he'd cleaned himself up this evening.

"I've heard that women don't like being scraped by a man's beard," he murmured, freeing his hand to explore.

She arched into him. "I wouldn't know," she sighed.

CHAPTER 26

Penrys flew in at mid-day under a gloomy sky to report a change in terrain. The track was cutting west through the low, mostly treeless hills it had been following, and the land was becoming better watered. They would be passing through sparse woodlands along a set of streams to some sort of gap in the ridge.

"I went ahead, far enough to confirm where the track was headed." She avoided looking at Najud when she said this, conscious that it was further than he liked.

When Penrys described this, the two senior wizards exchanged looks. Jiqlaraz said, "That's the entry to the long vale of Silmat. It's in between us and the Mahab tribe to the west, and just far enough away that neither of us use it for grazing on the *tarizd*. Both of us go there for wood, though—it's well forested."

Khizuwi added, "I've been there myself. Wood, water, and protection from the worst of the western storms. I can think of worse places to winter up."

The two of them turned to Najud. The argument the night before had been settled somehow in the wizards' shared *kazr*, and Khizuwi had told Najud this morning that they were content to combine their task with the needs of the Kurighdunaq and accept Najud as the *zarawinnaj*.

Najud had nodded soberly at their decision, then commented privately to Penrys, "They don't say what they'll do once we find her—probably be another fight with them then, but I'll take this compromise for now. Anything that gets us there with some hope of finding survivors."

Now Najud asked her, "How much more of the steppe do we have, before the ground rises to the gap?"

"About twenty-five, thirty miles. What are you thinking?"

"We can burn wood, but I can think of better uses for it. Any bodies?"

"Not on this stretch," she said, "not that I could see, but I found horses, about a dozen of them. We'll pass near them, and soon."

"They can't be from our tribe," Jiqlaraz said, "Too far away."

Ilzay spoke up as he put the remains of his meal away in his saddle pack. "More of our herds, seems likely." He turned to Najud. "We should pick them up."

"It'll slow us down," Winnajhubr objected.

Najud looked around the little group and considered. "Here's what we're going to do. We're going to scoop those horses up and bring them along. I also want every bit of fuel we can find while we're still in the grasslands. Use some of the large empty packs for that."

Winnajhubr opened his mouth to ask questions, then glanced up at the threatening sky and shut it again. Najud noticed and with a little smile he explained. "I think it's very interesting that horses managed to get away from this *qahulajti* after all this time. All we've seen until now, since the *zudiqazd*, have been injured beasts, abandoned and left behind. Is she tired? Does she have too much to control?"

He waved a hand at the lowering clouds. "Is she going to stop moving soon? If she's looking for a place to hold for the winter, this vale sounds ideal for her. And if horses escaped, surely some of the people can, too."

He smiled. "These horses will let us bring more fuel. We'll pick up some of the wood as we go along, and make pack frames tonight. Once we remove the *qahulajti*, we have to help whoever's left survive the winter—that was always the most uncertain part of our plan. We can carry the worst of them, with these horses, if the rest can walk. Or we can send the best of them to fetch help from your clan." He tipped his head to Jiqlaraz.

"And if we have to winter in the vale ourselves and are forced to it, well, we can eat them, or any of the remaining herds we find."

Watching the roundup from the air provided Penrys with sufficient amusement to make up for the cold. The young *nal-jarghal* Munraz volunteered to help and was surprisingly adroit at it.

Must've been his job before he turned apprentice wizard.

Munraz and Winnajhubr worked the herd from behind to encourage it to accompany the rest of them as they walked the track. Penrys let them know when they'd gotten them all together, and then landed to remount her own horse.

Ilzay confirmed that the horses belonged to the Kurighdunaq, and Winnajhubr recognized the lead mare of the bunch as one of his father's. He left Munraz as rear herdsman and rode alongside the mare, with his pack-string, talking to her in a low voice.

Even after they had been settled into grazing near their evening camp, Winnajhubr walked off from his *kazr* and kept the mare company for an hour or so, by himself, one hand always in contact with her, as though he could reach his father better that way. Jirkat and Ilzay left him alone, but Penrys noticed Munraz walking out to him in the twilight, with a dish in his hand.

The threat of the dull, overcast skies was finally realized when the snow began to fall, before they settled for the night, each group warm in its own *kazr*, working on pack frames. Penrys looked out at it sifting down before she dropped the door flap and closed the door.

It was still snowing lightly in the morning, with that steady fall that presages inches to come, though only half a foot had accumulated overnight.

Najud had scolded her the night before for flying further than a day's ride ahead to confirm the gap, and this morning they were still arguing in low voices about the distance in front of them.

"I can get to the gap—easily," Penrys said," The visibility isn't too bad, it's not that kind of storm. I've got to make as much distance as I can, *while* I can, before we lose the trail. We're still too far away."

"Not out of the reach of your mind-voice. Do it in batches of about five miles. Won't take any longer."

She bristled at the feel of a leash, but kept her mouth shut.

He tried to soften his tone. "There's no sun or stars for direction, the landmarks on the ground are being buried, and how can you find the trail if you can't see it?"

She pulled her neck scarf up around the bottom of her face and yanked on her gloves, before running a few steps and launching into the air.

Najud's mouth quirked. She hadn't actually confirmed she would cut the flight short. *She'll play fair—if she was going to disobey, she'd have said so. And then left anyway. I better let her cool down. Shouldn't be hard, in this weather.*

Khizuwi had watched their byplay from a distance. When Najud returned to his horse to mount up, the *bikraj* commented, "Impatient, is she?"

"Like a hound after a wolf," Najud said.

"Good. It takes a pack of hounds to bring down a wolf, and that's what we need." He glanced upward at the snow drifting down. "And luck with the weather, or the scent will be buried."

He kicked his horse and led his pack-string along behind him into place.

Najud grunted and changed his mind about mounting. He pulled his knife from his belt and walked to the nearest tussock of grass, sticking out of its new bedding of snow, and started cutting.

It was only an hour later that Penrys returned, arriving without warning and landing in front of the expedition.

Najud raised an eyebrow at her and got a reluctant explanation.

Sorry. I had to work off some frustration.

I understand, Pen-sha.

He could feel her relief at the dissipation of the quarrel.

"Could you make out the trail?" he asked.

"It still shows, but I had to set down a couple of times to be sure it was really there, underneath the snow."

It was a tacit acknowledgment of some of his concerns, he understood.

"It's fresher, now," she said. *Ilzay's expertise helps me read it better.*

"I have something for you," he said, and pointed to the first horse in his string. "There, on the left of his packs."

She walked up to look and broke into laughter at the sight of his new broom, all the strain between them tossed aside. "For me? When did you make it?"

"Something to do while we ride after you." He decided not to tell her how cold his hands had gotten. He'd make the next ones inside his *kazr*, where it was warm.

"We thought, when you needed to land and confirm the track, that you might find it handy."

"I will," she said, still smiling.

She brushed the snow off of her own horse, lifted the piece of canvas that had kept her saddle dry, and shook it off. Then she folded it and stuffed it into a saddlebag.

Once mounted, she turned to the others and described the next few miles for them.

While she spoke, Najud noted the same eagerness in her face as the other *bikrajab* showed, particularly the two older ones. He himself had never been on an official pursuit like this, any more than Munraz had, but their urgency to find this *qahulajti* and kill or control her matched what he'd heard about pursuits of this kind.

They really are hounds on a trail, aren't they—tenacious on the hunt.

He wondered why he felt differently. He agreed with their mission, but his heart was in the finding of the captives, not the killing of their captor. When he'd been pulled into the Voice's captive *bikrajab*, in Neshilik, he was more focused on their survival than on the destruction of that *qahulaj*, partly because they were too weak to hope for that.

Penrys is more like these bikrajab now than I am, intent on the hunt. This is her second chained qahulaj, and she a lion hound who seeks only lion. It's like my tulqiqa, my journeyman travels working on my nayith, my masterwork. She's driven to this, to pursuing these chained bikrajab. And there must be more of them.

She can no more settle into the quiet life I've been offering her than I could have.

The realization struck him like a blow. *I'm going to have to make my own decision—to begin the rest of my life here, now that I am a master, a jarghal, and let her go, or to help her.*

He thought of children, with an ache in his heart. No *bikraj* wanted to marry the mind-deaf, if he had a choice, but there weren't many *bikrajti*. Either you lived alone, watching your relatives raise nephews and nieces, or made what life you could with what partner you could find.

The elation of winning Penrys, not just a *bikrajti* but someone who captured his thoughts, his body, his soul—that was an unexpected gift.

But what about children?

It's only been a couple of months, not enough time to prove anything. But what if she's right about being too much of a "monster"?

He'd heard her, in darker moments, speculate that pregnancy might just be another thing to "heal" for her body.

The wings and the chain—those aren't really her. But what about the rest of it? The furry ears?

Despite himself, he smiled, recalling how sensitive those ears were to touch.

He remembered how competently she'd held the toddler that Tak Tuzap had found, after her family died—how upset she was when she dwelt on the possibility that she might have left a family behind, three years ago, before she was chained and abandoned with no memory.

She must want children as much as I do.

Maybe she's right, that no one can give them to her.

But me, I could marry someone else. Like she tells me to do. She's worried I could be giving them up deliberately, staying with her.

She was still describing the route ahead to the others, but she glanced at him with a raised eyebrow as if puzzling over where his thoughts were.

What of the force that put her in Ellech, three years ago? Could it take her away again?

This was no safe woman, and a life with her wouldn't be a safe life. But, by the sun and the moon, how could he possibly let her go?

And how was he going to convince her he wouldn't leave, that he didn't want to ever leave?

Whatever the cost.

CHAPTER 27

The snow was light, but it was enough to turn the ground white and to obscure the trail they were following—not entirely, but enough that Penrys had to land frequently to check that she hadn't lost it, as the wind blew the snow into uneven drifts.

Najud's broom was handy for that, though rather worn after two days of use.

The worst of it now was the frequent landings. The hardest part of flying was lifting her weight off the ground, heavier now for all the layers she had on, and this constant landing to check for the track was wearing her out.

She didn't bother Najud about it, since it couldn't be helped.

Now she looked up at the low, dull sky, the clouds heavy with snow. Up aloft, where she'd been moments ago, she'd felt the beginning of gusty winds that threatened worse than just snow.

I think we should stop early today. Don't like the looks of this weather at all. We called these sorts of clouds kemellangar in Ellech, featherbeds, for the snow they dump and the place you want to be while it lasts. It's a decent spot—there's a stream, partly frozen over but flowing underneath, and it's still on the sheltered side of the gap, about halfway up. Some trees to help break the wind, and it looks like some grass under the snow for the horses.

Najud's response was prompt. *How far? We need enough time to beat the weather and get the camp set up.*

She estimated the distance. *Three miles, maybe. An hour. Add another hour for the camp.*

She glanced up again and considered. Even if it started snowing soon, it would take a while to begin accumulating.

I think you have enough time. I'll stay here and prepare the ground.

She sent him an image of sweeping the snow from a circle of grass for the camp with his worn broom.

His chuckle came back in his mind-voice. *I'll make you more brooms, if you wear this one out. Anything to keep you busy.*

She looked around for tasks to do while it was still daylight. *I should go aloft one more time and check the lay of the land. Our horses could be here for a couple of days. And what does that track look like, once it crosses the gap? Better find out now, while I can still sort of see it.*

The *kazrab* were erected in record time, closer to each other than usual, and Penrys approved the strong ropes that were pegged to the ground, in expectation of a storm. So far the snow had held off, but the sky was much gloomier than a little while ago and threatened to start burying them at any moment.

Ilzay and Jirkat weren't in camp yet—they'd handed off their pack strings and peeled off a couple of miles back to see if they could pick up any fresh meat.

Other preparations were different today, Penrys noticed. Usually only the personal packs were brought in out of the weather at night, and the others were tied down under canvas to keep them dry, but this time each *kazr* was crowded along the walls inside with as many packs as it could hold. The remainder were piled at the base of the largest tree, a solitary pine on the perimeter of the camp, marking the edge of the track, and several layers of strong canvas were tied down over them, pegged to the ground like the *kazrab*.

Penrys had helped settle the horses down within reach of the stream a couple of hundred yards away, in a meadow sheltered on two sides. When Winnajhubr made a small pile of heavy rocks at streamside, he explained to her how it was handy to have something near at hand to use to break the ice and keep the water accessible to the horses.

"Will they stay?" she asked him.

"Once the deep snow falls," Winnajhubr said, "it costs them more effort to roam than to stay with each other. As long as we keep giving them some of the grain for encouragement, they'll scrape through the snow and make the best of it."

He looked around at the grassy field, guarded to the west and south by low ridges. "This is good spot you found us, *bikrajti*. Too small for more than a few days, but they'll be fine for as long as this storm is likely to last."

When Penrys returned to the *kazr*, she discovered all the fuel and food inside, ready to hand. Leaning up against the doorframe were two shovels, assembled from wooden poles bound onto cattle shoulder-blades. She laughed out loud to see two more brooms there, too, just as Najud had threatened.

When he walked in and caught her, he grinned. "For the roof of the *kazr*," he said, "To brush off the snow."

"Ah. Of course," she said. "Think it'll be that bad?"

"Maybe not, but best to be ready." He set down the two canvas buckets of water he was carrying.

"Won't we have snow to melt?" she said.

"Well, and we may be here for days, if I'm any judge, and the solstice celebrations are tomorrow—we'll want to be clean, and water already warm in the *kazr* is better than snow."

She saw the wisdom of that. "What's the solstice ceremony like?"

"We all of us miss the heart of the *magham*, the festival camp, where all the clans of the tribe gather for two weeks to sing, and drink, and dance. No one lives there the rest of the year, not like in the *zudiqazd*. We send our young men and women to put it in order when they return from the *taridiqa*, there at the center of the circle of the winter camps. Those who were betrothed a year ago bring their marriage gifts and seal the bond, and the *tayujdajti* brokers new marriages for the following year."

He leaned toward her. "We say, if you can remember everything that happens at the *magham*, you didn't have enough to drink."

"So," he said, drawing himself upright, "if we can't travel tomorrow, we'll do what we can to honor the solstice anyway."

"We are four Zannib clans and a stray," Penrys commented. "Think we can come up with a suitable compromise?"

He grinned. "Not a compromise, a combination. We'll do everything."

The snow-muffled sound of cantering horses brought everyone outside to welcome Ilzay and Jirkat. Their shaggy horses scattered the snow on the ground and puffed plumes into the air, looking for a moment like something out of an illustration Penrys had once seen in the Collegium in Ellech—barbarian horsemen from Zannib back from the hunt.

The horses' flanks were bloodstained in places. Across the back of Ilzay's was one of the steppe antelope that Penrys had seen from a distance, and Jirkat had three of the stubby marmots that popped up curiously when they rode through the right terrain.

"Well done!" Najud said as he surveyed their success. "Something to celebrate the solstice with."

He checked the sky to estimate when the snow would start. "We've got enough time to butcher them, and we'll roast some of it for supper tonight. Winnajhubr, take care of their mounts."

Ilzay and Jirkat dropped off their horses and helped strip them of their tack before turning them over to Winnajhubr to clean up and shelter with the rest of the herd.

Najud trampled out a station for the butchering under a tree with a convenient branch. The antelope had been bled out on the spot when killed, but otherwise left intact, so they ran a rope through the tendons of the hind feet to hoist it up so that any residual blood could drain out through the slashed throat.

The two hunters stripped off most of their clothing and bared their arms in the freezing air to skin the hanging carcase, lowering the hide onto the snowy ground directly underneath, fur side down, to use as a place to lay the meat. Then they gutted it carefully, setting the heart and liver on the hide and reluctantly packing the rest of the innards into the snow at the edge of the woods and scooping more snow on top.

Najud explained to Penrys. "Not enough time to clean the rest of it, and no way to boil that much all at once. We're not starving—we'll leave the gut for the animals that can use it, but we may be here for days, so we'll freeze it now to keep it from attracting predators."

After that, the antelope was divided into a joint for the celebration tomorrow, skewers with small, fatty pieces for their meal tonight, and the production of thin slices for drying under the roofs of the *kazrab*, where the air would circulate freely. The work occupied everyone else in the camp, except for Jiqlaraz who avoided most of the mess by offering to get the fire started. Najud and Penrys, bloody to the elbow and shivering in the cold, exchanged looks with his nephew Munraz and laughed out loud with him at the adroit maneuver.

Khizuwi, as filthy as the rest of them, contented himself with a comment. "Perhaps he'll cook it for us, too, while we get cleaned up."

Ilzay muttered darkly, "After we're done cooking tonight, let's ask him to dig the fire pit for tomorrow underneath it, to take advantage of the thawed ground."

"Won't the snow keep us from cooking outdoors tomorrow?" Penrys asked him.

"No, *bikrajti*, we just need hot rocks and a pit in the ground. It has to be covered anyway, so the snow won't matter."

As they neared the end of the antelope meat, Jirkat took care of the three marmots. He cut off the head of each and then, before Penrys's horrified eyes, he thrust his arm down the neck and pulled out the organs, adding them to the antelope's gut pile. After that he broke the ribs from the outside with a rock, and reached in to remove them, too.

She questioned Najud discretely. *What's he going to do with them?*

We'll fill them with hot rocks, sew them back up, and add them to our fire pit to roast with the antelope tomorrow. The fire will burn the hair off the hide.

He laughed at her expression. *They're very good that way.*

Ilzay scrubbed his hands in the snow, then ducked into his *kazr* and returned with several goatskins. He divided the thinly sliced meat strips into three even piles, each on its own goatskin. The skewers for this evening's meal were placed on another skin.

Najud provided silent commentary for Penrys. *The joint and the heart will be wrapped up in the cold air tonight outside to finish cooling, then brought into a kazr so they don't freeze. Tomorrow, the joint will roast in the fire pit for hours, with the marmots, and someone will cook the heart in a pan inside a kazr, for everyone to share.*

The liver was sliced now, threaded on its own skewers, and just in time, the clouds having thickened appreciably since they'd started, though evening was still more than an hour away.

Ilzay presented one goatskin of meat strips to Najud, and another to Khizuwi. "Do you have everything you need for this?" he asked them both.

Penrys looked to Najud for guidance. He nodded confidently and took the skin. "Come along, I'll show you what's next," he told her,

"Do we get cleaned up now?" she asked, hopefully.

"Not quite yet."

CHAPTER 28

In a surprisingly short time, they were done inside the *kazr*.

Najud had washed his hands superficially in the snow, and then dug through his packs until he turned out a pouch filled with double-ended hooks.

He rigged cords across the rafters in the two back quarters of their *kazr*, near to the walls where they would be most out of the way, and showed Penrys how to pierce a meat strip with one end of the hook, and then drop the other end of the hook over the rope. The air was dry enough with the heat from the stove that the strips were already past the dripping stage.

"Try not to let them touch anything else, even each other," he said.

"How long does it take?" she asked. "And what happens when you move?"

"The whole autumn slaughter's done this way, back in the *zudiqazd*. Takes at least a week until it's completely dry, but then they don't move while it's happening. We'll just wrap and rehang it all if the snow doesn't pin us down that long."

Penrys's arms were sore from so much reaching over her head, and still filthy. Najud smiled down at her and kissed the tip of her nose, counting on her dirty hands to keep him safe from revenge.

"This is nothing," he said, waving his hand at the meat strips which were already starting to acquire a sheen as the surface dried. "*Shabz* is our biggest source of meat for the spring and summer. A family needs a cow or two and several sheep to get them through the winter, and more to supplement their supply until the next autumn. It'll last a year or more, and they make a year's worth of it now."

Penrys contemplated ten times as much meat, or more, hanging from her rafters and shuddered. Najud laughed at her expression.

"It shrinks in a hurry. They say you should be able to fit the *shabz* from a cow into the cow's stomach, when it's done."

"Surely not," she said, picturing that in dismay.

"No, no—we store it in something that lets the air in, to keep it dry. It's just a saying."

He hung the last piece and picked up the goatskin to wash it. "It's a comfort to see one's food secure inside the *kazr* at the start of winter. Of course, this would only last us a week or two, but still…"

"Outside now," he said briskly, looking at his hands, "and let's clean off the worst of this. The water's been keeping warm near the fire, but snow's the thing to scour with."

Their firelight reflected off the low clouds as though it were keeping them at bay, but no one had attention for anything but the sizzling meat they pulled off of their skewers, trying not to singe their fingers in the process.

The antelope bits were crisp on the outside, and greasy, and delicious. Penrys watched as the men smiled and rubbed the fat on their hands and face, and tried not to let her face betray her thoughts. Khizuwi caught her anyway and walked over to her with a chuckle.

"The grease is very good for the exposed skin," he said. "Keeps it from cracking in the cold, dry air."

She nodded, with reservation. "But doesn't it smell?"

He held his hand up to her nose. It glistened with fat. Obediently, she sniffed at it. Other than the faint odor of the cooking smoke, she couldn't detect anything other than the scent of human.

"The skin absorbs it and leaves nothing behind after a few minutes, not even finger smudges." He touched her cheek, lightly.

"I'm surprised you bear so few marks from all those hours flying in the cold air."

She froze with surprise. *How observant he is. Even with the face wrappings, some of her skin always seemed to get chapped or mildly frostbitten, but it healed by morning.*

"Good advice, Khizuwi. Thank you."

Najud joined them, and Penrys suspected he'd noticed her reaction and wondered about it.

Khizuwi finished the rest of his current skewer and tossed the stick with its charred end into the fire.

"*Bikrajab*," he said, addressing them both with a nod, "Please, come visit our *kazr* tonight. We would like to speak with you about *bikraj* things."

After Penrys and Najud cleaned up from dinner, they stepped out of their *kazr* to obey Khizuwi's summons. Penrys saw that ropes had been tied to stakes at waist height, three of them. They ran from the doorway of each *kazr* to the next. She nodded to herself—in case it snowed so hard you couldn't see, you could hope to blunder across a rope and follow it.

Najud tapped on the doorframe and then entered the wizards' *kazr*, but Penrys hesitated in the doorway. She could smell the promise of snow in the air, and the warmth of the interior was appealing, but it still felt like a trap to her. She smothered her uneasiness and followed Najud all the way in.

The *kazr* was about the size of the one that Umzakhilin had gifted them with, but older and a bit faded. Like theirs, the back half was hung with drying meat and there were packs thick along the walls, out of the weather. Two equal-sized bedframes faced each other from opposite sides, and a roll of bedding on the floor attested to Munraz being displaced from his bed for the benefit of Khizuwi, their senior guest.

The two older wizards and the apprentice all rose to welcome them. Even for so short a walk, Najud had insisted they wear their heavy hooded cloaks and gloves, and they removed those as soon as they stepped inside. They gratefully accepted *bunnas* or *kassa*, kept hot by their fire. Penrys and Khizuwi were alone in their preference for *kassa*— everyone else warmed their hands around a cup of *bunnas*.

After a few appreciative remarks about the antelope and the coming storm, the conversation lagged. Najud ignored the awkwardness of the silence, apparently willing to let them raise the purpose of this meeting at their leisure, but it made Penrys nervous. She blew on her scalding *kassa* and sipped it cautiously, and waited.

Jiqlaraz set his cup down finally and spoke. "It's unfortunate that the first storm is likely to obliterate the trail."

"I flew through the gap while I was waiting for all of you," Penrys said, "just to see where the track was headed before the snow hit. It definitely went down into the vale you described."

"Good, good," Khizuwi said. "We'll know where to pick it up again, in a few days."

"How long before we can travel?" she asked.

"That depends on the storm," Jiqlaraz said.

When Penrys waved her hand in irritation at the obvious reply, Najud said, "As soon as the winds are gone we can move, but everything will take longer if the snow is deep. We'll have to ride more slowly, and check the trail more frequently."

He paused. "If they're wintering in shelter on the other side, you might be able to find them directly, if you get close enough."

She smiled, tightly. "I don't have to worry about the snow."

"Yes, but we do, and you can't get too far ahead of us."

Penrys felt the familiar, frustrating urgency. "They've got to be dying in this weather, in their summer clothing. Every day we wait…"

Khizuwi broke in. "The weather is the weather, *lijti*. There's nothing else we can do. If you find them, all by yourself, what then?"

He raised his hand in question and Penrys reluctantly nodded and sighed.

Jiqlaraz cleared his throat.

Penrys watched him. *Here it comes, what he really wants.*

"We have not forgotten your description of Najud as one who knows how to organize *bikrajab* to work together, and we'd like to hear more about that."

Najud smiled faintly and nodded.

"In addition," Jiqlaraz said, "we'd like to hear more about what we can expect from someone like this *qahulajti*, so similar in some ways to you." This last was addressed directly to Penrys. "If we have the opportunity, perhaps we can study her for some time before…"

Munraz stared at his uncle, his eyes wide. Khizuwi confined himself to a sideway glance so brief the Penrys wasn't sure she'd seen it.

Jiqlaraz ignored them both. "After all, we need to plan how the four…" His eyes flicked to his nephew's face. "…the five of us will overpower her, when the time comes."

Khizuwi said, "You're hoping that our colleague will just allow us to experiment on her, to see what we need?"

"No," Najud said, flatly, half rising in anger.

Penrys put a hand on his shoulder and drew him back down. She lowered her eyelids sleepily and drawled, "Now, then, let's just try this idea of Jiqlaraz's for a little while, see what he advises to capture her."

To Jiqlaraz she added, "You can go ahead."

She'd raised her shield by this time and was scanning all of them. Compared to a room full of hostile Rasesni mages, this was likely to be straightforward, but she'd never met any Zannib wizards besides Najud, and there was no reason to take chances.

As she expected, Jiqlaraz pounced almost before she'd stopped speaking, with no effect on her defenses.

Khizuwi bowed his head with a little salute of the hand as if to apologize for the necessity of participating, and attempted his own assault without success. He smiled ruefully as he continued, and invited Munraz to join in. "You may as well find out what it feels like to fail."

Penrys could feel Najud's worry as he watched with her. She told him, "They're a lot like you, even Munraz. You're all about the same strength, though your experience must be rather different."

With amusement, she observed Munraz's shy smile. He must've wondered if he was as strong as his uncle, or would be, someday.

"Enough," she told them. "We calibrated this sort of thing in Gonglik with the Rasesni mages. The way we counted it, wizards like Najud were about a level ten in strength, that is, ten times stronger than the weakest of them. The best of them were about a twelve."

Jiqlaraz puffed up a bit in satisfaction.

Najud commented, "We figured Penrys was about ten times stronger than the best of us."

And, just like that, Jiqlaraz's expression curdled.

"I can teach you to combine your strengths," Najud said, "and that will make you more effective. Then, when we add in Penrys, we might have enough."

"Or not," she said. "The Voice, the wizard-tyrant in Rasesdad, was stronger than me. How much was the power he stole from his wizards, how much the chain, and how much just him... well, that I couldn't tell you."

She shrugged. "This girl may be stronger than me, too. What may be working in our favor is that she might not have met wizards yet, since none of her captives seem to have been *bikrajab*. So maybe she doesn't have the practice and skills that the Voice did. Does she know how to shield herself? What would have triggered that?"

"Does she have wings?" Munraz's voice popped up unexpectedly, and Penrys smiled at him.

"I don't know. Don't know if the Voice did either, but his chain looked like mine, and he had the ears."

Into her mind, involuntarily, flashed the image of the Voice's head rolling in the road, one furry ear bloody, and one dusty. "He died too quickly for us to find out more," she said, without going into the details.

Khizuwi asked, "How did he steal power from *bikrajab*?"

"He drew on the core of their power and left them just enough for survival, like tapping the sap from a tree for sugar." She ran her tongue over her lips, recalling the taste of the syrup from the north of Ellech.

"How did he do that?" Jiqlaraz leaned forward eagerly.

This is not a man to gift with power. If I trusted you before, which I didn't, I wouldn't now. Penrys was pleased that the truth wouldn't help him any. "It feels like this," she said, and sucked lightly at the root of his power until it was about half consumed.

He staggered up white-faced and backed away.

Najud frowned at her, and she restored Jiqlaraz's power to him.

Munraz hastened to his uncle's side for support and gave Penrys a wide berth as he passed.

"The power is stored in the chain, somehow, I think. He held wizards captive for almost three years like that, as well as a horde of others," Penrys said. "Let's hope this young one hasn't discovered how to do it yet."

Najud commented mildly, "We already know she's stronger than you in at least one respect—her reach to the High Pass from the summer encampment."

"And I've never tried to control people," she said.

A sudden slap of the wind against the wall of the *kazr* added punctuation to her statement, informing them all that the blizzard had begun.

Hostile weather, and newly hostile wizards, now that they have a better idea of what they're up against and how dangerous I might be to them. I suppose it was only a matter of time. Penrys could feel her shoulders sagging, but Najud gave her a quick nudge with his elbow.

"Let's teach them some of the basics of how to join together," he said, "before we go out and brave the storm, eh?"

CHAPTER 29

Necessity forced Penrys awake in the morning, and she bundled up and braved the windblown snow in the dim daylight to deal with it.

Ilzay and Jirkat were up before her, she saw, fussing with the fire pit they'd dug the night before into the ground softened by their cooking fire. Off to the side there were lively flames, freshened by the wind gusts, and strong enough to beat off the falling snow for now. As she watched, they maneuvered cobbles out of the fire with sticks and rolled them into the open pit. When they landed, they sent up a shower of sparks that fought against the snow flurries, and Penrys realized there must be a roaring fire in the pit, too.

She waved at them as she ducked back inside. Najud stood near the entry, rough-dressing for the same purpose.

"Looks like Jirkat and Ilzay are starting the cooking already," she told him. She chuckled. "Didn't see Jiqlaraz helping."

"I just hope they put a good stake in the ground so we can find it again in a few hours." He licked his lips in anticipation.

He waited a moment to watch her peel off her coverings and hang them from hooks on the lattice walls to dry. "Going back to bed?" he asked, hopefully.

"Sorry." She smiled. "Maybe later."

He made a show of disappointment and went out into the storm, securing the door behind him.

Penrys didn't know how many days this storm would last, but she knew they'd want to get moving again as soon as they could. If she wanted to clean anything in the snow, now was the time, storm or not.

She dressed more thoughtfully for the day, and started piling up the rugs from the back half of the *kazr* near the doorway. Then she bundled up again and brought an armful out into the snow next to the wall of the *kazr*, along with one of Najud's new brooms.

After laying the rugs on top of several inches of snow, she used the broom to sweep snow onto the tops of the rugs, then swept them hard, using the snow as a sort of scouring powder to absorb dirt and freshen the fibers. She shook each one free of snow when she was done and dropped it back into a pile near the door of the *kazr*. Najud joined her, relaying the carpets back into their proper place and lifting the ones in the front half for the next batches.

By her third load she'd acquired an audience. Khizuwi watched her in silence for a few moments. "Where did you learn to do that?" he asked.

Penrys straightened up and realized he was not alone. Winnajhubr and Munraz had joined him, and Jirkat had drifted over. When she glanced in the direction of the fire pit, she could no longer see any flames at all—just a stake in the ground, from which another rope ran to the doorway of Jirkat's *kazr*.

"This is something they do in Ellech, the country folk. The servants at my patron Vylkar's hunting lodge would do it in the winter after several inches of new snow had fallen—though not, of course, in a blizzard." She grinned. "When it's this cold, the snow cleans without soaking them in water. Works for blankets, too. You can even scrub them with brushes for stains, but it's awkward without something to push against."

She saw their interest and expanded. "I've seen them do this for ordinary clothing, too, when it's not easy for them to wash or dry it in wintertime, in the small huts. But with all that meat drying inside, I don't want to add wet clothing, so I'll see what I can do with our clothes out here after I finish the heavy stuff."

As if yoked together, Jirkat's head turned to Winnajhubr, and Khizuwi's to Munraz. The same apprehension showed on the faces of both the young men, and they heaved identical sighs.

Penrys burst into laughter at the performance and told them, "It's not so bad. You'll be happy for fresh bedding tonight."

She asked Khizuwi, "What do *you* normally do to clean blankets and rugs?"

"We hang them over lines in the sunlight, and beat them to drive out the dust," he said.

"And in winter?"

"Once the *shabz* is finished, we can do the washing, but this..." he gestured at the rugs, "waits until the spring. When the *taridiqa* starts, the folk left in the *zudiqazd* begin their cleaning, and the *taridaj* do the same as soon as they set up the spring encampment."

Penrys shrugged. "I didn't know when we might be stopped again—thought I better get to it while I could."

Najud had returned outside sometime while this was going on, and at that he stepped up and threw an arm around her shoulder possessively. "This one's mine, but I might be able to arrange for the borrowing of brooms for the rest of you."

It took a couple of hours for Penrys to satisfy her fit of cleanliness.

As much as possible she did the work outside, on the lee side of the *kazr* where any dirt from the cleaning would be blown away or covered with snow.

The stove and the few bits of furniture were scrubbed in place with wet cloths, and all the bedding down to the ropes stretched across the frames had been stripped off, and the ropes themselves retightened. The cushions, like the thin *umaqab* on the beds and the small scattered ones, had at least been freshened by an external scrub and a limited airing, which consisted of Penrys gripping them on her back, one at a time, while the wind gusted against her and she tried to hold on.

When she could think of nothing left to attack, she came inside and hung up her outer garments for good.

Her eye fell upon three canvas buckets full of water, warming by the fire. Najud straightened up from remaking their bed, and she saw that the other one was already tidily assembled, too.

He was freshly-shaven and the ends of his hair dripped, and he wore only what was needed in the warmth of the *kazr*, a riding-length robe over breeches, and the simple slippers they used inside.

She stopped to appreciate her work. Everything was reasonably clean, and the bright colors of the painted woodwork, too fresh to have faded much yet, were echoed by the more subdued hues of the carpets and the accents of cushions and Najud's little squares of fabrics that he used for special occasions. They reminded her of when she first met him, traveling in a supply wagon for the Kigali cavalry.

When she glanced down at her own dirty hands, she sighed. *One more thing to clean up.*

Najud walked past her and opened the door to drop the outer flap and tie it down. Then he closed the door and looked at her sternly. "You've forgotten one thing," he said, and drew her over to the stove, where he'd arranged soap and a towel nearby. He began to unfasten her clothing. "I'll help you with this myself."

CHAPTER 30

"Do we have to get up?" Penrys mumbled. After the morning's work, Najud had rubbed the soreness out of her muscles. He hadn't stopped there and, what with one thing and another, she was disinclined to move.

"It's solstice," he said, cheerily, and swatted her through the blanket by way of encouragement. "*Durmiqa bul.* We'll all be eating in here—don't you want to be up to greet them?"

"What, now?" she said, in alarm.

"No, but soon. Better get dressed."

He was wearing the best robe he'd packed with him, and the cleanest of his turbans. Penrys thought he looked like some barbarian lord, except for the grin.

"When Winnajhubr and Munraz return from checking on the horses, Ilzay and Jirkat will dig out our dinner."

Penrys scanned for the two youngest. "They're on their way," she told him.

He opened the door and rolled up the flap to make it clear that visitors were welcome. The draft of cold air brought snow in with it, and it was unexpectedly dark outside.

"What time is it?" she asked.

"Who can tell exactly in this weather?" Najud replied. "The middle of the afternoon. All the *kazrab* are still standing—a fine thing—and there's only a couple of feet of snow so far. Still, looks like it will go on till morning at least."

He went on outside and left her.

There was nothing as fancy as Najud's robe in her pack, but she donned her newest and cleanest clothes and checked that everything was tidy for company.

Najud had brought the low worktable into the front area and laid his *binwit* on it, the rolled leather bundle that made up his mead kit. It only held two small bottles, and Penrys wondered if he'd managed to top it up since they'd celebrated the turn-home in his borrowed freight wagon on the Kigali plains.

Others were providing the food, so she added water to the pot on the stove and set it to boil. She visualized the meat—it would make a mess wherever she put it. *That doesn't make any sense. They would always be celebrating this indoors in the winter. How do they deal with that?*

A knock on the door was her only warning, and then she was invaded by bulky men and cold air. Some of them busied themselves hanging their coats and capes on the lattice by the doorframe, but Jirkat and Ilzay came in bundled and singing. Each carried a crude wooden platter made from a rough-hewn fallen trunk. One held the antelope joint, already hacked into smaller chunks, and the other held the marmots, each one lying on its back, the belly sliced open to form a bowl of its own meat. The hot stones had been removed, but cooked root vegetables and chopped cabbage had been added to soak up some of the liquid.

The platters were deep and heavy, but they did the job of containing the juices, and the worktable was large enough to hold them, once Najud cleared off his *binwit*.

Winnajhubr came forward with a bag of wooden plates which he presented to Penrys, and behind him Khizuwi walked, carefully, using folded cloths as well as his gloves to carry a covered pot of something savory. He placed it on the stove to stay warm before he returned to the door to unwrap himself.

They lined up tightly in a crowd by the door once their outer clothing was removed, and Najud separated from them to stand next to Penrys, by the stove.

Khizuwi came forward first and bowed to the pair of them. "Greetings for *durmiqa bul*, to the *zarawinnaj* and his *lijti*. Today our day is dark, but we welcome the return of the sun."

He carried a *binwit* with him, and when he took his seat, on the rug near the stove, he laid it carefully down before him.

Jiqlaraz was next, with a nod to Najud, and a moderate wish for the well-being of everyone present. It looked to Penrys like he, too, was carrying a *binwit*. When she glanced at the rest of the men, she saw that every one of them had a bundle like that.

What do they drink when they're not drinking mead? Is it just that they didn't bring anything with them? It suddenly struck her how odd it was that she hadn't noticed before, but then it had all been emergencies, grief, and travel since they'd crossed the High Pass.

She was so used to alcohol not lasting very long with her that she didn't miss it herself.

The rest came forward in order of age, with Winnajhubr last. Najud recited what was clearly a traditional welcome "to all our family and friends, and to strangers met along the way."

When he paused and looked at her expectantly, she panicked. "Health to the herds," she said, "and to absent kin." Then she smiled and added, "And a thank you to the cooks!"

Penrys leaned against the leg of her bedframe and watched the party. Her constant sips of Najud's mead helped her stay inebriated, but her body disposed of the alcohol quickly and it was impossible to match the others. She was surprised that Khizuwi's dish of sliced antelope heart and onions had been the first to be emptied—something about what heart was good for, along with a good deal of humor at trying to make Najud eat more of it.

There seemed to still be a meal's worth left for the next day on the platters, despite the efforts of all to demolish the feast down to the bones. Before his mind turned to other things, Najud had told her she should wrap the remains in goatskins and bury them in the snow near the door where they could be found the next day.

A meat-eating people, these Zannib, when they got the chance, and that reminded her of Ellech, too.

The point of this celebration seemed to be food, drink, and stories which, come to think of it, was true for most holidays. Winnajhubr was currently describing how he and a friend had blackened their faces and donned bearskins to ambush a young friend, when it unexpectedly turned out they'd targeted the girl's mother instead, and she with a broom in her hand. Jirkat and Ilzay, who'd been witnesses of the resulting commotion, provided expert commentary on the dancing bears that had fled, complete with apologies, while the camp around them roared with laughter.

"For youngsters, we thought you two showed promise," Jirkat told him.

"But we weren't sure you would survive until morning," Ilzay added.

Jiqlaraz's stories were unexpected—reminiscences of his wife, now dead. As if to counter any maudlin tendency, Khizuwi then launched into a long, picaresque tale about the adventures of a goat and the havoc he created as he wandered from *kazr* to *kazr*, seeking adventure and uncovering illicit affairs, mysterious thefts, poor housekeeping, and plenty of food.

Penrys knew this had to be a traditional story not a personal experience—for one thing, it came with a chorus everyone repeated after the punchline of each episode, "the goat, the goat, the curious goat, who can evade the curious goat." Since each chorus included a swallow of mead, it was clear that part of the challenge was for the drinking tale-teller to make it to the end. In the final chapter, the goat ended up providing the feast, and tranquility was restored, with the homily that the less you know about your wife and the neighbors, the happier you will be.

Ilzay told the tale of his *binwit*—the father who had given it to him, and his father, taking the tale of fathers and brothers back five generations. Munraz continued the theme, his shyness lost under the influence of the mead. Instead of a single person giving him his *binwit*, he said, it had been the whole family, each one contributing a part to welcome him to his adult life with them.

Penrys felt the nostalgia they all experienced in the silent moment that followed that story. *They all remember a similar thing, a similar emotion, as they were welcomed into their family, their clan, on a new level.*

The unbecoming spike of envy that it generated in her was strong enough to make Najud turn his tipsy head in concern. She patted his shoulder and smiled at him. "Never mind," she murmured.

When they called upon her to tell a story, she took her cue from Khizuwi, and avoided her personal life. She told them instead how the herd-girls in rural Ellech stayed with their flocks in the mountain meadows all summer long. "These are girls not quite fully grown. Each summer they go up with their family, herding the sheep or the goats or the cows, and then they leave the girl behind all by herself to look after them. She milks them, and makes cheese, and works on the clothing she will bring to her wedding someday, when she marries. Then her family comes and brings her back with the flocks. And the cheeses."

She waved her hands in the air and took another sip of mead. "But these are *girls*, you understand. They have to talk with each other." That brought a chuckle from her audience.

"So, if the mountain valleys are narrow enough, and the next cabin is close enough, they can sometimes call to each other. You can't hear words that far, but they have some particular phrases, with melodies. If you can hear the song, you know the words. They have other tunes they use when they call the animals, looking for strays."

The men asked for an example. The *kazr* was a muffling environment for sound, but she stood up and pitched her voice into that front position of her face that let it carry a long distance, and sang them one of the teasing fragments.

"What's that mean?" Najud asked.

"Well, they get up at dawn to do the first milking. So when a girl goes outside and can't see her distant neighbor outside the cabin yet, she calls, 'Are you alive? Are you alive? I thought you must be long, long dead.' To poke fun at her, you understand."

They looked interested, so she continued. "When they see a wolf or a bear, or even fire, they have traditional alarm calls for spreading the word. For that, they use a very long wooden horn they make out of hollowed halves of a softwood, wrapped around with birchbark to hold them together. It takes practice, but you can get several different notes out of them. One call means 'bear', another 'wolf', and so on."

She made a low rumbling noise in her chest and gave an example of the four-note call that meant 'bear'. "You have to hear it. The notes are very low, and they don't seem to be that loud, but they carry a tremendous distance. Miles. From far away, it sounds as if it's the mountain speaking, or the forest."

Winnajhubr said, sleepily, "You'll have to tell my sister about that. She'd like it."

Penrys looked more closely and saw that more were in danger of just dropping off, and she had no plans for sharing her *kazr* for the night with six more snoring bodies.

Stepping carefully, she hauled Winnajhubr and his friends to their feet. "All right, men—time to go home." She bundled them into their outer garments and made sure they had gloves.

The gust that hit their faces when she opened the door woke them up a little, and she made sure that each of them had a grip on the rope guide to their own *kazr* before she shoved them out to stagger into the snow flurries.

She stood in the doorway with the door almost closed to watch their progress until they disappeared into the dark, and she remained there until her mind-scan showed them safely back inside their own *kazr*. When she turned, she found Khizuwi had risen and was watching her. He raised an eyebrow and she nodded, so he shook Jiqlaraz into alertness and together they got Munraz up.

Khizuwi managed another bow as he left with his companions, all three gripping their rope and each other. Penrys waited until they reached their *kazr* before closing her door, glad to let a little fresh air into the space.

Najud was dozing sitting up, and she tried not to wake him as she wrapped up the remains of the feast in goatskins and stashed it in the snow two feet to the left of the doorframe. It was visibly deeper than before, almost three feet now, and the wind blew it into higher drifts in places, but it was too dark for the light inside the *kazr* to show very much. She stood in the doorframe and lowered the flap, then closed the door.

She surveyed the damage from there. The cooking pots had long been removed from the stove to the standing table used for food preparation. Those who had thought about it had taken their mead-kits with them, but some remained—the whole *binwit*, or just a cup or bottle. She gathered all the bits and put them on the low worktable next to the empty platters with their congealed juices for sorting out in the morning. The wooden plates Winnajhubr had brought joined them, along with any stray utensils that threatened bare feet in the dark.

She glanced around in the light of the flickering lanterns and the stove. Her long morning nap had disoriented her and she couldn't tell if it was early in the evening or late. The colorful, warm interior still smelled of cooked food and laughter to her, a timeless place, a bubble sheltered from the storm, with the sharing of stories that bonded them together.

Three years in Ellech, two months in Kigali, a month here. Winnajhubr with his pranks had more tales to tell than she did—the ordinary stories of growing up, making friends, irritating his elders. Soon he would add falling-in-love stories.

What were her stories? She was maybe ten years older—where were her ordinary stories, the tales to make others laugh?

The anger that rose in her pleased her more than the self-pity of her previous mood. She would find the man who had ripped her life from her before dumping her on a mountain in Ellech, naked in the snow, and she would ask him "why?" before she took her revenge.

She shook with the emotion, and it disturbed Najud who blinked himself awake. "What's wrong?" he asked.

She unclenched her fists, and calmed herself before walking over to help him up. "Nothing important," she said. "Let's get you to bed."

He glanced around the empty *kazr* as another gust bounced off the lattice wall. "They went home through that?"

"I watched all the way and made sure they got back safe," she reassured him. "It's just us, now. Flap's down."

His face lit up at that and then took on a woeful expression. "Too much to drink, Pen-sha."

She smiled. "Never mind, it'll wear off. I'm not worried."

Later in the dark, with no light but the gleams from the stove, Penrys wrapped herself around Najud's back, hugging him close. She checked the locations of all the people, asleep in their *kazrab*, and moved outward to the horses to do a count. They were huddled together, dozing.

They seem to be used to this sort of weather. Look how they think about it—the warmth of their neighbors, the security of the herd, confidence in food and water.

She expected that would change if they ran out of grain or if it became too hard to find grass or water under the snow, but horses don't plan for the future and for now they were fine.

She knew Najud was still awake. "Want to see what the horses think of the snow?" she asked him. "Take a look…"

He peeked into her mind and she showed him what the horses felt.

"I've been experimenting with keeping them from straying," she said. "Should I tell the others? I don't want them to get used to someone else watching for them."

Najud snuggled up closer to her, as if he could pull her arm over him like a blanket.

"They already know you do this, and they're grateful."

She grunted. "Hmph. Go to sleep, nothing to do until morning."

Halfway to dawn he woke her up to prove her wrong.

CHAPTER 31

Once the door flap was lifted, there was a constant stream of visitors from mid-morning onward, despite the continued battering of the storm.

Most had mead-kits, in whole or in part, to sheepishly retrieve. Winnajhubr rescued the wooden plates his group had supplied, and went off to clean them in the snow. A few blows of Najud's hand-axe outside split the greasy platters into kindling small enough for their stove, where the aroma of last night's feast as it burned made Penrys stomach growl.

The leftovers had already been divided into a marmot and part of the antelope for each *kazr*, so all Penrys had to do was to hand the lightly frozen packet to someone from each of the other groups and bring her own in to thaw again. She went to the trouble of stripping the meat from the bones so she could reheat it without the clumsy marmot hide and bones, and those she discarded entirely, walking them a distance into the trees before flinging them away.

"How much longer will this blizzard continue?" she asked Najud, when she came back in. Two days was a long time, even in Ellech, but she wasn't sure what to expect, this far to the south.

"Could go on for days," he said. He'd been doing his own cleanup and now sat crosslegged on his narrow unused bed, his back supported by a cushion against the lattice wall. He patted the spot next to him, and she picked up the other cushion and walked over to join him there.

He draped his left arm over her shoulder companionably, and she made herself comfortable with her legs tucked in sideways instead of crossed. "You see," he said, "the weather comes from the west and it brings the water from the Wandat Sea with it. There's always more snow in the west of *sarq*-Zannib than in the east, as the water drops out of the sky on the way."

He waved his free right hand. "The wind has a long reach over the Wandat, and it's open ocean west of that, so there's not much to stop it. The ridges a hundred miles west of here which divide the central steppe from the western farms, they're the first real barrier it finds. So it blows and snows on both sides, more on the west than the east, but enough for both, and keeps blowing and snowing all the way from there."

She leaned on him. "So this is a winter storm on the ocean, come to land, is it?"

"That's right."

Her head could feel the rhythmic rise and fall of his chest, and his arm was a warm weight. He felt like shelter to her, as if he and this *kazr* had always been there, safe from the storm. She shivered a bit at the unexpected feeling of security.

"Hmm?" He looked down at her.

"Nothing. I just…" She swallowed. "I don't want this to end. To lose you."

His right arm wrapped around her, too, and he hugged her to him.

"We won't let that happen, Pen-sha," he promised.

"I'm not what you want," she said, "Not what you deserve. If I were the only chained wizard, well, perhaps this could be my life…" She waved a hand at the interior of the *kazr*. "But I'm not. I have to find out about the others, have to help stop them, if they're monsters. Otherwise I'm one, too."

She lifted her head to look into his face. "D'ya understand?"

He nodded reassuringly. "I know. You have to do this like I had to pursue my masterwork."

Penrys broke into a smile. "Yes! That's it, exactly." Then her smile vanished. "But you deserve children and a home."

"So do you," he murmured.

She shrugged without looking at him. "I don't think I have a choice. But you do."

"No, I don't, Pen-sha. That's what I've been trying to tell you. Children or not, you're what I want, what I need, and that's a price I'm willing to pay."

His grip around her tightened and he gave her a little shake. "And I know you feel the same way, so quit fighting it."

What am I being so stubborn about? This man is dear to me—my heart would ache if he were gone. He's made his own decision, in spite of warnings. Can't I accept that? She could feel his tense emotions, underneath the deceptively smooth surface of his voice.

She couldn't speak for a moment.

He leaned over her and pulled the hair back from one of her animal ears. "You know you want to," he whispered into it, and then warmed it with his breath.

She giggled. "What, you've been auditioning for the job, all this time?"

"If the door flap were down, I'd do it again," he said, with a leer.

"Must be all that heart meat they forced down you yesterday." Her smile faded, and she turned to search his face again. "Are you sure, Naj-sha?"

"I'm sure. My life for yours. Your enemies are my enemies."

She stopped breathing for a moment at that.

He lay his right hand along her face, and she leaned into it.

She was silent, her mind still, and then she finally yielded. "All right, then."

The explosion of relief and joy from Najud overwhelmed her. He dropped his shield entirely and let her see the full effect of her agreement. It frightened her—what had she done to deserve it? But she was glad, so glad, that he wanted to find a way to make it possible, too, whether she deserved it or not. It was her job to make sure he didn't regret it.

She sat there quietly with him for some time, all uncertainty vanished. It was a magical moment, and she knew it couldn't last, but she wanted it to.

Inevitably, a thump on the door ended it.

Winnajhubr stuck his head in. "We're going to knock down the load on the roofs and sweep a path along the ropes. Again. Can we borrow your brooms…"

He paused. "Najud?"

There was nothing indecorous in the way they were sitting, but Penrys was amused to see how slow Najud was to give Winnajhubr his attention.

"Leave me one. I'll come out and join you in a moment," Najud said.

Winnajhubr lingered, maddeningly. "We haven't checked on the horses since morning, *bikrajti*."

The suggestion was clear. "I'll take a look and tell you," Penrys said.

A quick smile flashed across the young man's face, and he hastened to grab a broom and leave.

She stood up and stretched, enjoying a remarkable sense of well-being. "Back to work," she told the bemused Najud.

He smiled at her and rose. "Whatever you say, *lijti*."

She snorted. "The first order of business is warmer clothes, if we're going outside."

CHAPTER 32

Penrys emerged from the *kazr* in her full winter flying gear. The gusts of wind were less frequent but the snow was still coming down thickly, and already starting to cover the swept canvas of the *kazr* roofs with a new layer, even as Najud and Winnajhubr were knocking the old layer off.

After much sweeping, the paths along the ropes were still negotiable, but on either side the walls of snow climbed to three feet. Jirkat was busy at his end with a shoulder-blade shovel rather than a broom.

When Najud raised an eyebrow at her clothing, Penrys told him, "The horses are all still there, but I can't tell how they're doing for food, or whether they're able to reach the grass. I want to take some grain out to them and see."

He nodded and waved her down to Jirkat for the grain sack. She trudged through the fresh snow on the path and told him what she wanted.

"Not too heavy," she said. "I can always make multiple trips, but I can't carry very much, especially with all this clothing."

Jirkat ducked inside and came back in a few moments with a pack partially filled. "If you can find a sheltered spot, where you can scatter it so they can eat it before it's covered, that would be best. You don't want them competing, so you might need several spots, or a long line."

She hefted it to feel the weight—about twenty pounds. "That can't be enough, surely."

"If you can relay, say, another two like this, it'll make a difference."

"Shouldn't be a problem," she said. "I'll let you know what I find when I get back." She glanced back at her own *kazr*. "If it's important, I'll tell Najud, and he can tell you." She tapped her forehead meaningfully, and Jirkat nodded his understanding.

Penrys thought about lifting another twenty pound as she launched, and it made her legs tired. "Tell you what, Jirkat… I'm going to use the path to get into the air, but could you then go stand in the middle with the pack up, and the straps where I can reach them? That way I can circle around and grab it from you. Easier that way for me." She illustrated what she meant with her hands.

His eyes widened. "All right, *bikrajti*. Whatever you need."

She needed a few running steps to launch, and the partially cleared path almost ran out before she got off the ground and pulled herself into the air. The wind was stronger above the ground, but she used it to increase her momentum and then cut lower to leave that wind current and circle back to Jirkat to snatch the pack. He held it up steadfastly as she swooped by and her hands closed around the pack straps like an ungainly eagle snatching at a fish.

It was only a couple hundred yards to the enclosed meadow that sheltered the horses. Penrys had been checking on them remotely while Jirkat and Ilzay had gone there in person until the height of the blizzard, and this was the first time she'd actually seen them in days.

She was relieved to find that at least half of the area had been trampled thoroughly, evidence that they were digging through the snow for what fodder they could find. The winter-hardy horses stood bunched together wherever they could get out of the wind, except for the ones taking advantage of the relatively calm air to continue foraging.

After she circled the meadow twice, she decided that the edge of the woods on the west was the best suited for laying out grain. The snow was shallow there, only a few inches drifted in, and the horses seeking food would soon dissipate that.

She landed in the meadow near the uphill side of the ground she'd chosen and thought about herd management. The trick was to start farthest away from the horses and work toward them. The hungriest or most motivated would be the first to investigate what she was doing, and once they found bits of grain, they would stay there looking for more, so she might be able to scatter it out lightly until she reached the weaker horses without causing too much competition between them.

This load of twenty pounds was nothing, but by the time she came back with more and repeated the exercise, maybe they'd have sorted themselves out adequately.

Her landing caught their attention, and when she shook the half-empty pack to let the grain rustle audibly, some of them started her way.

She shuffled her way through the snow under the trees as quickly as she could and dribbled the grain out in handfuls as she went. When it was all gone, she stepped back into the meadow and ran a few clumsy steps downhill to launch again.

A quick pass around confirmed that the herd was slowly converging on the grain in a line, the way she'd hoped, and she headed back to the camp.

This time she found Najud waiting with the next load of grain. *Everything all right?*

They're fine. Stay there, and I'll circle around.

As she swooped by him, she dropped the empty pack from one hand and grabbed the new one with the other.

After her last load, Penrys walked up the grain line to look the horses over one by one. Their concentration was on muzzling up the last bits they could find, so she was able to check each one for injury or fitness, at least superficially.

They were losing weight, as Ilzay had told her would happen all winter long until they could gorge again in the spring, but this was normal for them. It wouldn't kill them, unless the winter was much harder than usual. She wondered how Najud's donkeys were doing, and the Rasesni horses, back in the *zudiqazd* with Umzakhilin.

This blizzard was full of snow, and that was a problem for the horses pawing for grass, but it wasn't terribly cold. That meant the stream was still a good water source, frozen over in spots but open in others. The marks of trampling made it clear that the horses could break through it as needed for water.

It was time to return for good. The winds were picking up again, and the snow was swirling instead of just falling.

She reported to Najud. *I'm finished here—anything else I need to do?*

Come on back. I think we're due for more of the storm.

When she launched and circled the meadow one last time to pull herself higher into the air, she checked for predators—a bear or two could wreak havoc among the horses. There was nothing that large within reach, but it reminded her she hadn't been able to scout for days, since they were pinned down by the snow.

The wind isn't bad yet, Naj-sha. I'm going to do a circle around the camp, to check for problems.

He didn't reply immediately, and Penrys bit her tongue as she pictured him discarding his first few responses.

Stay within range. I mean it.

Agreed.

She started at an angle downwind, to the southeast. When she was done, she wanted to come back to the camp from the southwest, which would be downwind again. That way, if the weather worsened, she wouldn't have to fight the wind on the way back.

A circle with a five-mile radius centered on the camp should tell her all she needed to know about any nearby hazards.

She flew as low as she dared, but the visibility was terrible through the falling snow. Her constant awareness of Najud tethered her circuit and she didn't push the extremes of her range, fearing to lose contact and thus any hope of orientation, with no sun visible and no recognizable terrain.

Her mind-scans found more of the antelope Ilzay had hunted, and many of the smaller predators that thrived in the snow which immobilized their prey. There was a bear in the northeast quadrant, not very near the camp, but she seemed very sleepy and almost undetectable. Penrys wondered if that's what hibernation felt like.

Most of the animals were waiting out the storm. No birds shared the air with her, and even the foxes she found felt warm, as though they were snug in a den somewhere.

Time for me to come inside, too.

She swung through the final western quadrant of her patrol, struggling to keep the wind from blowing her off course. Five miles from camp - she checked she could still detect Najud. Five miles outward... nothing. She slanted slightly to the south—the gap was down there somewhere—and then... People! Several people— cold, starving, dying.

People. A group of them, in bad shape. I think they're some of ours, the captives.

The response was immediate. *Where? How far?*

You can feel my direction. West-southwest. I think it must be the trail through the gap. I can't see them, and they're not moving much. I'm not sure how far—they're not between us, they're on the other side. That's why I couldn't sense them before from the camp. Maybe two more miles? Seven altogether.

She thought about the contact problem.

If I land there, I'll be out of range.

Don't do that. Wait a moment while we talk about it.

She glided with the wind and probed her find more carefully. They were moving in this weather, but very, very slowly. There were no wizards in the group, anyone she could reach directly. She could feel determination in some of them, but everything else was confused and very strange—she couldn't make sense of it. Was it just that they were dying that distorted their emotions, or something else?

Pen-sha, here's what we're going to do. Most of us will come, on horses and leading horses, with blankets. We're going to take them back to camp to wait out the rest of the blizzard.

She waited for him to continue. There was something else.

Can you reach anyone in camp, not just me?

You're worried about direction?

She felt Najud's confirmation. *If we leave the camp in this weather and can't find it again...*

His image of a snowy trail buried in new snow was clear to her. *I understand. I can feel everyone in the camp from here.*

Then we're going to bull our way out on the trail and leave Khizuwi behind. Once we get about three miles out, we'll set up someone as an anchor that you can find, and then you can go to these survivors and get them ready. Once we reach you and start back, then you can find whoever we left on the trail, and once we reach him, you can find Khizuwi. Do you understand?

Even with no one to see her, circling in the air, she nodded. *Clever of him.*

Yes. That'll work. Better leave two people together, not just one, in case of accident.

CHAPTER 33

Two hours later, once the riders from the camp had gotten about three miles from her, Penrys rose from her snowy shelter and trampled out a short path so that she could launch into the air for most of the final two miles.

All the time she'd waited, sitting on the tail of her coat with the rest of the skirt forming a pocket of trapped warm air around her crossed legs, she'd kept up her contact with Najud. Every few minutes she shook the accumulated fresh snow off her upper body, grateful it wasn't much colder, not like the deep of winter in Ellech, in the lower mountains.

Najud chose Munraz to remain behind as an anchor on the trail, with Winnajhubr. He wanted someone Khizuwi might be able to reach, if they needed to retreat to the camp three miles back, and Penrys had convinced him to make it two people, not just one. They were under orders to stay there as long as they could.

The four men who were coming the full distance led three horses each, breaking new trail all the way and switching out the leading horses to rest frequently.

Penrys wanted to walk up on these new people, not just land amongst them and scare them. Happily the thick falling snow cut visibility, and she was able to set down fifty yards away without triggering any surprise in the minds she was scanning.

They still made little sense to her. They moved as a group, but their emotions were reduced to little more than determination and fear, in varying balances.

She checked to make sure her chain was covered—the last thing they needed was a reminder of their captor—then she laboriously made her way through the snow, and called out to them over the noise of the wind as they got closer to each other.

"Hello, the Kurighdunaq," she cried, and felt no one respond. The sound of them pushing slowly through the deep snow reached her, carried by the wind, and she backed up along her path a short distance. "Over here," she called. "This way!"

This time, she felt a reaction from two of them, and the party paused and shifted her way. She repeated her call to guide them, and the leader soon broke into the crude path she'd made and stood, as if bewildered, until the press of the rest of them forced him further down the path, where they staggered to a stop.

They were something out of a terror tale told late at night around the campfire. The seven men and five women wore rags so little resembling clothing that it was difficult for the eye to make out the outlines of their bodies. Most of them had some sort of blindfold covering their eyes, and all were tied to each other by short lengths of fabric or leather strips.

"M'name's Penrys," she called, as she approached. Several of them turned their heads in the direction of her voice, but even the ones without blindfolds couldn't seem to quite focus on her.

"I'm a *bikrajti*, and there are more of us in our camp, with some of your clan-kin. We've been tracking you, trying to find you."

They stood still, their heads turning from side to side as if to listen more carefully. No one spoke.

"Jirkat," she said. "Ilzay, Winnajhubr. Umzakhilin sent us, and Hadishti." She tried the names she expected them to know.

Their inhuman lack of reaction raised the hair on her arm, but she made herself come closer to the leader.

Najud, I'm talking to them but they're not reacting. Watch.

She felt him join her. "People are coming, with horses. We'll take you to our camp. They're coming through the snow, from the east. That way." She pointed down the trail, and when she looked that way herself, she winced at the obvious dead end, where she'd landed.

What will they make of that?

It didn't seem to register with them.

She stopped moving and tried to look deeply into the leader, while Najud watched. The man saw daylight and clear skies. His body felt snow, the flakes fell onto his face, but that wasn't what he saw.

It's like the illusion I gave Winnajhubr, but much worse. He knows his body is right and his mind is wrong, but he's been fighting it too long to be quite... sane.

Najud's reaction was swift. *Don't get any closer until the rest of us get there.*

Some of them reached out to others, and clung to them, as if for reassurance. When she scanned outward, she couldn't find the other chained wizard in range, but she wondered if that was just her own limitation. When she raised a shield for herself and extended it to cover these survivors, it made no difference to the illusions the leader saw.

Someone was going to have to take the first chance. Ignoring Najud's advice, she walked slowly up to the leader, talking the whole time. "I see you all, standing in the deep snow, in the blizzard that's gone on for two days now. It's afternoon, and dark from the storm. My friends with horses will be here in an hour or so, and I'll stay with you until they come."

The leader's head tilted to follow her voice.

She took a few more steps. "We'll ride back along the path they're making, back to our camp. It's warm there, and we have food for everyone. It will take a little while to ride that far—the horses have been working hard to break the path."

The leader was interested in her voice, if not her words, and she tried to reassure him as she would a wounded animal, with a low, quiet, non-threatening voice.

"D'ya think you can ride? It would mean cutting you apart— you can't ride all tied to each other."

She felt a reaction of fear to those words. "It was clever of you to bind yourselves together, to fight the illusions you couldn't trust."

One more step, and she stood directly before the leader. "I'm going to touch you now," she told him. "I'm real."

His eyes still didn't focus on her, but she took off her glove and gently clasped his bare hand. He jumped back a half-step, then froze.

"Yes, I'm real. You're with friends." She clutched his shoulder and held it, and the man shook.

One by one, Penrys spoke to each of them and touched them gently to try and convince them of her reality. They were all thin, walking skeletons with no fat on them, and she wasn't sure of their ages—they must be younger than they looked, she thought, to have survived this long. But no youngsters, no one not fully grown.

The rags they wore were a combination of summer garments, both whole and in pieces, and untanned skins used as cloaks and crude shoes. No one was barefoot.

Anyone without good footwear has probably already died.

Penrys was startled to hear Najud's comment—she'd forgotten his presence. *They still have knives, some of them. Why would she let them keep knives?*

You don't defang your dog, once you've tamed him.

The implications of Najud's observation struck a chord in her. *She's treating them like the rest of her animals, not like people. Leaving them as she found them, but making sure they come along with her. She must assume they can take care of themselves.*

She spent the time while they waited for the riders to get there describing everything around them—the trees with their heavy weight of snow, herself and the clothing she wore, and eventually each of them. She joined the hands of two of them, already tied together, and described them each to the other, and repeated this throughout the group.

No one resisted her, and level of fear she felt from them diminished.

Her voice was getting hoarse by the time the riders broke through to the end of her own short path, with Najud in the lead, and she started to describe them as well.

Jirkat and Ilzay dropped from their horses in haste, and then stumbled to a halt when Penrys blocked their approach to give everyone time to adjust.

She cleared her throat and told the survivors, still peering about like blind moles, "Here are Jirkat and Ilzay of the Kurighdunaq. Your clan-kin." Then she stepped aside to join Najud as he approached.

The astonishment on Jirkat's face quickly turned to resolution. "Dhalmudhr," he said calmly, "It's good to see you alive." He picked up the leader's arm and clasped it.

Ilzay was already moving through the group, naming everyone and touching them, murmuring his name and Jirkat's, over and over.

"Can you still find Munraz and Winnajhubr?" Najud asked Penrys as they watched this tiny remnant of the clan reunite.

"Clear as a bell," she said. "How long will it take to get back along the path you broke?"

"Two hours, at least, all the way to camp." He looked up at the unchanging falling snow. "I think we'll still have daylight. The faster we can get them mounted, the better."

Penrys looked at the horses that had been led by the riders and realized they carried nothing but the pads that would be cinched under the pack frames.

Najud followed her gaze. "We don't have spare saddles, but they've ridden since they could walk. They'll be fine."

Jiqlaraz watched them and the survivors with equal attention.

"No horse for me?" Penrys asked.

"Better for you to go ahead to the boys. Maybe you can talk to Khizuwi from there, tell him what's coming in detail. Then once we reach them, you can jump forward to Khizuwi and help get things ready."

He looked her over as if to judge how tired she was. "Think you can do all that?"

"I'll manage."

CHAPTER 34

Penrys tried to mind-speak Munraz before she landed, but she wasn't sure how much got through. It must have worked, for he was standing expectantly with Winnajhubr when she swooped in upon them through the falling snow, like some great owl.

"Twelve of them," she called, with a smile. "Did Najud tell you? I'm going to stay long enough to guide him in, and then go on to Khizuwi and help him get ready. How are you two holding out?"

They'd picked a spot at the edge of some trees, and used long tethers on the horses, not wanting to hobble them and hinder their ability to paw through the snow in search of fodder. The snow under the trees was only a couple of feet deep, in drifts, and they'd trampled out a place for a cheery fire of fallen wood.

"We're fine, *bikrajti*," Munraz said. "My uncle told me everything until he got out of range." He stared at her. "How far away can you reach Najud?"

"He's got maybe a mile or two, I think, but I can reach about five miles now. Used to be less."

She smiled at him. "That's why we had to set up this way station with you two. I couldn't find the camp from where the survivors were, but I could find you."

Munraz blinked. "It's complicated." He yawned involuntarily and Winnajhubr poked him.

"Nothing to do to pass the time," Winnajhubr apologized for him. "So we took naps."

"I know—it's been a long wait." She asked Munraz, "Could you bespeak Khizuwi from here?"

"I tried, but…" He spread his hands in uncertainty. "Can you?"

"Want to watch?" she offered. His eyes widened and he nodded.

You can hear this, yes?

It's as clear as my elders, when they talk to me!

Penrys suppressed a smile. *Good. Now, watch and listen.*

She felt his hesitation. *Will my uncle approve?*

I don't know. That has to be your decision. She gave him time—there was no real hurry.

It was hard to lie to someone this way, where they could feel your own emotions, if not your unvoiced thoughts. Penrys tried to keep her mind still enough for him to become comfortable with a stranger, someone not of his family. She wasn't sure how long he'd been an apprentice—perhaps he hadn't been able to mind-speak for very long.

She felt his excitement return. *Yes, please, bikrajti. I want to learn.*

Good, because I like to teach. She grinned at him, and he hesitantly smiled back. *All right, first I'll show you Najud and the rest of them.*

She reached back to Najud then. *Just checking in. I've got Munraz with me.*

Najud's surprise was as obvious as if he were standing next to her, and then Munraz's reflected surprise at being able to feel it.

Calm down, you two. Najud, I'll talk to Khizuwi next and then wait until you get here to go on and join him. Anything you need me to warn him about?

Yes—there's one stranger, a young man. I wondered if Khizuwi might know him.

Penrys's eyebrows rose. *I'll tell him. They talking yet?*

She could hear the emotion behind his simple negative. *No, and we've stopped troubling them about it for now.* He paused, and then returned his attention to her. *We're leaving. Stay out of trouble until we get there.*

His worry and affection were clear enough to her and also, apparently, to Munraz who broke off his contact with her, blushing.

"I'm sorry, bikrajti," he stammered.

"Husbands and wives," she told him. "Nothing to apologize for, I'm the one that invited you."

"Truly?" Winnajhubr interrupted, with a grin. "You and Najud?"

When she smiled and nodded, he whooped. "I told them so. Jirkat owes me that chestnut mare of his, and Ilzay a knife."

"What, they didn't approve?" she asked, a bit tartly, and Winnajhubr sobered.

"Oh, no, *bikrajti*—they thought you wouldn't want to stay with us and live as we do. Foreigners…" He coughed. "We've never heard of one who did. They thought Najud couldn't do it…"

His voice trailed off.

"Couldn't persuade me to stay?" She watched his young face redden as he pictured the implications and realized just how inappropriate this conversation was with an older woman, betrothed to someone else, and both of them wizards.

"He can be very persuasive," she added, with a hint of a leer, just to embarrass them further.

"Now, if we're all quite done with poking into my affairs, let's go tell Khizuwi the news." They nodded, chastened. "The news about the survivors, mind, not about things that don't concern you."

Inwardly, she couldn't stop her own heart from singing with the reminder of how the day had begun. She tried to keep it from Munraz as she let him watch while she reached out to Khizuwi.

Khizuwi, can you hear me?

After a moment, he replied. *Bikrajti? Where are you? Anything wrong?*

She did her best to broadcast reassurance. *I'm at the intermediate point with our two young men, and Munraz is watching us talk.*

Khizuwi's amusement came through clearly. *And can you hear us, nal-jarghal?*

Munraz's reply was unsteady but determined. *Yes, bikraj. I'm learning from Penrys. It's very interesting.*

I'm sure it is. Khizuwi's sardonic comment was tinged with approval, Penrys thought.

To business, now. Khizuwi, Najud thinks it'll take two hours to reach camp. As soon as he gets this far, I'll come on ahead to help you.

What do we need?

They're starving. We need meat broth, and cabbage in it. It's not likely they've eaten any greens for weeks. Twelve of them—I doubt they'll be able to eat much right away.

Khizuwi paused. *Injuries?*

There must be some, but they were all walking and nothing was obvious. We can assume frostbite, at least—their clothing is wretched.

Now it was her turn to hesitate, conscious of the young Munraz listening in. *I'm more worried about their minds. They're not talking, and… I think their minds are showing them falsehoods, so they've stopped trusting their senses. That's the only way I can think to put it.*

Khizuwi's inarticulate grunt managed to reach her through mind-speech. *Best worry about that once their bodies are safe.*

Agreed. Oh, and one of them isn't of the Kurighdunaq. Najud wondered if he might be one of your young men. From the story about the caves.

His surprise was clear, and then followed by hope and caution. *We'll see.*

The track they'd trampled through the snow when they left the camp to get the survivors four hours ago was still visible in the failing light as Najud led them all back to the camp. The storm's gusty winds were much reduced from the day before, and though snow continued to fall, it hadn't blown and drifted enough to erase the trace.

Khizuwi and Penrys came out of their respective *kazrab* to greet them before Najud could call out. Najud wasn't sure if Khizuwi had heard them coming, or if Penrys had told him. Khizuwi walked past the survivors, drooping on their led horses, and searched their faces.

"Here," Jirkat said, and he raised his hand to point at the last one in his own string. Khizuwi pushed through the snow to look at the man, and broke into a smile. "Ariqnas! It's Khizuwi. We've got you back."

He walked alongside him, his hand on the man's thigh, as Najud led all the horses into the space between the *kazrab*. Penrys finished coiling the guide rope between their *kazr* and Jirkat's that she'd lowered to make that possible, and walked over to him when he stopped.

"How are they?" she said, looking up at him.

"Unresponsive, but alive," he told her. "What's the plan?"

"We'll have to divide them among us, of course. Khizuwi and I, we thought it would be best to keep the women together, and the numbers are right, so we're taking the women, since we've got the most space, and I suppose Khizuwi will take his clansman—that leaves three more for him, and the rest in with Jirkat.

"We've got broth keeping warm in each *kazr*, and warm water, too, along with cloths for bandages and washing, lotions for their skin, and so forth. So, feed 'em, wash 'em, check their injuries, then everyone to sleep, I think. It's been a long day."

He swayed in his saddle. *A long day, indeed. But a good one for the Kurighdunaq.* He summoned up the effort to dismount and clung to his saddle from the ground after his unsteady feet sank into the snow.

"Winnajhubr," he called, "Let's get the horses stripped and back to their shelter, and bring some more of that grain with you. They've earned it."

Keep an eye on him, Pen-sha. Wouldn't want him to get lost as we lose the light.

Penrys's wordless assent echoed back to him.

Between them, they sorted out the survivors in a hurry to get them inside, out of the cold.

Penrys ducked into their *kazr*, and Najud walked over to the first of the women. "Come with me, *lijti*, we're going inside now. Penrys will help you."

He tugged her gently by the arm. Her blindfolded face turned first to follow his voice, and then from side to side, as though she were using her ears instead of her eyes to track her surroundings.

Jirkat and Ilzay had given him their names, and as he guided this one over the threshold and into the warm *kazr*, he told Penrys. "This is Anah-Zul."

Penrys stepped up and took over, cocking her head at the doorway to dismiss him. "Welcome to our *kazr*, Anah-Zul. Please, come sit over here." He heard her continuous patter for the comfort of the woman as he left to bring in the next one.

A couple of hours later, Najud sat on his bed and looked around his little flock, wrapped in blankets and huddled within reach of each other on the rugs.

Penrys had given each one a few mouthfuls of broth, right at the start, holding the spoon for them. One had broken into weeping at her first taste, she'd told him, but the rest had just swallowed.

Then, one by one, she had taken each woman back behind a curtain for privacy. She stripped and washed them, cleaned and bandaged any obvious sores, and smeared a thick layer of ointment bound in fat over chapped and frostbitten skin.

One of them, Luram, looked to have once-broken fingers, now mended awry, but there was nothing to be done about that. For the rest, Penrys told him, they were thin, very thin, but whole.

I'm going to feed them again and let them sleep.

He could feel Penrys's weariness in her mind-speech.

She went round and sat with each woman, spooning more broth into them and talking constantly, in a low reassuring voice. The ones that had been blindfolded were bare-faced now, but Najud wasn't sure how much they actually saw.

It was strange that they hadn't spoken yet, hard to remember that they were people, since people were never relentlessly quiet like this. They refused to be separated, even to let one of them take the unused bed, and Najud thought that was a promising sign, that they were at least that aware of their surroundings. They turned their heads to follow Penrys's voice, and his own

Penrys didn't have enough clothing for five women, of course, but everyone had gotten some of her spare socks and enough undergarments for decency.

As he watched, she cocked her head as if listening to one of the silent women. Then she rose and put her bowl down by the stove to keep warm, and helped the woman stand up and wrap the blanket around herself more securely. They walked to the doorway, where Penrys guided her hands to their collective footwear. Once the woman's hands had recognized her own boots, she helped her put them on and then they went together, out into the snow.

Of course. He could help with that task, but he thought they'd be more comfortable with another woman than with him. Instead, he stood up and made himself useful inside, finishing the job of feeding them, cleaning up the bowls, and readying the *kazr* for the night.

When the last of them had made her guided trip outside and returned, he waited for Penrys to finally slip into their bed and lower the rarely-used curtain around it.

All done, Pen-sha?

He could feel her halfway to sleep already, snuggling up against him for warmth. She muttered something unintelligible, and he smiled.

A little song danced through his mind as he remembered how the day had begun. *She agreed. She's mine, now.*

He wrapped an arm around her and pulled her closer, and she relaxed completely.

Mine.

CHAPTER 35

By the middle of the next morning, Penrys had completed her rounds. Each of her charges had been fed again, but they still weren't talking—cooperative when she or Najud moved them, but initiating little movement unguided.

Najud had left a few minutes ago to see how things were progressing in the other *kazrab*. She'd wanted to see for herself, but there was no leaving these women alone, not with a hot stove she wasn't sure they could perceive. She also wasn't sure how they might react if both their new guardians vanished at the same time.

She talked to them constantly, trying to keep her voice from going hoarse as it had the day before when she'd wanted to make herself heard over the storm. The damage had healed overnight, but she expected to be talking like this all day, as a sort of therapy.

It was very strange listening to herself going on and on in the otherwise quiet *kazr*, where only the faint noises of the stove were normally present. The women weren't deaf—she was sure of that, both from their physical reactions and from what she could monitor of their minds—but she didn't think much penetrated beside the calm emotion and the sense of another person.

She could never see another person's thoughts explicitly, but their emotions and a few images were there for the looking, and sometimes their deeply learned skills. These women knew textiles and weaving, dairy and food preservation. Most of them knew child-rearing. Bimal reminded her of Inghiti, the apprentice herd-mistress that the Winnajjinza had loaned to Umzakhilin—perhaps that had been her job. Najud only knew their names from Jirkat and Ilzay, not their roles in the clan.

The images she saw in their minds had little association with the world around them. Just behind them, they felt terror and fire. In front of them was smooth grass and pleasant walking. They sat in the *kazr*, in the midst of deep snow, and saw bare grasslands everywhere they looked.

The women themselves were hiding behind these images, and she couldn't reach them.

What if the images they saw matched reality?

Penrys gently pulled Bimal around on the rugs until she faced another woman, and then sat next to her. She looked at the other woman, and tried to project what she saw into Bimal's mind, to override the vision of sunlight and grass.

"This is Anah-Zul. This is real."

She lifted up Bimal's hand and extended it to touch Anah-Zul's knee.

"This is you, touching Anah-Zul. This is real, too."

Twice, and three times she repeated the exercise. Then she turned Bimal's head gently in the direction of the other women. "We're here in my *kazr*, all of you. The men are here, too, in different *kazrab*. See the stove, keeping us warm?"

Maybe there was a faint reaction, but Penrys couldn't be sure, so she turned Bimal's head back to look at Anah-Zul, who reacted not at all to the exercise.

Once again, Penrys stretched the woman's arm to touch the other woman, describing what she was doing and actively pushing the image into Bimal's mind.

"You. This is you, touching her. Pay attention to it. The grass isn't real—you already know that, it's why you ignore it—but this is real. The woman is real, and the *kazr*. I am real, moving your hand and talking to you."

When she guided the woman's hand back to her lap, she encountered resistance for the first time. Bimal raised her other hand and felt for Penrys's, where it rested on her arm.

"Yes! I'm real. Look, you can take my hand and move it. See?"

She let her hand be examined, and projected the image as strongly as she could. Even for what Najud described as the mind-deaf, she thought some of it was getting through.

Bimal blinked and turned her head independently, keeping her grasp of Penrys's hand. Penrys turned with her to supply a version of what she was seeing over the grassland vision, and that stale image in Bimal's mind... flickered, reappeared, and flickered again.

Unexpectedly, Bimal lurched to her feet, and Penrys held her arm. She slowly rotated in place, and Penrys stopped supplying alternative visions to let her own eyes take over. When she faced the stove, she stretched out her hands to it and took a step in that direction, and Penrys supported her until they stood just a couple of feet from its solid, undeniable heat.

Bimal touched Penrys's face lightly with her stove-warmed hand, and jerked her hand back as if she hadn't been sure Penrys was real.

"I'm Bimal," she said, in a voice rusty with disuse. "*Dirum* for the Kurighdunaq." There was wonder in her voice, as if she were only just now awakening.

"Yes, you are," Penrys confirmed, "and it's a pleasure to meet you. Welcome back." She took the woman in her arms and hugged her, and the stiff body relaxed into a single shudder before straightening again.

"What happened to us?" she asked, as she pulled back from the embrace.

As she spoke, Najud opened the door of the *kazr* and caught the end of her question.

His grin was infectious. "You're talking!"

Bimal smiled back tentatively.

He turned to Penrys. "What did you do?"

She shrugged. "Hard to explain. Showed her the real world, and made her believe in it, I guess. Ought to work on most of them, I imagine."

"What's that you've got?" she asked Najud, when she noticed the bundle in his hands.

"Shirts or robes for all the women, courtesy of the men in camp. We'll make something out of the blankets, maybe, for breeches, but this'll do for a start."

"Good. I'll work on the rest of them, and you can tell Bimal the story."

By mid-morning, all the women had been broken out of their hallucinations and started to recover. Luram had the most trouble with staying focused in the real world, and Bimal took charge of her, talking to her constantly and leading her around the *kazr*, touching things.

Khizuwi popped in early in the process. "What's this Najud's been telling me?"

He stayed and watched for a while, making observations to Najud, then the two of them ducked out together.

Penrys led each of the women outside, one at a time, to look at the camp. Luram and Bimal came out together, and Bimal made a ball of snow and put it in Luram's hands. "You used to be good at this, Lusha," she teased her. "Bet you can't hit me now."

A sly expression crept over Luram's face and she threw the snowball directly at Bimal who scrambled away from her. Luram bent down of her own will and scooped up another handful, and then stopped, looking at the walls of the *kazr*, at the other two *kazrab*, at the trampled snow… Then she turned and looked at Penrys, and touched her face, with the hand full of forgotten snow, and Penrys flinched as it dropped down her neck.

"You *are* real. This is the snow we walked through," Luram said, then shuddered. Bimal trudged back and held her, and cocked her head at Penrys. "I'll take care of her, *lijti.*"

Movement caught Penrys's eye, and she saw Najud emerging from Jirkat's *kazr*, followed by everyone who'd been inside.

Bringing you guests, Pen-sha. Your method's working the best, Khizuwi says.

Penrys did a quick calculation of what the *kazr* could hold. *All of them at once?*

She felt his amusement. *Khizuwi's, too.*

She spun to look. He was right—there they came.

"All right, ladies, we're going to be crowded. Better get back inside and pick out the best seats."

Luram ignored her and ran down the path to one of the men in Najud's group. She grabbed his hand and started talking earnestly into his ear, keeping him company as they came. He wasn't responsive, as far as Penrys could see from a distance, but that didn't stop her.

Bimal watched with her, and told her, "That's her brother." She shook her head. "So many of us dead. How will we ever rebuild?"

CHAPTER 36

"You show them the real world, in here," Penrys tapped her forehead, "reinforcing what their eyes are seeing, which they're currently ignoring. They've got a habit of sight now, of ignoring the image in their heads which they know is false. That's what you've got to break through—make them trust their eyes again and ignore the old compulsion."

Penrys was trying to explain her method to the other wizards. The women on the outer edge of the crowd in the *kazr* nodded their agreement, but Khizuwi voiced the problem.

"We believe you, *jarghalti*, but how do you do it?" he said, spreading his hands.

"I'll show you again."

She invited them to watch through mind-touch while she worked with Dhalmudhr, the leader of the survivors. Bimal came forward and offered to be the familiar face he would first see, and Penrys went through the same process as before, showing him what was in front of him, projecting that vision into his mind, until finally he reached out to test it for himself, with a tap on Bimal's knee, and a bewildered emotional release.

Bimal tugged at him until he stood up and followed her back to the recently recovered women. She talked quietly but earnestly to him there.

"Do you see how that worked?" Penrys asked her colleagues.

Najud said, "I saw what you did well enough, but I can't do that, put an image in someone's mind, a living model of the world they see. I wouldn't know where to start."

He looked at Khizuwi and Munraz, and they shook their heads, too. "Looks like this task is yours, *bikrajti*," Khizuwi said. "The sooner we can break the illusion for all of them, the sooner we can help them, and find out what we need to know."

It took more than an hour to work her way through the rest of them. Some were much smoother than others—the illusion was easier to break. None were even as difficult as Bimal had been, and

Penrys learned quickly that she could predict how the process would go as soon as she first touched a mind.

Only one was a problem. Jirkat called him Haraq, and he was Umzakhilin's cousin, related through their mothers. Penrys shifted him to the end as soon as she touched him, and when she returned to him it was as she'd anticipated—the imposed illusion was ingrained so strongly into his mind that she couldn't successfully overlay it with reality.

When it gradually became apparent that she was not winning this one, at least not on the first attempt, the survivors nearest to him guided him back to sit in the middle of the group, and all who could reach him touched him, absorbing him back into their midst protectively.

Penrys watched their actions with an impassive face, but behind that mask her mind was busy. *These are probably a random set of people from the clan, but this disaster has bound them together into a family. See how they look after their own. They're not going to be absorbed into this camp easily.*

Najud stood up and bowed deeply to the eleven survivors who could see him, barring Haraq. "I'm Najud, son of Ilsahr of clan Zamjilah, of the Shubzah tribe, and I'm the *zarawinnaj* of this expedition on behalf of the Kurighdunaq. Here's what we know…"

He took them through their finding of the summer encampment, the fate of Umzakhilin, and the addition of the other *bikrajab* as the word spread. He avoided mentioning Penrys's chain, or her unknown relationship with the *qahulajti* who had enslaved them, for which she was grateful. Nor did he mention such strange things as wings, not yet anyway—he was unspecific about how Penrys had found them.

Her hand crept up to her throat to check the coverage of her scarf there, and she caught Jiqlaraz's eye on her while she did so.

When Najud finished his summary, he waited expectantly. Dhalmudhr rose unsteadily, and Najud sat down again on his portion of the rug, next to Penrys.

"I'm Dhalmudhr, son of Bajushaz, of the Kurighdunaq. I recognize Jirkat, and Ilzay, and Winnajhubr here, my clan-kin, but I'm dismayed by this tale, and sickened. We have been lost in this nightmare for three months, you say?"

Najud nodded.

"Where are my children? Where is my wife? My father?" Dhalmudhr's voice broke, and only the muffled crackling of the fire in the stove was audible while they waited for him to recover.

Ilzay stood up, with a hand on the horn around his neck that recorded the tally of the dead. "We've found many who died along the way, and Umzakhilin will have found others between the summer encampment and the *zudiqazd*. Some of the dead we can name to you and perhaps you can name more of them. Others have eluded us, and we hope more are still to be found, alive, held by this *qahulajti*. Only you can tell us that."

Dhalmudhr nodded. His face was so lean and wrinkled that it was hard to guess his age. It carried little expression—they were all that way, as if they'd grown unaccustomed to communicating with their faces to those who couldn't see them.

"There are others, we know there are, but we couldn't see them. At night, there was only darkness for us—no stars, no moon. In the daytime, she spun lies of green fields with terror and fire behind us to keep us moving."

Penrys watched Winnajhubr nod along as if this reminded him of her experiment with illusion.

"We found each other by chance," Dhalmudhr said, cocking his head at his fellow survivors, "and once we did, we tried to never let go. There were more of us once..." He swallowed. "But they were lost. Some died—from cold, from injuries no one could treat, from sickness, from hunger. From worn-out shoes, sometimes—it's so easy to hurt your feet when you can't see what you're walking on, and if you couldn't keep up, well, you were just another injured beast."

"Some wandered away and lost contact with us." He nodded at Bimal. "It was her idea to tie us together, a long time ago. A good idea."

Clearing his throat, he added, "We tried to get others to join us, or to at least make their own groups, but many of them couldn't hear us, and most of us couldn't speak."

He paused again, then continued. "We were lucky. We all had good shoes or boots, if not at the beginning, then from the dead. We could sometimes talk to each other, at first, at least a bit— talking got harder and harder. And we had knives. With knives, we could eat."

He looked around his audience as if begging them to under-stand. "*She* wouldn't tolerate us killing a beast from the herds, even when we chanced upon one in our reach. But every now and then one would die, or her wolves would make a kill. And that was our chance, if she moved slowly enough for us to carve something off before all the herds passed, or if it was near the time for the night stop. After we checked the carcase to make sure it wasn't one of us."

After a moment of silence, Jirkat asked, "How did you get away?"

Dhalmudhr turned around and looked at the little remnant of the clan he'd broken away with.

"We'd just eaten what we could find of a sheep, before the wolves got to it, and the darkness started. That very day we'd been brought south, down a hill, after many days of going up and west."

He swallowed. "We were never going to be stronger, and I thought it might be possible to retreat the way we'd come, and put some part of the land between us. We had hours of night to retrace the rise of the land, and if we succeeded, we could turn east when we reached the top, into the sunlight, warm on our faces. Then we could at least die free and together."

His unused voice was hoarse now. "And then came the blizzard. Walking downhill gave us something to do, with the wind at our backs, through all those green fields our minds told us were there. I don't think anyone wanted to be the first to stop. Or, anyway, no one said so." He smiled sardonically at the notion of conversation, and the unexpected expression on his blank face transformed it.

He swayed unsteadily on his feet. "When will you break camp so we can go get the others?" No one answered him, and he sat down again.

Khizuwi called upon his clansman, the young herdsman Ariqnas, to tell his part of the earlier tale.

Penrys thought he looked ten years older than his age-mates Winnajhubr and Munraz.

When the young man stood up to speak, he kept his eyes on Khizuwi. "Barshhubr and I were with the horse herds, up in those well-watered meadows, near the caves," he said. "You know the place? Wayat mar-Zarqash?"

Khizuwi nodded his understanding, and Ariqnas continued. "Wishkazti rode out to join us for the afternoon, and we all decided…"

"To go exploring inside," Khizuwi suggested. "You're hardly the first."

"None of us had done it before. We'd heard the tales but we didn't really believe them—it was the sort of thing we told the youngsters around the fire at night and we were too old to be frightened by that."

He continued in a monotone as if he'd told himself this story over and over again for months.

"We made torches and went inside the big one, the one whose opening you can see from a distance. There was even a sort of path there to it, and sheep bones. Wishkazti was worried about the bones and wanted to turn back, but I… I told her we weren't cowards and the *zarawinnaj* would want to know what we discovered. We'd be… we'd be heroes when we got back to the camp that night."

He added bitterly. "And she believed me, and we kept going. And then *she* found us."

After a couple of shaky breaths, he continued. "She was just a kid, younger than me. Maybe thirteen or fourteen. It was hard to tell, because her face never changed. She wore hides, just cut up or tied on. And a chain, a thick chain made of something, didn't look like gold exactly, around her neck. She was no Zan, not with that light brown hair.

"We introduced ourselves, but she didn't talk to us—she never did talk to us. She listened when we spoke, to her or each other, but she never spoke. She looked at the torches, too, as if she'd never seen anything like that before.

"Barshhubr complained that his head hurt, and he started to back away, and he stumbled. It was just a little fall, but when he went down we heard the growls behind her for the first time, and her wolves took him."

He swallowed. "He got his knife out in time to hurt one of them, but it didn't do him any good. Wishkazti and I, we couldn't move. We tried!"

Penrys could hear the anguish in his voice breaking through the monotone.

"*She* held us in place. While the wolves were eating… she walked in among them and picked up the knife and felt the sharp point. She looked at us, at the knives on our belts, and she poked through… what was left and found the sheath and the belt, and took those, too. The wolves never bothered her—they got out of her way when she… growled at them.

"Then she walked over and stood in front of us. There was some blood on her from the injured wolf and Barshhubr—I couldn't take my eyes off of that. She stared at Wishkazti and when she screamed, she turned to me but… I felt nothing. Then she just… walked away, back deeper into the tunnels, as if nothing had happened. The wolves ignored us, but we still couldn't move. I couldn't touch Wishkazti, not even to hold her while they… cracked his bones. It was him she'd come to see when she left the camp, you understand, not me."

The silence was complete in the *kazr*.

"She held us for a couple of days, I believe. It was hard to tell the time, in the cave and its tunnels. I think she studied us. Wishkazti interested her more than me. She would sit down in front of us, with her wolves. We could move now, but we couldn't leave the chamber we were in. There was just a glimmer of light to tell us where the big entrance was, but the darkness didn't seem to bother *her* any. It was like she could smell us.

"Anyway, she'd sit down in front of Wishkazti, and they'd both go still. I… I tried to make myself invisible. She did it to me, too, but it didn't really bother me.

"Then, the last time, when she left, Wishkazti wouldn't talk to me any more. She just sat there and hugged her knees to her chest. When I woke up, I found her there in the dark, her knife still in her hand and the smell of her blood thick in the air."

Penrys felt Khizuwi's grief, as strong and sharp as Ariqnas's, if hidden from his face.

"I don't know how long she kept me. I think she learned her control on me—the visions she sent were strange, then she settled into something like she used later, with the grasslands, and the fire, and the darkness. When she left the caves, we climbed the hills to the northeast, up onto the trading trail, and went east from there, until she found the Kurighdunaq camp."

He bowed his head, and then turned resolutely around to face the rest of the survivors. "I and my friends, we woke this horror and brought the disaster upon you. I couldn't tell you about it before. If my life will offer you any relief, it's yours."

Bimal stood up and picked her way among the seated people until she reached him. "You are no more at fault than the spark that lights a fire. If not you, then it would have been another. The fire would have come eventually anyway." She wrapped her arms around him, and he wept like a child.

"Come back here," she urged him, and guided him into the heart of the group, and they all touched him and welcomed him.

Najud waited a moment, then stood up and spoke to them. "We've heard enough for now. Please go with Jirkat and Ilzay and Winnajhubr for a little while. They'll make you something to eat, and you've got the other two *kazrab*. We need to talk about *bikrajab* things now, before we continue."

The three Kurighdunaq young men led them all back outside, and they moved in a group as if still bound to each other, careful to keep the unresponsive Haraq with them. Penrys wanted to try again with him, after everyone's emotions were more settled, but for now her hands were shaking and she clasped them together to hide it.

Khizuwi was the first of them to speak, after everyone else was gone. "A story to tell the youngsters around the fire, eh?" He shook his head.

Jiqlaraz came straight to the point, his mouth set grimly. "Yes, and what are we going to do about this?"

CHAPTER 37

Jiqlaraz began with a question that had been bothering Penrys. "How can this *qahulajti* impose a vision on these multitudes, day and night? I'm willing to grant the act itself, since our own chained *bikrajti* can clearly do it." He waved a hand at Penrys. "But doesn't she ever sleep?"

"Maybe she only does it while she's awake," Penrys said. "Maybe the rest of the time it's what they called 'the darkness.' Their grassland illusions lasted without her, so why not the darkness, too? They may have fought against that blindness to escape, but perhaps everyone just got used to sleeping when she did.

"I noticed something else," Khizuwi said. "Barshhubr's complained about his head hurting before he fell. The *qahulajti's* interest in Wishkazti… Several of Wishkazti's relatives have been *bikrajab*. Some of Barshhubr's, too."

Najud lifted his hands in a shrug.

Khizuwi explained. "Umzakhilin carries the *bikraj* blood, you said. Well, whom did you fail to wake, *bikrajti*?" Haraq? Jirkat told me he is *tamalba nazum*, sister-son, to Umzakhilin's mother. It's in his bloodline. Of the others, who was the most difficult to break free?"

"Bimal," Penrys said. "by far, but Luram had trouble, too. She's Haraq's sister."

"And are there *bikrajab* in Bimal's family?" When no one answered he beckoned to the silent Munraz and told him, "Go and find out," and Munraz went.

"Ariqnas survived three months of her close attention. He seems to have been careful, for a young man, but what I think also saved him is that there's not a drop of *bikraj* in his family."

"What are you saying, *jarghal*?" Najud asked. "That she finds those with *bikrajab* blood more interesting? That they're more vulnerable to her?"

Penrys answered him. "That she can take their power directly from them, weaken them, use it to force her control more deeply."

Jiqlaraz said, "You speak as if you are familiar with these things, *lijti*."

His tone raised her hackles, but she tried to reply evenly. "I am," she said, omitting his title. "I've seen wizards do it before."

"Perhaps even you," he said.

That brought Najud to his feet beside her. Before he could retort angrily, Munraz returned with Bimal. Oblivious to his interruption, he told Khizuwi, "She wanted to come herself, to help."

Najud sat down again, muttering, while Khizuwi asked her, "Bimal, what do you know about *bikrajab* in your family?"

She looked at the assembly of wizards in puzzlement. "Everyone knows Umzakhilin's story, the choice he made."

Khizuwi nodded, and she continued. "Haraq's his cousin, and his sister Luram, but I'm his *namalba*, too, back in our grandmothers' lines somewhere. I've never heard the voices."

"Did you know," Khizuwi said, contemplatively, "that it's often thought among the *bikrajab* that a bit of the bloodline makes for a good *dirum*?"

Penrys shifted in surprise. *The herd-mistresses have a little wizard in them? Makes them better with the animals, maybe.*

"No, *bikraj*, I'd never heard that," Bimal said, thoughtfully.

"Nor I," Najud said. "One of my own sisters is a *dirum-malb*, an apprentice."

Jiqlaraz looked most surprised of all. Penrys couldn't work out why, and then a thought occurred to her. *Maybe he's realized there's another source of bikrajab blood suitable for marriage alliances.*

"Thank you, Bimal," Khizuwi said, and waited until she left. "So, we have one theory—the stronger the trace of *bikraj* blood, the better this *qahulajti* can control them."

Penrys was distracted by the thought. She looked more carefully into Bimal's mind as she walked through the snow, and thought she saw something like a wizard's core of power, but small and faint. It was stronger in Haraq and Luram.

She returned her attention to discover Khizuwi regarding her with interest. "Yes, *bikrajti*?" he said.

"You're right," she told him. "They do have a small version of what a *bikraj* has. I've never seen that before."

He smiled. "You've never known what to look for, before."

Munraz said, as if reluctant to state the obvious, "But doesn't that mean all of us are just the sort of slaves this *qahulajti* finds easiest to manage?"

"It sure does," Penrys answered him. "Think what a *dirum* she would have made."

Following a knock on the doorframe, Dhalmudhr stuck his head in to see if he was interrupting, and then marched in to stand before Najud.

Penrys thought he looked much better than before and wondered why—she decided it was the human animation in his face.

"There are matters we should discuss," he said, politely. "The storm is blowing over. The snow has stopped and I don't expect it to return."

He spread his hand eloquently. "We could leave tomorrow, *zarawinnaj*, and begin heading west. After all, we've already broken that trail. Seven miles, Ilzay said—that's a good start.

"And that means we have to prepare clothing, and food. Jirkat tells us you planned for this, that there are hides and canvas and blankets. We could cut and sew gloves, make breeches—many things. We still have daylight for that, if we begin now."

Without waiting for a reply, he turned to Penrys. "Would you be willing, *bikrajti*, to try again with Haraq? His sister said it was hard for her, but she's sure you can do it, break through to him."

"I'd be glad to," Penrys said. "It's what I planned on."

Dhalmudhr nodded to her, and looked around at the others. "I know you've been talking about what you should do next, as *bikrajab*. We, all of us… we wanted to tell you that we're going back, as soon as we can. On foot all the way, if you won't come and can't lend us horses."

Najud listened to all of this calmly. "What is it that's spurred all of this haste, when you can barely walk, any of you, and need more time to recover?"

Dhalmudhr swallowed, but if anything his expression became more determined. "We've spent the last hour or so with Ilzay, *zarawinnaj*, going through the remembrances of the dead. We matched some of your unknowns to names, and mourned all the ones we knew. It's hard to explain to someone like you, who wasn't with us these long months…"

Running a hand through his hair, he said, "We're past grief, in a way—grief is for later, for after we've gotten all of the living back from *her*. We can't leave anyone behind, trapped in that nightmare, not and live with ourselves afterward. We all agree. If you won't come…"

Najud interrupted him. "We haven't said we wouldn't come. And however you go, it will be with horses. But I will *not* sanction your starting tomorrow."

When Dhalmudhr opened his mouth to protest, Najud held up his hand. "You'll slow us all down. If you can't help yourselves, how can you help anyone else? And we need time to prepare. The earliest… the *earliest*, mind, would be the next morning, so that we have all day tomorrow to get ready."

Khizuwi spoke up. "We're only perhaps fifty miles due south of clan Umbazul's *zudiqazd*. I've traced three sides of a square, coming here. A journey of two or three days would see you all there, or at least the weakest of you."

"My clan's *zudiqazd* isn't much further," Jiqlaraz offered. "A straight walk to the east, away from this *qahulajti*."

Dhalmudhr's head was shaking as they spoke. "It doesn't matter about us, that's not what we want. I don't know how many are left, but it must still be dozens." He clenched his fist. "My blood boils just sitting here, doing nothing, don't you understand? Bimal has already sworn to free enough of the horses the *qahulajti* took to mount everyone."

Regretfully, Penrys pointed out some uncomfortable facts. "As soon as you're within range, this girl is just going to capture you again, and then what? Now I agree that maybe you can find some other people lingering at the back of her herds and out of her reach, if she hasn't noticed. But maybe not, too."

She gestured at the other wizards. "What we were just talking about is that we might not be strong enough, even as a group, to stop her. And if we can't, you've got no shield at all."

Jiqlaraz added, "And this *bikrajti* should know, for she is similar in nature."

Penrys inhaled in shock at this rough exposure, and Najud glared at Jiqlaraz.

When Dhalmudhr turned to her in puzzlement, she reluctantly unwrapped the scarf around her throat and exposed the chain. "I've never met her, but she's not the only one of her kind."

Dhalmudhr backed up several steps and his mouth worked for a moment. Then he paced forward again resolutely and spoke to her. "I remember hearing you talking, yesterday, for hours, and then today, in my mind, showing me what was real and what wasn't. You are *not* the same—I do believe you."

A strange emotion convulsed her. *What is this? Relief? Gratitude at his acceptance?* Whatever it was, her mouth quirked.

Najud broke the tension. "We brought four more large *kazrab*, without their furnishings, for special shelters. We'll set one up now, as a place for all of you to work and sleep, unless the women want to be separate."

Dhalmudhr nodded his thanks. "I'll ask them, *zarawinnaj*, but I think they will want to stay together. We're a family, now, of sorts."

He examined Najud's face, and conceded authority, at least provisionally. "We'll abide by the one day delay, but we'll have a decision by tomorrow, and with you or without you, we're going back after that."

CHAPTER 38

Penrys buried her chain again under her scarf, and then wrapped up in her sheepskin coat and followed Dhalmudhr out in search of Haraq and his sister. Najud came with her to get some help erecting one of the empty *kazrab* for the night.

She found Luram in her own *kazr*, with the rest of the women, and Haraq was with her. Their quiet conversation stopped when she opened her door, and Luram looked up hopefully.

At Penrys's gesture, Luram stood up and gently pulled her brother up, too. They wrapped themselves up and followed Penrys back outside.

"We're going to go out and see the world," Penrys told her, "and try to convince your brother to give up these illusions." Luram's grateful smile panicked her—what if it didn't work? But confidence was half the game, and Penrys didn't let her face change.

Movement at the door of Jiqlaraz's *kazr* caught her eye. Munraz stood there looking for someone and, when their eyes met, he set off determinedly in her direction.

He eyed Luram and Haraq, but spoke directly to Penrys. "I apologize, *bikrajti*, on my uncle's behalf." He bowed to her. "My grandfather would have beaten me for manners like that."

"He's your uncle and your master," she told him, hiding her bemusement. "You must be loyal to him."

"I am! But not to the point of blindness."

"Or bad manners." This time she smiled. "Never mind, it had to happen sometime. I just wanted to wait until everyone was freed, first. It would interfere with their trust."

"Dhalmudhr wasn't afraid," Munraz said.

"No, he wasn't."

Penrys noticed the bewildered look on Luram's face at this conversation, and told her, "I'll explain it all after we take care of your brother."

Her face brightened, but Munraz's fell. "Want to come along and watch, *nal-jarghal?*"

He glanced at the work already started, a few yards away, to erect the new *kazr* in the trampled space enclosed within the other three.

"They have plenty of people to help," she said. *Was Najud ever this hesitant? Not likely.*

"Come on," she said. "Let's all go for a walk."

For a while they stood inside the yurt being raised, hoping the familiar activity would help, but it made no difference to Haraq, and Penrys led the other three back outside and they walked through the camp. Every time she showed Haraq the snowy scene in front of him, his vision of grasslands flickered back.

Penrys stopped them by Jirkat's *kazr*, out of the way of the activity.

"Munraz, close your eyes and think of the steppe. What do you see? Describe it."

Obediently, he stood still and shut his eyes. "There's a rising slope near the *zudiqazd*, at the edge of our northern winter grazing where you can see a long ways to the south. *Inghiqa* has started, the snow is mostly gone, and we'll be leaving soon for the *taridiqa*. The new grass is green against the snow."

"When you turn your head," Penrys asked, "do you see the same thing, or does your point of view shift?"

He tried it, then opened his eyes and looked at her, puzzled. "It moves, of course."

"And you?" Penrys looked at Luram.

"Mine is on the trail home from the autumn camp to the *zudiqazd*. No matter where the camp was, there's a place, a gap between the hills where we always pass through, on the way home. It's as though we leave the wild *khijr*-Zannib and return to our settled *zudiqazd*."

"I know the place," Penrys told her, and thought.

"Haraq's is different, too. Everyone has a different idea of what grasslands means to them. If we each dreamed of the steppe, all the places would be different, yes?"

Munraz and Luram nodded.

"So the *qahulajti* can't be sending them a vision, or they'd all be the same. She can't tell them 'see this,' like I've been doing. Instead she must be sending them something more like a command in a dream, more like 'dream of this.' And so their minds provide whatever version of that dream makes sense to the dreamer. When their heads turn, the dream landscape turns with them."

She shuddered. "Was it like that, Luram?"

"More nightmare than dream, *bikrajti*, but it sounds right," Luram said.

"So the visions I imposed on you were stronger than your dream, finally, but they weren't the same thing."

"I… I couldn't say, *bikrajti*. All I know is that when I started to pay attention to what you were showing me, the… dream released me."

"Hmm." Penrys thought about the implications of that theory. Was it something as simple as "See the dark—dream of the dark," really? All the herds the girl stole would tend to stay put at night, and the people could be made to stay, too. Only people who had given up using their eyes could break free of that one. They didn't blindfold themselves not to see what was around them—they did it to ignore their eyes altogether. No trigger, no dream. Would that work? It worked for these survivors—they walked away at night.

Add to that "See the day—dream of grassland in front of you, terror behind you." You don't talk to people, when you're dreaming, though you might sleepwalk. But they managed to plan, a little. What would that do to someone, months of this? It's a wonder they're sane.

Suddenly she smiled broadly. But they *are* sane, once they stop dreaming. The rest of them would probably recover, too, if they could be rescued.

"What?" Munraz asked, when he saw her expression.

"I think I know what to do," Penrys told him.

"Let's go," she said, pointing west to the woods just behind her own *kazr*. "We're going to wake Haraq up and give him something else to pay attention to."

They stopped under a large mountain cedar. The camp was visible through the trees, but the snow was only a foot or so deep at the base of the tree, sheltered by its sloping snow-laden limbs that shed the powder away from the trunk.

Penrys caught her breath from breaking through the deeper snow to get to this spot and then pressed her face close to the bark and inhaled the familiar scent. "I learned something today, Luram. The only Zan I knew was Najud, and he a *bikraj*. I haven't met any others until recently. I thought you were either a *bikraj*, or you weren't, but today I discovered that people who carry the blood may show it in small ways, other ways. Did you know that?"

Luram shook her head.

Penrys said, "I learned that sometimes a *dirum* comes from *bikraj* bloodlines, for example. And for the first time, I looked for that." She tapped her forehead to indicate her meaning.

She turned to Munraz. "There's a core of power inside every *bikraj*—have you seen that?"

"No, *lijti*," he said.

"Let me show you, then. Come, watch." She felt him tentatively join her. *See, here is Najud.*

She showed him the core of Najud's power, trying to keep it impersonal.

And here is how you look to me. This time she gave him a glimpse of himself.

See how you are roughly the same? That's what I meant when I told them you were all four about the same strength.

Munraz ventured a question. *And you, jarghalti?*

I can't show you, because I can't see that. You can try to look for yourself.

She felt him panic and flee out of her mind.

"What, did you try it?" she asked him, aloud.

"It was like staring at the sun—I couldn't do it."

"Nonsense. Najud doesn't have any difficulty. Ask him to show you."

But it made her wonder. *Does he have a problem, and hasn't told me?*

"Come on back, there's more to the lesson," she told Munraz.

Now, look at Luram, the same way you looked at Najud.

She could feel his surprise. *She has power, too—a little. Haraq, too.*

And your friend, Winnajhubr? She guided his search.

No. None at all.

"That's right." Penrys turned to Luram. "You know Umzakhilin carries the *bikraj* bloodline. Well, you two, and Bimal as well... you all have a little bit of it, too. Not enough to be *bikrajab*, but enough that Bimal is *dirum*, and that you and your brother are more trapped into obeying the *qahulajti*'s orders than the others are."

Penrys puzzled about how to explain further to her. "I can shield myself from a *bikraj* attack of the mind, and can shield others, too. I tried that when I found you, in the snow, but it didn't make any difference. I thought the *qahulajti* was still imposing visions upon you, but she wasn't. That probably stopped a while ago, or she only renews her commands when she needs to. Instead, you were just following her commands, and you're better at that than your companions are."

"What can you do about it, *bikrajti?*" Luram asked.

Penrys sighed. *What indeed? Here's where they start to fear me again.*

"I can… drain his bit of *bikraj* power, and that might let me wake him. Then I can give it back."

"Can't you just take it altogether from him, and me, too?" Luram asked.

"Not a good idea, *lijti.* You'd miss it, I think, just as Bimal would miss it as *dirum.*"

She glanced at Munraz, his face eager to watch this next step.

This is done using my chain, nal-jarghal, and that skirts the Zannib prohibition against devices.

He looked indignant. *Aren't your wings devices? Khizuwi doesn't stop you flying as a scout. I'm only watching.*

She hesitated. *I fear what your master would say to you.*

I don't. Besides, doesn't the qahulajti bear a chain? Shouldn't I learn what she can do?

Penrys wasn't comfortable with it, but his people considered him an adult, and Haraq had to be cured.

"All right," she told him. "Find me a cone from this tree. The snow should have knocked some down."

He pushed his way through the snow until he reached one, lying on the surface in the powder.

She led Haraq to the cedar and turned his face toward it. She pulled off his gloves and gave them to his sister to hold.

Come watch, nal-jarghal.

She waited for Munraz to join her, then she drained Haraq's power into her chain, leaving him just a flicker. Munraz tried unsuccessfully to suppress his shock, but she focused more on Haraq, whose visions of grasslands weakened.

"Smell this," she told him, holding his face against the rough tree bark. "Take a deep breath—you know that scent, its freshness. Feel the bark against your cheek."

She took one of his hands and wrapped it around the cone. "Feel the shape of this cone, how it prickles against your fingers."

Laying his other hand flat on the trunk, she said, "Feel how cold the wood is, the stickiness of the sap."

His mind was confused, like a man disturbed from a deep sleep, but the grasslands still flickered behind it all.

I need something more. But what?

Everything was buried in blank, useless snow. She knelt down at the base of the tree and pawed the snow away like a dog digging a hole, until she reached the wet soil. As she'd hoped, the tree's roots had pushed rocks up as they grew. She grabbed one, smaller than her hand, and stood up again.

She opened the hand that held the cone and pressed the stone into it instead, dirt and all. "Feel this—it's a piece of the mountain. Feel the sharp edges, broken the way rocks break, worked on by water and ice. Once it was a mountain, and someday it will be dirt, but not now. Now it is cold, and heavy, and *real.* Wake up! Look at it!"

She snatched her glove off and slapped his face with her bare hand. The sharp crack of it bounced through the trees. His hand clenched around the stone and he stiffened, his eyes alert. They looked at the stone in wonder, and then up at all their faces, stopping at his sister's. She rushed to him and folded her arms around him, but he kept hold of his stone and stared at Penrys over Luram's shoulder.

Penrys restored his power from her chain, and he shivered in response. "What did you do, *lijti?* I heard you, I think, in my dreams."

"Your friends will be glad to see you again, Haraq," she said.

Luram took her brother's hand and led him back toward the camp. "I'll explain," she told him. "Let's get you some food."

Penrys watched them go, and Munraz stayed with her.

"Well," she said, "We should get back."

Munraz laid a hand on her arm to stop her. "I was watching, still, when you showed him the tree and the rock. I think you could have just commanded him to wake, like *she* made him dream. Why didn't you?"

Penrys grimaced. "What, and become his new *qahulajti,* instead of the one he had? Don't we have enough of those already?"

MISTRESS OF ANIMALS

CHAPTER 39

Najud straightened up from leaning over his worktable in the *kazr* and stood up to stretch his back. The pouches of seven of the dead, previously unknown, now hung from the rafters near the stovepipe with their names neatly painted into the engraved leather.

Dhalmudhr's "family" needed the table, now that he was done with it. All of them were gathered in their new *kazr*, even the Umzabul boy, Ariqnas, with borrowed lanterns and the other two tables, working as quickly as they could to prepare winter clothing for themselves and as many others as possible from the supplies that had been carried from the Kurighdunaq *zudiqazd*.

They can have our worktable now. I'm through with it.

Penrys's reply was immediate. *I'll come get it.*

He was glad for the quiet inside the *kazr* after the noise of all the women this morning. Once Luram had returned with the recovering Haraq, he'd gone outside for relief, feeling like a stranger in his own *kazr*.

He could see nothing good coming of letting them all go back, especially the women, but Dhalmudhr was right—they were all determined to do it. When they'd left to join the others in the new *kazr*, he'd returned to his sad task with the pouches and tried to use the peace and silence to think of a better way.

The door opened, and Penrys came in with Munraz while Najud was making his way through the hanging *shabz*, testing the dryness of the meat strips. She smiled at him and picked up the light table. "I'll leave him with you," she said, cocking her head at Munraz, and carried it easily out of the door.

Munraz closed the door behind her and removed his outer garments, then he turned to face Najud, nervously.

"Do you have a little time, *bikraj?*" he asked. "I have questions, and I don't think my uncle will have the answers."

Najud raised his eyebrows, but he sat down by the stove and invited Munraz to join him. It was unusual for a *nal-jarghal* with a master to seek information from another *bikraj*, and likely to cause trouble if the master were jealous and came to hear of it.

"Did the *bikrajti* tell you how she woke up Haraq?" Munraz asked.

"Not all the details, no. We haven't had the time," Najud said.

"She let me watch—it was very kind of her to allow it."

Just like her. She must know it's an intrusion to another bikraj's relationship but she doesn't care. And she doesn't much like Jiqlaraz. Well, can't blame her for that—I don't like him either.

Najud kept his thoughts to himself. "Why don't you tell me about it, and ask your questions?"

As Munraz described what had happened, he was startled to hear that both of them had peeked in on him as an example of a *bikraj's* core power.

"But then I asked if I could peek at her for a comparison, and she let me." Munraz ground to a halt.

"Let me guess," Najud said. "Hard to look at?"

"Blinding," Munraz conceded. "You must see that all the time, *lij*, how do you…?"

"She doesn't know, *nal-jarghal*," he said. "At least, I don't think she does. I'm not sure if she saw the other chained *qahulajti* clearly, the one she killed, during that fight, but she can't look at herself, of course."

It was embarrassing, but the apprentice needed an accurate answer. "I don't look at her that way very often, but when I do, I think of her like the sun, and me the tall sunflower facing her." The young man's cheeks flamed, and Najud added, "I don't think *you* should do that very much with her, do you?"

Munraz evaded that remark. "Are all *bikrajti* like that, *lij*? I haven't met many, not young ones." He cleared his throat, then said, "If they are, then I can see why my uncle wants one."

Najud didn't like the sound of that. "What's it like at home for you, *nal-jarghal*, with your family? Aren't there several other *bikrajab*?" He pinned him with a hard look. "Why didn't they come, too?"

Munraz was silent, and Najud waited. Twice he opened his mouth to speak, and stopped, as if ashamed. Finally he looked down and muttered, "I asked my uncle that. He said, 'They're all married already.'"

That sent a chill up Najud's spine. "And Jiqlaraz is a widower, is that it?"

Munraz blushed, and looked away. "Or me, if she was as young as the messenger said."

Nothing could be heard except voices outside and the quiet hissing of the fire.

Najud asked him, bluntly, "A *qahulajti*, and unwilling? How did he think to do it?"

"I don't know." Munraz looked up. "It's wrong, I know it, but now that I've met Penrys I think I understand why he would want to."

"What you are telling me is contemptible, Munraz. What the messenger brought your people was a call for help, for hundreds of people, not an opportunity to... breed."

"I know," Munraz said, miserably. "You're right, but I have to do what they tell me."

"Do you? Even if you don't think it's right? Why?"

Najud let the question stretch on and on unanswered into the silence, and Munraz hung his head.

Penrys broke the tension when she walked in, smiling and rosy-cheeked.

Munraz scrambled to his feet and ducked his head to both of them before grabbing his coat and leaving.

Penrys stared after him. "What's the matter with him? I told him to talk to you—did you lecture him?"

Najud, still seated by the stove, considered how much to tell her. "I think he has a case of calf love."

"With me?" Penrys laughed as she hung her cape near the doorframe. "Well, that's harmless, at least."

Najud could feel his face freeze, and Penrys stared at him.

"You don't think so? You're not jealous of someone Winnajhubr's age, surely."

'It's not that, Pen-sha." No good would come of not elaborating, Najud decided. "He tells me Jiqlaraz came to try and capture the girl, if he could, for himself or for the boy."

"What, as a... wife? Chained and all?"

He could see how that surprised her. "Well, he didn't know that, of course, or what it meant."

He cleared his throat. "Worse, we've introduced him to another one."

She burst out laughing. "Oh, yes—that's likely. I wouldn't pass that man a piece of…"—her eye roamed the *kazr* for inspiration—"of *shabz* if he were dying."

"I don't think he's too particular about approval from either of his candidates," Najud commented dryly.

Penrys sobered. "You're not serious? You think this is a real threat?"

"It would be wise to avoid being alone with him. I don't think he's quite corrupted his nephew yet, though the boy wanted to know if there were others like you."

Her mouth quirked. "Well I'm flattered, but he doesn't know what he's asking, does he?"

"It's no laughing matter, Pen-sha. If you were taken unawares…"

She raised a hand. "I hear you. I'll be cautious about my dealings with Jiqlaraz. I've no great desire to spend time with him anyway."

She sat down on his unused bed to remove her boots, and replace them with the slippers she used inside the *kazr*, then she carried her boots over to the bare canvas patch near the door to drip.

Her chain was exposed around her neck, and the scarf underneath it. When she caught Najud's surprised gaze, she explained. "I waited until everyone was in the new *kazr*, and took the scarf off, and told them the whole story. I think Dhalmudhr had warned them already, so it wasn't too bad."

"It's time they were told," Najud said, and she nodded.

"Yes, I think so, now that Haraq's on the mend. Oh, I haven't told you. D'ya know how I ended up showing him a cedar tree and a rock?"

"They talked about little else when they got back," Najud said, remembering the chatter.

"Me, I thought it was the slap on the cheek that did it. My hand still stings." She chuckled. "Anyway, he's made himself a little pouch to hold the rock. Says it's a *lud*, that I made him a *lud*. It doesn't work like that, does it?"

Najud was startled. "No, it doesn't. No one can make a *lud*, only find one. Maybe you just happened to find one for him."

"Doesn't seem too likely to me," she said, unconcerned. She topped up the spouted pot and put it on top of the stove to heat for *kassa*. "I thought you had to find your own. That it was between you and the *lud*."

"Yes…" Najud let his voice trail off. "Must be a coincidence."

"Maybe he was just receptive. I had to drain his core to break the hold of the visions—he was just reinforcing the command with his own power. Then I gave it all back, of course."

The description sent an alarm through Najud. "You didn't give him any extra, did you?"

"No, why?" Penrys stared at his face. "What's wrong?"

"I never told you…" he muttered.

"Told me what?" she said, giving him her attention fully, the box of *kassa* forgotten in her hand.

"When you found the captive *bikrajab* back in Neshilik, and me with them, and you restored our power…"

"From my chain, yes." She waited for him to continue.

"When you poured it in, four of them didn't survive, Pen-sha."

In silence she lowered herself onto his bed. There was a look of shock on her face, then it was replaced by outrage. She shielded her mind from him.

"And you were going to tell me this when?" she asked, her voice low but rising.

"There was too much going on at the time." He spread his hands helplessly.

"And afterward? Or the next day? Or week?" Her voice was cold now, and contained.

"Or only after I killed someone else by accident, like Haraq today?"

"It wasn't your fault," he said.

She slashed her hand through the air. "That's not the point. What happened during a battle is one thing. I can live with that, I suppose. I'll have to. But not telling me, that's… that's unthinkable! That's helping it happen again when it could be avoided."

She rose and stood over him. "How can you do that? How can you keep that from me, make that decision for me? What am I, a child?"

He watched despairingly as she turned her back on him and hugged herself. His stomach churned, and he stood up and wrapped his arms around her stiff and angry back.

"I'm sorry, Pen-sha, it was the wrong thing to do. I just didn't want you to be hurt any more."

She was silent, and even with her mind shielded he could feel through her shaking body how she was trying to rein in her emotions. He tried to convey to her the sincerity of his apology. "Please forgive me."

In a serious voice, she finally responded. "You can't be hiding things from me for my own good, Naj-sha. It's not… respectful. It means I can't trust you to tell me the truth. How can we be partners without trust?"

"I know," he murmured into the top of her head. "I'm sorry." *She called me Naj-sha, it'll be all right.* He kept repeating that to himself, part assurance, part wish. He could feel his pounding heart beat begin to slow.

"And it's dangerous. Look what might have happened today."

"Yes," he said. He turned her around and pried the box of *kassa* out of her hand and dropped it on the empty bed. She unfolded her arms to let him do it, and he took advantage of that to hug her again, this time from the front, tightly, as if he had no intention of ever releasing her. He made sure her ear was pressed against his chest.

"I won't do it again," he told her, and hoped the magic that made her knees weak when she heard his deep voice conveyed through his body would still work. "Forgive me?"

She lowered her shield against him and sighed. **As if I have any choice in the matter when you hold me like that.**

CHAPTER 40

"Can't we kill her from a distance? Lay in wait, with bows?"

Penrys broke into the debate wearily, again. "Not unless you can shoot a few miles. That's how far I can sense you, if I look. Or maybe you're thinking to sneak up on her while she's asleep. Through the wolves."

The man who'd made the proposal sat down again.

Dhalmudhr's family had the largest *kazr* in the camp now, and everyone was gathered there, trying to come to some resolution about actions. The smell of leather working still lingered in the air. Three packs along the walls were stuffed with the clothing they'd worked so hard on the day before, as well as the food they were planning to take with them when they left tomorrow, still determined on a rescue.

Penrys was tired, not just from the lack of progress in any sort of feasible plan, but residually, from yesterday's quarrel with Najud. *So easy to damage trust, and so hard to overlook it.*

She forgave him—how could she not? He'd meant well and she knew he was sorry, but she hadn't wanted to face the reality that all men make mistakes, that there was no magic place in the world where two souls have perfect communication and perfect knowledge. Her heart was sore, but it was directed inward rather than at Najud.

Maybe I am a child, without experience. Grow up! He doesn't owe you perfection, and you certainly don't have it to offer, yourself.

She sighed, and caught Najud's worried look. *It's not fair to make him worry about something he couldn't help.* The effect her smile had on him was almost worth the turmoil of the day before—he brightened like a full moon and beamed back at her, and her smile broadened.

Then she noticed the silence in the *kazr* and glanced up at the others. Khizuwi was standing at the front and looking down at her, over the heads of several people. "If the newly betrothed would care to rejoin us…"

She felt the heat in her cheeks, and when she eyed Najud, she saw he was in no better case.

"My apologies, *jarghal*," Najud said. "Happy thoughts."

Khizuwi's mouth quirked. "I understand. Blizzards are always good for marriages and child-making."

Jiqlaraz's stiffened posture caught her eye. *Was this news to him? Didn't his nephew tell him?*

Suddenly Najud's warnings took on an unexpected weight. *There is something very wrong about that man. He can't seriously have expected me to join his… breeding program, can he?*

She shifted uneasily and returned her attention to the discussion.

At the next impasse in the planning, Penrys stood up. "Here's what we can't do. Let's be clear on that so we can concentrate on what's possible."

The side conversations quieted.

"I can't scout to find out where she is, not without being detected. My range is about five miles, but hers must be longer since she reached your clan-kin at the High Pass."

She pointed upward. "That includes flying. So, unless I can sneak in while she's sleeping and attack her from the air before her wolves notice, let's assume we can't sneak up on her or ambush her."

Looking at their outraged expressions, she sighed. "I know you're all fine warriors—this has nothing to do with that."

She let them settle back down. "I think I've heard some good ideas here. There must still be plenty of horses with her, and Bimal's notion of swooping down to round up a herd and forcibly mount all the prisoners has merit. I can even help with that, by weakening any residual *bikraj* power they have so that the illusions are easier to resist."

She left unsaid her fear of what would happen if she drained them and was then killed before she was able to restore them. Their core power, such as it was, should gradually refill, as it did for true wizards, but she wasn't sure it would work that way.

"That means, Bimal, that you might find it harder than usual to function as *dirum*, for a while. I don't know how that works for you…"

She trailed off and looked a question at Khizuwi, who just shrugged in response.

"And there's another possibility. Perhaps I can shield you when you go back and keep her from just controlling you again."

That brought a look of hope to several faces, and she shook her head to discourage them. "There's no way to test that without alerting her. I don't even know if I can shield myself. So if I try that and it fails…"

She glanced at Najud, and saw him straighten up and frown as if he suspected what she would say next.

"Or we could try distracting her. She has a lot to handle, all those animals and people. She lost lots of animals along the way, especially at the beginning, but even now, after all that experience, she lost those horses we found. And you—you escaped her. And she hasn't come after you."

She had their attention. "She's not invincible. She can be killed. And I can give her something else to worry about while the rest of you do a raid through her herds and scoop up the people.

"The *bikrajab* have been learning to shield as a group. If they go with you, that should make it harder for her to recapture anyone, and if you stick together, you might make it out to the gap. And I'll see how well she can manage to attack on two fronts simultaneously."

She sat down and yielded her place as speaker. Najud glared at her and she dropped her eyes, while Khizuwi rose to his feet.

"This is not the way that *bikrajab* deal with a *qahulajti*, when there are people in the way who might be hurt. But there are too few of us…"

Penrys noted his expressionless stare at Jiqlaraz.

"… and even if there were more, this is different sort of *qahulajti*, this chained *bikrajti* girl. I don't know that ten of us would make any difference to her. It may be better to split our forces in this way, to try and save the most lives."

Jiqlaraz rose abruptly and interrupted. "But even if our distinguished *jarghalti* here succeeds in the distraction and escapes herself, what's to prevent this *qahulajti* from pursuing us? We must capture or kill her eventually."

"Capture?" Najud asked, from his seat on the canvas floor.

Jiqlaraz flushed and turned to him. "If possible. By all accounts she is just a youngster, a *yathbantudin*. Perhaps she can be… tamed."

He glanced pointedly at Penrys who stared blandly back, then showed her teeth in a little snarl. "I don't think you'd find that rewarding," she commented.

Jiqlaraz turned away from her.

Khizuwi said, "She hasn't pursued these people from her lost herds. Perhaps, as the *bikrajti* suggests, she has more than she can handle. The blizzard alone must have caused her difficulties, as it did us. Clearly she can't control the weather, too, or we'd have seen sunny days instead."

The subdued chuckle around the room helped ease the tension, and Jiqlaraz sat down again.

Najud rose heavily and joined Khizuwi, in his role as *zarawinnaj* and in the unstated and possibly disputed role as leader of the wizards. Khizuwi's presence at his side muted any issues the wizards might have with that, and Penrys admired the maneuver.

"And so, we have a plan. To go a distance into the valley from the gap, that distance yet to be determined. Penrys to seek out the *qahulajti* and distract her,"—the faint quaver in his voice shook her—"and everyone else to gather people, by force, and tie them to horses, while the *bikrajab* shield them all. Bimal and others will round up horses and bring them to the people. We'll need saddle blankets and girths, clothing, and little else."

He paused. "We'll set up the other three *kazrab* before we go and leave everything else behind. If she catches us, there's nothing we can do, and if she doesn't pursue, we'll need the shelter to treat everyone."

Najud looked over at Penrys, who tried to share her sympathy with him. "This is what we will do."

He turned his attention away from her again. "Now, let's talk about the details."

"You can't protect me from harm," Penrys told Najud, late that evening, in the privacy of their *kazr*, its lowered flap ensuring no interruption. "Not really. No one can."

She lay in his arms in the dark, her back to him.

"It's what I swore to do," he replied eventually, in a low voice.

Silence from him again for a moment, then he gritted out, "I understand the logic of the plan." He was tightly shielded from her, and it dismayed her.

Finally he throttled a cry of frustration. "I didn't expect it to be so hard." He turned her toward him roughly, making his claim on her survival desperately, in the only way he could, and she responded in kind with a fierceness that surprised her.

Afterward, he dropped his shield, and held her, tenderly. *Did I hurt you, Pen-sha?*

Never. You couldn't. But I'm hurting you, going into this fight alone, and I'm sorry for it.

She tried to show him her love for him, how he filled her senses and her heart, but she wasn't sure how much got through. *You're mine as much as I'm yours, Naj-sha, and I want you to be careful tomorrow. It would grieve me beyond telling if any harm came to you.*

She ran her fingers lightly down his chest, marveling as always at the firm male muscles, and he shivered.

"We won't think about it, then," he muttered, leaning over her. "I know of an excellent distraction."

CHAPTER 41

Penrys watched Najud survey his little troop of impromptu warriors at the top of the gap. She closed her eyes to rest them—the day was sunny, and the snow blinding.

The trail broken by the horses when the survivors were discovered was still quite clear and eased the work of the animals, but from there to the gap itself was another three miles, and the residual track through the snow left by the escapees hadn't been as wide.

She reached out into the valley and felt herd animals, and a clear group of people about three miles away, with a faint whisper of more further out. *The first of many, I hope.*

They'd brought every horse they had, tied in long strings behind the ridden ones. The camp was empty, every *kazr* erected, including all four of the big shelters—their fires damped—and the *shabz* still hanging in the rafters of the original three *kazrab*.

This first ten miles and all the preparation had eaten half the morning, but they were ready now. *All except the wizards. They'll never be able to fight her off by themselves.*

Before they left, Penrys had tested the joint shield raised by the other four wizards, with even Munraz helping. It was reasonably made, for so little practice, but she tore through it, as gently as she could, with ease. Privately, she'd told Najud, "You can't rely on it for defense. There are just too few of you. Better use it for stealth." She'd been doubtful it would help even there, but there was no good reason to discourage them.

She took a deep breath now and held it for a moment, then exhaled with a sigh and dismounted.

After leading her horse to the end of Najud's string and tying him on there, she trudged forward through the snow until she reached his leg, and looked up at him briefly.

"The first group is there." She pointed with her entire arm, giving him the direction. "No more than three miles, I think. Ten of them, and plenty of horses nearby. There are others just beyond—I'll have more to tell you once I get into the air."

His hand came down on her shoulder and gripped it, hard, through her sheepskin coat. "Be careful, my heart."

She raised her own gloved hand up to cover his. "And you. Good luck."

With that, she raised her scarf over the lower part of her face and checked that the knitted cap from Neshilik was firmly in place. Then she backed a little distance down the now flattened path between the horses, and took a few running steps to launch into the air, her wings exploding as she invoked them.

She circled the group once, then headed down into the vale.

Once aloft, Penrys quickly outdistanced the riders. She glided over the first cluster of people to confirm them for Najud. *Ten people, where I said. Alive but not moving around much. Horses to the east of them, dozens, about half a mile away.*

For the next hour or so, she continued south further into the vale. Every time she located another bunch, she made sure she circled back within range of Najud to tell him. Altogether she located fewer than fifty people, and there were no groups smaller than six. As she passed overhead, she drained any fragments of wizard power she found, to make it easier to break their holders from the commands imposed upon them, just as she'd done for Bimal, Luram, and Haraq before they started.

Horses were abundant, if the riders with Najud could herd them and keep using them for the rescue. *That's his problem now, not mine. My problem… Where is she?*

She probed everywhere in a five mile circle and found no trace of the girl who'd caused so much grief.

By then, Najud had moved on to the second group she'd identified for him, and she extended her distance from him one final time to its maximum range. *That's all I can find from here. Don't go any further—anyone else will have to take their chances. I'm moving on.*

His reply came back faintly. *No matter what happens, come back to the camp. I'll wait for you there.*

I hear you, Naj-sha.

There was a pause, and at the last moment she heard his *Good hunting, beloved.*

And then he was out of range.

She tried to put him out of her mind and concentrate on what she was seeing. *They must be right—she's staying in this valley for the winter. The snow isn't as deep, and the horses have reached the grass in lots of places, so they've been here a while.*

Miles went by while she shielded herself and scanned for someone else on the ground, someone like her, like the Voice. There was nothing, nothing but the chilly air on her face and the occasional herds below, in the snow. The woods that lined the western edge of the valley were visible to her right, a couple of miles away or so, and they stretched southward before her for miles.

Several animals caught her attention from the same direction, animals new to her. In the instant it took her to realize they must be wolves, she felt her shield blasted away, and a strange mind-voice intruded. *My animals. Mine! You must fight for them.*

Penrys's vision was overlaid with grasslands to the southwest, where she knew there were woods, and in all other directions were fires, the fires she'd seen once in Ellech when an entire grove on a mountain slope burned after a lightning strike.

It's not real. The ground is flat and snowy.

She fought away from the southwestward pull, disoriented. She could hear the roar of the fire approaching, the crack of trees falling, where no trees existed. The hot air around her in all directions except from the southwest made her body disobey her in panic, and she twisted and flailed in the air trying to regain control. All of this took time.

The feel of air rushing up at her penetrated past the struggle into her conscious thoughts.

Which way is up? Where's the ground? I can't see the ground!

Najud stored Penrys's information as it came in and monitored the shield the *bikrajab* were clumsily holding over everyone.

The first group of ten people set the pattern for the rest of them. Dhalmudhr and his companions walked through them and told them, over and over, "Rescue. This is a rescue. We're going to put you on horses and take you away."

Some of the meaning must have penetrated, since everyone stopped and let themselves be moved around. Like Dhalmudhr's people, they were ragged and very lean, but tough. They each had some sort of footwear, but Luram and others supplemented their clothing with gloves and blankets from the packs a couple of the horses carried.

Quick teamwork saw Bimal and Winnajhubr rounding up horses from the nearby herd Penrys had told him about, while Dhalmudhr's people got each person mounted on a led horse, even if all they had was a saddle blanket from the pack frames cinched on and some rope loops for simple stirrups.

They filled an entire string of the led horses this way, not even bothering to untie them first, while Jirkat and Ilzay helped the returning Bimal and Winnajhubr tie the newly retrieved horses into a string to replenish the supply of mounts. A couple of months of unharnessed freedom had taken their toll, but the horses were less energetic in their winter semi-starvation than they might be and most of them submitted to being put to work again. Any horse that wouldn't cooperate was turned loose—speed was paramount.

The first batch of survivors was ready in half an hour and Najud put Haraq and Luram in charge of them. "Back to the gap. Take them all the way into the camp and settle them down."

He watched as they got started, and then led his diminished force on to the next cluster, based on Penrys's reports.

There'd been no interference from the *qahulajti* yet, and Penrys hadn't found her. How long could that last?

It was mid-afternoon by the time they worked with the last group of people Penrys had located before she flew out of range, and there'd been no word from her. She was well overdue.

Najud fought to keep his mind on the people they were rescuing, but he was numb, obsessing over her silence. *She found the qahulajti, clear enough. Must have. Where? Is she alive? Why hasn't she come back?*

This last set of survivors made five batches, and they still had horses in strings ready for more, but no way to find them. They were ten miles from the gap by now, he thought, and ten more to the camp, and these wouldn't get there until well after dark.

Each group had been hastened back with two leaders in charge, and as he sent this last bunch off, he looked around at what was left, mounted and waiting for him—all the *bikrajab*, worn out from concentrating on the continuous shielding, Dhalmudhr and Bimal from the survivors, and the original three Kurighdunaq trackers, who'd refused to leave. He'd tried to send Munraz out with this last group, but Jiqlaraz wouldn't let him go.

"Now what?" he asked them. "Your *zarawinnaj* seeks your advice."

The long day working together had worn off Winnajhubr's youthful shyness. "No word from the *bikrajti?*"

"No." Najud swallowed. They all needed to know details. "Not since the second stop. She was fine when she flew out of range, but that was hours ago."

Khizuwi said, "There's been no sign of the *qahulajti* or her wolves. That can't continue. Do we know where the next people are?"

Najud shook his head. "This is the last she found before going on. There may be more, or not—we don't know." He glanced over at Dhalmudhr, who spread his hands and shrugged.

While Jirkat argued with Dhalmudhr about going on, Najud felt an ominous pressure, as though a thunderstorm were building up rapidly on the horizon, and all of nature noticed and hunkered down. It came from further down the valley, from the south.

He remembered the frisson he'd felt when he'd been tied like a goat in the path of the Voice, in Neshilik, and had felt him approach.

"Run!" he cried, acting on instinct. "Run for the gap. She's coming."

They obeyed him in an instant, all uncertainty banished, and pulled their strings of horses behind them in a clumsy trot through the snow.

Najud and his companions quickly caught up with the latest batch they'd sent ahead and hurried them along.

After a couple of miles, the pressure he felt vanished. He called to Khizuwi, "I think she must be on foot and we've just gotten back out of her range, but I'm sure that was her. No one we've spoken to mentioned her riding—perhaps she doesn't."

Ilzay circled his horse to trot alongside him. "That's not as good as you think. The snow will slow the horses, too—tire them out. Normally they could outpace someone on foot, but now? How far away is she?"

"Penrys thinks she can reach about twenty-five miles," Najud said.

"So. Let's figure it. We're maybe twenty miles from camp, ten to the gap and ten from there. By the time we get to camp, in the evening, the *qahulajti* will have come about ten or twelve miles. We'll gain on her tonight."

"But we have people to see to. We can't go on tomorrow. If she gains on us, if she gets this far… she can reach the camp from here, maybe by tomorrow night."

"If she keeps coming," Khizuwi interjected. "If she's traveling alone or with her wolves, she can be fast. If she decides to bring herds along, it'll be slower. Remember how slowly she traveled when you were tracking her."

Najud's thoughts darkened. *And how fast will she be if she's dragging Penrys captive with her? Penrys must be why she's been slow to come after us.*

"*Zarawinnaj?*" Ilzay said, softly, and Najud recalled himself to his responsibilities.

He looked up at and estimated the amount of daylight remaining. "We've got to hurry, keep 'em at the trot. I want you in front, Ilzay, once it gets dark, to lead us in the moonlight."

"Jirkat, Winnajhubr," he called. "Ride ahead to the camp. Tell them we're coming, as fast as we can. We'll need to pack up and move out tomorrow."

Ilzay objected. "The horses might need a rest before we can run for it, *zarawinnaj.*"

Najud muttered, half to himself. "If she catches us, nothing else is going to matter."

Pen-sha, where are you? You can't just be gone. But you must be, for the qahulajti to be free to come after us.

CHAPTER 42

Najud sat alone in his *kazr* that night, the darkness held at bay by a single hanging lantern.

He'd done what he could to settle the newly rescued survivors. Khizuwi and Jiqlaraz took the lead in trying to help banish the illusions they saw, and several of the first group were surprisingly effective, too. The rest of them had been busy, batch after batch, with feeding, cleaning, clothing, and finally bedding their clan-kin in the four crowded *kazrab* they shared. The old survivors insisted on looking after the new ones, getting them through their first night of freedom.

The camp was quiet now, everyone exhausted.

All through the activity, the people who knew him had been careful to avoid mentioning Penrys. He could feel the bubble of silence that surrounded him wherever he walked, until finally it drove him away into his private darkness.

He sat upright on his own narrow bed, not the one they shared—he wouldn't sleep there. His stomach hurt, and his mouth was dry, but he couldn't make himself get up and dip a cup of water.

At one point, Winnajhubr had told him that Yardiqurti had been found, Khashghuy's betrothed, the one he'd asked his brother to save. "Jirkat was all smiles," Winnajhubr had said. Najud had felt his own face break into an imitation of shared pleasure and watched Winnajhubr falter to a stop as he remembered Penrys's absence.

Remotely Najud was ashamed of his envy, but couldn't muster up the energy to do anything about it. *It's good that not all the news is broken families and death.* But right now he didn't care. A place inside himself, a place of strength and resilience, was damaged. He wanted to push past it, but it was too much trouble. Even lying down to sleep took too much effort.

A knock on the doorframe drew his dull attention. He hadn't lowered the flap, he realized. He couldn't—that meant something else to him, now, with Penrys, and he couldn't stand the reminder.

Khizuwi opened the door and walked in. He carried a covered pot in his gloved hands and set it carefully on the stove. The smell of meat and spices leaked from the lid and Najud's stomach growled.

"I didn't notice you eating," Khizuwi said. He rummaged through the cooking area at the back of the *kazr* and retrieved a wooden plate and a spoon for the pot. He scooped some of the savory stew onto the plate, and laid it on the warm piece of metal that supported the stove.

Then he folded his legs on the carpets in front of the stove. "Come, sit here," he said, patting the rugs beside him. When Najud was slow to respond, he added, "I'm not leaving until you sit down and eat something, so unless you want me snoring in here tonight…"

Despite himself, Najud felt his mouth quirk. He roused himself to stand up, surprised at how stiff his muscles had become. He stumbled to the indicated spot, and lowered himself down.

Khizuwi leaned to his left and pulled a blanket off the bed Najud had just been sitting on. Without getting up, he flung it over the younger man's shoulders, and Najud welcomed its warmth, realizing only then how low he'd let the fire go and how chilled he was.

"Eat," Khizuwi said, without further comment, and Najud obediently leaned forward to pick up the plate and chase the bits of meat with the spoon from his belt pouch. His eyes strayed to the *shabz* hanging from the back rafters.

"Yes, it's *shabz*," Khizuwi said, "Not dry yet, quite, but we're already eating it. Sixty people is a lot to feed, in a hurry."

Najud noticed his eyes sliding sideways to watch his face. His body had seized his attention, telling him how hungry it was.

"That's sixty people we've rescued in a few days," the older man said. "What's that, a quarter of the Kurighdunaq clan? You've saved the clan today."

"It…" Words stuck in Najud's throat, so he coughed and tried again. "It wasn't me. It was…"

"Penrys," Khizuwi said, and Najud flinched from the name.

"Yes, it was, but it was you, too. This was a great thing that was done today. A great thing."

He gave Najud a moment to respond, then continued. "And it will all be wasted if we don't get out of here as soon as possible. Wasted. Do you want that?"

"No!" It tore from his throat, despite himself.

Khizuwi nodded in satisfaction. "Good. Then we need you, all there is of you. We're not done. Grief will have to wait."

He levered himself up and looked down at Najud. "We all grieve for her, but it's the living we must save." He let himself out of the *kazr*, and Najud finished the meal alone.

After he was done, he stepped outside to scour the plate with snow and glanced at the sleeping camp, so much larger with the bulk of the four big *kazrab*, like giant nests holding the hopes of the clan. *Get them out of here, then stop the qahulajti. And if I survive that, then what do I do with the rest of my life?*

He lifted his head and blasted out, as loudly as he could, *Pen-sha!*

Nothing but silence came back to his mind.

"Can't we go any sooner?" Najud's nerves twitched as he listened for the subliminal feel of the *qahulajti*, the storm on their trail.

Everyone except the survivors was meeting in Najud's *kazr*, at mid-day. The *bikrajab* had done all they could to heal the minds of the new batch, and outside this *kazr* there was a whirlwind of activity as they prepared for a multi-day journey.

"You know how far she can compel obedience." Najud had spoken to a woman who'd been at the grandfather *lud* and unable to escape. All of her companions who had fled for half a day from the *qahukajti*'s momentary inattention during the chaos of the summer encampment had been forced back on foot before evening, and she was the only one still alive.

Ilzay stood firm. "Half the grain we carried went to the horses today, and little enough it was, after all the work they did yesterday. We can't expect them to last several days in footing like this—they have to rest today."

"And so do the survivors," Jirkat added. "There are still a dozen, confused by their surroundings, and all the rest need as much food as they can hold, and warm clothing. A lot's been done but..."

"Ilzay," Najud said, "We're depending on her speed from before, when she didn't care about it. If she moved quickly yesterday, she could be here tonight."

Khizuwi's words echoed in his mind. *Wasted.*

Ilzay shook his head. "It doesn't matter, *zarawinnaj.* If she reaches us today, she can reach anyone we send out now or catch them tomorrow if the horses founder. We stand a better chance waiting for morning and getting them truly out of her grasp."

"Them?" Najud asked. "Oh, no. You three are going with them yourselves. That's certain."

Winnajhubr's voice rose in protest. "There won't be anyone to defend you here."

Najud took a breath and stood up. "There are only two things we have to consider—where to send them, and when. The rest of it, who stays and who goes, that's already decided."

Khizuwi nodded from his place, encouragingly.

"We can send them only three places. Khizuwi has suggested the *zudiqazd* of the Umzabul. It's the closest. Jiqlaraz has also offered clan Rashaban. But the *zudiqazd* of the Kurighdunaq isn't much further, taken in a straight line instead of the way we came, and that's where they're going— four to five days, depending on the depth of the snow and the endurance of the horses."

There were protests, but he held up his hand. "All the Kurighdunaq will go together, and that includes the three of you." His eyes sought out Ilzay, Jirkat, and Winnajhubr. "This is the task Umzakhilin laid upon all of us, and you've fulfilled it. Now it's time to bring them home."

He looked at the others. "If we send them anywhere else, she might follow them there, and it's not right that other clans take that risk. And if we send them out into the wild, sooner or later she'll find them, or they'll die."

He settled himself firmly, his feet wide apart. "No, what we have to do is stay and hold her, here. Keep her from following."

Jiqlaraz said, "And if we're not strong enough?"

Najud shook his head. "We're going to have to be. There's no one else."

He looked around the *kazr.* "All right. We strike the *kazrab* at dawn and load the horses. They can eat while they ride. Jirkat, you're in charge."

Khizuwi seemed unperturbed at the prospect of remaining behind. Munraz was both worried and excited, but it was Jiqlaraz's thoughtful look that puzzled Najud, though he could make nothing of it.

It makes no difference what they think, as long as they stick and fight. Besides, I told Pen-sha to come to the camp, no matter what. I can't leave.

CHAPTER 43

Fire and ice. The sensations didn't make any sense to Penrys. Her head pounded, as if it would fall off if she moved, and her right leg screamed and throbbed.

She still saw grasslands in one direction and forest fires from Ellech everywhere else, but there was no sensation of the wizard who had contacted her. She was shielded again.

I'm not dead? How long have I been here?

What's the damage? What's broken?

She lifted a hand and froze in agony the moment her body shifted to compensate. *What's wrong with my leg?*

She couldn't see over the hallucinations. Very, very cautiously she removed her glove and skimmed her fingers slowly down her right leg. The knee was bent awkwardly. Without applying any pressure, she tried to understand the problem by touch alone as she continued down. She had to contort her body to reach that far, and the movement made her break into a sweat.

What is that? Sharp, cold… That's a bone! It's broken through the skin, and I can't see it.

I've got to bind that. I'm going to have to pull the bone back in. How?

She jostled the leg accidentally, and underneath the pain she felt something disturbing—it moved as a unit, not as if it were dangling broken.

It's started to heal this way! I can't fix that, not by myself. How long has it been?

She felt around her with the ungloved hand and discovered she was in a deep pocket of snow, lying on evergreen needles.

I must have fallen through trees into snow. Why hasn't she found me?

The hallucination of fire pushed her again, and her head pounded back.

This time she raised her hand to her head. The knitted cap on her head and the hair around it was matted and stiff, all over.

Blood, dried blood.

She felt all around her head, gently. She couldn't find any surface injury, and her skull felt normal enough.

Must have cracked it, but not completely split it open.

She put her glove back on and lay back, giving herself a little time to recover from the activity that had set everything throbbing. Then she tried to order her thoughts.

Against all odds, I'm not dead yet. I've got to get my mind back before I can do anything else.

She remembered the problem with Haraq. *My own power is reinforcing the hallucinations. How can I stop it? I took Haraq's power into my chain. Can I do that to myself?*

The thought made her shudder, and that triggered pain. She forced herself to calm down and control her reactions.

It would be like cutting off my hand. What if I can't get it back? Will I lose my wizard abilities altogether?

She breathed shallowly. *If I can't break the hallucinations, I'll die anyway—infection, cold, starvation, discovery. Haven't got much to lose by trying.*

It was awkward focusing her perceptions on herself. She sapped her own core strength and, as she did so, the visions weakened. She opened her eyes, and saw the snow in front of her, the surface of it two feet above her, and the sky beyond. Pines swayed overhead—that was a puzzle, but maybe she'd glided towards the woods while she was under attack.

She looked down at her leg and almost wished for the illusions back. Her right calf was rigidly bent at an angle partway down, and an inch of bone stuck out through the leg of her breeches where it changed direction. The blood on it was dried and frozen, as much as the blood on her clothing. *Not just one bone, then, but both of them. Must have hit a branch on the way down. Two branches, considering my head.*

Time to try restoring her power. *Not too much, just what was there before.*

That was an even stranger sensation than draining it, but she felt stronger when she was done. The hallucinations and the compulsion failed to return.

Why didn't she kill me? Couldn't she find me, once I fell? I must have gotten close before she noticed, for me to find her wolves. Maybe the shield is good for stealth, at least.

She felt herself getting sleepy again. *No! Do something about that leg, then get out of here, even if you have to crawl.*

Her sheepskin coat had pockets, deep ones—she could do without her belt. She unfastened the coat and pulled her belt off without moving. She stuffed the pouches that came free into the coat pockets, all except the skin of water which she hung over her neck, after she took a deep swig. Her stomach growled but she ignored it for now.

Next she lifted her tunic and slipped her knife under it to slit through her shirt around the armholes, pulling at the fabric until she could reach it all. Once the sleeves were detached she was able to pull them off by the wrist. If that wasn't enough, she'd cut the rest of the shirt off, too.

With the two ragged sleeves and her belt, she considered the problem. There was no point worrying about whatever infection she'd already been exposed to. What she wanted to do was immobilize the fused ensemble and pad it to protect it from further injury and exposure. Might as well leave it clothed—nothing much she could do about it now, and the boot would help keep her foot from frostbite. At least the toes still moved.

She almost passed out when she sat up. Her head spun and pounded, and the position strained her broken leg. When she was able to see again, she folded the sleeves into pads. Not thick enough.

She cursed, and cut off the rest of the shirt under her tunic. This gave her sufficient material to build up a support around the protruding bone as a foundation for another pad on top. She wrapped her belt around it twice, as much as it would go, and hoped the whole thing would hold well enough that she could crawl out of her snow hole. She couldn't think of anything as ambitious as standing on one leg until she could find a stick to lean on. If then.

Now what? What's the plan?

She knew what part of it was—get back to the camp somehow.

Penrys sat in the snow with her back supported by the trunk of a small pine on the edge of the woods, and reconsidered. She was only five or six yards from the pit she'd made in the snow, and her trail crawling here was broad. What scared her was that she'd passed out twice in the process.

Won't get far this way.

She giggled at the thought, and that scared her more. *Infection, and fever. Well, that'll take a while to kill me. What's the distance to the camp? Can't walk it.*

I've got to be at least twenty or thirty miles from the gap.

She couldn't dodge it any more—she had to know where the girl was. She dropped her shield and scanned as widely as she could reach. No girl, no wolves. No people, either. Plenty of herds, though.

Could she ride? She thought about that for a while. Her leg would be agony, dangling down a horse's side, and mounting would be... a challenge. But even if she found a suitable stick, walking would be just as bad, and much slower. Too slow.

The trees around her were a small cluster of outliers from the real woods which started a hundred yards to the west. Just a little further, and she would have fallen into the mass of trees and broken her neck, instead of a encountering a mix of trees and snow. She could see the broken branches of the tree that she must have hit.

Lucky. I was very lucky.

She glanced down at her bundled calf, at the leg stretched out before her at its sickening angle, and snorted. *Some luck.*

I wonder if the rescue succeeded.

She shied away from thoughts of Najud. She thought of the camp, instead—that was her goal. She had to get back. If she focused on Najud, who must be thinking her dead, it just weakened her.

The notion of flying kept recurring—such a quick way of covering the distance. But she couldn't launch standing still, she had to run, so that was impossible.

She was afraid to check her wings to see if they were damaged. They were flesh, after a fashion—they could bleed and feel injury—but she couldn't sense them unless she invoked them. If they were badly hurt, the additional pain might be enough to stop her altogether. *And then what would I do? Leave well enough alone.*

I'll die before the wings do. Despite her situation, she cocked her head and considered. *What'll happen then? Do the wings come out when I'm dead or remain... wherever they are when I'm not using them?*

She visualized someone someday stumbling across a few bones, an ugly chain, and a pair of crumpled wings. Maybe they'd be bones by then, too, or a pile of whatever's inside them. She mused over the possibilities until her head tilted and she forced herself upright again.

Stop that!

Too many tasks to consider, and she had to focus or she'd paralyze herself.

All right. No girl and no wolves. Good. Horses in range. Good. Seems simple enough. Maybe forty miles to camp. No problem—do it in a day.

She thought about trotting bareback, with that leg, and shuddered, and then she glanced at the sky. *Two days? How long have I been out? It's afternoon, but it's not the same day.*

Her bladder hadn't held. She'd cleaned up with snow, but the evidence was clear that it was more than a day.

She remembered the girl's voice—she'd wanted to fight for her herds. Maybe she'd missed Penrys when she fell out of the sky and knocked herself out, and was still around, or maybe she'd gone north to get her flock of people back. *And I've lost at least a day. If I make it back to the camp, what will I find?*

She savagely dismissed the vision of torn *kazrab* and dead bodies, and began calling with her mind for horses.

CHAPTER 44

The little herd of five horses was just what she wanted. They looked at home in the snow, shaggy and alert, visibly thinner with the loss of some of their autumn fat. Best of all, they were short, though still too tall for Penrys to mount easily.

She liked the look of a leopard-spotted mare—the brown dapples on the cream coat matched the bold temperament she sensed from her.

Penrys had never tried using her mind on animals directly, until the experiments she'd done recently—it had never been necessary—and she disliked the compulsions that the girl had used. Was there a better way?

Come, Leopard-cat. Come help me. It was a continuation of the call that had brought them here out of curiosity.

The summoned mare took a few shuffling steps forward in the snow while the rest hung back. Penrys held out her bare hand for the mare to sniff, then pulled it back gradually to bring her nearer after it, until the long mane near the shoulder was within reach.

"There, there," she crooned to keep the mare calm. "Come on, lie down here." She tugged on the mane to encourage her.

This was much more alarming to the horse, so she continued to speak soothingly while trying to show the horse mental pictures of lying down, secure in her herd, just to the right of Penrys.

Eventually the mare folded her knees next to Penrys, while the other four horses looked on. "That's a girl, everything's fine. You just stay right there."

She rolled left and swung her right leg over the horse's back, and almost blacked out as it touched the ground on the other side. Her hands gripped the mane above the shoulder, and the mare lurched upright with her, and then spun and shook her off onto her bad leg.

❧

Warm breath and tickling whiskers on her neck woke Penrys.

She clenched her teeth and held back a scream as the red-hot pain in her leg reminded her of what had happened. Her breath came short and quick until she could suppress her reaction a little.

The horses had stayed, and the little leopard-spotted mare was nuzzling Penrys curiously.

Let's try again.

She rolled over on her left side and, when she'd recovered from the movement, she repeated her invitation to lie down, and the mare cooperated.

One more time.

She swung the bad leg over more cautiously and took a good grip on the mane. This time, when the mare pushed herself up, she seemed less alarmed by the peculiar method the rider had chosen for mounting, and didn't try to toss her off.

Penrys contented herself with sitting still, her head bowed until her right leg had reached some point of relative equilibrium of pain. When that was over, she felt weakened but elated.

I've got a horse. I can move.

She used her knees and weight to guide the horse, and turned her toward her little herd.

Maybe the girl couldn't find me, unconscious, but that's changed. Maybe I should become a horse, instead.

She sampled the minds of her new companions and built herself a persona. Not a boss mare, no, just an ordinary horse, not worthy of a second glance. One with the herd.

She kept them headed north at a brisk walk, the fastest pace she could handle. They wanted to graze as they went, but she pushed them.

Whenever she dozed, she found them stopped when she woke, pawing through the snow for grass. She started singing to them, to keep herself awake and entertained—simple songs out of Ellech, which were all she knew. She made up new ones, with nonsense words and silly choruses, anything to keep her going.

She ate half the food she had with her, a few bits of not-yet-dried *shabz*. When she ran out of the water in the skin slung over her neck, she had to dismount by pulling her right leg over and dropping onto her left to balance, leaning against the horse, while she scooped snow into the skin to melt, and took advantage of the support to relieve her bladder. The mare lay down for her to ease the remount, as if she'd done it all her life, and Penrys rubbed a handful of snow on her face to stay awake as they ambled forward.

The cloudless night, when it came, changed nothing. It was colder, but she steered the herd north by the stars.

When she woke up, on horseback, for the last time, the false-dawn was just beginning to show in the east. The horses were stopped and drowsing, standing.

She swung her bad leg over one more time and, once she'd gotten her balance, she lowered herself all the way down, in the trampled snow, and wrapped her coat around herself to sleep.

"Get 'em mounted, Ilzay. Hurry up."

Najud tried to hasten the survivors out of the camp. Only two *kazrab* remained in the early morning light, his own and Jiqlaraz's. Twenty horses were left for riding and pack-string, and all the rest were lined up on the trail with sixty people and more than ninety horses.

Jirkat trotted back along the whole length of the mounted survivors to Najud who was overseeing the last string, and he brought Haraq with him.

Najud ignored Haraq and addressed himself to Jirkat. "Get going. You can tidy it up later. I can feel her, I tell you. Don't stop for anything except night camps."

Ever since dawn he had sensed that same thunderstorm on the horizon feeling that had so spooked him two days ago. If they moved out in a hurry, they ought to be able to stay out of reach, but they had to get started.

Ilzay called over to him. "That's the last one. We're done." He trotted over to join Jirkat and looked curiously at Haraq.

"We're ready, *zarawinnaj*," Jirkat said. "Ilzay's going to take the lead, and I've come back to steady the rear. But Haraq here…"

"I'm staying," Haraq interrupted. "I've already told my sister."

Ilzay just shook his head, patently leaving it for Najud to sort out, and trotted up the line. Jirkat took up his position at the back of the column.

"You can't stay," Najud told Haraq. "We're all *bikrajab*."

"And you don't think that's going to make any difference, do you?" Haraq said.

Najud grimaced at the bald truth.

"Besides, you're going to need another good archer," Haraq said.

"A lot of good that'll do if you can't lift a hand against her," Najud muttered. "This is madness—go with them."

"No, *lij*. I would dishonor my *lud*."

That stopped Najud. He understood it. Haraq felt he needed to live up to the perception that helped him break free of the *qahulajti*. And it was also partly for Penrys.

"But she's… dead." *Probably.*

"Doesn't matter, *bikraj*." Haraq dismounted and began stripping the simplified tack from his horse.

Khizuwi had observed the conversation from a distance, and he shrugged when Najud caught his eye.

Najud turned without further comment and watched the cavalcade leave. All the Kurighdunaq had been freed of their compulsions, and survival now was a matter of luck and sufficient time. If they ran short of food, well, there were horses to spare.

The last of the grain they took with them would be handed out tonight when they stopped, to hearten the beasts for the remainder of the journey. Jirkat understood how to switch the lead horses out frequently while breaking through the virgin snow to give them each a rest.

The forward impulse of the column finally traveled to the rear where Jirkat waited, and then they jerked into motion, too.

Najud looked around at what remained—three strange *bikrajab* and himself, and one foolhardy Kurighdunaq survivor, too stubborn to dissuade—and he shook his head. They should all be leaving with the others, if it weren't necessary to keep the *qahulajti* from following. The problem was, you could keep ahead of her on a horse, but you couldn't rearrange all the rest of the people in the area just to avoid her. She had to be stopped.

Jiqlaraz strolled over with Munraz. "When do you think the attack will come?"

"I think she's probably in range now, or almost," Najud said. "But that doesn't mean she'll strike from there. If that's twenty-five miles, and she prefers to wait until she gets here, why she's still fifteen miles from the gap and we won't see her until tomorrow. If not," he shrugged, "she could start now."

"You mean we'll have to wait on guard all day?" Munraz said.

"And night, too, *nal-jarghal*," Khizuwi said, as he walked up. "A man could lose his balance, waiting like that.

Haraq joined them. "Then let's take the time to see if we can better our defenses. Maybe you can't hold her off of us," he nodded at the rest of them, "but if you can, I want to choose the ground we attack from."

Najud shrugged. "Might as well. Not a lot else we can do."

CHAPTER 45

By mid-morning, Penrys was blearily awake again, and the herd was still keeping her company. Once again, the leopard-spotted mare cooperated to let her mount from the ground, and Penrys pushed the whole herd forward at a brisk walk.

Whenever her head nodded, she started talking to the horses again, telling them everything that came into her head. Sometimes she startled herself awake, hearing words from her mouth that made no sense to her, babbling silly little songs.

When she bobbed awake around mid-day, she thought her horse felt tired. "Leopard cat, kitty-cat, I'm sorry. I'll find someone else to ride, one of your friends."

She slipped off the mare and called a dun over, his back stripe prominent and echoed in the thinner stripes on his rear legs. She got the idea across to him easily, now that she was practiced in it, and he lurched up with her on top.

"That's a good boy, my Dundun, Dunsiedun. You just keep right on going north there."

When she blinked again, it was mid-afternoon and everyone had their head down, looking for grass. "No, no, that won't do. Tell you what, I'll eat the rest of my food and then we'll both go without. How's that?"

She demonstrated and let the empty pouch fall behind her, and they all moved on. After a while, her first horse sidled over, curious about her non-stop talking. When the mare bumped the right side of her mount, Penrys caught the bad leg between them and screamed herself lucid.

The horses bolted a few steps in surprise but she managed to hold on, and gradually the herd reassembled.

Penrys trembled on top of the dun, bathed in sweat. She was alarmed to find her coat was off, held to the horse only by her seat, but she wasn't cold. She must have taken it off, but the snow wasn't melting, it wasn't actually warm.

What if she'd lost the coat? She'd need it later, after the fever receded. There was nothing to tie it on with, so she shrugged her arms back into the sleeves. Then she leaned to the right and touched her leg below the knee. Dull fire came back.

This is… not good. I'm getting worse, not better. Easy pickings if the girl finds me.

She pushed her mount to the fore in an effort to get them all moving persistently. There were lines in the snow ahead of her. Tracks! The snow was too deep to actually see a print, but one looked like it might be human, and there were several others, all the same. Wolves?

It's her! How long ago? Am I too late?

What's happened at the camp?

Thoughts of catching up occupied her, and when she crossed a broad trail of many horses, she thought they must be part of Najud's rescue, and she cheered.

"Hooray for us. He got them!"

She might not be very far away. Don't forget—you're just another horse.

She managed to pin that thought in her wandering mind. Every time she woke up, the whole long afternoon, she explained to her horse.

"Dunsiedun, now remember, I'm just one of your mares. Just a boring old bay. Well, no, why can't I be a blue roan? Somethin' interesting?" She swayed with her horse as he walked, and the stars overhead bobbed with her.

Nighttime already? Well that's no reason to stop.

The trail before her couldn't be clearer, trampled in the snow.

"Come on, Cat, let's show them how to walk uphill."

She thought she'd been riding with these horses for years. Her mind had become adept at shying away from anything that might distract her, like the camp in ruins, or Najud dead, or the wrongness in her right leg.

When the sun rose at last, she saw the gap a few miles ahead of her, at the top of the rise.

And when she reached out, she found the girl was there, on the other side, and her shields snapped down.

"Just a shaggy old bay horse, don't pay me no attention. Me and m'mares, we're just walking along." She shivered, and held her coat tight around her.

Gotta catch her before she reaches the camp. Her walking, and me walking, and her never looking back to see anything but horses.

Najud rose from his sleepless bed, the narrow one he'd never shared. The *bikrajab* had divided the watch all day long among the three seniors. They'd all come to feel the foreboding that Najud did, the pressure from the west that was slowly approaching.

We're well within her reach, even if she's not within mine. Why hasn't she attacked?

At least one *bikraj* had shielded the five of them all day and through the night. The practice was improving their skill at working together, and even the *nal-jarghal* was holding his own at it. Najud was glad, now, that Munraz had stayed—his young presence had made everyone else work harder at maintaining good cheer, to give him a model to follow.

The wait was exhausting. They couldn't keep a state of heightened tension all day long without cost. In the morning, when the survivors had made it past the limits of his ability to detect them, he'd settled down into acceptance of the fight ahead of him, one he hadn't expected to survive. But then it didn't come.

They snatched a bite to eat at mid-day, and it didn't come.

In the long sunny afternoon they sharpened blades and arrow points. Only Haraq and Munraz had bows, but all the *bikrajab* had *khashab*, the curved swords of the Zannib-*hubr*, even Haraq—a gift from Winnajhubr. It wasn't a physical fight they expected, though if the *qahulajti* brought her wolves or other animals, they had to be ready.

So the rasping of stones on metal kept them company in the afternoon, but the attack didn't come.

They'd tried not to lower their guard when they ate their flavorless food at night, all their attention outward. At last they'd retired to their separate *kazrab* and traded off the shielding work for the night.

Now Najud belted on his *khash* and made his stealthy way to the doorframe, trying not to wake Haraq, curled in his blankets on the rugs. No one slept in Penrys's bed—it was never discussed. Najud had dropped the curtain on it, as if she were still there.

As he reached the door, Haraq's voice lifted quietly. "Is it time, *bikraj?*"

"Not yet," Najud muttered, and he stepped out into the false-dawn.

He turned west and strained his senses. There it was, the gathered storm, stronger now. She was still coming.

Behind him the tip of the sun cleared the horizon and his long shadow stretched before him. He heard Haraq open the door behind him.

Give them back. They're mine.

The force of it in his mind drove him to his knees and he couldn't speak. Haraq took one startled look at him and ran for the other *kazr*.

I've been here before.

It felt like an old, stale thought to Penrys, one she'd been chewing on for a while. She pushed her leopard-spotted mare back into her fast walk and checked that the other horses were still with her, before she hauled the thought out again and examined it.

Then she lifted her head. The trampled trail was broad before her—many horses had passed. The slope of the ground was downhill. This must be the last stretch, before the camp.

Her litany of "I'm just a horse" had been interrupted.

Where is she?

Her leg still hurt, not so harshly any more, but with an ominous dull feel that terrified her. She'd rather the sharp agony—at least that meant it was still alive, still part of her.

She wiped the sweat off her face with a gloved hand and scanned toward the rising sun. *There she is. No shield. What's she doing?*

She reached out further and felt no one. *Am I out of reach of the camp, still, or are they gone? Or...*

No. She would not contemplate the other alternative. She must still be out of range, with the girl between them. *Be my anvil, Naj-sha, I'm tired of chasing her. I'll be the hammer.*

CHAPTER 46

Najud pushed back against the force that questioned him and staggered to his feet. He couldn't reach through his shield to alert the others, but he saw them run from their *kazr* in haphazard clothing, armed and headed for their predetermined positions.

Haraq pushed by him again, into the *kazr*, and emerged seconds later with his bow and *khash*, and swept towards the woods where he hoped to be concealed behind the *qahulajti* when she finally arrived.

If she ever did. It was all Najud could do to stand upright, despite the shields reinforced by all four *bikrajab*, and she must be miles away. He made sure that Haraq stayed protected, but this couldn't last for long.

Where are they?

It was like standing in front of the war horns when they blasted out a challenge. He was only surprised his hair didn't blow back. How far away was she?

He scanned, with a faint hope of finding Penrys with her, captive but alive, but the girl was out of range, and Penrys was surely gone.

It was time for the plan. He braced himself, since she seemed to have settled upon him as the leader.

Come and talk to us.

He felt an inarticulate snort of surprise, as if a horse had suddenly spoken to her.

I can understand you. You're not like the others.

Her attention turned from him for a moment. He could hear the horses a couple of hundred yards away whinnying, and then a general probing test against their united shield.

You're a different kind, like goats and sheep. Stay. I'll retrieve the rest of the herds you stole, and bring you back with us. It's a good valley, good for the flocks.

Najud swallowed. This was like throwing out a net for bait fish and finding a toothy monster bigger than your boat, in that moment before it realized it could tear apart the net, and the boat, too.

Come and talk to us. We can tell you things you want to know.

She ignored the invitation. The concept of learning things from her beasts must be too strange for her.

Where are they? This time the push was stronger, and Najud swayed as if it were a physical wind. Was this what Penrys would have been like, if she'd ever probed him?

Time for the bait. *Behind us, lijti. They're behind us. We can show you the way.*

That pleased her, he could tell, and for a moment he was ashamed of fooling someone so naive, but he couldn't spare pity for anything so deadly.

The pressure on him lessened, and she was silent in his mind. He waited for several minutes, then moved to the center of the camp, to the deeply flattened circles of bare grass where the big *kazrab* had been.

He called out, "She's stopped, for now. I think she's going to come here directly, but she's further away than I can reach, still."

One by one, they left their positions and returned, all except for Haraq. Najud knew where to look and felt his mind, but it was calm and quiet, almost like one of the trees he hid with. *Better to let him stay there, if he wishes. I can barely feel him, and I know where he is.*

The girl's unshielded mind-speech reached Penrys, but she couldn't hear the replies.

The camp must still be there. They should have left!

Nothing seemed real to her, not the endless snow and trees, not the shifting of her body as the horse moved under her, not the emptiness of her stomach and the heat of her flesh, melting off her like butter. Her coat was gone and she didn't miss it.

"Sorry, kit-cat, little leopard—it's now or never."

She urged the mare into the running walk that so many of these shaggy horses could do. *It's not right—she's starving, too. But I have to get there, I have to!*

The rest of the herd joined in, and she extended her shield over them, thinking of the horse that had trampled Umzakhilin. *None of my horses will do that, not while I'm still alive. I won't let that happen to them. They're my horses, my herd.*

Not hers. Mine.

She shook her head to try and clear her thoughts. She felt the girl, not far ahead of her, and her wolves with her.

It wasn't long before Najud could feel the *qahulajti* directly. "She's coming. Half an hour?"

The pressure from her hadn't strengthened so much as broadened, until she seemed inescapable, like a storm. All the *bikrajab* could feel it, and Najud's audience in the center of the camp barely moved in acknowledgment of his announcement.

"Wish she'd just get here and finish it," Munraz muttered.

Najud spared a thought for Haraq. He believed he'd escaped notice and might continue to do so, focused as the *qahulajti* had seemed to be on the *bikrajab*. He wished him well. Maybe someone would survive to tell the tale.

The survivors by now would be out of range, and he was sure Jirkat could be trusted to keep them moving. The snow, however, would give them away. Once the little barrier of this camp had been swept aside, it would be easy for her to follow the track. All that work for nothing. And Pen-sha.

His stomach clenched. *No! There are four of us. We can do this.*

"Back to your spots and wait. Watch for the wolves, but try to wait for her to appear before killing any of them. She has to get within our reach first."

He watched them find their positions and vanish, leaving him alone in the center of the camp, like the bait he was.

Seized by impulse, he made a show of pawing the snow with his foot and baa'ed loudly, like a sheep.

The chuckles from the hidden men around him made him smile in return.

If I die here, I die. Better than being captured. And maybe snow will hide the trail of the survivors. Anything could happen.

The wolves found him first.

They paced into the camp from the west, seven of them, and Najud moved to attract and hold their attention, worried about them scenting out the others. They behaved more like dogs, sniffing him and growling but not attacking.

Trained them, did you? Didn't want them tearing up your herds, eh?

He could feel the fear sweat breaking out—this many wolves could take down a man in moments, even with a *khash*. The leader, a dark male, snarled at him but left him alone.

Can't let them find the others.

"Can you hear me?" he called out, but the answer came back in his mind.

Be quiet. I am here.

His tongue froze, and he stood, immobilized, as she strode into the camp.

At first she seemed to him almost like a small bear. She was dressed in skins, crudely pieced together, all except her boots which looked like typical Zannib summer boots, worn and falling apart. She wore a belt and on it was a sheathed knife, the gleam of the metal on the hilt a shocking bit of civilization.

There was the chain, the chain he was so familiar with, but on an alien neck, and the face… It was expressionless. He had to look past the deadness of the face to see how young she was, and foreign. He'd never seen freckles in quantity before, and light-brown hair was very strange, outside of travelers at the ports. The hair was matted and hacked unevenly to keep it off of her face.

He thought her skin might have been pale, but it was so uniformly coated in grease and ingrained dirt that he couldn't tell.

His tongue wouldn't work, and so he continued in mind-speech.

Welcome to our camp.

She stared at him, before replying, as if puzzled by a talking animal.

Do you eat meat, like the others? My friends won't like that.

Turning her head casually, she sent her wolves to the hiding spots of the other three *bikrajab*. *Come out where I can see you.*

Najud avoided thinking of Haraq while he heard Jiqlaraz and Munraz come up on him from behind.

Khizuwi's eyes flickered to Najud, when he staggered to his side, but he didn't speak. Perhaps, like Najud, he couldn't.

It puzzled him that she didn't make them drop their weapons— Munraz's bow and all the *khashab*. *Doesn't she recognize what they are?*

You look like the others. Why do you feel different?

Najud tried to explain. He needed a distraction to make her free them. *We're bikrajab. You are, too.*

She backed away in revulsion. Najud could see it in her mind, and her body confirmed it, but only a wrinkled nose on her face echoed the emotion.

You're animals. I'm nothing like you.

And she broke their pitiful shield to show them the truth of her claim.

CHAPTER 47

The savage girl's words expanded to fill his mind.

Where are the rest of my herds? Show me.

It was so strong, it actually inhibited his ability to reply. She must have sensed it, for she backed off the pressure slightly and issued the command again.

Clearly she spoke to all of them, not just Najud, because Jiqlaraz answered her. *East and north, back the way you came, lijti.*

Najud felt his hackles rise. Any man could succumb, but to give her a term of respect?

In that instant, a wolf yipped behind her, and the *qahulajti* turned around. A second arrow appeared in the wolf's chest, and he fell. The girl howled at the death.

It was the first sound Najud had heard from her.

With a sweeping gesture of her arm, the girl flung the remaining wolves out to seek their target and followed them. Two more sprouted arrows, one after the other.

Najud pulled at her control but couldn't free himself. It took little of her attention to pin him down, just a nuisance while she dealt with other problems.

Then the *qahulajti* stopped suddenly, turned to face the trail, and screamed.

Najud felt the draining of her power and regained his independence. He knew that somehow, impossibly, it must be Penrys, but there were more urgent dangers to deal with. "The wolves," he shouted to the others, "Kill the wolves."

He heard the twang of an arrow behind him from Munraz's bow, and then he drew his own *khash* and finished off a wounded one. In a few minutes, all the wolves were dead or dying. Jiqlaraz nursed a bite on an incautious hand, but the rest were unbloodied.

The *qahulajti* stood immobilized as he had been, facing upslope to the west, and all of them crept around her cautiously, *khash* in hand. Haraq emerged from the trees with an arrow nocked to his bow, ready to shoot.

The girl ignored them all, and trembled.

Najud's ears finally registered the sound of hooves in snow, and five horses ambled into the camp.

His broad welcoming smile faded as he took in the sight. Something rode the exhausted leopard-spotted mare, and it moved, but his eyes failed to recognize the details. The face was hardly visible through the hair glued onto it, and he couldn't tell the knitted cap from the hair. The chain—he could see the chain—and his faltering smile returned, but the rider had no glance for anyone but the *qahulajti*.

She walked her horse up to the girl and stopped. "No, they're mine." Her voice was hoarse, barely a whisper.

Penrys's horse jolted at the howling of the wolves, and the commotion woke her to action.

She scanned and found them all—the girl, the wolves, fighting and dying, and Najud and the others, captive. The camp's horses were untouched.

There was no time for finesse, and she had nothing left in her but brute force, anyway. She drained the girl's core of power into her chain, all of it, and heard her scream. She grinned tightly at the sound.

She returned a tiny trickle, enough to let her mind-speak, and no more, and then she spoke to her. *Wait for me. We will discuss this issue of you and your herds.*

One more push. "Come on, my dearie, good little horse. We're almost there, and then we can rest."

It seemed forever before she took the last bend around the old pine, and there they were. The blood of the wolves was vivid on the snow. She'd felt them die and felt a distant regret, but it had to be done.

When she stopped in front of the girl, she swayed a moment and then reinforced her whispered claim with her mind. *My herds, all of these.*

The girl refused to agree. *What did you do? Who are you?*

Penrys saw her youth, vividly. *I'm you. Another version. It doesn't have to be this way.*

She scanned her as deeply as she could, clumsy in her weariness. There were no answers there. Her skills were exactly what you could expect—animals and survival. She was curious—Penrys could feel that—but damaged, so damaged.

Do you have a name? Perceiving the girl's confusion, she offered, *Shall I give you one?*

What's that mean?

M'name's Penrys. Someone gave me that name, too, when I first woke up.

There was no reply for a moment. *No one was there, when I first woke up.* This was followed by images of the wolves who'd found her and fed her, before she weakened beyond recovery. Her wolf family, now dead.

I'll call you Vylkerri, to honor a man I respect.

There was no reaction from the girl. *Too little, too late. She's not really quite human any more.*

Penrys could feel the simmering, frustrated rage, powerless but undiminished. *I can't just keep her drained forever. Too tired. It'll have to do for now.*

She swayed again in her saddle, and looked down at Najud. There seemed to be a light shining behind him, and he looked worried. "I came back to the camp, like you said."

Her lips were dry and she moistened them. "She'll be all right until the power comes back. Don't know how long." A thought furrowed her brow. "Look after the horses, will ya? They took real good care of me. They're awful tired."

The thought of dismounting scared her, distantly. "You just let me stay here for a while, Naj-sha. I'll be better when I wake up."

Behind him, Najud heard Khizuwi take charge. "Bind the *qahulajti*, Jiqlaraz. Munraz, you help him."

He couldn't move for a moment. Pen-sha was alive, but could he keep her that way? His eye traveled down to her right leg, and his skin chilled when he saw the angle made by her calf.

"Haraq, I need your help." He walked around to the other side of her horse and she turned her head to track him, blearily.

"Don't you worry," he told her, his voice as calm as he could make it. "We'll take good care of you. You'll be fine in no time."

She grabbed his shoulder and repeated her warning. "You can still see the core power of a wizard, yes? Like that one?" She cocked her head at the captive girl. "You've got to watch her while I take a little nap. It's gonna come back, her power, and I'm gonna have to drain it again, but I need a little rest right now, m'mind can't focus on it…"

"Shush, now, Pen-sha. I'll take care of it, you can count on me. If there's anything I can't handle I'll wake you up."

She looked as if she hadn't slept in days. There were lines in her face, under all the dirt. Up close, it looked like dried blood.

"And m'horses… I asked a lot of them and they kept me company."

The hoarseness of her voice as she muttered her urgent messages thickened his throat.

Behind him, he heard Munraz asking Haraq quietly, "Why is she so worried about the horses?"

"They're like warriors who've fought together. She wants to make sure they're taken care of, like any good commander. People who've been fighting a long time, they get like that."

"I promise, Pen-sha," Najud said. "Now you be quiet. We're going to take you off your horse."

She shook her head. "Better if I do it m'self." She leaned forward until she was almost flat along the horse's neck, and then dragged her right leg over.

Najud stood behind her to support her, but she managed to land on her one good leg before he scooped her up and carried her away, with Haraq in his wake.

His eye took in the *qahulajti*, and Jiqlaraz standing over her. Her hands and feet were bound and her knife had been removed. Najud wondered if he could see her core power, as he'd told Penrys. He'd done that with the Rasesni mages.

He looked at her now, and it was plain to him. Where Penrys was bright, this girl was dim, but it was true—the power would return. If they couldn't wake Penrys when that happened, they'd have to kill their captive.

Khizuwi walked out of Jiqlaraz's *kazr* with a piece of canvas and a leather satchel, and he laid the canvas on the bare grass where one of the big *kazrab* had been.

"Lay her here, *zarawinnaj*." He raised his voice. "Munraz, take the pot in your *kazr* and add more water to it, and heat it until it boils. While that's happening, find Najud's warm water and some rags and bring all that here."

Haraq helped Najud lay Penrys down on the canvas in all her dirt. She was still conscious but drifting off.

Najud masked his fear and smiled down at her. "We're going to get you clean, Pen-sha, and take a look. Then we'll fix you up."

A grimace crossed her face. "Don't think so. Leg's... bad. Sorry, Naj-sha."

He patted her cheek. "You let me worry about that. Now be quiet."

Her eyelids drooped, and then reopened. "Did it work?"

"What, the rescue? We sent almost sixty people back to Umzakhilin yesterday."

A faint smile flickered on her lips, and this time her eyes stayed closed.

CHAPTER 48

All attention now focused on Penrys's leg.

They'd cut off her clothing and washed her roughly before draping a blanket over most of her to give her some warmth. Khizuwi had shooed Najud away from his examination of the leg, and he busied himself with washing her face and hands thoroughly, and soaking all of the blood out of her hair. They never did find the skull fracture that had generated the blood, but since it seemed to have healed cleanly, they ignored it. She slept unmoving through all the attention, though she whined when Khizuwi poked at her leg.

"Come look," Khizuwi finally said.

Najud crouched down where Khizuwi pointed, and swallowed. It had taken a while to soak the cloth padding off of the injury, and for the first time he saw it clearly.

"The bones are firmly set," Khizuwi said. "That doesn't normally happen in just four days but..." He shrugged. "You can smell infection, but the blood is still reaching her foot—that's a good thing."

He looked Najud in the face. "We have three choices, and you're going to have to make one for her. We can just clean it up and leave it like this, maybe cut the bone down even with the skin. I don't advise it—the infection is hiding inside and will probably get worse. Just because she can heal flesh and bone quickly doesn't mean she can't be killed by fever. And, besides, she would be badly crippled the rest of her life, if she survives."

Najud nodded.

"Then there's the possibility of just taking the leg off, below the knee." Khizuwi's voice was calm and rational. "I saw her fingers, how they grew back. Can she grow a leg?"

"I don't know," Najud said. "She said the fingers were the first time she'd actually lost something, instead of more ordinary injuries."

"So. The good part about this choice is that it would probably stop the infection and she would live. The bad part is that it would be permanent, at least for everyone else, and maybe her, too. No coming back from that decision."

"And the third choice?"

"The third choice is more complicated." He peered at Najud's face as if to gauge his reaction. "We break her leg again, both bones. Then we cut into it and find the pockets of infection and kill those. And then we let it heal normally."

Najud could feel the blood draining from his face.

"Would that work?"

"Well, if we cut one of the tubes that carries blood, we might kill her. If we don't get all the infection, we might still have to cut it off. But if the shock didn't kill her, it would probably heal cleanly. It would take the longest to recover from—we'd have to hold her flat on her back until the bones set firmly and the cuts closed."

"But in her case, that might not be too long—maybe a few days instead of weeks." Najud could see the logic of it, and it gave her the most certainty of a complete recovery.

Then a thought struck him. "There's no way to soften the pain for her."

Khizuwi lifted an eyebrow, and Najud explained. "You might not remember from the drinking at the *durmiqa bul*, but mead doesn't work on her for long. Nothing does."

"That's... unfortunate. We'll have to tie her down, then. Can you explain it to her? It'll take a while to prepare, and we have to be ready to cut it off if something goes wrong, to stop the bleeding."

Najud raised his head. Haraq was just returning from leading Penrys's horses to the camp's herd and settling them down with a few handfuls of the remaining grain. Munraz hovered around, waiting for more orders from Khizuwi, and Jiqlaraz... Jiqlaraz was crouched on the ground, talking to the *qahulajti*.

Najud stood up and watched him. When he scanned the girl, he could see her core power had brightened. She didn't speak, but that didn't seem to be stopping Jiqlaraz's one-sided conversation.

Khizuwi followed his gaze and nodded grimly. "We'll deal with that, after. One thing at a time."

"Munraz," he called. "I need you to bring me some things. You, too, Haraq."

A finger stroking her cheek woke Penrys. She was lying on the ground and the first thing she noticed was that she felt… clean. It was wonderful.

Pen-sha, wake up.

She smiled to hear Najud's voice in her mind. *Hmm?*

A savory smell passed beneath her nose, and she opened her eyes. Najud sat on the ground next to her holding a bowl of broth. "Haraq is going to prop you up and I'm going to give you as much of this as you can hold."

"Sounds good." She yawned and tried to push herself up with her arms, but strong hands lifted her shoulders from behind and Haraq pushed his crossed legs beneath them so she could lean on him.

She managed about half of the bowl before pushing it aside.

"No more? Well, that's all right—you take it slow." Najud put the bowl down beside him on the grass.

"Now, there's something else. I think it's time to tap our *qahulajti* again."

She reached out to look at the girl's core power which was starting to trickle back. Najud was right, better to be careful. Once more, she drained it into her chain, and then blinked back up at him.

He shook her lightly before she went back to sleep.

"One last thing…"

She waited, but he didn't continue. When she scanned his mind, she felt his fear. *What is it, Naj-sha?*

"We're going to have to work on your leg. I'm going to get you as drunk as I can, but it's going to be bad. We'll have to… to tie you down."

Her stomach clenched and she worked on keeping the broth down.

"What are you going to do?" she whispered.

"Khizuwi's done this before. We're going to…"

"Break the bones again and try to fix it right this time," she supplied. "I thought you'd have to, when I saw what had happened." She kept her voice cool and calm, but her skin chilled with dread.

Her hand stretched out to clasp his arm. "It's all right. Do what you have to do."

He paused. "I'll wake you up again when it's time."

Penrys was a quiet drunk, at least in these circumstances. Najud had worried that she wouldn't be able to keep it down, but she worked on it methodically. The four men had sacrificed what was left of their mead, but it wasn't enough to knock her out. He could only hope it would dull the pain.

Haraq finished tying her body and upper arms down to pegs pressed into the grass to keep her from moving. The lower half of her body was already secured.

Khizuwi had forbidden Najud the close work. Instead, he'd been assigned to trying to keep Penrys distracted as much as possible. He sat crosslegged next to her head and blocked her view.

Behind him, he heard Haraq slip into place next to Khizuwi, an extra pair of hands. Khizuwi had tools and liquids ready. Najud wasn't sure which turned his stomach the most—the sharp knives or the crude rock for a hammer and scrubbed stone as a chisel that would break the bones in just the right place.

"Now, Najud," Khizuwi said, quietly.

Najud grabbed her hand and held it. *Here it comes, Pen-sha. You hold on to me and yell all you want, if you have to.*

He felt, through her, the sickening horror of her skin being cut along the calf. The pain was dulled with the mead, and she tried to hold her body still. But then came the thud of the rock against bone, twice, and she screamed. Through it all her hand crushed against his, but she held her leg still.

He kept up a low patter to her the whole time. "You're doing fine, it's almost over."

The sting of fiery liquids deep within the open leg left her gasping for breath, and she began panting. Haraq pushed him aside to make room for a long stick with a padded fork which he tucked up under her arm. He bound it to her naked torso high and low with leather straps. When he backed up, Najud saw he had a shorter stick of similar shape—but this he jammed against her pelvic bone, and bound them both on either side of her right thigh. They jutted out several inches below her foot, and Haraq bound a short cross stick across them near the ends.

Khizuwi was bent over the calf, sewing, and Haraq helped him steady the leg. When he tied off his thread, he poured something on the skin which made Penrys's hand clutch Najud's again, and then he wrapped the wound round and round in clean cloth.

Haraq tied the two stout sticks together below the knee, around the calf below the dressing, and again above the ankle. While Khizuwi shook his hands in the air to relieve them of the strain, Haraq tied a rope around her ankle and ran a twisted cord from there to the cross stick, tying it as tightly as he could.

"Ready?" Khizuwi asked him.

Haraq nodded and picked up a small stick to insert between the twisted cord, and twisted it further and further to pull the leg straight, while Khizuwi eyed her good leg and the broken one and felt gently along the wrapping, until he felt the bones were as much as possible in their proper positions. Then Haraq bound the twisting stick in place to maintain the tension.

"We're done, Pen-sha. It's all over." Najud listened for a reply but heard only the faintest acknowledgment before she fled into sleep.

He helped Haraq release her from the cords that pegged her down, and she didn't move. Then there was nothing else to distract himself with, and he faced Khizuwi. "How did it go?"

"None of the big tubes that carry blood were damaged, and that's very good. Her foot is warm, not pale and cool."

"But?" Najud waited.

Khizuwi nodded. "But... the bones had started to fuse together. Extra bone, not like a fresh break. I had to cut that away, scrape it raw..." He caught a look at Najud's expression and stopped explaining. "Anyway, I didn't find any loose pieces to cause trouble later, and it ought to heal fine. Unless we didn't get all the infection. There's honey under the dressing, and some of the mead in the wound. That may be enough."

He looked down at Penrys, the blanket covering most of the two sticks holding her leg in place. "We should get her indoors out of the cold. I expect her to be out for hours, and then immobile for days."

Najud watched Jiqlaraz still talking to the *qahulajti* and said, "And then we need to deal with that."

CHAPTER 49

Najud and Haraq improvised a carrier out of the low worktables from each *kazr*, bound end to end, and used that to bring her into Najud's *kazr*.

"Leave her on it?" Haraq suggested to Najud. "Easier to tend her that way."

Najud shook his head. "Too hard to lie on for long. We've got room in here—let's just stretch some canvas on the rugs and put her there, then stash the tables in the back. I'll take care of her."

He scanned her mind—she was asleep, almost unconscious. That was the best thing for her. He made sure she was warm enough, and then left her there.

As soon as he emerged back into the afternoon sunlight with Haraq, his eye fell on a tableau of Munraz arguing quietly with his uncle. Jiqlaraz had a cup in his hand and had just been crouched down giving the girl a drink. Her hands had been rebound in front of her.

Najud felt Munraz's distress easily, and he gathered up Khizuwi to finally put a stop to this fascination with the *qahulajti*.

He walked directly up to Jiqlaraz. "Convinced her to go home with you yet, *bikraj*?"

Without a particle of shame, Jiqlaraz answered him. "She's harmless now, even you will admit. What's the point of killing her?"

"A hundred or two people dead," Khizuwi commented. "Isn't that enough of a reason?"

Najud probed her. Enough power had trickled back that she could mind-speak. *What's your name?*

That's what the female wanted to know, before you cut her. She gave me a name, Vylkerri. What does this male want? He won't talk to me like this. Only babbling noises.

It gave Najud pause, to have her speak in his mind, her face still expressionless.

He wants to breed with you.

The girl turned her head to look at Jiqlaraz and pushed him away with her bound hands.

Tell him I refuse. She turned her face from him with what dignity she could maintain, seated on the ground and tied like a prisoner.

"She's a child," Jiqlaraz said. "Look at her, sulking. Couldn't your *bikrajti* just, oh, burn it out of her, make her safe? We'd give her a home, in my family. Give her a useful life."

Munraz looked at him with horror on his face and Najud spat at his feet.

"Or do you begrudge me one, now that you've got one of your own?" Jiqlaraz said.

Haraq intervened to grab Najud's shoulder before he'd even realized he'd taken a step forward with his fist clenched.

Jiqlaraz continued to taunt him. "If you think she's so unredeemable, why do you keep one, yourself? Or if you reconsider, now that she's damaged, I'll be glad to take care of her, too."

"Enough!" Khizuwi glared at them both. "It is forbidden, what you propose, Jiqlaraz, and for very good reason. You cannot let a *qahulaj* survive."

Reluctantly, Najud told Khizuwi, "I'm not sure any of the deaths were quite intended, though. They all seem to be the by-product of gathering the herds or just finding out about people. The worst she seems to have done on purpose was the trampling of Umzakhilin."

He glanced at Haraq apologetically as he spoke, then continued. "You could ask her about it." He tapped his forehead.

Jiqlaraz was quick to seize the opening. "Your *bikrajti* has deliberately killed more people than this poor child. No one would want the girl to roam freely, of course, in this dangerous way, but there's no reason to harm her, surely."

Khizuwi was unmoved. "Any *bikraj* is a danger. It's the assertion of their own will over any other consideration, an indifference to the harm it causes, that marks a *qahulaj*, and that usually leads directly to death—in this case, many deaths. This girl is clearly such, whether she understands the connection or not."

He cast a look back at Najud. "And your *bikrajti* is not."

"Not yet," Jiqlaraz muttered darkly.

More loudly, he said, "And what of any children she might have? They'd be innocent, wouldn't they?"

Munraz backed away from his uncle, shaking his head. "Is this really what you wanted, uncle? Anything for the bloodline? And who would you give her to?"

"Does it matter? If she's not to your taste, I could manage. She's a little young of course, but think of the children she would have. She doesn't have to remain a danger if she's only needed for breeding."

The girl's incomplete comprehension of their dispute turned Najud's stomach.

"The rumors of your family are true, I see." He was no longer furious, only disgusted.

"*We* get stronger with each generation. What have *your* people accomplished, in clan Zamjilah?"

Najud forced calm upon himself. He didn't respect this man enough to let him provoke his anger, or so he tried to tell himself. Ignoring him he turned to Khizuwi. "One of us will have to take turns watching her, and we'll have to monitor her to make sure her power stays low enough."

Munraz stared at them and shook his head incredulously. "You don't understand, do you? He'll free her tonight and leave—you don't know him. Might even make a try for your *bikrajti*, while she can't fight back. And then it will all be to do over again, and more people dead."

He sputtered to a stop and confronted Jiqlaraz. "Our own family, this time, uncle, once her power returns—or don't you care?"

Najud could feel the wrath seething in the older man, though he kept it off his face.

"There are ways to make her safe," he hissed. "Would you betray your family?"

"Worse than that," the young man said. He pulled the knife from his belt and stepped behind the girl, then with a smooth motion he bent down and drew it across her throat before anyone could react. He dropped the bloody knife with a sob. "No more monsters, uncle. Not this time. Not even she deserves that."

At least it was quick. Najud was too shocked to think of anything else. Khizuwi shook his head, but didn't seem surprised.

"I sanction this killing," he intoned, "Though I would have waited for a more proper judgment."

"And I," Najud said, following the traditional formula.

"Not me," Jiqlaraz spoke through clenched teeth. "You are no family of mine, Munraz, son of no one. You are dead to us, dead to our clan, dead to our tribe." He spat on the ground three times and turned on his heel.

Haraq moved aside to let him pass, and he vanished into his *kazr*.

Najud exchanged glances with Khizuwi. *What now? I've never heard of dissension like this over a qahulaj.*

He walked over to the corpse and cut her bonds to lay her out decently. He cleaned Munraz's knife and gave it to him, avoiding his face and giving him the privacy of his tears. Then he returned to the girl and knelt beside her. Brushing her hair aside, he found the same small, fox-like ears that Penrys had, and the other *qahulaj* she'd killed, in Neshilik. Khizuwi witnessed it, and he let the bloody hair fall back.

A stir at the doorway to Jiqlaraz's *kazr* drew Najud's eye, and he watched the man stump around angrily, untying the knots that held on the roof canvases.

Haraq raised an eyebrow to Najud, but shrugged and walked over to help him disassemble the *kazr*.

The three *bikrajab* stood around the body and watched in silence as the *kazr* melted away. Eventually everything was stacked neatly, ready for the pack horses, all except for Khizuwi's possessions, and the personal packs of his nephew, which sat forlornly off to the side, unwanted.

Haraq went with him to the horse herd and helped him bring back his horses, seven of them. Munraz commented under his breath, "Left me my riding horse, anyway. And whatever I brought with me that's mine, which isn't much."

He wiped his face and snorted. "What's he going to sleep in? My old *kamah*, all the way home? He can't raise a *kazr* by himself."

Khizuwi cleared his throat. "You acted correctly in difficult circumstances, *nal-jarghal*. I would be pleased to take you as apprentice, but we are neighbors with your clan."

"My ex-clan," Munraz said.

"Yes. Well. It would be source of contention for both our clans all your life," Khizuwi said

"But not for me," Najud said. "I am new as a *jarghal* and hadn't looked to take an apprentice for many years yet. But if you don't mind someone without the experience of Khizuwi here, or of your uncle…"

Munraz spat at the mention of his uncle. "I would be greatly honored if you would accept me, *jarghal*, if your *lijti* will also permit it."

"We'll ask her later, but I'm sure it'll be fine. Khizuwi, what do you think?"

"It's a good solution," Khizuwi said. "I'll spread the word."

By now, Haraq had helped Jiqlaraz load his pack-string, and he led the six horses away from the camp, following the trail broken yesterday by the Kurighdunaq survivors. He never looked back or bid any of them farewell, not even Haraq.

The sun was casting long shadows in the camp, but there was still a body to deal with.

"We'll build her a cairn," Najud suggested, "Over by that old pine."

He looked down at the corpse. "What about the chain? We can't just leave it there."

He told them about the fight over the chain the Voice had worn, how it had exploded, and Penrys had the surviving fragment. "She says it didn't happen because the bearer was dead, but because someone had tried to do something forbidden with it." Devices were forbidden, in the tradition of his *bikrajab*.

Khizuwi questioned Munraz. "Would your uncle come back for it?"

The young man shrugged. "If it occurred to him. If he thought he could do something with it. He might bring more of the family… *his* family with him."

"The news will get around," Khizuwi said. "It may not be safe to take it, but it's surely not safe to leave it behind."

His eyes turned to the one *kazr* left standing in their camp. "The *jarghalti* should take charge of it, as she did for the other one."

Munraz asked, in a very small voice, "But how will we take it off?"

Haraq spoke up. "It's not fitting for *bikrajab* to do such things. I'll take care of it. In repayment for the debt I owe her for my *lud*." He cocked his head at the *kazr* where Penrys lay.

Khizuwi nodded his thanks and turned to the *nal-jarghal.* "Munraz, the body is just a shell, it doesn't matter. Come with me—we'll pick a spot and start gathering rocks."

Dinner had been a simple affair, and quiet. The long, eventful day, occupied all thoughts in Najud's *kazr.*

Munraz was yawning, but not everyone was quite ready to join him. He lay in his blankets in the front of the *kazr*, not far from Haraq. Najud had yielded his narrow bed to Khizuwi and taken his place on the rugs next to the sleeping Penrys. She muttered occasionally—her face was warm to his touch.

Khizuwi commented, "Fever. There's always some. Nothing to worry about if it gets no worse."

"Are you going to change the dressing in the morning?" Najud said. "She didn't want me to stitch her hand, said it might interfere with the healing."

"Hmm. I was going to let it wait another day but maybe that would be a good idea. Soon as we wake up, then."

Najud wondered what troubled her dreams. There hadn't been time to get the story from her yet, but he thought, from the distance and the injuries, that she must have been knocked out of the air somehow, and fallen. What about her wings, then? Were they broken, too?

He'd seen them bleed when an arrow pierced one. Could they get infected, and contaminate the rest of her? She didn't seem fevered enough for that. They were devices, she thought, and he wasn't sure just how they were connected to her body. It was beyond her understanding, and his, too.

He drifted off, holding her hand.

In the middle of the night, she spoke clearly, "Good little Dun, Dundun, my Dunsiedun. I'm just one of your mares, just another horsie. Keep going—don't stop."

It trailed off into silence, and Najud understood how she'd hidden from the *qahulajti* as she'd followed her back to the camp.

He wiped her face dry with the cloth he'd kept handy for the purpose, and picked up her hand again. *I have her back.* He hugged the thought to himself as he settled back into sleep.

CHAPTER 50

A strange plucking sensation irritated Penrys until she couldn't ignore it, and she opened her eyes.

She was in her *kazr*, on the floor, daylight streaming through the *zamjilah* over the stove. Something was still tickling her leg, and she tried to lift her head to see what it was, but her right shoulder was jammed by some sort of stick. When she lifted her left hand to explore, it was seized by someone, and Najud's face swam into her view.

"What's going on?" she said, faintly alarmed to hear the slur in her speech.

"Ah, you're awake, *bikrajti*." That was Khizuwi's voice. "Good. You can tell me what I want to know."

"But…" she said.

"This first. Explanations later." Khizuwi's voice was firm.

She looked up at Najud, and he nodded. "Do what he says."

Khizuwi was still mostly hidden, seated by her leg—she couldn't lift her head far enough to see him clearly. Munraz stood over him, holding a lantern.

Khizuwi held up a fragment of thread on tweezers where she could see it. "I'm taking stitches out, from yesterday. Do you remember?"

It came flooding back, and she blanched. She wiggled her toes on both feet. They seemed to be in the right place, one set next to the other, not scrunched up sideways the way it had been.

"Good. I was going to ask you to move your toes. Now lie still while I finish this."

Najud bent over her. "I can see why you didn't want me to stitch your hand, that time."

She envisioned her skin growing right over stitches. "Is he too late? Is it… bad?"

Khizuwi's voice drifted back. "It's been less than a day, nothing to worry about. But your wound doesn't need the help any more, so it's time to get the stitches out." In a lower voice he muttered, "While I can."

She giggled. "Sorry, *jarghal.* Did it work, yesterday? What're all these sticks doing?"

"Not comfortable, eh? You'll just have to put up with it for a while. They're holding your leg in the right place while the bones grow together."

She tried to twist her ankle slightly against the tension to test it, and got a stinging slap on the thigh for her pains.

"Stop that. Those bones haven't knit yet."

For Najud's ears alone, she murmured, "I wouldn't bet on that." But she held still obediently and smiled. There was a deep, dull, throbbing pain in her calf, but it was easier to bear than the original sharp agony, and it all felt alive to her.

"Don't know what I might have said yesterday, but I take it all back. This was worth it."

Her stomach growled. "We'll get you some more broth when he's done," Najud told her.

How would she eat it, flat on her back? And then another, more urgent thought struck her, and her cheeks flamed. "Um, Najud… broth in, broth out."

"Don't worry, we've got that all taken care of. You just go ahead."

He turned his face away, and she did what she had to, red with embarrassment. She discovered he'd made a hollow in the rugs she lay on and slid a shallow pan there. He briskly ran a damp cloth over her when she was done and took the pan away while she tried to recover her dignity.

Khizuwi distracted her with a series of probes and questions. She felt his hands working carefully over the muscles and bone. "The skin is closed and I can already feel the muscles smoothing out. The change from yesterday is… remarkable. No wonder your face never showed the bite of the wind—that's nothing by comparison to this."

"Were the other…" he coughed. "Were the two *qahulajti* with chains also like this?"

"Don't know. Couldn't ask the first one, but I can question the girl." She reached out for her, to check how much of her power had returned so she could drain it again, but she couldn't find her, anywhere—just Munraz and Haraq, outside.

"Where is she? What happened? Did she escape?" *Why aren't they alarmed?*

Najud came back into her view and sat down next to her. He dropped something onto the blanket over her stomach. It... clinked. He guided her hand down to it, and when she felt metal links, she tightened her grip around it. She didn't need to lift it to her eyes to know what it was.

"She had ears like yours, Pen-sha. Didn't see any marks on her, but then we left her in her skins, with the knife and boots she stole, so I can't say there were no scars anywhere."

"But why? She was under control. She was a child! Think how alone she was. It wasn't her fault."

"Could she have been changed, Pen-sha?"

She opened her mouth to protest and stopped, remembering how damaged she had seemed.

"I don't know. But that wasn't my call to make. I would have tried."

"No," Najud said, "It was the judgment of a group of *bikrajab*, as it should be."

Khizuwi said, "Jiqlaraz wanted to take her home and breed her. You, too, if he could think of a way."

That silenced her in shock, then she chuckled weakly. "That wouldn't have worked out very well for him."

No one replied, then Khizuwi said, "There are ways, *jarghalti*, that perhaps you don't know, to destroy the mind and leave the body. It could be done."

She had no answer for that.

"What happened?" she whispered.

Najud told her. "Munraz revolted against his uncle and cut her throat, to thwart him and to give the *qahulajti* a quick death. It was well done."

"Poor Munraz," she murmured. "And poor girl. She didn't ask for this."

"It's just us, now, with Haraq. Jiqlaraz disowned his nephew and left."

He cleared his throat. "I've taken him on as *nal-jarghal*, if that's all right with you."

She thought of the young man, blood on his hands and exiled from home. She didn't like the death, but she understood their reasoning and couldn't disagree with them.

It might be a while before she stopped picturing him standing over a chained girl with a bloody knife. But if he hadn't sacrificed his family ties that way, what would have happened?

It was too hard for her to sort out now. "As you like, Najud."

Two evenings later, Penrys was in revolt.

"I'm getting up and sleeping in my own bed if I have to unstrap all this myself."

"Six weeks to heal a broken leg, *bikrajti.*" Khizuwi's patience was wearing thin. "Even for you, three days is not enough."

"I'm not planning to dance on it. I won't put any weight on it at all. But I don't need this… maddening contraption on me any more. The bones are knit, if not yet strong. All they need is reinforcement and padding, and all I need is a crutch. And clothing. And some of whatever that is that smells so good on the stove, upright, like a civilized woman. And a good night's sleep." She could hear her voice rising.

She couldn't see their faces, flat on her back—they had a maddening habit of staying out of her sight—but she felt them all. Amusement from Haraq and Munraz, concern from Khizuwi. And from Najud?

Najud surprised her. "Everyone out," he said.

She felt the air movement when the door opened, and even Khizuwi left without further objection.

"Here you go, Pen-sha. Let me get that off you."

She almost wept in relief. "I was afraid you'd keep me caged up forever like this."

"Not me. I know how long your memory is. You'd pay me back eventually."

Her laugh was shaky. He released the twisting stick that held her leg in tension, and the tug on her ankle relaxed. She twisted her foot left and right for him.

"See? It may take a couple of weeks to be usable, but it's working again."

"I'll unbind the braces, but you will sit there until I find you some clothing or I'll tie you up again." Najud untied the straps where he could, and cut them where he must until they were all gone.

"That's wonderful. Such a relief." She raised herself up on her elbows and cracked her neck, watching Najud poke through her packs. "There's not much left," she warned him.

He laid out her last pair of breeches, a shirt, and her oldest tunic, along with underclothes, and pulled her up on one leg to support her over to her bed, and help with the awkward bits. When she was all assembled, she sat there, one leg braced on the floor and the other just lightly touching, and leaned on him to recover from the effort.

"Thank you," she told him, and touched his arm.

"What, for treating you like someone who knew what they could handle?"

She snorted.

"Now be nice to these men," he said. "They've been listening to you snore for two nights, and no respite in sight."

She punched him lightly in indignation, and he threw an arm around her.

"I do not snore" she said, her voice muffled against his chest. "Now go away and let them in. I'm hungry."

CHAPTER 51

Penrys wasn't able to sit easily on the ground, so she perched on the edge of her bedframe, her weak leg wrapped between knee and ankle with cloth bound around two pieces of the shorter stick that had pulled it straight, all of it resting on a pack that Najud had maneuvered into place. She couldn't eat much of the dinner—chunks of squirrel, fresh killed, and the ever-present cabbage—but the luxury of handling her own bowl and her own spoon was very welcome.

After the meal, Haraq whittled on the longer of the sticks she'd discarded, and presented her with the crutch she'd demanded. He'd reduced the fork at the top to a flat stub, thoroughly padded, and once he'd held it against her to check the position, he bound a hand-grip into place, stout and easy to hold with a gloved hand.

"Help me up," she told him. She placed it under her arm and tried a couple of steps, away and back, and then kissed him on the cheek, to the amusement of all. He backed away, his face flaming and his eye on Najud who smiled benevolently.

She got herself up afterward to go out, and Najud went with her. She eyed him as he followed her to the doorway but forbore to comment. "I'll just wait here," he said, after they got outside. "You'll let me know if I'm needed."

She stumped off with her crutch in the moonlight, delighted to be left in such privacy as this was, and when she returned, Najud stopped her before she would have reentered the *kazr*.

"Now might be a good time to look at your wings," he suggested. "There's enough light for the basics."

"I… haven't dared to look. I don't remember hitting the ground at all."

She remembered vividly what it had been like falling through the sky not knowing where the ground was.

"That's what a bump on the head can do." Najud's quiet voice calmed her. "Don't you think it's time?"

"Yes. You're right." She stepped up close and faced him, thinking that she might need something to grab if she were suddenly struck by the pain of a crumpled mess, and invoked her wings.

They swept out of nothingness with a flap, and there was no sensation of injury. She stretched them to their fullest, and spread the tail to match, and felt nothing wrong at all.

A weight she had hardly been conscious of was lifted from her mind and she beamed at Najud. "Look at them," she said, pleased with the exotic look of the feathers, banded like an eagle's and silvered by the moonlight.

"Wish I knew how they were made," she commented.

When Najud didn't reply, she realized just how worried he had been, too, on her behalf. "It's fine, I'm fine," she told him tenderly. "Or I will be, soon enough." She wrapped the wings around him in that way he loved, and he held her tight for too short a while before releasing her and stepping away.

"Time we went back," he said, his voice hoarse.

He preceded her through the doorframe, then stood aside to let her in. She stepped over the threshold and stopped. In the few minutes they'd been gone, the whole *kazr* had been tidied. The spot where she'd been stuck for days was now indistinguishable, the scraps of leather straps, the shavings from Haraq's work—all gone. The air had lost some of that musty feeling of long occupation, there was a lingering sharp scent of something pungent, and all the surfaces were clean.

The three occupants were back in their places as if they'd never moved at all, their expressions bland and innocent.

"I see the little folk from Ellech have been here." Her voice was dry, but her eyes were damp. "Too bad I haven't any milk to leave for them."

Haraq looked up casually and said, "Just a small bit of respect to our hostess."

"And it's grateful she is," she said. She picked her way carefully to her bed and lowered herself back down to the edge of it. Najud dropped to the carpets at her feet and leaned on the frame.

"I have a question," she asked, after her muscles stopped quivering from the unaccustomed exercise and the strain of maneuvering on the crutch. "How long has it been since Jiqlaraz left, and how soon might he return, with others?"

"He's been gone three days," Munraz told her. "I think he'll come back, and I don't think we should be here to meet him."

"That wouldn't be wise," Khizuwi agreed. "It's fifty miles or so, the way we came, to the point where the trail from the Dhajtawhaz *zudiqazd* met our path, and another sixty or so miles from there to his people."

"So we need to get to the junction and head north before he returns, if he does, and then he'll have to choose whether to come after us, or come here to see what he can find, yes?" Penrys shook her head. "We should leave in the morning, should have left already."

She looked directly at Najud and declared, "I can travel now."

He pursed his lips and nodded. "We go in the morning. What's the count of the horses, Penrys?"

She scanned the herd, glad to slip back into her old duties. "I make it twenty-six." Her heart sang when she recognized her little herd of five that had brought her out of Silmat.

"That's your four, Khizuwi, and four for the rest of us to ride, and eighteen to pack with, a superfluity considering there's just the one *kazr* now." Najud was clearly deep into his role as *zarawinnaj* now, Penrys amused to see.

"There's almost no grain left, so the horses will suffer," he said, "But we can take it in easy stages, and they won't have much of a load. Have to be sure to camp where Jirkat didn't, so they can still find grass under the snow."

"How far to the Kurighdunaq *zudiqazd?*" Khizuwi asked.

"Maybe a hundred fifty miles, the way we came, but Ilzay was going to take the survivors directly, and we'll follow his trail as long as the weather is clear and we can see it. He thought it would be more like a hundred ten or twenty, that way."

Haraq said, "Six days at worse, three or four days at best. Don't need a lot of food for that, just for five of us. Even if we have to sit out another storm."

He looked up at the rafters in the back of the *kazr*. The *shabz* hanging there was their entire remaining supply, but it was more than enough. Most of the food they'd brought with them had gone to Jirkat's group, but they were in no danger of shortfall.

Khizuwi nodded. "Tomorrow it is. Now, *nal-jarghal*, let's review again what you have learned about the mending of bones. Haraq, if you'll assist us by the loan of your body for an example?"

Penrys suppressed her smile. "I thought he was *your* apprentice, Naj-sha," she murmured.

"We agreed, Khizuwi and I, that he would teach as much as he could before he had to leave. I've been learning from him, myself."

She waved her hand over to the lesson, to encourage him to continue, but he shook his head. "It's just to make sure he remembers what he was taught already. We'll need an early night tonight if we plan to travel all day tomorrow."

"Too bad the Kurighdunaq couldn't pick up the rest of their herds while they were here."

Najud smiled up at here. "Those animals won't leave that valley until the snows are gone, if then. You'll see the Kurighdunaq back in Silmat as soon as they can manage it, to bring the rest of them home."

She was silent for a moment. "D'ya think there are any people still there? I didn't find any, but I could only see a narrow part of the valley, and I wasn't in the best of shape. And we didn't go very far into it."

"I don't know." His voice was somber. "Hope not, but there's no more we can do with what we have."

She looked around at the fragment of their team, and was forced to agree. "At least, with the girl gone, they might recover and survive on their own."

Najud nodded. "Some of them will have knives. If they can coax one horse within reach, they'll be able to get anything else they need. It's a good spot to winter over."

He was warm against her good leg, and they sat there in silence, listening to the quiet voices in the front of the *kazr*.

CHAPTER 52

The four men had the *kazr* disassembled in the morning faster than Penrys could have imagined. There was nothing useful she could do with one hand occupied with a crutch, so she took herself out of their way and waited.

When they brought the horses in at last from their sheltered meadow, she swung herself over to greet her five horses from the valley, and the leopard-spotted mare and the dun almost knocked her off her crutch in their enthusiastic shoving.

They couldn't fatten on the poor winter grazing, but they seemed livelier for the rest of several days. "We'll make those your string," Najud said, as he began rigging the pack gear. "Not the two you rode—those'll go bare."

She grimaced. "I had to put them through a lot. I don't know who they belong to, but I'll buy them if we can figure it out. They're mine, now."

As her eye tried to match the horse packs being assembled with the available animals, she did a double-take. "How did we end up with two of those low tables?"

Najud chuckled. "We tied them together to bring you into the *kazr*, and Jiqlaraz was in such a hurry to leave, he never got his back. He was careful to take everything he could lay his hands on that wasn't Khizuwi's. He left Munraz his clothes and one horse, and took the old family *kamah* away from him."

"But he didn't take his table back?"

"I think he was afraid to walk into our *kazr* and claim it. After all, you were there."

"Dead asleep." She snorted.

"Even so." A steely glint came into his eye. "And if he'd tried, I would've cut him down before he reached the door."

She stared at him, but he bent down again over his work and didn't notice.

Everywhere she turned there were busy hands, and none of them hers. *Time to move again.*

She hobbled to the old pine on the upslope trail to the gap. The cairn was fresh, the rocks bare except for the lichens that coated many of them. She looked back at the camp, with its seven empty circles, trodden down to the grass, and the mess of pathways within it.

So little to mark the spot. Only the cairn would remain after the spring growth took hold. A young corpse, its head separated from its body, as if they were afraid she would somehow walk after death.

The chain was buried with Penrys's most precious possessions, in the little pack that traveled on her own horse when she rode, the one that contained her *lud*, and the matching one from Najud— they were different minerals and unbalanced, separately, but they fit together in one enigmatic and complex piece.

She should show it to Khizuwi, on the way—see if he'd ever heard of a two-part *lud* like that.

Footsteps in the snow made her turn and, as if her thoughts had conjured him, Khizuwi joined her at the cairn.

"Dark thoughts?" he asked her.

"More like puzzled ones," she said. "I was lucky, and she wasn't. That's almost the whole of it. I could've died in the snow on my mountain in Ellech, if Vylkar hadn't heard me, or been raised by wolves and feral. Why me, and not her?"

Khizuwi shrugged. "The world is a chancy place."

"No," she said, shaking her head. "That's not the answer. We're not some accident of nature. Someone is making us and then dumping us into the world to live or die, heedless of what might happen to us, or to anyone we encounter. This girl would have been maybe ten years old when it happened, when her life was destroyed. What kind of person would do that to a child?"

"It kills us." She gestured at the cairn. "And it kills almost everyone we touch. Who's doing it, and why? Why?"

She glared at him as if he were responsible. "And what was I, before? Before they took my life from me and made *this* out of me?"

She invoked her wings and raised them above her. "A monster for his family to try and tolerate." She cocked her head at Najud standing obliviously below and helping Haraq bind the rafters of the *kazr*. "A threat to other wizards. A menace."

"A woman who loves a man and is loved," Khizuwi rejoined, unimpressed. "A *bikrajti* who risked her life to free others and to capture a *qahulajti*. A *jarghalti* who will help a *nal-jarghal* escape a dark life and become useful to others."

She had nothing to say. Her wings drooped, and she put them away, wherever it was they went.

"You must learn to live with it, *lijti*," he said, and patted her shoulder. "It'll eat you alive, else."

She turned back to the cairn and listened to his footsteps as they receded down the slope. When her breathing had calmed, she bowed formally, in the Kigali manner, and slashed her hand through the air. "*Sennevi*. It is finished, young Vylkerri. I wish it could have had a different ending."

After two days on the trail, Penrys's leg ached and her temper was short.

The track of the survivors was as broad as a highway, and as clear. They'd passed Jirkat's first encampment with its eloquent empty *kazr* circles, and gone another easy five miles before stopping and setting up their own. On the second day, they'd managed almost thirty miles.

The necessary distance between the riders with their pack-strings had kept conversation to a minimum. Even the mid-day breaks had been hurried and urgent. They'd finally passed the trail to clan Rashaban and pushed themselves another five miles beyond it before stopping.

Penrys had scanned to her limit as they rode, but five miles wasn't far, and she'd felt hemmed in, and blind.

The best thing was the weather—it held cold, but sunny. The snow remained crisp with just a bit of a thin crust from the sunshine. The broken track they rode was still powdery, and easier for the horses to push through than breaking new trail.

Now, in the dim light of the *kazr*, Penrys itched for something to do, other than keeping an obsessive count of the horses, foraging as best they could under the snow.

Haraq was mending a leather strap for a pack frame, and Munraz was sitting in front of Khizuwi for his evening lesson. The low drone of their voices was constantly in her ear.

She'd noticed Najud keeping a wary eye on her after she'd snapped at him in mind-speech on the trail today. She'd apologized, but something was singing along her nerves and she couldn't shake it. It had left her tense and curt most of the afternoon.

A phrase of Munraz's to Khizuwi caught her attention. "But what is wrong with the Zannib-*taghr*, that they should want to live such a tethered life in the east? Why would anyone want to be a merchant?"

She heard a subdued snort from Najud, but he left the question unchallenged.

That was not her inclination, not tonight. "Merchants, is it?" She glanced at Khizuwi in apology for her interruption, but he gestured to her to continue.

"Tell me, Munraz, do you carry a sword?"

"Of course, *bikrajti*. I received it when I became a *tushkzurtudin*, an adult."

"And where did it come from?" she asked.

"From my father, *lijti*." His voice faltered as he mentioned his family, but he kept on gamely. She waved him on in encouragement. "And before that it was carried by his uncle, and then the younger brother of his father, and then…" His voice trailed off as he ran out of the weapon's lineage.

"I see." She waited a moment. "And who made it?"

"I… I don't know, *lijti*."

She nodded. She was beginning to enjoy herself.

"And where did the metal come from?"

"I don't know that either, *lijti*."

"Do they mine for iron, the Zannib-*hubr*, your people? Do they refine it, pound it into steel, twist the billets together?"

Munraz shook his head.

"Najud, where do the swords come from? Can you tell him?"

She felt as if she were back in the library at the Collegium of Wizards in Ellech, where they'd never let her teach a class.

Najud half-bowed to her in amusement and began. "Most of the trade iron is mined in the hills north of Yenit Ping, the Endless City. That's in the Galat, where wars have been fought for centuries with Ndant, to control the source of the best iron. From there, it travels to Yenit Ping where entire neighborhoods are devoted to the crushing of the ore, the mixing with charcoal, the purifying of steel. At each stage, others buy the results. Some merchants trade the raw materials, some trade the unshaped steel, and some buy swords."

He glanced over at Penrys to confirm that was what she wanted, and continued with a smile. "A few of those swords are shaped into *khashrab*, the way the Zannib prefer, with the curve common to horsemen. Perhaps you don't know, *nal-jarghal*—on foot, most people use straight swords. While every young man in Zannib would prefer an ancient *khash* of famous lineage, many a younger son must be satisfied with a new one, brought by ship to Ussha or by *biziz*, on the backs of animals, to Qawrash im-Dhal."

He leaned forward. "From those places, some smaller trader, picking up a few goods for his profit, travels west into the central regions, and there, in a small clan where a young man is soon to be sixteen years old, some proud relative buys him a *khash* of his own, a new one, suitable for a fourth or fifth son."

Penrys took over. "Every *khash* in *sarq*-Zannib originated in this way, even the old and famous ones. Either the steel billets were brought and a Zannib smith made the sword from them, or the sword itself was made in a foreign land."

"That is what merchants do. They make sure that warriors like you have swords." She was amused by the appalled look on Munraz's face. "Arrow points, too, though you *can* make those out of flint if you prefer. And the stove of your *kazr*, and its chimney-pipe, so much better than an open, smoky fire. And your very pots and pans and knives and axes. You have silver in your hills, in Zannib, and precious stones, but little gold and no iron."

She glanced at Khizuwi, who nodded approvingly. "I have a task for you, Munraz. Tomorrow evening, I want you to tell me where *bunnas* comes from, and how it gets from the plant to the pouch you carry, and what other nations use it, and how they get it. The same for Khizuwi's *kassa*. And you know the carpet you're sitting on? Tell me where all the dyes come from that give it color and life—what are they, how are they made, and where do they come from? Why are some colors common and others rare?"

Najud added, "And what do they cost, compared to *bunnas* and *kassa*, both here in central Zannib, and in a foreign country. And finally, what do *bunnas*, *kassa*, and the wool dyes have in common with each other that make them excellent trade goods?"

"But... How can I do that?" Munraz said.

Haraq chuckled. "Just like the rest of us, young *bikraj*—by asking questions, thinking about it, and asking more questions. I'll help you—I'd like to know more of those answers myself."

The lesson cleared some of Penrys's bad temper and she made an effort to be more sociable.

While Munraz, a bit shaken, continued his session with Khizuwi, she turned to Haraq. "What will you do when you rejoin your sister?"

His face was still lean from weeks of inadequate food, the lines deeply drawn, but she had yet to see him lose his dignity. He paused, as if to consider before speaking, and she waited patiently.

He nodded to Najud and her, and answered. "None of you can understand what it's like for the Kurighdunaq to be gutted of so many of its people. No family will be left intact. I have my sister Luram, my cousin Umzakhilin, but what of my other sister, and my two brothers? I had a wife..."

His voice trailed off. "We've all lost parents, but that happens in the natural course of things. It's the children... There were no children sent back to the *zudiqazd*. You raised cairns for some of them, I was told. I can guess what happened to the others.

"What is a tribe without children? We've lost an entire generation. I understand you saved much of the property of the clan, *zarawinnaj*, but what is wealth without people?"

Najud said, quietly, "I have no answers for you, Haraq."

"No, I know that—how could you? You've done enough, the two of you, strangers as you are. The *qahulajti* is gone and the first part of the nightmare is over, and I'm glad I was there to witness it. But the nightmare has only just started. I don't know that the clan can survive the rest of it."

Penrys gave him a sympathetic glance, but there was nothing she could do to help, any more than Najud.

Her nerves tingled again, and she looked up, trying to trace the source of her irritation. It nagged at her like the buzzing of a persistent fly.

What is it, Pen-sha?

She couldn't answer him. It teased at her, just out of reach, but this time she felt a direction—south.

"We're about five miles past the trail to Rashaban, right?"

Najud nodded.

"There's something... Could it be Jiqlaraz? Already?"

Munraz's head turned when he heard her. "My uncle?"

"I don't know. It's too far away, but something's been bothering me for hours. If it's him, it's more than just one person."

Haraq said, "If he hurried, he probably had enough time to get there and return this far. Maybe he's camped for the night with others, as we are."

"They had a way of working together, my ex-family." Munraz's voice was bitter. "They hadn't shown me how to do that, yet."

"Like the Rasesni mages, joined together?" Penrys asked Najud.

He shrugged. "I've never heard of Zannib doing that." He glanced at Khizuwi, who shook his head.

"There will be trouble with those *bikrajab*," Khizuwi said. "It's been building for decades, from before my time."

"There'll be trouble sooner than that," Penrys said, "if they follow our trail in the morning."

CHAPTER 54

Late the next morning, they parted from Khizuwi, after confirming that nothing was trailing them. If it was Jiqlaraz and others that Penrys had sensed, they'd gone somewhere else, presumably to the abandoned camp site. She hated to think of them tearing the cairn apart, but there was nothing she could do about it.

"I know where I am. Easy to find my way from here," Khizuwi said. "Three days at most will see me home."

"Sure you won't stay with us for the winter, or at least visit and we'll bring you back with an escort?" Najud said. "I know Umzakhilin would want to thank you."

"No thanks are necessary for us to do what's needed, *jarghal*—you know that." He smiled at Najud's rueful acknowledgment. "No, you just send back Ariqnas when he's ready to come, and I'll let his family know the good news."

Penrys leaned low over her horse in a bow. "Thank you for your care, *jarghal*. I've learned a great deal from you."

"Not, I think, in *bikraj* matters," he said, dryly.

"In matters I value just as highly," she said, shaking her head. "You've given me much to think about."

"Take care of your *nal-jarghal*, you two."

He twisted in his saddle to face Munraz. "And you, young *bikraj*—listen to them. You don't know how lucky you are to have escaped the toils of your family, though you may not think so right now. And these teachers of yours, I do believe they will lead interesting lives. Go on as you have begun, and do great things."

Haraq had held himself back in this farewell of *bikrajab*, but Khizuwi singled him out.

"Haraq, I wish peace on you and all your comrades. The world will be better for all of you in it, rather than lost as you were. Find a way to rebuild and make it so."

Haraq bowed to him from horseback, in silence.

They sat their horses for a few minutes and watched him breaking trail to the northwest, and then returned to the broad track pointed northeast, to the *zudiqazd* of the Kurighdunaq.

In the evening, after they'd all eaten in the *kazr*, it was time to see how well Munraz had done his research.

Penrys had heard him quizzing Khizuwi all morning, before he turned off on his own, and he'd asked questions of everyone the rest of the day. She'd answered everything he asked, narrowly, and left it up to him whether or not he probed for more details. Najud did the same.

Haraq, as he'd promised, was sometimes the questioner, and sometimes a man with answers. She'd heard him speculating with Munraz much of the afternoon, before one or the other would return on a quest for more details.

On the whole, she was pleased with the ground covered by the research for a young man new to such things, but she wanted to hear what he'd learned and digested, not just what he'd heard, to get some feel for his mind.

She settled herself on the edge of her bedframe, with Najud on the carpets at her feet.

"It's time, *nal-jarghal*," she said. "Haraq, I'll hear from you, too—the both of you together."

"But *bikrajti*," Haraq said, "This is the *nal-jarghal*'s lesson."

Najud said, "It's for anyone who wants it."

He started with Munraz. "So, tell me about *bunnas*, as if you were a merchant or a trader."

Munraz looked from one of them to the other, and decided it was more polite to respond to Najud first.

"*Bunnas* is a plant that grows on the low hills around the southern shore of the Hilj Wandat, to the west." He paused as if unsure how to continue, and Penrys prompted him.

"Does it grow anywhere else?"

Munraz shook his head. "No, *bikrajti*."

Haraq opened his mouth and then shut it.

"Yes, Haraq? You have something to add?"

The man glanced at Munraz in apology. "Not that we know of, *bikrajti*. It might grow somewhere else."

She nodded in approval. "And why does it grow there, do you think?"

Haraq volunteered, "It's like any other plant, surely. There's something about the soil, maybe, that it favors. It doesn't get as cold there, with the inland sea to its north, and the hills behind it shelter it from the cold ocean current to the south."

Munraz nodded in agreement. "And there's more water in the air around the shore of the sea, I was told. Perhaps it likes that."

Najud nodded. "All true, and no one that I know of has tried seriously to grow it anywhere else. Perhaps it could be done, and it would no longer be a specialty of Zannib. Perhaps it could grow as well, or better, on the steeper slopes of the northern shore, in the hands of the Rasesni. Are we sure they've never tried?"

Munraz looked at Haraq and shrugged.

"And the preparation of the drink from the growing plant?" Penrys asked.

"Farmers take ripe berries from the plants and use the seeds. It's the seeds that they sell." Munraz clearly felt on firmer ground here.

"And are those seeds what you carry in your pouch?" Najud asked.

"No, *jarghal*. The women in my family roast the seeds, and grind them, and *that's* what's in my pouch." This was said with a note of triumph, of having found his way to the end of the answer.

"Hmm," Penrys said, noncommittally. "How do the farmers strip the fruit from the seed? Do they dry the seed? Does it rot easily in that form? If you wanted more *bunnas*, could you induce them to grow and process more of it, if they had a more profitable market? Or would the price drop if they grew more? Is there enough land for that? Are there enough farmers? Could the women of your family roast more of it if you had more of the seed? Do they have enough time, or would professional roasters be needed?"

She glanced at Najud, and he continued. "How would you confirm that no one else was growing the plant? Can it be grown from the seed? Should the seed only be offered after roasting to prevent that? Should the growing conditions be kept secret? If you sell the seed to foreign buyers, should you explain how to prepare it? Or should you only sell them the roasted seed, to make it easier for them? Which keeps longer, the seed before or after roasting? Which weighs less, and which takes up more space?"

Haraq had kept his head under the blizzard of questions. "I can answer that one. It keeps longer before it is roasted, much longer.

It should only be roasted just before using. The roasted seed weighs less, of course, but I'm not sure about space…"

Penrys looked at Najud and burst out laughing. "As you can see, we can probably come up with a day's worth of questions."

Munraz looked stunned. "I've been drinking *bunnas* all my life and never thought about any of this."

"I did not expect answers to all of this from one day's study, *nal-jarghal*," Penrys told him. "I don't know all those answers myself, because I've never seriously studied it. I knew, from the questions you asked during the day, that the two of you were trying to find out what we already knew, and that's a good start. But you also need to discover what we don't already know, and that means you must use your imagination to envision possibilities.

"For example, I don't even like *bunnas* myself, so I can't personally appreciate the fact that there are different strains with different flavors, like vintages of wine. But I know about that, and so I can learn about it if I need to."

Najud added, "And I, who do know something on this subject, can intrigue my more sophisticated buyers with the romance and flavor of the different kinds, make them feel like experts who can congratulate themselves on their superior understanding, while I congratulate myself on the superior capacity of their pockets."

Penrys nodded. "This would be true understanding of the subject of *bunnas*. And there would be many, many more things an expert could know about it. This one plant—admittedly an important one. This one trade good."

She leaned forward. "I wanted you to see how there is depth in this subject, as far as you care to go, endless, like an onion. There is depth like this in *every* subject, and many subjects have no expert. Any farmer can tell you something like this about the plants he grows, to the degree he knows their history and uses. Your own people know your herds this way, the lineage and capacities of the different varieties, if not how they might be useful to others in different lands for different purposes you haven't imagined."

'I can't learn about the entire world, *bikrajti*," Munraz cried. "There aren't enough years in my life."

"No, you can't. Well said." She beamed at him. "But you can learn *how* to learn. *That* is the point of this lesson—to introduce you to this concept."

"I thought this was a *bikraj* matter," Haraq said.

"The work of a *bikraj* isn't much about secret things, Haraq." Najud included them both in the explanation. "What a *bikraj* can do is born inside, and what's done with it, well, that's where skill and technique can help. That's not exactly secret, it's just that without the power the rest of it is meaningless, so someone not a *bikraj* doesn't care about it. But then, what? What use is a *bikraj* without understanding?"

He looked at Haraq. "Your clan has no *bikraj* at the moment, but mine does. When there is an intractable dispute, it is sometimes only a *bikraj* who can settle it, one who can see clearly how the emotions of the people are involved and what would be the smoothest path to a resolution, the balance between strict justice and acceptance."

Munraz nodded at this description.

"When a child is lost, it may be the *bikraj* who has the best chance of finding it, not necessarily because of a mind-scan for any great distance, but because he understands where the child might go and what might have happened. Imagination and understanding, both."

"When there's a death," Penrys said, slowly, thinking of Khizuwi, "A *bikraj* can help the survivor work past sorrow to a better acceptance. Not just understanding, but sympathy."

She looked at Munraz. "The *qahulajti* was a *bikrajti* without understanding. I will maintain, despite the great harm she caused, that it was not entirely her fault, but in the end it doesn't matter. You must understand people and the limits of your own knowledge, and then learn as much as you can, if you want to be a *bikraj*."

"Or a leader of the people," Haraq added.

Najud nodded. "Yes, indeed."

Munraz ventured one more question. "What about the forbidden subjects, *jarghal*? Is there a limit to what we should seek to understand?"

Penrys and Najud exchanged looks.

"This is a subject about which you will have to make up your own mind." Penrys turned to Haraq. "What he's asking about is the difference between *bikr mar-shimiqa*, the magic of thinking, and *bikr mar-thulj*, the magic of things. In *sarq*-Zannib, *bikr mar-thulj* is forbidden. It is not that way in Rasesdad, nor in Ellech where I studied."

She fingered her chain and told Munraz, "This is a *jurqal*, a device, something forbidden. So are the wings, I believe. I didn't make either one, in fact they are far too advanced for me, but I have made devices, many of them. I studied them, at the Collegium in Ellech. It was not forbidden.

"Here, however…" She pursed her lips. "Khizuwi understood this and said it didn't make me a *qahulajti*. I doubt many of the *bikrajab* in Zannib would agree with him."

"I know my uncle did not," Munraz muttered.

"So. You see. You have plenty to learn without having to make your own choices in this matter. No one will try to influence you, one way or the other."

"And you, *jarghal?*" Munraz asked.

"I've watched her at work," Najud said, soberly. "I have not myself made devices. Not yet." Then he smiled and his whole face lightened. "But I think it is only a matter of time before I will ask her to teach me. That is *my* decision, not yours.

Munraz nodded as if filing that away. "Then what about the rest of my assignment, the *kassa* and the dyes?"

"Can you summarize it in a few sentences so we can get some sleep?" Penrys yawned in illustration, and Haraq chuckled.

Munraz straightened his spine. "I know less about *kassa* than I did about *bunnas*, and all I learned about dyes is that it is a very big subject about which no one here knew very much, beyond their names, uses, and trade values." He cocked his head at Najud, his source for that information.

"But I think I understand what they all have in common, for a trader or a merchant."

Penrys made him a go-ahead gesture.

"They're small, lightweight. They have a lot of value in small amounts. They don't take up much space in packs. They keep well, if you can preserve them from damp and heat. They're hard to come by, the sources are limited, and you need a lot of knowledge about how to acquire them and who would use them. You need to give instructions with them, when you sell them."

Haraq added, "And once you have a customer, he'll want more and more of them."

"Oh, and that's why red is so common in our rugs and not blue—too expensive," Munraz threw in.

"Well done, both of you," Penrys said. "That's plenty, for a start."

CHAPTER 55

Najud was impatient to be done with traveling. *Winter's for catching up on sleep and gossip, not for freezing fingers and toes.* Four mornings on the trail, and they still didn't expect see the end of it tonight.

He was in the lead, at the moment, not that there was any mistaking the path. Haraq and Munraz held the middle position. *No cairns along this route, it's not the way we came. Won't be any bodies, either, to be trampled heedlessly by the horses.*

Penrys rode last, with her pack-string of horses out of Silmat. She was still on the watch behind them for Jiqlaraz, in case he decided to bring trouble north. She must be scanning forward as well, for she suddenly bespoke him. *Visitors ahead, Naj-sha. It's all three of them! Jirkat, Ilzay, and even Winnajhubr. If no one stops, we should see them in forty minutes.*

Najud twisted in his saddle to tell the others the news. "Looks like our Kurighdunaq guides are coming back to see what's taking us so long. Can't say I blame them. They'll be on us before we're even thinking about the mid-day stop."

Both Haraq and Munraz brightened, though Haraq snorted. "As if we can't find the *zudiqazd* with this to follow." His arm took in the twenty-foot wide trail. "Still, it'll be good to hear about the others."

They walked forward at a brisker pace, until Jirkat must have spotted them at a distance and dropped his pack rope, for he popped up ahead of them, galloping his horse to meet them. The other two appeared and stopped, prepared to wait for Najud's party to reach them.

Jirkat circled them, trilling like a madman, waved at Penrys as he passed with a broad smile, and fetched up with Najud in front. "We thought you'd gotten lost, *zarawinnaj*, since it's well known you can barely find your way from one *kazr* to the next."

He glanced at the other three. "Khizuwi wouldn't come back with you?"

"He wanted to go home instead," Najud said. "That was yesterday."

"Why have you got the young *bikraj* with you, and not the old one?"

Munraz overheard and looked away. Najud said, "That's a long tale, Jirkat, and should be told to others first."

Jirkat nodded, unoffended. "And the *qahulajti*? Is she behind you?"

"No, she's no longer a threat." *Jiqlaraz, now, was another story, but not for right now.*

By then Najud's party had reached the others and the greetings were general. Najud broke into their conversations. "How far are we, Jirkat?"

Ilzay answered him. "You'll get there this evening if you don't stop. We left from the *magham* this morning, as all the clans were going. And a sad festival camp it was—like ghosts at the party, we were—better if we'd all gone on to the *zudiqazd* and stayed there."

"Then that's what we'll do. Save your chit-chat for the trail, everyone," he called. "We're going to press on and sleep in the *zudiqazd* tonight."

Around mid-day, their trail took them by the site of the *magham*, with its handful of permanent buildings for the group gatherings. It was deserted—nothing was left but three clusters of *kazrab* circles, of which the middle, more northerly one, was pitifully small.

Najud shook his head at the sight. *What must it have been like when Jirkat led in almost sixty survivors? Joy, at first, surely, but then sorrow, for the tally of the dead and the list of the missing.*

The survivors knew who was back in the zudiqazd, waiting for them— they'd had days on the trail already to begin to mourn their dead—but it would have been fresh grief to the others.

And what did the other clans think, in the midst of the winter celebration, about this sharp reminder of death and the fragility of life?

Ilzay rode beside him and noted his silence. "We arrived in the evening, *zarawinnaj*, and there was a great feast. Shelters were offered on all sides, but they would only sleep in the four large *kazrab* we'd brought, as they had for a week. Dhalmudhr was their spokesman, and he explained to Umzakhilin..."

He paused and took a deeper breath. "He said no one else could understand, that it would be some time before they could settle in again. Some of those few who had family still living tried to share with them, but no one slept away from the rest of the survivors, that night."

Najud said, "They've made new families, haven't they, families of necessity. All their lives they'll remember having been together like this, wherever else they go. Like a band of warriors after a long and hard battle."

Ilzay nodded. "After a couple days, four of them moved to the *kazrab* of their relatives. I've heard it's not going very well, that they stop in the middle of conversations and stare at things that only they can see."

"It'll get better, Ilzay," Najud said. "Everyone alive feels guilty about it. It's not sensible, but we can't control such thoughts."

"As you say, *zarawinnaj*. It was sad, though. They knew how out-of-step they were with the spirit of the *magham*. They stayed away from the weddings, not because they begrudged the joy of others, but because they didn't want to spoil it for them."

His shoulders sagged. "This was the first *magham* I can remember where the Kurighdunaq had no weddings at all, or even betrothals. As if the whole clan were a wounded beast and could spare no time for such things."

"The clan *is* wounded," Najud said, "and no wonder. I'm surprised it stayed for the full *magham*."

Ilzay smiled faintly. "Some in the clan wanted to return to the *zudiqazd* altogether, instead of just doing the periodic check on the herds and the ones who couldn't travel. Umzakhilin wouldn't permit it. He said the Kurighdunaq were too proud to let an enemy win while there were still warriors to defend it, that it would not allow itself to give up in defeat just because a blow had been struck." He sighed.

"He will be a great *ujarqa*, Umzakhilin—a clan leader to remember. To see him, with his cane, talking to the survivors… That gives me hope."

"He's a survivor himself," Najud said. "If anyone can reconcile the fragments of the clan together, it's probably him."

"And Hadishti," Ilzay said. "She was everywhere, making things easier. No one realized what she was capable of, before."

"People are strengthened by the work they do," Najud said. "I've seen it before, many times."

CHAPTER 56

Half a mile before they reached the edge of the *zudiqazd*, Jirkat took charge of Winnajhubr's pack-string and sent the young man ahead in the partial moonlight. Then he returned to his quiet conversation with Haraq. Penrys heard the name 'Luram' mentioned, Haraq's sister.

She glanced aside at Munraz, who was licking his lips nervously. When she raised an eyebrow, he blurted out, "It's not my clan. They won't want outsiders here."

"Not my clan, either," Penrys said, matter-of-factly. "Umzakhilin adopted Najud in, so I suppose it's his clan—I'm not sure how these things work in *sarq*-Zannib."

An outsider's perspective on the possibly quaint customs of his own people served its purpose in distracting Munraz from his anxiety.

The first faint fires of the evening came into view ahead. Everyone was indoors, of course, but each time a door opened, it shed light from the *kazr* onto the trampled snow, more and more by the moment, the light occluded briefly by people emerging.

Ilzay steered for the dark bulk of four large *kazrab* on the edge of the settlement, and then stopped, and everyone pulled up behind him. Out of the gloom appeared the two herd-boys Penrys remembered, the ones that had taken care of Umzakhilin.

"Come take these horses, Zabrash," Ilzay called. Right behind them were Bimal, the lost *dirum*, and with her the young *dirum-malb* Inghiti that the sister clan Winnajjinza had offered Umzakhilin.

Winnajhubr, on foot now, side-stepped the activity and trotted straight to Jirkat and Ilzay. "He wants to see you, Umzakhilin does, and then I'm to bring the *bikrajab* when they're ready."

Penrys stayed back a bit with Najud and Munraz, and let Jirkat and Ilzay get sorted out first. Then she kicked her left foot from her stirrup, balanced on her hands, swung her right leg over, and dropped to land on her good leg, holding onto her horse until she was stable. Her crutch was strapped to her back, as the most convenient place to carry it on horseback, and by the time she'd untied it and gotten it under her right shoulder, Bimal had come to greet her.

"You're looking well, *dirum*," Penrys said, and indeed it was clear that she was in her element, overseeing Birssahr and Zabrash, with Inghiti's help.

"These five horses…" Penrys said, indicating her string. "I want them. I'll buy them, whoever's they are. They saved my life."

Bimal smiled. "I know how that can be. I'll find out about them for you, *bikrajti*."

Najud roped Winnajhubr into helping him erect their *kazr* with Munraz, and Penrys stayed out of the way. Just beyond the activity, she could dimly see in the partial moonlight that more people had come outside, quietly, just to watch.

They made quick work of putting up the *kazr* and laying out the rugs, and then their packs along the walls. Najud gave it all a glance, then shooed Penrys and Munraz out.

"Zabrash will get the fire started and keep an eye on it so we don't all come back to a cold bed," he told them.

Winnajhubr was waiting for them nervously outside, and beckoned the three of them to follow him to Umzakhilin's *kazr*.

All along the way as they went more deeply into the *zudiqazd* people gathered in ones and twos and watched them go by. When Penrys reached out and sampled their mood, she felt curiosity and tension, fear and hope.

She followed Najud as he ducked into the big, central *kazr* that was shared now by Umzakhilin and Hadishti.

"Welcome back," Hadishti said, warmly, and her children, Sharma and Dimghuy, found them places to sit, struggling a bit with Penrys until Najud simply lowered her down onto her good knee and left her to arrange the healing leg straight out in front of her from there. They glanced curiously at Munraz.

The place was fully furnished now, Penrys saw, and looked as if it had been this family's home for generations. Hadishti brought fresh mutton and beans to each of them, and when she'd given Penrys her share, Penrys grabbed her arm to stop her for a moment. "Thanks for all your advice," she said, "Not to mention the cooking lessons. Made things easier."

Hadishti beamed at her. "Eat, now, and relax. Plenty of time to talk afterward."

Umzakhilin was chatting with Jirkat and Ilzay closer to the fire while his new guests ate. He looked much better to Penrys, though she saw a sturdy cane on the rugs beside him.

Najud had just laid his meal aside, when there came a knock on the doorframe. Umzakhilin looked at his clansmen. "Did you tell him?"

They shook their heads and tried to hide a smile. Hadishti told Najud, "We have a surprise for you, *bikraj.*"

The door opened, and a young woman stepped in over the threshold, her head bare and covered with black curls.

Najud scrambled to his feet. "Rubti! What are you doing here?"

Penrys looked from one face to the other as they hugged. *She must be his younger sister, the one he said was a dirum-malb. How wonderful to have a family to greet you.*

But this is my family, too, now. What a strange thought.

Najud grabbed her left arm and hauled her up, steadying her until she could balance with her crutch. "*Nurti,* this is my betrothed. Penrys, my middle sister, Rubti."

The girl took in her broken leg and obviously foreign appearance with a startled blink, and then smiled up at her brother. "You always leave the most important news out of your letters, *tigha,* don't you? I want to hear the whole story."

Najud grinned. "But why are you here? Anyone else with you? Is everyone all right?"

"They're fine, and it's just me. I'll tell you about it later."

Najud helped Penrys settle back on the carpets, then plunked down with his sister, side by side.

Umzakhilin cleared his throat, and all eyes switched back to him. "So, *zarawinnaj,* you've done as I asked and brought us back our clan. I'm told the *qahulajti* is no longer a threat, and this is fine news. I've heard part of it from these men." His gesture encompassed Jirkat, Ilzay, and Winnajhubr. "And part from many of our returned clan-kin."

He paused and looked expectantly at Najud. "Now, if you are not too tired, perhaps you could give me your full report."

Najud drew a deep breath and let it out. Then he straightened his spine and told the tale. He took Umzakhilin swiftly over the first few days of camps and cairns and tracking, and Jirkat and Ilzay contributed the occasional bit. Winnajhubr maintained a discrete silence befitting his relative youth.

Penrys told the story of the meeting with Khizuwi, and then the next meeting with Jiqlaraz and Munraz. She introduced Munraz as Najud's *nal-jarghal*, and hers, and that raised eyebrows, but she saved the explanation for its proper place in the report.

Najud took a moment to outline the rumored marriage practices of the Rashaban *bikrajab*, and Munraz nodded to verify the details. Then he continued with the blizzard, the same that had dumped the snow all around the *zudiqazd*, and which gave Umzakhilin a clear date for when things happened from there.

Penrys explained how they found the first survivors, and what she thought the *qahulajti* had done to them, and how the effect was dismissed.

It was harder for Najud to maintain his even tone when he outlined the expedition into the Silmat valley, where Penrys located the pockets of survivors and then flew off and didn't return. She reached out and gripped his hand, and he continued to describe, with Jirkat and Ilzay's help, how they hastened group after group of them back to their camp. "None of this could have been done without the fine men you sent with us, *ujarqa*. We needed every one of them."

Penrys hastened over the details of her slow chase and what she made of the *qahulajti*'s movements.

While Jirkat told of gathering all the survivors and making what speed he could with them, Penrys caught the open-mouthed looks Rubti gave her brother as she listened to this tale, and the occasional glances directed her own way.

Najud took time for a deep draft of mead. Then he braced himself and described the fight about the *qahulajti*, and her death. Penrys could picture it all. *And me unconscious in the kazr the whole time.*

"Munraz upheld the judgment of the *bikrajab* present, and for this he has paid with exile from his family and clan," Najud said.

"And so the *bikrajab* of Rashaban are now declared enemies?" Umzakhilin asked.

"That's not entirely clear. Khizuwi speculated that it would happen, if not now, then soon. Penrys thought they crossed behind us, back to the camp and its cairn, a couple of nights ago."

Penrys shook her head. "I can't be sure that's what I felt."

"And young Munraz here?" Umzakhilin's voice was carefully neutral.

Najud said, "He killed the *qahulajti* to keep his uncle from claiming her, and it cost him everything. We will vouch for him, as our *nal-jarghal.*"

"I will think about this," Umzakhilin said. He leaned back and stretched a moment.

"And so there may yet be survivors in Silmat, and certainly more of our herds. We must send another party soon, but I don't like to call on the other clans in our tribe for yet more help."

Ilzay said, "It may be, *ujarqa*, that clan Umzabul, Khizuwi's clan, would be willing to help. We need to escort young Ariqnas there anyway. Perhaps that could be an opportunity to strengthen relations with them, outside our own tribe, and the distance from there to Silmat is hardly any further."

"That's an interesting suggestion."

Penrys could see that Najud was pleased with Umzakhilin's reaction.

I don't understand what's going on.

What's happening, Pen-sha, is that the ujarqa may be considering the caravan base I've suggested, where alliances beyond the tribe will become important.

Umzakhilin clapped his hands together. "This is enough for one evening." He spoke to his audience of *bikrajab*. "I have been waiting until the fate of the *qahulajti* was known. Tomorrow morning we will have the grand tally of the living and the dead. And in the afternoon, we will do our weddings, here in the privacy of our own *zudiqazd* instead of the *magham*, where we can manage our own grief." He glanced over at Hadishti.

"There will be five of them, all at once," she told them. "Jirkat's brother Khashghuy and the rescued Yardiqurti—he waited for his brother to return. And four more, newly announced among the survivors." Her lips quirked. "They're determined to weld family fragments back into new families."

Najud looked at Penrys and raised an eyebrow. She smiled and nodded.

Hadishti watched them and told her husband, "Six couples, I think it will be."

CHAPTER 57

Rubti walked back with Najud and Penrys to the *kazr* they shared with Munraz. She greeted everyone she met along the way by name and they smiled back at her.

Najud noticed. "How long have you been here, *nurti*, that you know so many people?"

"Only a few days, *tigha*. I got here in time for part of the *magham*, before Jirkat and Ilzay came back. After that, they started worrying about what was keeping you. I wanted to go with them, but Umzakhilin wouldn't allow it."

They ducked inside through the doorframe and startled Zabrash who'd been dozing on the rugs by the stove. When the boy saw Rubti, he grinned. "I didn't tell him."

Najud commented sardonically, "How is it that so many conspired with my little sister to keep me in the dark, eh?" He chased the boy out of the *kazr* in pretend wrath, and shut the door behind him.

"Now, sit down, *nurti*, and tell me the whole tale."

The two siblings sat across from each other, in front of the stove, and Munraz observed from near the door, silent. Penrys suddenly realized that she didn't know if he had brothers and sisters himself.

Penrys moved over to her bed so she could sit on its edge, and watched her… sister-in-law. *How strange that felt. Was it her youth that gave her such self-possessed confidence? But no, Najud has that, too. What must the rest of the family be like?*

"It was four weeks ago, two months after I celebrated becoming a *tushkzurtudin*. A message came special for you, over the Low Pass, with your lineage and clan, and we accepted it for you."

She reached into her winter robes and pulled out a stiff wrapped packet of paper, still sealed and bound with cords. Najud glanced at it, then handed it to Penrys and she stretched forward to take it.

It was addressed in both Kigali and Rasesni script, very formal, and beneath that someone had written the Zannib version, more casually. When she held it up to her nose, the scent of paper, ink, and seal were overlaid with some sort of Zannib spices, no doubt from whatever pack it had shared while it traveled. She laid it aside on the bed.

"We didn't know what to do with it," Rubti said. "Our father thought it likely that the message itself wasn't written in Zannib, judging from the address, and was reluctant to open it. And, in any case, we didn't know where you were. Last we heard, it was somewhere in Neshilik."

She looked up at Najud accusingly from under her brows, and he threw his hands into the air in helpless apology.

"Then a week later," she said, "Hazimjilah arrived, from the west. He said he'd been sent by Zamharshat, *gharqa* of the Undullah tribe, and he had a message for your family, from you. And it had *my* name on it, in someone else's handwriting."

She laughed. "Now, I had heard of the Undullah tribe, over by the High Pass, but how would they know my name?"

"Donkeys," Najud said, promptly, and her eyebrows climbed.

"Are those *your* donkeys?" she asked, distracted by enthusiasm. "No one told me. I haven't had a chance to look them over seriously, but there's this one jack with a bad temper…"

Najud and Penrys interrupted her in unison. "Demon." Rubti glared at them as they laughed.

"Never mind," Najud said. "We'll get to that. But that's how they know your name—I mentioned my *nurti*, a *dirum-malb*, and they remembered."

"Oh. Well, we guested the man overnight, and he was ready to return the next morning. And… I decided to come with him."

"But why, *nurti?* It's such a long way, and with a strange man…"

"We had separate *kamahab*," she declared, indignation strong in her voice. "He was just a companion for the road. He took me to the *magham* and returned to his own clan there."

Najud just continued to look at her steadily.

"I'm grown now, I can travel when I want to," she said, her chin high.

Najud's unchanged silent regard worked on her. Penrys carefully kept her face expressionless.

"Oh, *tigha*, I was so *bored*. Hazimjilah told me what had happened here, and he told me about you, too, *bikrajti*." That last was addressed to Penrys, across her brother. "Though he didn't say anything about a betrothal."

Najud responded to the accusation in her voice with a mock whisper. "You see, *nurti*, I hadn't convinced her yet."

"Why not? Didn't she like you?"

Penrys could see her hackles rising in defense of her brother. "No, Rubti, it wasn't that. It's complicated... I thought he deserved better..."

"And I told her she was wrong," Najud said.

Rubti subsided. "Oh, in that case... If that's all, then whoever he wants is fine with me, *nagha*."

She turned to Najud. "What do I call her? Is she older than Yukjilah? She looks like she might be."

Penrys bit her lip. *She called me 'older sister.' A sister!*

"We don't know, *nurti*," Najud said. "Probably, since Yukjilah's almost as young as our Ghuruma."

"Ah," Rubti nodded sagely. "*Naghayin*, then—oldest sister." She giggled. "That'll make Yukjilah unhappy—all those years as a youngest *nurtin* in her own family, then a *naghayin* in ours when she married Butraz, and now just a *nagha*. She loved being oldest for a change."

"She'll adjust," Najud said, dryly. "Now, seriously, *nurti*, why did you want to leave?"

Rubti's face sobered. "You left when you were my age, *tigha*, remember? Everyone says it was different for you, doing your *daril* work, traveling as a journeyman *bikraj*. I'm just a *dirum-malb*, but there're others in the clan. It's work I want to do, but not as an apprentice, forever. And then, there's no one unmarried there that interests me, not that way."

She took a deep breath. "I wanted to see more of the world, just like you, find my own place in it. So, when we heard where you were and what you were doing, and there was this foreign letter to deliver, I just... decided to go."

"Our parents allowed it?"

"I'm old enough, they couldn't stop me. And our mother gave me this, for you."

She leaned over and kissed Najud on his cheek.

Penrys spoke, to cover Najud's surprised silence. "Surely you're not still sleeping in a *kamah* in this weather."

"Inghiti invited me to share her *kazr*, *naghayin*, and I'm helping with *dirum-malb* stuff. They don't have enough winter herdsmen yet, though some of the ones you rescued are starting to help."

She leaned forward. "Do you know what Bimal said to Inghiti? She told her she should stay, since her own *dirum-malb* was dead. Maybe she might take me on, too. I could learn a lot here."

"You should move in with us," Najud declared. "Family."

Rubti laughed. "What, the night before a wedding? I can wait a little while." She called over to the silent Munraz. "We'll find you a place, too, *nal-jarghal*, for the next few days."

Wedding! Penrys looked ruefully at her broken leg and mentally reviewed the filthy clothing in her pack.

CHAPTER 58

"I *like* her," Penrys told Najud, after Rubti bounced out of the *kazr*. "Are they all like that in your family?"

Najud laughed. "No, she's special. Of course, I don't know the last two very well—the youngest wasn't even born when I started my travels. But Rubti fastened on to me every time I came home, and it got so I didn't feel right if she was somewhere else. It'll take me a while to think of her as a *tushkzurtudin*, but don't tell *her* that."

"Munraz," Penrys called, and waved him over to join them. He rose from his quiet spot and sat down closer to the stove.

"I just realized I don't know much about your family. Are you the oldest? Do you have brothers and sisters?"

"I was the only child of my mother born alive," he said, "before she died."

Penrys's mouth dropped. Before she could sputter anything, he continued. "That was my father's second wife. His first wife died in childbirth, and the babe with her. The elders wouldn't allow him a third wife."

Najud asked, quietly, "Were they cousins, your parents?"

Munraz swallowed and looked away. "Mine were," he muttered. "His first wife was a half-sister."

"Are they all like that in Rashaban?" Penrys asked, appalled.

"Not in the rest of the clan—that's one reason they won't wed with us. Just in my family. Some of us are… mad. That's dangerous in a *bikraj*, so those are kept quiet and controlled. The men still have uses for the women in that condition. They marry them, hoping for children. Sometimes there are daughters, sane ones, to raise for the next generation."

Penrys remembered Khizuwi's warning about ways of destroying the mind while leaving the body, and she shuddered.

"Oh, *nal-jarghal*…" Najud said. "And you escaped this? Were there others who escaped?"

Munraz stared down at the carpet. "There were stories… I had four cousins my age—boys, of course, the girls were kept apart for eventual marriage. We traded stories we'd heard late at night."

He cleared his throat. "One of my cousins is dead, one vanished—I think he's probably dead, too. He never came back after a training session with his father. The other two are married and their wives are pregnant."

He lifted his head and his eyes were bleak. "One of the wives you could even talk to."

Penrys swallowed, and then said, briskly, "And you were next, eh? Well, we're both orphans now. It's not so bad, considering."

He glanced at Najud shyly and looked back at her. "It seems like a nice family you're joining, *bikrajti.*"

"You'll find one, too, someday," she told him, with the strongest conviction she could muster.

He flashed a half-smile and drew himself upright, burying his feelings again.

She picked up the much-traveled document and tossed it to Najud. "I think you better read this."

"I think you're right," he said, and proceeded to untie the knotted cords and break the seal. He unfolded two papyrus pages of tidy handwriting, and two paper sheets of different manufacture, one of which had a wax seal in which short ribbons were embedded, while the other had square stamps in red ink along the bottom.

He looked at the odd sheets first. "This is a permit for a *biziz,* a caravan," he said, his voice rising, waving the one with the red chops. He read aloud, "For anywhere in the western half of the nation. This permit may be copied anywhere in Kigali, for any caravan owned in full or in part by the Zan Najud, son of Ilsahr, of clan Zamjilah."

He looked at Penrys. "It's signed by Tun Jeju on behalf of the King of Earth and Sea."

Munraz choked, and Najud turned to him. "It sounds less preposterous in Kigali *yat.*"

He tossed the sheet with the wax seal to Penrys. "Here. Your written Rasesni is better than mine, I expect."

She unfolded it and looked it over. "Not sure about a couple of the words without that dictionary Dzantig gave us, but I think it's the same sort of thing. This one's signed by Menchos."

"Of course it is." Najud shook his head. "You should see the letter. It's marked 'number 1:3.' Tun Jeju's work. Means he must've sent at least three copies."

He thought about that a moment. "One to Jaunor, maybe. This one through the Low Pass to clan Zamjilah. The other one... where? To Ussha? Just in case?"

"What does he want? You didn't get those permits for free," Penrys said.

"You. They want you." Najud read it over twice and handed it to her.

Penrys scanned the letter, then started over and considered it more slowly. "...present yourself and the Ellech woman Penrys to the Office of Imperial Security in Yenit Ping as soon as the first Grand Caravan arrives from *sarq*-Zannib, or as soon thereafter as may be possible, with the permission of the Circle of Speakers... on a matter of the security of our nations."

She looked up. "He doesn't say outright 'come or you can bid these permits farewell,' does he?"

Najud smiled tightly. "He doesn't have to. You ignore something like this at your peril. I don't say that he could reach into *sarq*-Zannib for us, not easily, but we'd never be able to visit Kigali again if we refused. Our names and descriptions would be known everywhere."

He nodded at the letter in her hand. "That's an order. And these," waving the permits in the air, "are the honey to sweeten it."

"But why?" she thought aloud. "I thought it was some peculiar coincidence that we should find another chained wizard after the other one, but now I wonder if they've found more of them. What else could it be?"

She looked at it again. "They're not very urgent about it."

"We can't get there any earlier, not realistically. No one travels any distance in winter by choice. We'll have to get to Qawrash im-Dhal in the east for the start of the first *Biziz Rahr* into Kigali, in about two months. The Grand Caravan doesn't leave until the grass is far enough along to support grazing. That's five hundred miles away, a month in good weather, plus another week or so to visit my family along the way. If we winter here, as I'd planned, that gives us almost a month to prepare. It's possible."

He broke off from his calculations to search her face. "But only if you want to, Pen-sha. We could stay in *sarq*-Zannib, join my family, live a quiet life." He smiled at Munraz, silent and fascinated. "Train the occasional *nal-jarghal*."

She snorted. "And give up your dream of a western caravan? And what about these chained wizards? They must be involved. There's no other reason they'd want me."

She folded the letter up carefully and handed it and the Rasesni permit back to Najud. "Well, we don't have to answer immediately. It's not like we can get a message to them any time soon." She turned to their apprentice.

"Any interest in traveling to Yenit Ping and seeing the sights, Munraz? You know, where the iron for your *khash* comes from?"

CHAPTER 59

Najud sat on his heels by his open pack and considered. The *kazr* that surrounded him, one of several that Umzakhilin had set aside for their goods and those of the summer encampment, was unheated and dark, its *zamjilah* covered against the snow. On the bare canvas, partially illuminated where his lantern shone directly, were two small leather pouches and the soft robe embroidered by Rubti for her *tigha* three or four years ago, a bit worn now by use.

He'd considered his formal ceremonial robes, the only other choice he had, but he'd glimpsed the clothing that Rubti had brought Penrys this morning, from Hadishti—good, clean, robes— but not the sort of thing intended for foreign cities, to represent the pride of his nation. It would embarrass her if he outshone her, and besides—holding the robe up against his newly shaven cheek—this soft robe was suitable enough, and it would delight his *nurti*, the only family who could stand by him today.

A little more rummaging in the pack turned up his best *anah im-ghabr*, the turban that could not be omitted for a traditional wedding.

He tied up the pack again, and counted all the packs, his and Penrys's, stored there, estimating the number of horses he would need. Plus food and fodder, their *kazr*, and extras, he reminded himself. Then he shook his head and rose to his feet with a creak of the knees. *Time enough for that later. There were more important events to focus on, today.*

Penrys stood with Najud in the flattened and packed snow that formed the inner circle of the handful of *kazrab* in the *zudiqazd*. The whole clan stood with them, dressed in the best of their clothing. They'd had two days to find their goods, retrieved from the summer encampment or stored from the *zudiqazd*, and they were clean and tidy, the clothing so much fresher than their worn faces and thin bodies that it broke Penrys's heart to see them.

And they were so few, not even enough to fill the half-perimeter that defined the open space before Umzakhilin and Hadishti who held possession of the center on real, wooden chairs—the first Penrys had seen in Zannib.

So someone has chairs, I see. Why don't they use them in the kazrab?

Najud snorted. *Practically speaking, why burden your horses with something you don't really need? But the true answer is, it's something the Kigali would do, elevating themselves over someone else. Only for very serious occasions will you see them in sarq-Zannib. For matters of weight, when a lisha is needed, a little king.*

He chuckled. *Though we do keep one chair for the use of the Kigali ambassador at the Ghuzl mar-Tawirqaj, the Circle of Speakers, in Ussha. He thinks it's to honor him, and we don't tell him what we really think.*

He pictured for her a standing turbaned speaker at the formal assembly of the country, all of his audience seated decorously on carpets, except for one person in a long Kigali robe, proudly occupying a decorated chair with a bored look.

Penrys kept her laughter to herself, and the voices muttering around her quieted as Umzakhilin raised his hand.

Canvas underlaid a small spread of felt pads in front of his seat, and another area of snow-protected felts to the side of the chairs held one of the low worktables, with Bimal and a survivor Penrys didn't know seated behind it. A pile of the wax-filled tablets that served for temporary records were piled before them. Behind Bimal were Inghiti and Rubti, supporting the *dirum* and learning from her.

"Who's that with Bimal?" she whispered to Najud.

"Quyubil, the *tarimkaj*, law-master. Must be a canny man."

"Why?" she asked.

"He's the oldest of the survivors."

Umzakhilin beckoned Ilzay forward, and the crunch of his footsteps in the snow sounded clearly in the dead silence of the observers. He shouldered the horse pack with the rainbow marking of his clan that Penrys well remembered, and laid it on the felt pads at the foot of the chairs. Another wave of the *ujarqa*'s hand called forth Khashghuy, with a similar pack. Penrys realized this one must be from the search for survivors between the *zudiqazd* and the summer encampment.

Ilzay opened the pack and took out one of the pouches that Penrys remembered Najud working on in the quiet of their *kazr*.

He called out the name on it, and a woman stepped out from the onlookers and walked forward. "My father," she told Quyubil, and he made a note on his tablet. She picked the pouch up reverently, and returned to her place.

Khashghuy took a pouch from his pack, and cried the name, and young Zabrash came to claim it. "My older brother," he declared, with a wooden face.

Name by name, the morning wore on. Penrys shielded her mind from the silent grief, but the keening that arose whenever a child was named couldn't be evaded so easily. So many were dead that the same people stepped forward again and again, and the fold of their robes that held the pouches bulged with the collection.

Every now and then the *tarimkaj* ruled on who the closest relative was, when the more obscure lineages were all that were left alive.

As each of the unidentified ones had been taken out of the packs, they'd been laid separately on the felts. Finally, as the packs were emptied, those were all that were left.

Ilzay opened one and removed its tag. "A man, left forearm broken once." Three people walked heavily forward to see if they recognized the cloth, and one man claimed it. "My brother," he declared to the *tarimkaj*, and choked out the name.

In the end, seven remained unidentified, all children except one. Not even the gender was sure for some of them. Penrys realized it meant that so many of their family were also dead that no one was left who could be sure who they were by the details of their clothing.

Najud stood by her side, his features desolate. His aunt Qizrahi and her son Zaybirs were among the dead in Khashghuy's pack, and he discovered there were two daughters, new to him, with her. Her husband's sister claimed them.

Umzakhilin himself had taken charge of his son's pouch, and that of the son's wife. Only his white-knuckled grasp betrayed his composure. Bimal, Hadishti, even the *tarimkaj*—no one in the clan was untouched.

At last, next to the seven lonely pouches, Ilzay laid the two tally horns, and Khashghuy a single carved stick—there had been no survivors to find in Khashghuy's journey. They spoke quietly to Quyubil about the numbers represented there, and he made notes on his tablets.

There were tears on some of the faces, but everyone waited stoically for the *tarimkaj* to speak. Penrys surveyed the crowd and saw no one younger than Zabrash and Birssahr, and none obviously older than Quyubil. *Their wisdom and their hope, both gone at once. How can they recover from that?*

"*Ujarqa*."

The word from Quyubil seized everyone's attention. "I have the tally of the living and the dead, if you would hear it."

"Speak, *tarimkaj*." Umzakhilin's face was remote.

"Clan Kurighdunaq was, at the time of the summer encampment, two hundred and eighty-four people, all told. We are now seventy-one."

A suppressed gasp from the onlookers sighed over the snow.

"We are sure of one hundred and eighty-two dead—three in the *zudiqazd*, fifty-four on the summer and spring trails, and one hundred and twenty-five between the *zudiqazd* and the valley of Silmat.

"Of the thirty-one remaining, we cannot speak. Most likely they are also dead by the trail, but not found, especially the young ones. But many of these are not children—our recovered clan-kin, and I, believe there may be some still alive in Silmat."

I wonder what the count of the Voice's dead was. Najud's mental voice conveyed his bitterness.

Penrys thought of the ease with which she had killed the men of the hill tribe that fought for the Voice. *We're a bloody lot, aren't we?*

Najud turned his head to look at her and squeezed her hand.

Umzakhilin spoke to his clan. "I declare the tally correct. We'll send another party to Silmat in a few days to look for anyone still alive, and to retrieve whatever of our herds may be wintering there. The tally cannot be final until that is done."

Heads nodded at the statement.

Bimal now spoke for the first time. "I have conducted a tally of the herds, though this will change after the proposed visit to Silmat. I will speak to each of the heirs about what is theirs once they are properly named."

She cocked her head at Quyubil, seated next to her.

"The total for clan Kurighdunaq as a whole is surprising, *ujarqa*. We have only lost at most one in four of our flocks, and the expedition to Silmat may improve that significantly. We have all the winter grazing we ever did, so there is no difficulty supporting them, and the harvested spring fodder, as well as some of the autumn. The only problem is herdsmen—I'll need more to preserve them over the winter."

Umzakhilin nodded to show he'd heard her. "*Tarimkaj*, please sort the heirs."

He looked out into the crowd. "This will be a preliminary declaration, not a final one—that must wait until the Silmat valley is explored. You may not dispose of any property beyond recovery, except for food, until that time."

Quyubil called out the name of one of the dead, and two men stepped forward, both of them nephews of the man, through different brothers. There was a brief discussion, and the *tarimkaj* added to his notes and made a declaration.

Penrys was appalled at how long this could go on and glanced at Najud in dismay.

Don't worry, Pen-sha. This is just the lineage of inheritance they're sorting out, not the substance.

He smiled at her puzzled look. *The tarimkaj is establishing who the heirs are, and to what degree. With so many dead and only obscure relations remaining for some, that is not a simple task. The actual possessions of the dead—their goods and herds—will take much longer to sort out. That's why the dirum is there, too, taking notes about special animals, breeding lines, and so forth. Since not all the herds are retrieved yet, and more people may be found, it's subject to revision until it's finally settled.*

She muttered, "It's as bad as a legal dispute in Tavnastok, where they grow lawyers like weeds."

"Why do you think Umzakhilin's doing this out in the cold snow, when all of them want to go into their *kazrab* and get warm, and will be quick about it in consequence?"

She smiled at the simple cunning of it.

"And besides," he said, "these decisions *will* be settled and final, soon enough. It will be as the *tarimkaj* and the *ujarqa* decide."

"Penrys, Najud." Umzakhilin startled her by calling their names. He waved them forward while the steady stream of clan survivors talked to the *tarimkaj*, and Penrys was careful of her footing with her crutch. He gestured to them to turn around and face the remains of the clan, and stood up behind them to place his hands upon their shoulders, one for each.

"These *bikrajab* have done great service to the Kurighdunaq, as much as if they had been *bikrajab* of our own. I have already declared Najud clan-kin to the Kurighdunaq, through his aunt Qizrahi. What shall I do with this foreign *bikrajti*, soon to be his wife?"

A few voices cried out, "Kurighdunaq!" and heads nodded in agreement.

"Then so it shall be." He turned them by the shoulders to face him again. "Najud, son of Ilsahr, and Penrys..." he paused for her to supply her lineage, but she shook her head and he continued, "You will always have a home with the Kurighdunaq, clan-kin like any other. You have come to our need, and we will come to yours—you have but to ask."

Penrys caught a glimpse of Hadishti beaming from her seat, then Najud bowed to the clan-leader in the Kigali fashion, and Penrys imitated him. Umzakhilin sat down again, and when they turned to walk back to their place, Penrys was warmed by the nods of approval from their neighbors.

Najud muttered to her, "This complicates matters, Pen-sha." There was concern in his voice, but when she looked at his face, he was grinning. "I never expected to marry a woman of such wealth." He glanced about to see if anyone could overhear his unseemly mirth in the midst of the somber faces.

"What are you talking about?"

I asked Umzakhilin what he would do about the yathzurazd, the clan's share. Every legacy donates one animal in ten, or its equivalent, to the clan for distribution by the wife of the ujarqa. It's a simple way to ensure no one goes hungry.

So?

So, Umzakhilin admitted there would be many animals whose owners would never be identified. Not the horses, mostly—everyone takes an interest in their neighbor's horses and can identify them—but the cattle, sheep, and goats are less individual. He plans to distribute those evenly to each member of the clan. That means you, too, now.

What would I do with a bunch of sheep, Naj-sha? I can't accept that.

His face sobered from its teasing look. *You must, Pen-sha. First, it would be an insult to the clan to hold yourself separate. And then, herds are the wealth of women, not men. The women control the animals, and bring them or the wealth they represent to their husband's family, where they continue to manage them, and their husband's flocks, too, for the sake of their children.*

Not being married yet... He winked at her. *I have herds, myself, with the Zamjilah, but they're managed by the women of my family. That used* to be Rubti—*I wonder who's doing it now? Anyway Umzakhilin knows you have no clan, and this gives you standing, wealth to bring to your marriage like any other young woman, so you won't be a pauper. For the respect of the clan.*

He laughed quietly at her stricken look. *Don't worry, there will be rapid trading of the yathzurazd until everyone has what they want. Many an orphan has built his wealth from such a foundation, going about in tattered clothing while his flocks increase.*

Now compose yourself, Pen-sha, like a respectable woman soon to be married, and stop counting your sheep.

CHAPTER 60

A few hours later, Penrys stood in the slanted light of the late afternoon, in the same cleared circle at the center of the *zudiqazd*. Najud grinned at her side, and the other five couples were spaced out evenly, surrounding Umzakhilin and Hadishti who were standing now, their chairs gone.

Behind her, Bimal and Haraq stood in support, while Rubti and Ilzay stood for Najud, and each of the other couples had friends to do similar service.

What am I doing here, in this alien place with its peculiar customs? In borrowed clothing and a borrowed language, pretending I'm part of it?

Her fingers of her right hand strayed from the crutch hooked under her shoulder to the brooch above her left breast, the silver eagle the size of her palm with its outspread wings. Najud had presented it to her, and she couldn't help but think of the first time they'd made love, her wings wrapped around both their standing bodies, until they got in the way. By the leer lurking on his lips when he pinned it on, it was in his thoughts, too—a private sharing between them, in the public view. She felt her cheeks redden.

She'd noticed that the other brides and the women attending them dressed in their finery all seemed to be wearing necklaces and little other jewelry. *Even in Gonglik or wherever he found this, he knew already that he couldn't give me a necklace to compete with this... this chain that brings horrors.*

She'd known that Najud had little gifts in his packs for all his family, and Rubti had been delighted with hers—a necklace of various animals, stacked like large beads, each carved from a different mineral. Horse and bear, lion and goat, raven and frog. "This came out of far Ndant," he'd told her. "I saw it in Yenit Ping and thought of you."

Najud glanced at Penrys now, in unaccustomed sobriety, and whispered to her, "You won't regret this, Pen-sha."

"Promise me you won't either," she whispered back.

"Never." He smiled confidently, and Umzakhilin began the ceremony.

Najud captured Penrys's left hand, lest she bolt in panic at the last minute. He smiled broadly at the sight of the silver eagle, a reminder for all to see but none to understand, except the two of them. His body tingled with the memory of that first night, in the northern hills of Neshilik, and he had to call himself back to attention.

"After death comes life," Umzakhilin intoned. "Just as our grief was a private matter for the clan, so this hope is ours to cherish as well, born out of hardship and determination…" His gaze fell on the four couples of survivors. "Out of good fortune…" This time he looked at Khashghuy and Yardiqurti, who clung to each other as if never to be separated. "And out of new blood." This last was accompanied by a steady look at Najud and Penrys.

Hadishti beamed at all six couples. "May your lives be fruitful and full of children."

Najud gripped Penrys's hand hard at that, knowing her fear. His eye fell on Munraz, standing with Winnajhubr among the other witnesses. *If not children of my body, then children of my choosing, and hers. It'll be enough. I hope I can make her believe that.*

"May you cherish your *jaram*—a comfort in hardship, a joy in living, a shield in danger, and a light in darkness. You have partners now, to share your life, and new responsibilities—to each other and to the clan."

"Go and rejoice!" Umzakhilin cried. "Witness, all ye Kurigh-dunaq, and celebrate!"

He clapped his hands loudly three times, and Hadishti struck the ancient ram's bell three times with a length of antler, padded at the tip with leather, waiting each time for the sound to fade. When the echo of the bell died away at the end, the onlookers broke ranks and surged over their friends.

Rubti hugged her brother, and then turned to embrace Penrys. "*Naghayin*, it should be my mother doing this, but let me welcome you to our family in her stead."

Najud looked down at the two of them, the dark curls of his favorite sister, and the rich brown hair and foreign features, now so dear to him, of his wife. "There will be a feast soon," he said, to quiet her nerves. "And then the new couples will sneak off, pair by pair, each into their own *kazr*, while everyone else drinks."

He pointed out to her the five small temporary *kazrab* broken out of storage for the newly married couples and now being erected by enthusiastic well-wishers. They were sited off to the side of Najud's *kazr*, out of the way of casual passers-by.

Rubti giggled. "The flaps will be down over the doors for days." Then she realized this would include her brother and his wife, standing right there listening to her, and her face flamed.

Najud thought Penrys's laughter was the result his *nurti* deserved. "Soon," he said to Penrys, over Rubti's head. "We have to take a few bites before we retire—it's expected."

He grinned at her. "But I find I'm not really very hungry. Are you?"

"Not for dinner," she said, dryly.

He felt his whole body surge at her response.

Haraq cornered Najud before the feast with questions about the proposed caravan based near the High Pass, and Rubti stayed to listen.

"It won't be this spring, Haraq," Najud said, "And maybe not the next either. It'll take time to prepare a base and spread the word to other traders. And Umzakhilin hasn't told me what he wants the role of the Kurighdunaq to be."

"But he's going to let you breed the donkeys and begin the first generation of mules," Rubti said. "Bimal told me."

Najud nodded absently, his eyes following Penrys as she spoke to Hadishti and the two of them shared a laugh.

"That means they'll still be too young in two years, but it's a start. And they have plenty of horses here."

Najud refocused on the face of his eager *nurti*, looking for her place in the world, and it struck a chord in his heart.

"The new *biziz* will need a *dirum*," he told her. "Would that interest you?"

Her face lit up. "Me? Yes! I'll learn everything I can from Bimal. I won't disappoint you, *tigha*."

"I know you won't, *nurti*."

"You'll be needing other folk for the *biziz*," Haraq said. "I'd like to be one of them."

"I would value your help, Haraq. We'll be here for a month or so. Plenty of time to talk things through."

"I know you have other things on your mind, *bikraj*," Haraq said, and he winked at Najud as he hooked an arm through Rubti's, to her surprise, and drew her away.

Najud barely noticed as his eyes sought out Penrys. As if she felt his gaze, she looked up from her conversation with Hadishti, and smiled at him wickedly.

Why are they taking so long laying out the feast? The sun's almost down. I don't care what they say about it, the bikrajab will be the first ones away tonight.

Penrys's eyes caught Najud's and he nodded. She had no appetite for the food, savory though it smelled, and put her bowl on the felt pad on the snow that she shared with him. It was awkward getting up without upsetting it, even with Najud's help, and she balanced on her left leg with one hand on him while he retrieved her crutch and handed it to her.

All of this drew everyone's eyes, and she reddened as she heard the chuckles make their way around the camp.

Najud yawned elaborately at the spectators. "Sure is late," he said, to the air at large.

"Why? You're not going anywhere tomorrow. Or the next day, neither." The anonymous joke pulled laughter in its wake, and other less polite suggestions followed.

Penrys raised her head high and pretended not to hear them, though her dignity was seriously impaired by the lurching of her pace through the trampled snow. They walked in silence, away from the eyes of the clan and the light of the fire, until they came to a stop in front of the door of their *kazr*.

Najud pushed the door open and she stepped over the threshold, while he busied himself lowering the flap and tying it down before shutting the door behind him. He knelt down to tend the fire in the stove, and then stood up again in silence, watching her as she swayed uncertainly near her bed.

"I don't know why I feel so nervous," she said.

"It means more now, Pen-sha." His deep voice soothed her. He unpinned the eagle brooch from her borrowed robe and put it in her hand, and she ran her finger over it.

"I have nothing for you, Naj-sha, nothing like this." She hung her head.

"It's not gifts I want from you. It's you."

She stood still while he helped her shrug off the robe. He folded it neatly and placed it on his narrow bed, and followed it with his own clothing. She rarely got a chance like this to admire him, the male shape of him, and it held her attention while he removed the rest of her own clothing.

"I've thought of something after all," she murmured. She took one step forward, until she stood, chest to chest, right up against him and invoked her wings to wrap all the way around his back until he was enclosed in sliding feathers against his bare skin. She slipped her arms around him, letting the crutch fall, and just held him while her wings worked their magic on him.

When his thickened voice reverberated through his chest to her ear, the one knee supporting her weakened, and he had to support her.

"Can't stand much more of this, Pen-sha," he said, a bit desperately.

"Sorry about the leg," she whispered, and he helped her hop back to the edge of her bed to sit.

"Oh, I don't think it'll bother us much. I don't think we'll notice it at all."

GUIDE TO NAMES & PRONUNCIATIONS

PRINCIPAL CHARACTERS & PLACE NAMES & TERMS

PEOPLE - ELLECH

Penrys (Ryssi) (PEHN-rewss)
The chained adept. Wizard trained at the Collegium of Wizards.
Vylkar (VIEWL-kar)
Senior wizard at the Collegium of Wizards. Patron of Penrys.
Vylkerri (viewl-KEHR-ree)
The name of the young wizard-tyrant who devastated the Kurighdunaq clan, given by Penrys in honor of her patron.

PEOPLE - KIGALI

Chang Zenju (CHAHNG ZEHN-joo)
The *laigomju*, commander, of the cavalry squadron sent from Jonggep to Neshilik.
Tun Jeju (TOON JEH-joo)
The *notju*, intelligence master, and imperial representative for Chang Zenju's expedition.

PEOPLE - RASESNI

Dzangabtig (Dzantig) (DZAN-gab-tig, DZAN-tig)
Priest and member of the Temple School in Kunchik. His god is Dzangab.
Menchos (Mene) (MEN-chohs)
Senior commander or intelligence master exiled from Dzongphan.
Surdo (SOOR-doh) - The Voice

The chained wizard-tyrant who wreaked havoc in Rasesdad. The name was given by the Rasesni—his actual name was unknown.

The Voice
See "Surdo."

PEOPLE - ZANNIB

Akshullah (ahk-shool-LAH)
A clan in northwestern central *sarq*-Zannib, part of the Undullah tribe.

Anah-Jilah (Anasha) (ah-NAH-jee-LAH)
The little sister of Yuknaj and Winnajhubr.

Anah-Zul (Zulsha) (ah-NAH-zool)
A survivor of the Kurighdunaq disaster.

Anitqizat (ah-neet-kee-ZAHT)
A master wizard.

Ariqnas (ah-rick-NAHSS)
A herdsman who survives his encounter with the Mistress of Animals, from clan Umzabul, tribe Maqurrah.

Bajushaz (bah-joo-SHAHZ)
Father of Dhalmudhr.

Barshhubr (barsh-HOOB-er)
A herdsman, from clan Umzabul, tribe Maqurrah.

Bimal (bee-MAHL)
The herd-mistress of the Kurighdunaq, a survivor of the disaster.

Birssahr (beers-SAH-her)
A boy who survived the Kurighdunaq disaster.

Butraz (boot-RAHZ)
Najud's older brother.

Dhajtawhaz (thahj-tow-HAHZ)
A tribe in the northwest central region of *sarq*-Zannib. One of its clans is Rashaban.

Dhalmudhr (thahl-MOOTH-er)
The leader of some of the survivors of the Kurighdunaq disaster.

Dimghuy (deem-GOOEY)
Son of Hadishti.

Ghayrbarsh (guy-er-BARSH)
Father of Jiqlaraz, of clan Rashaban, tribe Dhajtawhaz.
Ghuruma (goo-ROO-mah)
Najud's oldest sister.
Hadishti (hah-DEESH-tee)
A survivor of the Kurighdunaq disaster. Mother of Sharma and Dimghuy. Her original clan is Umzabul, tribe Maqurrah.
Haraq (hah-RAHK)
A survivor of the Kurighdunaq disaster, brother of Luram.
Hazimjilah (hah-ZEEM-jee-LAH)
A messenger sent to clan Zamjilah.
Ilsahr (eel-SAH-her)
Najud's father.
Ilzay (eel-ZYE)
A friend of Jirkat.
Inghiti (in-GHEE-tee)
An apprentice herd-mistress of the Winnajjinza clan, tribe Undullah.
Hubrahi (hoob-RAH-hee)
A young man of the Kurighdunaq clan.
Jiqlaraz (jeek-lah-RAHZ)
A senior wizard from a family of wizards, from clan Rashaban, tribe Dhajtawhaz. Uncle of Munraz.
Jirkat (jeer-KAHT)
A survivor of the Kurighdunaq disaster.
Kazrsulj (kahz-er-SOOLJ)
Najud's mother.
Khashghuy (khahsh-GOOEY)
Jirkat's younger brother.
Khashjibrim (khash-jeeb-REEM)
Father of Kazrsulj and Qizrahi.
Khimar (khee-MAR)
Daughter of Suragh, playmate of Anah-jilah.
Khizuwi (khee-ZOO-wee)
A senior wizard from clan Umzabul, tribe Maqurrah.
Kurighdunaq (koo-REEG-doo-NAHK) - World-bow (Rainbow)
A clan in northwestern central *sarq*-Zannib, part of the Undullah tribe.
Luram (Lusha) (loo-RAHM)
A survivor of the Kurighdunaq disaster, sister of Haraq.

Mahab (mah-HAAB)
A tribe in the northwest central region of *sarq*-Zannib.
Maqurrah (mah-koo-RAH)
A tribe in the northwest central region of *sarq*-Zannib.
Mishajmarzuwi (mee-shahj-mar-ZOO-wee)
Jirkat's father.
Munraz (moon-RAHZ)
An apprentice wizard, nephew of Jiqlaraz, from clan Rashaban, tribe Dhajtawhaz.
Najjilah (NAHJ-jee-LAH)
The oldest son of Umzakhilin.
Najud (nah-JOOD) - Lucky, Fortunate
A master wizard of the Zamjilah clan, in the Shubzah tribe.
Qizrahi (keez-RAH-hee)
Kazrsulj's sister, married into the Kurighdunaq clan, in the Undullah tribe. Her original clan was Zamjilah, tribe Shubzah.
Quyubil (koo-yoo-BEEL)
The law-master of clan Kurighdunaq.
Rashaban (rah-shah-BAHN)
A clan in northwestern central *sarq*-Zannib, part of the Dhajtawhaz tribe.
Rubti (ROOB-tee)
Najud's second sister.
Sahrzay (sah-her-ZYE)
Clan leader of the Winnajjinza clan, in the Undullah tribe.
Sharma (SHAR-mah)
Daughter of Hadishti.
Shubzah (shoob-ZAH)
A tribe in the northeast central region of *sarq*-Zannib. Zamjilah is one of its clans.
Suragh (soo-RAHG)
Mother of Khimar, from the Kurighdunaq clan.
Umzabul (oom-zah-BOOL) - Sun-arrow
A clan in northwestern central *sarq*-Zannib, part of the Maqurrah tribe.
Umzakhilin (oom-zah-khee-LEEN)
The *zarawinnaj*, migration leader, of the Kurighdunaq clan.
Undullah (oon-dool-LAH)
A tribe in the northwest central region of *sarq*-Zannib. It has three clans—Winnajjinza, Kurighdunaq, and Akshullah.

Urqudham (oor-koo-THAHM)
Khizuwi's father.
Winnajhubr (wee-nahj-HOOB-er)
A young man, brother of Yuknaj.
Winnajjinza (wee-nahj-JEEN-zah) - Cloud-rider
A clan in northwestern central *sarq*-Zannib, part of the Undullah tribe.
Wishkazti (weesh-KAHZ-tee)
A friend of Barshhubr, from clan Umzabul, tribe Maqurrah.
Yardiqurti (yar-dee-KOOR-tee)
The betrothed of Khashghuy.
Yukjilah (yook-jee-LAH)
Butraz's wife.
Yuknaj (yook-NAHJ)
A young woman, sister of Winnajhubr.
Zabrash (zahb-RAHSH)
A boy who survived the Kurighdunaq disaster.
Zamharshat (zahm-har-SHAHT)
The tribal leader for the Undullah tribe.
Zamjilah (zahm-jee-LAH) - Eye of Heaven
Najud's clan, part of the Shubzah tribe.
Zaybirs (zye-BEERS)
One of Najud's cousins, son of his aunt Qizrahi, from the Kurighdunaq clan, in the Undullah tribe.

PLACES - ELLECH

Drosenrolkentham (DROH-sen-rohl-ken-thahm) - Wizard-learning-place
The Collegium of Wizards in Tavnastok.
Ellech (ELL-ekh)
A northern nation tucked along the southern margin of the Dunnarfeol mountains, with precipitous timber and grass-covered slopes running down to a deep-water port. Famed for industry and research, with a well-armed merchant navy to seek out new markets.
Tavnastok (TAV-nah-stok) - City of Wealth
Inland city based on river commerce and industry, in the Asuthgrata region.

PLACES - KIGALI

Galat (GAH-lat)
A disputed region between Kigali and Ndant, with significant mining resources.

Gonglik (GOHNG-lick) - The Steps
The largest city in the Neshilik region, named for the extensive stretch of rapids and waterfalls on the upper reach of the Seguchi River which inhibit navigation. It lies south of the river and extends to the north at Kunchik, with the first permanent bridge over the Seguchi River, 1800 miles from its mouth.

Jaunor (JOW-nor) - Cold Wall
The trading village at the base of Tse Jan, the High Pass, at the extreme south of Neshilik.

Jonggep (JONG-ghep) - The Meeting of Waters
The largest inland city, at the junction of the two main branches of the Junkawa River: The Seguchi and the Neshikame.

Junkawa (joon-KAH-wah) - The Mother of Rivers
The longest river in the world, with two main branches: The Seguchi and the Neshikame. It finds its outlet at Pingmen below the walls of Penit Ying.

Kigali (kih-GAH-lee) - Land of the Ki Dynasty
Set in the mid-latitudes of the southern continent, Kigali is a wealthy and hard-working nation with a history of political stability and expansion. The Junkawa River and its hundreds of tributaries provide internal communications, and well-placed ports support its strong mercantile interests.

Neshikame Jun (neh-shee-KAH-mee joon) - Little Sister Water
The northern branch of the Junkawa River. It is navigable well into the western regions.

Neshilik (neh-SHEE-lik)
The western district of Kigali, surrounded by mountains and traversed by the Seguchi River. Often disputed with Rasesdad.

Pingmen Hanjong (PING-men HAHN-jong) - City View
The bay or series of harbors carved out by the Junkawa River.

Seguchi Jun (seh-GOO-chee joon) - Seguchi River
The southern and main branch of the Junkawa. It finds its source in the Mratsanag Mountains in Radesdad above Nagthari, and Gonglik in Neshilik is the site of the last downstream bridge. All crossings are by boat or ferry below that

point. It is navigable up to the Steps at Gonglik, and navigable again above the rapids to Dzongphan.

Yenit Ping (YEH-nit ping) - Endless City
Capital city, on both sides of the Junkawa River, overlooking Pingmen harbor.

PLACES - RASESNI

Damsnag (DAHMS-nahg) - The Right Horn
The southern encircling range at the eastern end of Mratsanag.
Dzongphan (DZONG-fan) - Temple Quarter
The capital city, which includes the mother temples of all the gods, in Nagthari.
Garshnag (GARSH-nahg) - The Left Horn
The northern encircling range at the eastern end of Mratsanag.
Mratsanag (m-RAHT-suh-nahg) - The Wild Ram's Horns
The second tallest mountain range in the world.
Nagthari (NAHG-ta-ree) - Between the Horns
The region between the eastern mountain pincers, bordering Neshilik.
Rasesdad (RAHS-ess-dahd)
The Rasesni nation includes the Mratsanag Mountains and the well-watered and fertile plains they support on two coasts. It is the western neighbor of Kigali, in the southern hemisphere.

PLACES - ZANNIB

Qawrash im-Dhal (cow-RAHSH eem-THAHL) - Well in the Steppe
The city in the eastern region from which the largest caravan to eastern Kigali originates.
(Jus) Shamr (JOOS SHAHM-er) - The Low Pass
Caravan route between *sarq*-Zannib and central Kigali, west of Jonggep, the Meeting of Waters.
(Mard) Shimiz (mahrd shee-MEEZ)
Important harbor city at the mouth of Yud Aziyal on Hilj Wandat, near the Rasesdad border.
(Jus) Sidr (JOOS SEED-er) - The High Pass
Caravan route between *sarq*-Zannib and Neshilik at Jaunor.

Silmat (seel-MAHT)
>A narrow, sheltered valley in between the Mahab and Dhajtawhaz tribes, claimed by neither but shared for resources.

(Mard) Ussha (mahrd OOSH-shah)
>Capital city, founded by Kigali, on Pago Bay on the east coast near the Kigali border, at the mouth of the Harin River. Also known as Zudiqazd mar-Sarq, the Winter Camp of the Nation.

(Hilj) Wandat (heelj wahn-DAHT) - Enclosed Sea
>Very large almost landlocked sea in the far west, bordered also by Rasesdad.

Sarq-Zannib (SAHRK-zahn-NEEB)
>The Zannib nation. It occupies the bottom of the southern hemisphere and is neighbored on the north by both Rasesdad and Kigali. The western third concentrates on fishing and small farm agriculture, while the remainder is steppe and grasslands.

Wayat mar-Zarqash (wah-YAHT mar-zar-KASH) - Zarqash's Corner
>A cluster of ridges that hold a cave system.

Zudiqazd mar-Sarq (zoo-dee-KAHZD mar-SAHRK) - Winter Camp of the nation
>See Mard Ussha.

WORDS & PHRASES - ELLECH

Kemellangar (KEH-mel-lahng-ar) - Featherbeds
>A down comforter and, by extension, a nickname for fat clouds that threaten deep snow over a wide region.

Sennevi (SEHN-neh-vee)
>"It is done." The customary final phrase that marks the end of a traditional tale, often accompanied by the slash of a hand.

Yrmur! (EWER-moor) - Broken, Wrong!
>A curse.

WORDS & PHRASES - KIGALI

Kigaliwen (kih-GAH-lee-wehn) - Kigali people
>A group of Kigali people, or the collective citizens of Kigali.

Kigali yat (kih-GAH-lee-yaht) - Kigali speech
>The language spoken in Kigali.

WORDS & PHRASES - ZANNIB

Anah im-ghabr (ah-NAH im-GAHB-er) - Flower of the head
The turban, common but not universal headgear among the Zannib.

Barqah (bar-KAH) - Friend
The common address for a person known to you.

Baijuk (bye-JOOK)
Mead, a drink fermented from honey.

Bikraj, Bikrajti (beek-RAHJ(-tee)) - Wizard, wizardress
The common title for a wizard.

Bikr mar-shimiqa (BEEK-er mar shi-MEE-kah) - Magic of Thinking
The Zannib term for mental magic.

Bikr mar-thulj (BEEK-er mar THOOLJ) - Magic of Things
The Zannib term for physical magic, not practiced by the Zannib.

Binwit (been-WEET) - Mead kit
The collection of materials for drinking mead ceremoniously. It includes the stoneware bottles and cups, often handed down within families, wrapped in an engraved leather rolled pack, usually presented at the transition to adulthood.

Biziz (bee-ZEEZ)
A merchant caravan.

Biziz Rahr (bee-ZEEZ RAH-er) - Big caravan
The Grand Caravan that runs three seasons of the year from Qawrash im-Dhal through eastern Kigali and *sarq*-Zannib.

Bunnas (boon-NAHSS)
A low wild shrub native to *sarq*-Zannib whose berries are collected and dried as part of the *taridiqa*, the annual migration. The infusion of ground, dried, berries in hot water is high in caffeine. Popular throughout the southern countries and a significant trade item for *sarq*-Zannib.

Daril (dah-REEL)
The title for a journeyman wizard.

Dirum (dee-ROOM) - Herd-mistress
The senior woman responsible for all the clan's herds while on *taridiqa*.

Dirum-malb (dee-ROOM-mahlb) - Apprentice to the Herd-mistress

A younger woman learning the position of *dirum*.

Dunaq wandim (doo-NAHK wahn-DEEM) - The World That Surrounds

The Zannib term for the world of reality that exists outside the ordinary world of perception.

Durmiqa bul (door-MEE-kah BOOL) - Sun is still

The solstice, the shortest day of the year.

Gharqa (GAR-kah)

The title for a tribal leader.

Ghuzl mar-Tawirqaj (GOOZ-el mar tah-weer-KAHJ) - Circle of Speakers

The national tribal assembly in Ussha.

Ishqa (EESH-kah) - One couple (two)

One of the old words used for counting herd animals in couples: *ishqa* (2), *imgha* (4), *nudi* (6), *nari* (8), *tadas* (10), *tari* (12), *tabith* (14), *tushur* (16), *shuwaq* (18), *shabir* (20), *jama* (22), *jalu* (24). A *mawik* is half a couple, thus "*nudi* and *mawik*" is 7. A complete set, 24, is a *jal* (flock).

Imgha (EEM-gah) - Two couple (four)

One of the old words used for counting herd animals in couples. See *ishqa*.

Inghiqa (een-GHEE-kah) - Spring

One of the four seasons.

Jal (JAHL) - A flock (twenty-four)

One of the old words used for counting herd animals in couples. See *ishqa*.

Jaram (jah-RAHM)

Spouse.

Jarghal, Jarghalti (jar-GAHL(-tee))

The title for a master wizard (wizardress).

Jibrim (jee-BREEM) - Burning Month

The month of mid-summer. The Zannib lunar calendar recognizes twelve or thirteen months in a year and is complicated to synchronize with their chief trading partner, Kigali.

Jukwit (jook-WEET)

The stoneware bottles used in the *binwit*. They have an indentation around the center to allow them to be hung from a cord.

Jurqal (joor-KAHL) - Device

A magical device, part of the *bikr mar-thulj*, the magic of things.

Kamah, Kamahab (kah-MAH, kah-mah-HAHB) - Tent, Tents
A small one or two person tent used for rapid travel.

Kassa (KAHS-sah)
A bushy plant grown on mountain slopes, the leaves of which are used, dried, for a stimulating infusion.

Kazr, Kazrab (KAH-zer, kahz-RAHB) - Yurt, Yurts
A structure similar to a yurt, made of a wooden framework encased in felt.

Khash (KHASH)
The curved sword that is the typical weapon of the nomadic Zannib.

Khijr-Zannib (KHEE-jer zahn-NEEB) - The grasslands of *sarq-*Zannib
The steppe terrain that dominates the northern territories of *sarq-*Zannib.

Khimar (khee-MAR) - Honey
Honey is a special substance, favored by the *lud* for its unusual locations and properties, and for its use in fermenting mead.

Kuliqa (koo-LEE-kah) - Turn home
The celebration when the *taridiqa* begins the last leg of the annual migration, to the *zudiqazd*.

Lij, Lijti (LEEJ, LEEJ-tee) - Sir, Lady
A term of respect. *Lij-mar-lij*—Master of masters. Derived from Kigali *li* and *ju*—Country-king.

Lisha, Lishajti (LEE-shah, lee-SHAH-tee) - Little king, queen
The diminutive of *lij*, used somewhat mockingly for clan and tribe leaders operating in their most formal manner.

Lud (LOOD)
Numinous objects or locations, often referred to as "little gods."

Magham (mah-GAHM)
The festival camp, the temporary two-week gathering of all the clans in a tribe in a central location within the ring of clan winter camps.

Mawik (MAH-week) - Half a couple (one)
One of the old words used for counting herd animals in couples. See *ishqa*.

Nagha, Naghayin (NAH-gah, nah-gah-YEEN)
Older sister, oldest sister.

Nal-Jarghal (nahl-jar-GHAHL)
The title for an apprentice wizard.

Nari (NAH-ree) - Four couple (eight)
One of the old words used for counting herd animals in couples. See *ishqa*.

Nayith (nah-YEETH)
The masterwork of a wizard, the transition between journeyman and master. So judged by another master wizard.

Nudi (NOO-dee) - Three couple (six)
One of the old words used for counting herd animals in couples. See *ishqa*.

Nurti, Nurtin (NOOR-tee, noor-TEEN)
Younger sister, youngest sister.

Qahulaj, Qahulajti (kah-hoo-LAHJ(-tee)) - Taboo
Wizard-tyrant, one who does taboo things.

Sarq-Zannib (SAHRK-zahn-NEEB)
The Zannib nation.

Shabz (SHABZ)
Dried meat, used as a winter staple food.

Shaimur (shy-MOOR)
Dried fish, used as a winter staple food.

Tabith (TAH-beeth) - Seven couple (fourteen)
One of the old words used for counting herd animals in couples. See *ishqa*.

Tadas (TAH-das) - Five couple (ten)
One of the old words used for counting herd animals in couples. See *ishqa*.

Taridaj (tah-ree-DAHJ)
The people who partake of the annual seasonal migration performed by the traditional Zannib of the central region.

Taridiqa (tah-ree-DEE-kah)
The annual seasonal migration performed by the traditional Zannib of the central region.

Tarimqaj (tah-reem-KAHJ)
The law-master of a traditional Zannib clan.

Tarizd (tah-REEZD)
The route taken by the annual seasonal migration performed by the traditional Zannib of the central region.

Tayujdaj (tah-yooj-DAHJ) - One who pairs for others

The marriage-broker who introduces potential partners and arranges betrothals.

Tigha (TEE-gah)

Older brother.

Tulqaj, Tulqajab (tool-KAHJ) - Traveler, Travelers

The greeting used for an unknown Zan.

Tulqiqa (tool-KEE-kah) - Wander time

The traditional wandering time when journeymen wizards travel to learn and to find opportunities to perform a *nayith*.

Tushkzurdtudin (tooshk-zoor-too-DEEN) - Has sixteen years

An adult, one who is at least sixteen.

Ujarqa (oo-JAR-kha)

The title of the clan leader.

Umaq, Umaqab (oo-MAHK, oo-mah-KAHB) mat, mats

An easily-rolled-up cushion used in place of a bed mattress for a *kazr*.

Wirqiqa-Zannib (weer-KEE-kah-zahn-NEEB)

The Zannib language.

Wishkaz (wish-KAHZ)

Hot spice.

(Yar mar-)yathzurazd ((YAR mar) yahth-zoo-RAHZD) - (Offering of) the tenth one

A tithe of one in ten of animals inherited, or its equivalent, given to the clan to be distributed to the poor and needy.

Yathbantudin (yahth-bahn-too-DEEN) - Has nine years

A child between nine and sixteen. Old enough to join the *taridiqa*.

Yuj (YOOJ)

A couple. Used for mated pairs.

Zamjilah (zahm-jee-LAH) - Eye of heaven

The central crown at the top of the *kazr* that holds the rafters together and lets the smoke escape.

Zan (ZAHN)

An individual member of the Zannib nation.

Zannib-hubr (zahn-NEEB HOOB-er) - Free or Swift Zannib

The Zannib who continue a nomadic tradition of annual migration.

Zannib-taghr (zahn-NEEB TAHG-er) - Slow Zannib

The Zannib who live a settled life.

Zarawinnaj (zah-rah-wee-NAHJ) - One who rides in front
  The leader of the *taridiqa*.
Zudiqazd (zoo-dee-KAHZD)
  The winter camp, from which the *taridiqa* begins and ends. It houses those who do not go on the migration.

IF YOU LIKE THIS BOOK…

MORE GOODIES

You can find **more information** and **maps** at: KarenMyersAuthor.com/link-mistress-of-animals/.

Continue reading for an **excerpt** of the first chapter of **Broken Devices**, the next book in **The Chained Adept** series, and find out more about it here: KarenMyersAuthor.com/link-broken-devices/.

Sign up for the **newsletter** to stay informed of new and upcoming releases and to get occasional bonuses, like free short stories: KarenMyersAuthor.com/signup.

Let other readers know what you think by leaving them a review where you bought the book.

CONTACTING THE AUTHOR

You can contact Karen Myers at KarenMyersAuthor.com or by email at KarenMyers@KarenMyersAuthor.com. You can also follow her on Facebook: Facebook.com/KarenMyersAuthor.

ALSO BY KAREN MYERS

The Hounds of Annwn

To Carry the Horn
The Ways of Winter
King of the May
Bound into the Blood

Story Collections
Tales of Annwn

Short Stories
The Call
Under the Bough
Night Hunt
Cariad
The Empty Hills

The Chained Adept

The Chained Adept
Mistress of Animals
Broken Devices
On a Crooked Track

Science Fiction Short Stories

Second Sight
Monsters, And More
The Visitor, And More

See KarenMyersAuthor.com for the latest information.

EXCERPT FROM BROKEN DEVICES

The Chained Adept: 3

Available from Karen Myers and Perkunas Press

The Grand Caravan arrived that afternoon in sunlight fresh enough with the spring season to ignore the dust of the travelers and settle on the bright colors of their exotic robes and turbans instead.

Outriders had preceded them into Tengwa Tep, and the merchants and citizens of that entrepôt that could spare the time gathered on the southwest outskirts of the city as soon as the news had spread that the Grand Caravan had come, as scheduled, and that the trading season with *sarq*-Zannib and upstream Kigali had begun for the year.

Penrys rode well back in the caravan, dressed in the riding-length robes that all the dark Zannib wore, men and women, on horseback. Najud, her husband, was near the front, but the rest of her companions, as new to the caravan as she was, chattered excitedly about their first look at a Kigali city, its yellow brick golden in the light from the west, varied by the colorful stucco of its many residential and manufacturing compounds. By comparison, the caravan's first stop, a few days ago, had just been a large market town.

She'd seen cities before, in Ellech, across the northern seas. Here it was the children that caught her eye—dozens and dozens of them, screaming with excitement. Some were with a parent, but mostly they ran free, the littlest ones trailed by irritated older sisters or brothers. Unlike their elders, with the long single braid that almost all Kigali not in the military used, the children wore their hair loose or, at the most, gathered into a tail.

"Did they come to see the riders?" Rubti asked.

Penrys smiled at her sister-in-law's eagerness, a ten-years-younger version of Najud. She was an apprentice herd-mistress, a *dirum-malb* in her own language, and she'd been fascinated by the rehearsal the night before of the entertainment the caravan would provide this first evening, to entice the crowds to trade for the five-day stop before it swung west, upstream paralleling the Junkawa, for the longest leg of its great circular route—to Jonggep, the Meeting of Waters.

Ilzay leaned across his saddle to catch Penrys's attention. "There's our setup place." The young man pointed to the left, into the open pasture that was bare of animals and clearly set aside for the use of the caravan, divided from the outermost commercial buildings on the west side of Tengwa by a well-used broad dirt road.

The caravan broke into its smaller components and the travelers began to unpack and erect their dwellings in the unchanging sequence they would maintain for the entire route. Penrys recalled Najud's advice when the caravan started from Qawrash im-Dhal to pick their neighbors well, since they'd be living with them for four months. That wouldn't be true for Penrys and Najud who would be leaving the caravan here tomorrow with their apprentice Munraz, but the other four would be hauling their two *kazrab* and trade goods on all but the final leg, parting from the caravan only once it had returned to *sarq*-Zannib and reached the land of clan Zamjilah on its way back home.

The six of them led their pack-strings of horses, five each, to their designated spot and began unloading their goods from the pack frames. Before the first of the three round *kazrab* had been raised, Najud trotted in with his own pack-string.

"Sorry, Haraq—we've been summoned. Can you take charge of getting our *kazr* up? Munraz can tell you where everything goes. I need to grab Penrys for a while, by order of our Imperial… hosts."

A grimace crossed his lively face. *Sorry, Pen-sha. They're waiting for us. I'll stall them until tomorrow—we don't want to cross the river in the dark, I assure you. But they want to make sure I brought you. As, um, requested.*

Penrys felt the mix of exasperation and tension in his mind-speech. "Shouldn't we change our clothes?" She beat her sleeve with the riding gloves clenched in her hand and let the eloquent dust rise to make her point.

"No time. They'll have to take us as we are, at least on this side of the river where we can always just leave again."

With a sigh, Penrys waved her hand at what was left of their unloading and smiled apologetically at Haraq. "Have fun watching the riding exhibition if we miss it," she told Rubti.

She brushed the trail dust off as best she could and remounted her horse. Najud led her at a trot to the head of the caravan, passing the large *kazr* of the *zarawinnaj*, the caravan leader, and then crossed the road to the Tengwa side and slowed to a walk. He searched through the crowd of Kigaliwen, adults and children, who were watching the camp going up in the field, until he spotted two men, dressed somberly, and turned his horse in their direction.

"That's the dark brown of Imperial Security," he told Penrys. "Apparently they've been watching for us."

When they reached the two men, they dismounted. Najud bowed in the Kigali fashion and Penrys followed his lead. When she noticed the older one staring at her neck, she raised her hand and unwound the colorful scarf she'd wrapped around it, a gift from a kind tailor's wife in far western Neshilik. At the sight of the heavy, brassy chain, settled close around her throat, with no method of removal, the official nodded.

"You are wanted as soon as possible in Mentsek Tep," he said. "Gather your things and follow us."

Penrys raised her eyebrows, and Najud shook his head. "We'll cross to Yenit Ping in the morning, Nip-chi, not in the darkness of night. By the time we load goods and horses, the sun will have long set."

He turned to Penrys. "Penrys, this is Nip Jochat, and Zep Pangwit who will be our guide into Yenit Ping, to take us to Tun Jeju. *Binochi*, this is Penrys of Ellech, my wife."

"So they didn't expect you to be married to my *tigha*?" Rubti was amused at the surprise Najud had described to her when they returned to their camp.

"News doesn't travel all that quickly," Penrys said. The scene of chaos that she'd left had fallen into order before she got back. The horses and other animals were tethered or herded in flocks on the far side of the camp, in the pasture set aside for the thrice-yearly visit from the Grand Caravan. In the middle rank were the *kazrab* of the caravan leader, the guards, and the permanent staff of the *Biziz Rahr*, scattered along its length, and then interspersed were all the traders traveling together in the caravan, one group after another. Some were regulars who undertook the journey every year and greeted each other like family, while others, like their own party, were strangers.

The final rank, along the frontage of the road, were the trading booths, still going up in the setting sun, bare and undecorated until the next day's early morning would see them transformed into colorful and enticing stops for the citizens and merchants of Tengwa Tep, and for any other traders who would rendezvous here before the caravan proceeded further into Kigali. Some would be buying, for the local region, and others would consign their own items for sale. Goods that went by water traveled in Kigaliwen hands, but the overland trade, along the route of the *Biziz Rahr*, was handled by the nomadic Zannib, by long custom.

Penrys had seen the process a few days ago in their first village, where the kinks had been worked out for the new travelers. The caravan's customers and trading partners would wait until tomorrow for their official business, but already they were gathering in the open space left beyond the *zarawinnaf*'s dwelling, waiting for the entertainment to begin.

As she approached the crowd with Rubti, Penrys could feel the exercise of the traders' professional skills, as much a part of them as the skills of a carpenter or soldier would be to another. She reached out with her mind and scanned the people—hundreds of them, in addition to those with the caravan. Across the road were the thousands in Tengwa Tep, and this, she knew, was just a small city, anchored by the caravan trade. The scale was overwhelming, and she concentrated on just the activity in front of her.

Over here, Pen-sha.

Penrys zeroed in on Najud's location from his silent call and steered Rubti in that direction. Along the westward-facing front of the talkative crowd, their little group stood quietly—tall Haraq made taller by his turban, and young Ilzay, his eyes never still as they drank in and filed the behaviors of the people as though they were an exotic species of animal. Najud was there, younger than Haraq, with his face that so resembled Rubti's, especially when a smile flashed across it as it did now, seeing them both. Munraz, their apprentice, stood by his side and smiled shyly at Rubti.

All the men wore the turbans that marked the Zannib, and as Penrys cast her eye across the crowd, she could see the colorful headgear bobbing like the blooms of tall flowers in a field of grass.

The Kigali men, some of them, sported the small emblematic caps of their rank or profession, perched moth-like on their heads. The universal single braid down the back for the adults, men and women, was in stark contrast to the exuberant curls of the Zannib women who wore their hair only casually restrained by scarves or pins, like Rubti.

Rima, the oldest of their party, had threaded the brightest scarf she owned through her own dark curls, until she seemed as youthful and uninhibited as Rubti. Penrys felt out-of-place in this crowd, with her shoulder-length brown hair in the sea of black-headed people. She hadn't stood out so much in Ellech, with its variety of hair colors, but here in the southern continent, any variation from black was unusual, and her skin tones and rounder eyes were all wrong, too.

All around them she overheard snippets of conversation. Promises of spices and rugs, jewels and wool, exotic fabrics and dyes. Pearls from the Wandat Sea. Bargains being struck for consignments further along the route.

Suddenly the noise quieted, and Penrys looked west, into the sunset. A single Zan on a white horse had appeared. He bowed, and his horse knelt, too, before rising up to carry him at a gallop along the front of the crowd. Hands reached out to grab children and pull them out of the way, but Penrys could both see and feel how much the rider was in control of his horse, and how often they had done this before.

She felt the arrival of more riders, coming out of the setting sun, before her eyes wanted to leave the first one. They split into two groups of three and rode with their arms crossed over their chests and no reins at all. For a few minutes they wove through each other in intricate crossings, their faces impassive, using only their legs to direct their horses. Penrys could feel their concentration as they performed, something between a dance and swordplay.

With a shout and a flourish, all six riders moved as one and drew their *khashab*, the curved swords of the Zannib, from the sheaths mounted to the saddles. What followed was a stylized sword dance on horseback, first one group of three slashing and their opponents ducking fluidly away, and then the other. After the synchronized exhibit, they broke off into three pairs and traded a flurry of blows that never connected. Finally, by what signal Penrys was unable to detect, they stopped and struck their swords against their partners' swords in a single ringing clang that died out in the silence of the fascinated crowd, until the first hand-clapping began, and the children shouted in delight.

All six riders lined up and bowed, and than circled at a gallop and vanished back behind the caravan leader's *kazr* on the left, just as the sun finished setting.

Penrys glanced down at Rubti whose eyes were shining. "Think you can learn how to do that, in three months?"

Waking up from her trance, the girl turned a serious face to her. "Do you think they'd teach me?"

"Why not? Seems to me like it would be a fine thing for a herd-mistress to learn."

That evening all seven of the travelers made themselves comfortable after dinner in the *kazr* that belonged to Najud and Penrys.

"Last time," Najud said, as he poured the *bunnas* for Haraq and then settled the pot on the metal plate that supported the stove. "No more *kazr* for us, in Yenit Ping."

He'd miss the comfort of the warm felt walls surrounding the round lattice-work shell, and all the colorful painted woodwork and textiles. It would all collapse down tomorrow into loads for two of the horses in his string, while the other two *kazrab* remained standing, for the four who would go on with the *Biziz Rahr* for three quarters of its circular route.

Tun Jeju, the Kigali officer of Imperial Security had requested his presence, and Penrys's, in Yenit Ping, and Najud knew it was more in the nature of an order, an obligation already paid for in the form of a permit for a new caravan in the west of *sarq*-Zannib. He'd brought his apprentice along, but the rest were there to learn how the grandfather of caravans operated, as a model for the new one Najud intended to found.

"It's not too late, Munraz," he said. "There are other *bikrajab* traveling with the caravan—I could probably arrange for you to study with one of them instead, if you wish it. They're all older than I am."

Penrys rolled her eyes, and he corrected himself. "Than we are."

He could see that Munraz actually considered the offer, before shaking his head. "I'd rather study with you two, *bikraj*, and see the great city."

"All right, then. You'll find it… interesting."

Proceeding in order of seniority, Najud turned to Rima. The widow of a trader from clan Umzabul, she'd wanted to experience the Grand Caravan, from its base in Qawrash im-Dhal to its trading cities in Kigali, the better to prepare the other traders in her clan once the western caravan became a reality.

Najud looked to her steadiness to counter-balance his volatile younger sister. "Is there anything else you need, Rima, before we part? You're comfortable with your trade goods? Your silver?"

"It's not my first *biziz*," she said, with a smile, "though there's nothing like the *Biziz Rahr*, it's true. Penrys can take her loads of *kassa* into Yenit Ping, but I'll seed the market along the way with mine, and see if we can't stir up a demand for it."

The herbal infusion was an alternative to the dark and popular *bunnas*, and not yet well know outside of the far west, around the Wandat Sea.

Haraq was still a puzzle to Najud, even after two months on horseback together. Neither he nor the much younger Ilzay spoke much, and they shared a certain sobriety of character.

Penrys had broken Haraq free from a *qahulajti*, a wizard-tyrant, a few months ago, when the Kurighdunaq clan had been so disastrously drawn into the grasp of a young girl with overwhelming powers. In the process, Haraq had stuck to them both, and declared his interest in helping to create the new caravan.

Privately, Najud thought Haraq felt he owed Penrys some sort of debt for his life. That was nonsense—others had been saved the same way, including Haraq's own sister—but Najud was no longer surprised, when he turned around to warn Penrys of something, to find Haraq there before him, tending to the danger.

Ilzay was different. The Kurighdunaq clan was now so reduced in size, that its *ujarqa*, Umzakhilin, the clan leader, was considering Najud's proposal to help build a caravan base on the clan territory, like a Qawrash im-Dhal in miniature, as a way of avoiding absorption into the other clans of his tribe. Ilzay wanted a place in that. He was here to learn how a mature *biziz* operated, to help plan the infancy of a new one.

"You have all the letters for Umzakhilin and the others?" Najud directed the question to both of the men.

"We have everything, *bikraj*," Ilzay responded. "If Umzakhilin says 'yes' before you return, we know what to do. The rest of the work goes forward either way—the breeding of the horses and mules, and the announcements for the merchants and traders in the west."

"Good," Najud said. "I'd rather start the trading base this year, for greater stability next year, but even without it I'm determined to try for a first, short caravan next spring as an experiment."

"And Rubti, that means I'm placing a great responsibility on you." His sister returned his look with unaccustomed seriousness. "Just getting our herds from Zamjilah to Kurighdunaq will be a trial, even if those we spoke with when we passed through still plan to come with you. It's no small thing to uproot so many animals and people, and bring them to a new clan for an... uncertain adventure."

"I can do it, *tigha*," she said. "I may only be a *dirum-malb* now, just an apprentice herd-mistress, but I'm sure I can do it."

Penrys laughed. "Don't you think you'll be a full *dirum* if... when you succeed? If that's not a masterwork, moving so many animals three hundred miles west, I don't know what would be. Talk to the *dirum* of this caravan and learn everything you can. Stick to her like a burr and make yourself useful."

Najud said to Rima, "Take care of her for me."

"Well, I will," the older woman said, "but I don't see the least need to worry about it. You go off and give that old Kigalino what he wants, and we'll see all three of you in a couple of months."

Najud and Penrys shared a look. *If only it proves to be that simple.*

Find out more about this book here:

KarenMyersAuthor.com/link-broken-devices/

ABOUT THE AUTHOR

Karen Myers is a fantasy and science fiction author, best known for her heroic fantasy novels.

After a degree in Comparative Mythology from Yale University and a career as an industry pioneer building software companies, she has devoted herself to writing speculative fiction. Her stories feature heroes in real and imagined worlds filled with magic, space travel, and adventure.

When she's not writing, she enjoys hunting, fishing, photography, and playing her fiddle.

Karen lives with her husband, dogs and cats in an old log cabin in the mountains of central Pennsylvania, surrounded by wildlife. Bears, coyotes, deer, and possums visit often, and when she fiddles on her porch, the wild turkeys talk back.

She can be reached at KarenMyers@KarenMyersAuthor.com.

www.ingramcontent.com/pod-product-compliance
Lightning Source LLC
Chambersburg PA
CBHW072203130726
47910CB00011B/1804